OUTLAW
COUNTRY

OUTLAW COUNTRY

A SMOKE JENSEN NOVEL OF THE WEST

WILLIAM W. JOHNSTONE
AND J. A. JOHNSTONE

PINNACLE BOOKS
Kensington Publishing Corp.
www.kensingtonbooks.com

PINNACLE BOOKS are published by

Kensington Publishing Corp.
119 West 40th Street
New York, NY 10018

PUBLISHER'S NOTE
Following the death of William W. Johnstone, the Johnstone family is working
with a carefully selected writer to organize and complete Mr. Johnstone's
outlines and many unfinished manuscripts to create additional novels in all
of his series like The Last Gunfighter, Mountain Man, and Eagles, among
others. This novel was inspired by Mr. Johnstone's superb storytelling.

ISBN-13: 978-0-7860-4725-3
ISBN-10: 0-7860-4725-9

First Kensington hardcover printing: February 2021
First Pinnacle paperback printing: May 2021

10 9 8 7 6 5 4 3 2 1

Printed in the United States of America

Electronic edition:

ISBN-13: 978-0-7860-4726-0 (e-book)
ISBN-10: 0-7860-4726-7 (e-book)

On board the Leopoldina, at sea—

Smoke Jensen stood at the railing, looking out over the gray, seemingly endless sea. His wife, Sally, was in their cabin just behind him, getting ready to go to the salon for dinner. Smoke liked to use the private deck that their first-class accommodations afforded them. He enjoyed moments of solitude such as this. He'd often experienced the same sense of peace in the high country that was his home.

"Why would I want to go to Paris?" Smoke had asked a month earlier, when Sally had first broached the idea of taking a passenger ship across the Atlantic.

"Because you won't get that many more chances to go," Sally had said. "And I would like very much to see the famous City of Light."

Smoke had smiled at his wife, as he usually did. "Well, sweetheart, that's all you really have to say. If you want to go, I'm all for it."

The day was overcast, and the breeze of the ship under way brought a chill to his bones. He shivered and pulled up the collar of his sheepskin coat.

"For heaven's sake, Smoke, do you intend to stand out there in the cold until you turn blue?"

Smoke turned to smile at Sally's admonition. "No, just until you're ready for supper."

"It's dinner, sweetheart. Remember we are first-class passengers on a transatlantic passenger ship, and first-class passengers don't 'eat supper.' They go to dinner, where they *dine*. It seems to me like we have had this discussion about a million times before," she added with a smile.

"Eat or dine . . . It makes no difference to me as long as I get some food. I'm starving to death."

Sally laughed. "And first-class passengers never starve to death. They merely acquire an appetite. They don't gobble like a hog."

"If I promise not to gobble like a hog, can we go to sup . . . uh, dinner now?"

Sally shook her head as she teased him. "I swear, we may as well have come in steerage. Come along. Let's get you fed before you waste away."

After negotiating their way through the ship's passageways and going down two decks, they were met in the salon at the bottom of the grand stairway by one of the stewards.

"Good evening, Mr. and Mrs. Jensen."

"Hello, Carl," Smoke replied. "Where will you be seating us tonight?"

"You'll be sitting with a young, newly married couple. Come. They are at the table now."

The steward guided Smoke and Sally through the dining salon and between the other passengers until they reached a table that was situated right in the middle of the room.

There a man, clean-shaven except for a mustache, was sitting with a very attractive redheaded woman. The man stood as Smoke and Sally approached the table.

"Hello. Welcome. It's good to have you join our table. My name is Ernest Hemingford. This is my wife, Hadley."

"I'm Smoke. This is Sally."

"Smoke?" Hadley said as the others sat down. "That's a rather unusual name."

"I suppose it is," Smoke said. "It isn't my real name, of course. It was given to me many years ago by someone who became my mentor and lifelong friend."

"I've read about a man named Smoke," Hemingford said. "Smoke Jensen, it was. And from what I've read, he led a life of adventure and derring-do."

"What happened to him?" Hadley asked.

"Oh, I don't know," Hemingford replied. "He was an icon of the Old West. I'm sure he's dead by now."

Sally smiled. "Your assumption that he is dead is a bit premature. He is here now, about to have dinner with you." Sally sat.

"You?" Hemingford said, his face lighting up with interest as he looked across the table. "You are Kirby Jensen?"

"You really have read about me, haven't you? Yes, Kirby is my name, though I use it only on official papers. Like on my passport," he added.

Hemingford stuck his hand across the table. "Mr. Jensen, it is a real pleasure to meet you."

They clasped hands, each with a strong grip.

"Why don't you call me Smoke? I'm a lot more comfortable with that."

"I can understand that," Hemingford said. "I think a

person should have a good name, other than the one they got from their parents at birth. I really don't like the name Ernest, and I've been thinking about coming up with something new."

"What about Papa?" Sally suggested.

"Why Papa?" Hadley asked.

"Well, he looks a little like my father did," Sally said. "And there is something warm and inviting about someone called Papa."

Hemingford smiled. "Papa," he said. "Yes, I like that. Papa Hemingford, it shall be."

"Why are you going to Paris, Ernest, uh, Papa?" Smoke asked.

Hemingford chuckled. "Ernest is fine. It will take me a while to get used to Papa as a moniker. I'm going to Paris because I have a job as foreign correspondent for the *Toronto Star*."

"Do you really think there will be enough news in Paris that would be of interest to the readers in Toronto?"

Hemingford shook his head. "You don't understand. I won't be writing news stories as such. My job will be to write features, human interest stories, articles that grab the reader emotionally when I come across one." He looked directly at Smoke. "And I think I have just come across one. I'll do one about you."

"Mr. Hemingford, I'm flattered that you would want to use me as your subject, but there have already been a lot of stories written about me. And some of them are even true," Smoke added with a smile. "But those days, when the West was young and when a person lived by his wits and sometimes his gun, are over. I don't believe you can find anything new."

"You are still ranching, aren't you? Sugarloaf, I believe it is called?"

"Yes."

"Let's make a deal, Smoke. I won't tell you how to run Sugarloaf, and you don't tell me how to write." Though Hemingford's response was almost a challenging statement, any edge it may have had was ameliorated by a wide grin.

Smoke laughed. "All right, fair enough. I'll be fine with that."

"We'll be at sea for seven days. If you don't mind, I'd like for you to spend a couple of hours with me each day. By the end of the voyage, I should have enough information to write a story about an icon of the American West. Would you be willing to start now?"

"All right. Where would you like to start?"

"You said that a mentor and old friend gave you your name. Why don't we just start with that and just let it flow from there?"

"He was called Preacher," Smoke began.

CHAPTER 1

The story

"You're a preacher?" Kirby Jensen asked when the old man told him his name.

"Didn't say I *was* a preacher. I said that's my handle. That's what folks call me."

Kirby laughed out loud.

"What you laughin' at, boy?"

"I'm laughing at your name."

"It ain't nice to scoff at a man's name. If I wasn't a gentle type of man, I might let the hairs on my neck get stiff."

"Preacher can't be your real name."

"Well, no, you're right about that, but I been called Preacher for so long now that I've near 'bout forgot my Christian name. So, Preacher it'll be. That or nothin'."

"Where do you live?"

"I live in the high lonesome."

"Where is the high lonesome?"

"It ain't so much of a where as it is a thing. It's whistling wind and the silence of the mountains. And I wouldn't want to live nowhere else."

Kirby and his father, Emmett, were traveling across the plains when they first encountered the old mountain man called Preacher. Shortly after that auspicious meeting, the three of them had been trailed and attacked by a Pawnee war party. It was during that battle that Kirby, then only sixteen years old, had discovered his amazing natural talent with firearms, especially handguns, dispatching one of the warriors with a .36 Colt Navy revolver.

Following that ruckus, Preacher had declared that Kirby, having gone through a baptism of fire, could no longer be called a boy despite his young age. And as a man, he needed a man's name.

"Smoke'll suit you just fine," Preacher had said as he looked at Kirby's ash-blond hair. "So Smoke it'll be from now on. Smoke Jensen." The old-timer had chuckled. "Kinda like the sound of it, don't you?"

That was Kirby Jensen's introduction to the man who over the next several years would become his mentor, friend, and surrogate father. The latter had come about because Kirby's real father had left him under the mountain man's care. On the day his pa had left, he and Kirby had stood in front of the trading post at dawn.

"You do understand my ridin' off alone, don't you, boy? There's some things you're goin' to need to learn 'bout livin' out here, 'n I cain't think of anybody more able to teach you them things than Preacher. Problem is, it's goin' to take you some time to learn all you need to learn, 'n me 'n you both know that I don't have that much time left. So I aim to leave you here to get your learnin', while I go out lookin' for the three men that kilt your brother. You got 'ny problem with that?"

"I reckon not," Kirby had replied quietly. "I know you're doin' what you feel you've got to do."

"Bye, boy."

With his father gone, Kirby lived with and studied under Preacher. He learned how to survive under the most extreme conditions. He could trap and hunt for food, he could make a fire without matches, and he could find water when the average man would give up in despair. He learned how to read, not just the written word—he could already read and write—but he learned how to read nature. He could predict a storm before any obvious sign; he could fathom and react to the actions of wild animals.

"I been seein' the way you can handle a pistol," Preacher said. "Ain't never seen no one your age that was that good with a handgun, and not sure that I've seen anyone full grow'd who was any better. That's another reason to call you Smoke, the way you burn powder faster and more accurate-like than anybody else I ever laid eyes on.

"All famous men needs 'em some kind of a handle, a name other 'n the one they was borned with," Preacher continued. "I've know'd some right famous men in my day, Big Cat Malone, Grizzly Adams, Liver Eatin' Johnson, Nekked Colter."

"Naked Colter?" Smoke asked with a laugh. "You really know someone who calls himself Naked?"

"John Colter his name was, 'n he was a part of the Lewis and Clark Expedition. Fact is, they used him to feed the party 'n to find mountain passes for 'em. Then, after that was all over he wound up someplace in Montana, where he was jumped by a bunch of Blackfoot Injuns in the middle of the winter. They taken off his clothes, a-thinkin' he wouldn't run off, but he done so, 'n he run for miles, nekked as a jaybird." Preacher laughed. "'N he kilt one of 'em, too. Like I say, all famous men needs 'em a special name."

"I'm not famous."

"You're goin' to be. Ain't no doubt in my mind. No doubt a'tall. You're goin' to be a famous man someday, the kind of man folks writes books about. I got me a feelin' 'bout that, 'n my feelin's ain't hardly never wrong."

"I doubt that I'm ever goin' to be famous," Smoke said. He smiled. "But I do like the name."

It had been two years since his pa had ridden off, and Smoke hadn't heard anything from him in all that time. He wasn't surprised by that, given that Emmett had written only two letters home the whole time he'd been away during the war.

There was nothing of the boy left in Smoke. He was now a man, fully grown, over six feet tall and with shoulders as wide as an ax handle. He was hard in body, face, and eyes. The bay he had ridden out here hadn't survived the first year. When his horse had fallen on the ice and broken his leg, Smoke had had to put him down, but Preacher had found another mount for him, a large, evil-tempered Appaloosa. The Indian Smoke bought him from had sold him cheap because he hadn't been able to break him.

That Indian, as well as the other Indians who knew the animal, were shocked to see the horse bond immediately with Smoke. He was a stallion, and he was mean, his eyes warning any knowledgeable person away. The Appaloosa had, in addition to his distinctive markings—the mottled hide, vertically striped hooves, and pale eyes—a perfectly shaped 7 between his eyes. And that became his name: Seven.

"Smoke, I've done learned you about as much as I

know how to learn anyone," Preacher said one summer morning. "There ain't no doubt in my mind but that you could light in the middle of the mountains some'ers and live as good as me or any other mountain man I ever know'd could. 'N I don't believe they's a man alive who could beat you in a gunfight or stand up to you with his fists. But truth to tell, the time of the mountain man is gone. It's been two years since we had us a Rendezvous, 'n I don't know if there'll ever be another 'n. Just be glad you got to see one of 'em when you did."

"I am glad," Smoke said. "If I live to be as old a man as you are, I'll still remember getting to go to that Rendezvous."

"Whoa now! Are you tellin' me that's all you're goin' to remember? That you ain't goin' to 'member nothin' else I learned you in all this time?"

Smoke laughed. "I reckon I'll be remembering plenty of other things, as well."

Shortly after that conversation, an old mountain man rode up to their camp, hailing them before he got too close to make sure he didn't get shot out of the saddle.

"You just as ugly as I remembered, Preacher," he said in the form of a greeting.

"I didn't think you was even still alive, Grizzly," Preacher said. "I heard you got et up by a pack o' wolves. No, wait, that ain't right. Now that I think back on it, what they said was that you was so old and dried up that the wolves didn't want nothin' to do with you."

Smoke had already learned that mountain men insulted each other whenever possible. It was their way of showing affection.

They were hospitable to each other, too, which meant

that Grizzly sat down and shared their food and coffee while he and Preacher swapped tall tales and more insults for at least half an hour.

Then Grizzly said, "I've got somethin' to tell the boy."

"He ain't no boy," Preacher said. "He's a growed man." He didn't seem surprised that Grizzly had brought news.

Smoke waited for whatever Grizzly had to tell him. He had a feeling that it wouldn't be anything good.

"A man rode into the Hole about two months ago. Strange man he was, 'n all shot up. Dug his own grave. When the time come, I buried him. He's planted on that there little plain at the base of the high peak on the east side of the canyon. Zenobia Peak, it's called. You remember it, Preacher?"

Preacher nodded.

Grizzly reached inside his war bag and pulled out a heavy sack and tossed it to Smoke.

"Seein' as it was your pa, this would be your'n, I reckon," Grizzly said to Smoke. "What it is, it's a right smart amount of gold."

Smoke knew that Grizzly could have kept all the gold and Smoke would have been none the wiser. He also understood the code of the mountain man and knew that if he made any comment on Grizzly's honesty, Grizzly would be very upset by it. Honesty and honor among such men were expected.

Once more Grizzly dipped into the bag. "And this is a piece of paper with words on it. What it is, is names your pa wrote down so's you would know what men it was that put lead in him. He said you'd know what to do, but for me to tell you, 'Don't do nothin' rash.'"

His business done, the old man rose to his feet. "I done what I give my word I'd do. Now I'll be goin' on."

Old North Church—Boston, Massachusetts

"One if by land, two if by sea." All the parishioners of the famous old Episcopal church were aware of their church's historic role in the Revolutionary War. They had gathered today for the funeral service of Gordon Woodward. It started to rain just as Father E. D. Owen began the funeral, and he used the rain as an illustration.

"You may think that this is nothing but rain falling outside," Father Owen said. "But if you do think that, you would be wrong. What it is, is God's tears. Yes, sir, even God is crying that he had to call home a good man like Gordon Woodward.

"Gordon left behind a fine girl, his daughter, Nicole. Nicole is all alone now, because it wasn't but six months ago that her mother, Edna, died. We must all pray not only that God receives Gordon into His arms, but also that He helps this poor girl get through her grief."

The rain continued for nearly an hour, and Father Owen, not wanting to subject his flock to the downpour, continued the funeral, talking about what a fine man Gordon was, what a fine woman Edna was, supplementing the eulogies with several random readings from the Scriptures. Then, mercifully, the rain abated, and everyone went outside to the church graveyard.

Fourteen-year-old Nicole Woodward stood at the edge of the grave, looking down at the several inches of water that had collected at the bottom.

The coffin was lowered into the open grave. Father Owen said a few words, then he gave Nicole a handful of dry dirt. She had no idea where the dry dirt had come from, but she was glad she didn't have to drop mud on her father's casket.

The ladies of the church had a gathering at the church after the burial, and amid the eating, everyone came over to Nicole to express their sympathy.

"Oh, you poor girl. What will you do now?"

"I will be joining my aunt Amanda and my uncle John in Illinois," Nicole said. "Just before he died, Papa made arrangements for them to take me in."

"Illinois? Oh, heavens, that is so far from here. How are you going to get there?"

"By train," Nicole replied. "I already have my ticket."

"You're traveling alone? Aren't you afraid?"

"No, I'm not afraid." She no longer had the luxury of fear, Nicole thought.

CHAPTER 2

Cairo, Illinois

When the train pulled into the Union Pacific depot, Nicole Woodward looked through the window at the people who were standing on the platform to meet the arrival. It took but a moment to find the person she was looking for, a tall, slender, very attractive woman.

Nicole smiled when she saw her aunt Amanda, and as soon as the train stopped, she stepped down from the car and hurried across the platform to meet her.

"Nicole, my, how you have grown!" Amanda said. "Why, you are a young woman now."

"I'm fourteen," Nicole said.

It was a short walk from the depot to the house occupied, but not owned, by John and Amanda Palmer. John worked as a hostler for the stagecoach line, and the house was owned by the company. Part of John's compensation was to be able to live in the house rent free.

"You poor dear," Amanda said. "Only fourteen, and having to take care of all the funeral arrangements for your father by yourself. The illness came upon Gordon rather suddenly, didn't it?"

"Not really," Nicole said. "The truth is, I don't think he ever fully recovered from Mama dying last year. It was as if after she died, he just didn't want to live anymore."

"Yes, my dear sister's dying was a loss to all of us. Tell me truthfully, Nicole, did Edna suffer at the end?"

"No," Nicole said. "Or, if she did, she bore it with such stoicism that nobody knew about it."

"Oh, how I wish I had been able to come to Boston so that I might have seen her one last time," Amanda lamented.

"She knew that it wasn't possible for you to come, and she was all right with it."

John came home soon after Nicole and her aunt arrived. He greeted Nicole effusively, then said, "I'm so thankful we're able to take you in, Nicole. I wouldn't presume to think that we can replace your own parents, but I will say this: as far as Amanda and I are concerned, you are now like the daughter we never had."

Nicole enjoyed her life in Cairo. It was a riverfront town, being located where the Ohio River joined the mighty Mississippi, and because of that it was a bustling settlement, with something interesting going on all the time.

Despite that, over the next four years she came to realize that her uncle was gripped by a certain restlessness. Because of that, she wasn't too surprised one day when he came in from his job at the stage line barn and shared some news with both Nicole and Amanda.

"I have bought a fine team of oxen and a stout Studebaker wagon. I've also given notice to the stage line. We'll leave Monday morning."

"Leave? Leave for where?" Nicole asked.

Amanda smiled at her. "Your uncle and I have been talking about this. We're going to Hell's Valley, in Colorado."

"Hell's Valley? Heavens, what a frightening name," Nicole said.

They might have discussed this move with her, she thought, especially if they considered her a daughter. On the other hand, they had provided a home for her over the past four years, and she was old enough now to be considered grown. They might be planning to leave it to her whether or not she accompanied them.

"There's free land to be had there," John said. "I can have my own farm."

"I know that you have lived only here in Cairo and in the city of Boston," Amanda said. "And the prospect of going to some remote place in the West might frighten you. But we have been planning on this for a long time, and John has his heart set on it."

"Oh, I'm not at all frightened by the prospect, Aunt Amanda," Nicole replied honestly. As she had realized back in Boston, after her father's funeral, fear no longer had much of a place in her life. To be honest, she had an adventurous streak she had never known about until that moment, and she felt it cropping up again now. "Why, I'm looking forward to the adventure."

"Oh, what a dear, courageous girl you are."

"We were hoping you'd want to come with us," John said with a grin. "I believe a whole new life awaits us!"

The Uncompahgre Mountains, Colorado

After learning of the death of his father, Smoke vowed to avenge him and see that justice was meted out to the men responsible for Emmett Jensen's death.

Preacher's wise counsel was that Smoke wasn't ready to set off on that quest for retribution just yet, however.

A man full-grown he might be, physically, but he still had much to learn about life on the frontier . . . and Preacher was the man to teach him those things.

As time passed, trouble found Smoke more than once, seeming almost to seek him out, and as he defended himself with the pair of Colt Navy revolvers he wore, his reputation grew. Inevitably, the time came for him to leave his reasonably comfortable life with Preacher and begin tracking down the men he had sworn to kill.

One of them was a big, ugly man with half an ear, Smoke had been told, and that description fit a man called Billy Bartell. Smoke followed his leads and found Bartell in a saloon in the little town in Colorado. With that description, Bartell was hard to miss as he stood at the bar, not twenty feet away.

Bartell sensed someone looking at him and turned toward Smoke. "What the hell are you a-lookin' at?" he asked in a snarling voice.

"I'm looking at the ugliest low-down varmint I've ever seen in my life," Smoke replied.

Bartell's response was a derisive laugh. "Hell, you ain't much more'n a boy—a big 'un, I'll give you. But with a mouth liken that one you've got, you ain't likely to live long enough to become a man."

"I'll live to see the sun set tonight," Smoke replied. "You won't."

"Why do you think that?"

"Because you're fixin' to draw on me, 'n soon as you do, I'm goin' to kill you."

"I'll say this for you, boy. You got a lot of grit for someone who's still wet behind the ears. Now, go away 'n just thank your lucky stars you didn't provoke me into killin' you."

Bartell turned back to the bar, as if dismissing Smoke,

and Smoke, upset that he couldn't provoke Bartell into drawing on him, began to wonder how he was going to handle this. He couldn't kill Bartell in cold blood, but neither could he just walk away from the grim task he had given himself to do.

Then Bartell solved Smoke's problem, because suddenly, and without warning, Bartell swung back toward him, making a grab for his pistol.

Bartell had the advantage of drawing first, and his many years on the outlaw trail had made him a formidable man with a gun. It wasn't until after Bartell had already started his draw that Smoke reacted, making a lightning-fast draw of his own. The gun in his hand roared and bucked before Bartell could pull the trigger. The bullet hit Bartell in the chest with the impact of a hammer blow, and he was slammed back against the bar before sliding down. He sat there, leaning back against the bar, his gun hand empty and the unfired gun lying on the floor beside him. He watched as Smoke approached him.

"There ain't nobody that fast," Bartell said. He coughed a blood-spewing cough.

"Don't die yet, Bartell. I want you to know why I killed you."

"I seen you lookin' at me, and figured out that you musta seen my picture on one o' them dodgers, so you don't have to tell me nothin'. I know this is for the reward."

"I don't give a damn about the reward. This was for my father. You hired on with the men who wanted him dead. Now, before you cross the divide . . . where is Angus Shardeen?"

Bartell coughed again, another body-racking cough, bringing up even more blood.

"You know what? I think I am goin' to tell you where he's at. Only I ain't doin' you no favors, boy, 'cause if you find 'im, he'll kill you."

"Where is he?"

"Rattlesnake Canyon," Bartell said. He tried to laugh, but it turned into another blood-oozing cough. "Yeah, you go on out there 'n after he kills you, me 'n you will be meetin' again, 'cause I'm goin' to be holdin' open a place for you in Hell. By that time, I will have made some friends, 'n I'll show you around the place."

There was a rattling sound deep in Bartell's throat, then his head fell to one side as his eyes, still open, glazed over.

"Anybody know where Rattlesnake Canyon is?" Smoke asked.

Bad Water, Colorado

Following a lead here and there, Smoke was able to trace Shardeen to a saloon in the little town of Bad Water, not far from Rattlesnake Canyon.

"Shardeen, do you remember a man by the name of Billy Bartell?" Smoke asked.

Shardeen, a big redheaded man with a purple lightning-streak scar on his face, laughed, but there was no humor in the sound.

"Yeah, I remember that dumb son of a buck. Why do you ask?"

"It took me a while to find him. I'm here to arrange a meeting between you and Bartell."

"Bartell wants to meet with me? Why? Does he need money?"

"Where Bartell is, money is no good."

"Oh? And where would that be?"

"That would be Hell."

"Hell?"

"I sent him there. And it's like I said, I'm here to arrange a meeting between the two of you."

Suddenly, Shardeen understood what Smoke was telling him, and with an angry shout of defiance, he jerked his pistol from its holster

Because there were several witnesses in the saloon, and he wanted to make certain that everyone perceived the fight as fair, Smoke didn't even start his draw until Shardeen had his gun out and leveled.

Shardeen, realizing that he had beaten his challenger to the draw, smiled in victory. Then that smile froze into a shocked look of horror as a clap of gun-thunder filled the saloon. Even though Shardeen had gotten his gun out first, Smoke was able to draw and shoot even before Shardeen could pull the trigger

Shardeen dropped his pistol, put his hands over the wound in his chest, then sank to his knees. He looked up at Smoke.

"Who are you?"

"It doesn't matter who I am. The only thing that matters is that I got the right man."

"Right man for—"

Shardeen died without finishing his question or learning why he was on his way to Hell. His face slammed into the sawdust-littered floor, but he didn't feel it.

Sometime later, Smoke stood at the grave of his murdered father, holding his hat in his hands. He was pleased to see that the markings he had chiseled in the rock-turned-tombstone were still quite legible. Preacher was standing some distance away, having told Smoke that he needed some private time with his pa.

"Pa, I've settled some accounts. I've killed two of the men who had it coming. I'd like to say that settled everything, but I can't say that just yet. Not until I take care of the ones truly responsible for your death. I've memorized the names. Wiley Potter, Muley Stratton, and Josh Richards. Someday I'll find them, Pa, and when I do, I'll make things right. I give you that promise."

Smoke stood there in silence for another moment, then he put his hat on and started back toward Preacher.

"Got things settled with your pa?" Preacher asked when Smoke walked away from the grave.

"Yeah."

"He was real proud of you, boy. Same as I am."

The lump in Smoke's throat wouldn't let him reply.

CHAPTER 3

The Palmer and Franklin wagons

They were in western Colorado now, nearly at the end of their long journey. To keep the extra weight down in the wagon, John Palmer was walking, just as he had walked almost every step of the way, sometimes but not very often trading places with Amanda, and sometimes trading places with Nicole. He glanced up at Amanda, who was holding the reins to the oxen team that had pulled the wagon all the way from Illinois.

There was another wagon traveling with them, belonging to Elmer Franklin and his two brothers, Linus and Sid. They had met in Western Kansas, and because they were headed for the same general area, had decided to travel together.

The Franklin wagon was being pulled by mules, and the brothers had teased John for using oxen.

"Tease all you want. You can't beat a team of oxen. They'll keep on a-workin' a long time after horses will give out on you, 'n even mules," John had told them.

Because John Palmer had worked as a hostler, he was well aware of the various attributes of horses, mules, and oxen. He knew that a team of horses would tire before a team of mules, and that a team of mules would tire before oxen. And while he could use oxen to plow his fields, they weren't that good at pulling a light wagon, so when they got to Hell's Valley, he would have to buy a team of horses or mules, whatever he could get the best deal for.

"I wonder how many people will be where we are going?" Nicole asked her aunt Amanda.

"Oh, not very many, I'm sure."

"Oh."

Amanda looked at her niece. "You sound unhappy about that."

"It's just that . . ." Nicole started to say, then stopped in midsentence.

"I know what's troubling you, dear," Amanda said, patting Nicole on the hand. "You are thinking about a husband, aren't you?"

"Well, I would like to get married sometime."

"I'm sure the Franklin brothers would, as well," Amanda said. She smiled. "Why, I'll bet even now, they are deciding among themselves which one will begin courting you."

"I . . . I suppose so."

"You don't sound very happy about the thought."

"I don't want to marry any of them," Nicole blurted out. "Don't get me wrong, they are all nice, I suppose, but Sid is the youngest, and he is thirty years old. I would like someone a little closer to my own age."

"Well, something will work out for you, I'm sure," Amanda said reassuringly.

It was now a little over a month since they had left Cairo, and the oxen had pulled the wagon all the way without giving them a bit of trouble.

John chuckled, then spoke to his oxen. "You critters have come a long way, but you don't have nothin' on me, 'cause I've walked near 'bout all the way from Illinois my own self."

"Did you say something, dear?" Amanda called down to her husband.

"I was just talkin' to the oxen, is all, tellin' 'em what a good job they've been doin'," John called back. "Critters like to be told when they're doin' good."

"Whatever you say, dear," Amanda replied with a smile.

"Would you like me to drive for a while, Aunt Amanda?" Nicole asked. "It would give your hands a rest."

"Why, thank you, dear. That is so sweet of you."

It was three days later when the Indians came. Sid Franklin saw them first. It was early afternoon, and they had just finished their lunch, when several Indians appeared on the crest of a hill no more than a hundred yards away.

"Elmer," Sid said. "What do you reckon that is?" He pointed to the Indians. Then the others saw them, as well.

"They're probably just curious about us," Elmer said. "I'll go see what they want."

Elmer had taken no more than half a dozen steps toward the Indians when an arrow came zipping toward him and buried itself in his chest. He let out a hoarse cry of pain and staggered back a couple of steps as he lifted his hands toward the shaft and stared down at it in disbelief.

Nicole didn't see the arrow until Elmer toppled over backward. Then she saw it sticking almost straight up from his chest.

"Get your guns!" John shouted, and he, Sid, and Linus reached into their wagons to grab their rifles.

Nearly a dozen flaming arrows flew through the air and buried their blazing heads in the side of the two wagons, setting them aflame.

Nicole heard the gunfire then, coming from the Indians as well as her uncle and the two Franklin brothers. She saw her uncle go down. The two Franklin brothers were still shooting as she crawled under the burning wagon.

"Aunt Amanda!" Nicole cried. "Aunt Amanda!"

There was no answer. Nicole couldn't remember where her aunt had been when the attack started. Amanda might have been killed by an arrow or a bullet already. She could hear them hitting the wagon above her as it burned.

She had believed that life had hardened her to the point that she was no longer afraid of anything. That was wrong, she realized now. She was still capable of sheer terror, and it welled up inside her, making her heart hammer madly and choking her.

Or maybe that was the smoke from the wagon, which was being consumed rapidly by flames. She couldn't stay there, she knew. She scrambled out from under the vehicle, on the side away from where the Indians had been, then ran for some bushes about fifty yards away.

The burning wagons and the smoke allowed her to escape unseen.

Very soon thereafter, all the shooting stopped, to be replaced by the savage, triumphant yelps and cries of the Indians.

Nicole still had not been seen. She slithered back on her stomach to get as far away from the Indians as she could, being careful not to make the brush move too much.

She closed her eyes to the horror that was playing out at the two burning wagons.

It was quiet when Nicole finally opened her eyes. The Indians were gone, and the wagons were blackened hulks. Nicole didn't know how long she had been here, wasn't aware of when the Indians had left. Had she gone to sleep? How could she have gone to sleep under such conditions?

Then she realized that she hadn't actually gone to sleep. She had fainted. She felt ashamed of herself for having fainted, but as she thought back on it, she realized that fainting may well have saved her life. Passed out as she'd been, she had not been a witness to the most debased acts of the Indians. Had she seen them, she didn't think she could have remained quiet.

Smoke hadn't given up his intention to find Richards, Potter, and Stratton, but he also felt that he had some obligation to Preacher, so he stayed with the old mountain man long enough to capture some wild horses and take them to market.

They were on their way back to their camp when Preacher began sniffing the air.

"What is it?" Smoke asked.

"Boy, are you tellin' me you don't smell that?"

"Yeah," Smoke said, realizing that he did smell something. "Smoke. I smell smoke and . . . Wait, it's not just smoke. Somethin's burnt."

"It's more like somebody is burnt," Preacher said.

"Somebody?"

Preacher pulled his long gun out and laid it across his saddle. "Let's go," he said.

Smoke, taking his cue from Preacher, snaked out his own rifle from the saddle sheath.

They came down a low-lying ridge and emerged from a copse of cottonwood trees. Then they saw the source of the odor. There were two blackened wagons sitting one behind the other. The vehicles weren't burning anymore; there wasn't even any smoke remaining.

That wasn't the case off to one side, where the flames of a small fire still crackled directly below the limb of a tree.

A naked man was tied by his feet to that sturdy limb, so he hung head down over the fire. His head and shoulders were black, cooked. The dangling body moved slightly, and Smoke figured it was blowing in the wind.

Only there wasn't any wind. Smoke's guts clenched as he realized the poor hombre was still alive.

But not for long. He let out a sound that was half gasp, half groan, and a great shudder went through him. That was the moment of death, thought Smoke, and the limp way in which the man now hung confirmed that.

"I didn't know there were any hostile Indians hereabouts," Smoke said.

"Most likely, it's a bunch o' 'Paches," Preacher said. "Danglin' a poor devil over a fire like that is one o' their damn tricks. They wander up this far north ever' now and then to raid the Utes." Preacher pointed to the other burned and mutilated bodies scattered around, including one man who had been tied to a wagon wheel and tortured. "There warn't no civilized Injuns never done nothin' like that, and 'Paches are about as far from civilized as you can get."

* * *

Nicole had laid there in the brush in a half-stupor for a long time, but finally something made her raise her head. She heard voices, and though they were too far away for her to make out what they were saying, she thought they might be speaking English. She rose up and looked out at them from her hiding place in the bushes.

They weren't Indians, but they were frightening looking. One had long hair and was wearing buckskins; the other one, who was younger and much taller, was wearing jeans and a plaid shirt. Both were carrying rifles, and she was undecided as to whether or not she should call out to them. Would she be jumping from the kettle into the fire?

Beyond them was a long, rounded mound of rocks. When Nicole saw it, she thought it looked like a grave, and a second later it came to her that that was exactly what it was. These two men, whoever they were, had buried those killed in the Indian attack.

Her aunt and uncle and the Franklin brothers. Nicole was convinced she was the only survivor.

The older man in buckskins wandered off, studying the ground around the site as if looking for something. The younger one walked over to the wagons and began poking around in the ruined remains. He reached into what was left of a trunk and pulled out one of Aunt Amanda's dresses.

"Preacher!" he called.

As the old-timer approached, the young man reached into the trunk again and retrieved another dress, this one belonging to Nicole. The old-timer rubbed the gingham between his fingers and said, "God have mercy on their souls. These men were damn fools, bringin' womenfolk out here."

"Maybe one of them got away," the younger one suggested.

"'Tain't likely. But we best take a look around anyway."

The young man jacked a round into his rifle and turned toward the nearby bushes.

Nicole still didn't budge. These men had buried the victims of the attack, which was the decent thing to do, but that didn't mean they could be trusted. The younger one was . . . not bad-looking, in a rugged way . . . but he seemed so fierce. Nicole could sense an aura of danger about him.

The two of them looked around for a while but didn't come near Nicole's hiding place. She wanted them to go away. She wasn't sure what she would do if they did—she would be out here in the wilderness alone, in that case— but that might be better than being helpless in their hands.

Then, suddenly, the young man turned and said, "Look, Preacher." He pointed at the ground, then walked directly toward the thick brush where Nicole was hidden.

"I see the prints, Smoke," the old-timer said as he joined he younger one. "Them's a gal's prints. Mayhaps she got clear and run away. Don't look like none o' the Injuns follered her. We best find her afore dark."

Oh! They are coming toward me! Nicole thought, her heart in her throat. The one called Smoke held his rifle ready.

Nicole couldn't control herself. She scooted backward, and the movement of the brush gave her away.

"Girl!" Preacher called. "You come on out now. You're among friends."

Unable to hold back tears, Nicole began to weep. All the terrible things she had experienced today came flooding out.

"We're not going to hurt you," Smoke said.

She wanted to believe him, she really did. But she couldn't do anything except cry.

"Lookee there!" Preacher exclaimed as he pointed into the brush. "There's a snake crawlin' in there with you!"

Nicole had a mortal fear of snakes. Without thinking about what she was doing, she leaped up and bolted out of the brush.

She ran right into Smoke's arms, which were outstretched to catch her. He folded them around her and caught her against him. For a second, instinct made her want to struggle, but when she felt the power and strength in Smoke's arms, she knew it would be useless to try to get away.

Instead she lifted her head and looked into his eyes, and as she did, she knew she had been wrong about him. Something she saw there in his gaze told her that he would never hurt her.

After a long moment, the old-timer called Preacher snorted and said, "This ain't no place for romance. Come on, let's get the hell outta here."

She was quite beautiful, with light blue eyes and a heart-shaped face framed by hair the color of wheat. She was young, but the soft curves of her body made it abundantly clear that she was a woman full-grown. Smoke was suddenly a little embarrassed. He let go of her and stepped back.

"What's your name?" Smoke asked.

"Nicole," she said. "Nicole Woodward. Are they . . . Is everyone dead?"

"I'm afraid so," Smoke said. He knew the news was harsh, but he spoke as softly as he could, trying to break it to her gently.

Despite Preacher's urging that they leave, Nicole stepped

over to the long, rock-mounted grave and stared down at it. Smoke wasn't going to interrupt her grieving.

"What about my . . . my aunt?" she asked.

"We didn't find her," Smoke said.

"Looks like the savages done took her," Preacher added.

Nicole drew in a sharp breath. "What will they do to her?"

"Was she a handsome woman?"

"She was beautiful."

"Then they'll keep her. They'll work her hard, but there's a good chance some fella will make her his wife. She'll be all right."

Smoke was a little surprised but grateful that Preacher seemed to be trying to spare the girl's feelings. Then the old-timer added, "Then again, they might trade her off for a horse or a rifle."

"Or they might just kill her."

It wasn't really a question, but Preacher said, "Yes, ma'am, missy, they sure might. Injuns is notional critters."

"I'll never see her again."

"Likely not."

Nicole put her face in her small hands and began crying. "I don't know what to do. I don't have any family to go back to. I don't have anyone."

Smoke put his arms around her and pulled her to him, and when he did, he became aware of two things. He felt intensely protective of her, and she felt soft and vulnerable in his arms.

"Sure you do, Nicole. You have us."

CHAPTER 4

Because she had nowhere else to go, Nicole moved in with Preacher and Smoke. Bedrolls and sleeping under the stars were all right for a couple of rough-as-a-cob customers like them, but a girl needed something better. Something permanent.

So they built a house of logs and rocks and adobe, and despite its rustic appearance, the place was actually quite comfortable. Smoke and Preacher erected an inside wall that gave Nicole some privacy, and soon she began thinking of this place as her home.

One day when both Smoke and Preacher were out of the house hunting for more mustangs and she was cooking supper, she moved the pots around on the wood-burning stove to regulate the temperature, and then she stopped for a moment, as nothing else was needed. She looked around the inside of the cabin. A deer's head was on one wall; skins covered another wall; and the door didn't actually open and close but was moved away, then replaced and held up by a support. There was a window, which Nicole enjoyed.

As she contemplated her situation, comparing this cabin

to the house where she had lived in Boston, she couldn't help but smile. In Boston she had been surrounded by people all the time, and now, considering the isolation of this cabin, she realized just how crowded the city was.

Oddly, she didn't feel a sense of nostalgia for Boston; the truth was, though she never would have thought such a thing, she enjoyed the isolation. And she wasn't completely isolated. She had Preacher and Smoke. Especially Smoke.

She recalled the conversation with her aunt Amanda, when she had expressed the concern that she might not find someone she would want to marry.

Well, she was no longer concerned. She knew now that she was in love with Kirby Jensen. It wasn't just that she found the tall, powerfully built man handsome; she did. It was also the way he treated her, with respect and tenderness. And when she learned that he had feelings for her as well, she was happier than she had ever been in her life.

Preacher, as he often did, left Smoke alone for long periods of time, going back into the mountains, just as he had been doing for more than fifty years, long before Smoke came to live with him. He was gone for the entire winter. Then one day in the early spring, Nicole told Smoke that they needed to talk.

Smoke chuckled. "What do you mean, we need to talk? Good Lord, girl, we talked all winter. We talk all the time."

"Yes, but as it turns out, Smoke, we have done something more than *just* talk all the time," Nicole said with a twinkle in her eye. "And that's what we have to talk about."

"I swear, Nicole, you aren't making any sense at all."

"We have to get married."

Smoke chuckled. "You don't have to propose to me, Nicole. I've already proposed to you, remember? You said yes, and we're going to be married as soon as Preacher comes back."

"When will he be back?"

"With Preacher, there's no telling. We'll just have to wait and see. It could be tomorrow. It could be six more months."

"We can't wait six more months. We can't wait six more weeks."

"What? What do you mean?"

Nicole smiled at him. "Smoke, what I'm saying is, I'm going to have a baby. No, *we* are going to have a baby."

Smoke sat, stunned, in the chair. "Nicole, you can't have a baby! Don't you know that we're better than one hundred miles from the nearest doctor?"

Nicole laughed. "Darling, you can't just say I can't have a baby, as if I can change my mind. It's already started. We're going to have a baby, but don't worry about a doctor. The baby is going to get here with or without a doctor. All I want is for us to be married. I want the baby to have a legal name."

"Preacher told me there is a little settlement of Mormons southwest of here, over in Utah Territory. We can probably find someone to marry us there. But it could be as many as two weeks there and another two weeks back. Can you stand the ride?"

She smiled and kissed him. "You just watch."

On the tenth day of their travel, Smoke figured they were in Utah Territory and probably had been all day, so the settlement of Mormons should be in sight. But all they found were half a dozen rotting, tumbledown cabins and no signs of life.

"Preacher said they were here in fifty-one," Smoke said. "I wonder where they went?"

Nicole's laughter rang out over the deserted collection of falling-down cabins. "Honey, that was over twenty years ago." Her eyes swept the land, and she spotted an old grave-yard that was overgrown with weeds.

"Let's look over there," she suggested.

They examined all the rotting grave markers, and the latest date they could find on any of them was from four-teen years earlier.

"There is no preacher, and I don't have any idea where one might be from here," Nicole said, obviously disap-pointed.

"We are going to be married today, Nicole, preacher or no preacher."

"How?"

"I'll show you."

Smoke built a fire and spent an hour heating and ham-mering a nail into a perfect circle. When it had cooled, he slipped it on her third finger, left hand.

"Before God, I take you, Nicole Woodward, as my wife," he said.

Nicole looked into his eyes. "Before God, I take you, Smoke Jensen, as my husband."

Smoke kissed her, then smiled. "Now let me ask you something. Would you feel any more married if a preacher that neither of us had ever met had married us?"

"Not at all. As far as I'm concerned, we are married," she said. "Come, husband. Let's go home."

Keene, New Hampshire

The president of Yale University, who chronicled his travels, had described Keene as "one of the prettiest towns in New England, situated as it is on an ancient lake bed surrounded by hills, which in the fall are ablaze with color."

A dark blue carriage, pulled by a team of matched white horses under the command of a liveried driver, rolled down Washington Street. Its only passenger was Sally Reynolds, a very pretty hazel-eyed woman, who was sitting in the plushly cushioned seat of the family brougham. She pulled the curtain back so she could look outside.

On the door of the elegant vehicle was displayed the Reynolds family crest, a silver shield with a portcullis and three blue bars, the shield flanked by lions rampant. The Reynolds family was one of the oldest in the city. Two hundred years earlier Adolphus Reynolds had been a hero of King Philip's War, a violent conflict between Indian inhabitants of New England and New England colonists that stretched from 1675 to 1678. Adolphus's significant contributions to the ultimate victory of the colonists were such that he was the recipient of a rather sizable land grant. Subsequent generations increased the landholdings, so that now the Reynolds family was one of the wealthiest and most influential families of the city.

Several pedestrians waved or nodded respectfully as the brougham passed them by. The beautiful young woman returned every greeting in a friendly way. After a short outing they turned off Washington Street onto a long tree-lined drive. At the other end was a large columned white house built in the Greek Revival style.

When the carriage reached the front of the house, the driver hopped down and hurried back to open the door for Sally. Sally had told him many times that she didn't need the door opened for her, but the driver had insisted that this was a part of his profession and that he would wish that she not deprive him of that act, so she acquiesced.

"Thank you, Mr. Witherspoon," Sally said as she stepped down from the brougham.

"My pleasure, ma'am."

Sally's mother, Abigail, met her in the foyer.

"Where's Father?" Sally asked.

"John is in the library."

"Good. I have something to tell him. You, too, Mother."

"My, you sound so serious," Abigail said.

"Yes, ma'am, I am serious. I want to talk to you both about something."

"All right, dear," Abigail said, though there was a hint of trepidation in her reply.

John Reynolds, who looked younger than his forty-seven years, was sitting at the library table, perusing an open book. He stood when his wife and one of his daughters came into the room.

"John, Sally says she has something she wishes to talk about," Abigail said, the tone of her voice giving away her concern.

"Oh? Well, what is it about, honey?"

"I've got a job," Sally said. "I have been accepted for the position of schoolteacher."

For several seconds, her father stared at her without responding. Then, "Why in heaven's name would you want to do that?" John asked.

"Father, I do have a teaching certificate, you know."

"Yes, but I thought it was just for the accomplishment. I never dreamed you would actually want to pursue that as an occupation. And why would you? There is no need for you to ever work. Your grandfather left you controlling interest in the bank. You are quite comfortable, you know. As a matter of fact, you are more than comfortable. You are a very wealthy young lady."

"Father, this is something that I very much want to do."

Sally's parents looked at each other in that way of long-married couples, as if they were communicating without saying anything.

"Very well, I won't stand in your way," her father finally said. "I'm sure that after a stint of teaching, where you will be . . . Well, I don't mean to sound snobbish, but you will soon discover that your social standing shall be so much higher than that of those who must work that you will have enough of it and want to resign."

"Which school has hired you, dear?" Abigail asked with a forced but hopeful smile.

"The Bury School Department."

"Bury School? I thought I knew all our schools," Abigail said. "Where is the Bury School?"

"It's in Bury, Mother," Sally said. She paused for a moment before she continued. "Bury, Idaho Territory."

Both Abigail and John gasped in chagrined surprise.

The Uncompahgre Mountains, Colorado

Preacher was sitting in front of the house in the mountains when Smoke and his new bride rode into the yard. He was spitting tobacco juice and whittling on a piece of wood.

"Howdy." He greeted them as if he had been gone only a day instead of six months. "Where you two been?"

"What do you mean, where have we been?" Smoke replied. "You're the one that rode off. Where have you been?"

"I've been around," Preacher replied, as if that was all the answer that was needed. "I told you I'd be back come spring."

"We got married," Nicole said proudly, showing him her ring.

"You with child, girl?"

"Yes, sir."

"I figured if I left you two alone, you'd get into mischief." The old-timer's bony shoulders rose and fell. "'Tain't no problem. I've helped birth dozens o' papooses. Woman does all the work. Man just gets in the way. Who spoke the marryin' words?"

"Nobody," Smoke said. "Couldn't find a minister. And we went all the way over into Utah Territory looking."

"Don't matter. It's what's in your hearts that counts." Preacher chuckled. "Knowed you was in love months ago, the minute I seen you fall off your horse."

"I never fell off my horse!" Smoke objected.

"I'll go fix supper," Nicole said with a smile.

When Nicole had closed the door to the cabin, Preacher turned to Smoke and asked in a low, serious voice, "You still got it in mind to find the rest o' them men that kilt your pa?"

"I haven't put it out of my mind," Smoke said.

"Yeah, well, here's something for you to think about. You can't be going looking for those men anymore, seein' as you're married now. You've got responsibilities to that woman, who is carrying your child."

"I reckon you're right, so I guess it can wait for a while. If they leave me alone, I'll leave them alone."

"It ain't going to work that way, though."

"What do you mean?"

"I figure they already know that you have been after them, and it's more'n likely they have found some people who will be a-comin' after you. They'll be paying them to do it, bounty hunters, you know, because a damn bounty hunter don't really care who he is after as long as he gets his blood money."

"I'm through with all that now, Preacher. I'm hanging up my guns. I want to raise horses and maybe run some cattle. You, me, and Nicole. We're going to raise a family, and our children will need a grandfather. And that's where you come in, you old goat."

"Thank you. That's the nicest thing you have said to me in months."

"Do you think maybe it's because I haven't seen you in months?"

"Well, yeah, I reckon that could be. When is the girl goin' to give birth?"

"November, she thinks."

"Just like a woman. Don't never know nothin' for sure."

The baby was born just after the first snow, and Smoke enjoyed sitting in front of the fireplace in one of the two rocking chairs he had made, warm and content, as he watched Nicole nurse little Art.

"What do you mean, you named him after me?" Preacher had asked. "You mean you are going to call him Preacher?"

Smoke and Nicole had laughed.

"No, we are naming him Arthur Emmett after you and Pa, and we're going to call him Art. That is your name, isn't it?" Smoke asked.

"Oh," Preacher said. "Yeah, I guess you're right. My name is Art, only I ain't never been called that by nobody in so long that I sometimes near 'bout forget. Seems to me like I been called Preacher 'most my whole life."

Bury, Idaho—spring

Wiley Potter, Muley Stratton, and Josh Richards sat in cushioned chairs in the PSR Ranch office. The gunmen Felter, Poker, and Canning were on the sofa; Stoner and Evans had each found a hard-bottomed, straight-backed chair; while Clark, Grissom, and Austin were sitting on the fireplace hearth.

"We'll give you eight thousand dollars," Richards said. "There are eight of you, so that works out to a thousand dollars apiece."

"You're givin' the eight of us a thousand dollars apiece to kill one man?" Felter asked.

"Yeah, well, he's not just any man. It turns out that he is much more capable than the average man, and I want to be sure the job is done," Richards said. "I found out not too long ago that he's been asking around about us. I don't know how the hell he ever found out that we were the ones that killed his old man, but I don't want to worry about him being on our tail."

"There are three of you," Felter said. "Are you saying that one man is better 'n all three of you put together?"

"No, I'm not saying that," Richards replied. "But there's something you've got to understand. Muley, Wiley, and I are important people in this town. Hell, we are important all over the West now. It wouldn't look good for us to get involved in some shooting scrape. Even if we killed him, and I'm sure we would, it just wouldn't look good for us. That's why we are hiring the eight of you to do it."

"Who is this man we're goin' after?" Felter asked.

"I'll give you all the particulars before you leave."

"Do you know where he is?" Felter asked.

Richards smiled. "I know exactly where he is. He has a

little place down in Hinsdale County, Colorado, livin' with some woman he found out on the trail. He may or may not be married to her. Anyway, the word is that she's had a kid by now, and that should give you men an edge. Not that you would need one.'

"A thousand dollars apiece?" Felter said.

"That's a lot of money, and I expect you to produce."

"We want half of it now," Felter said.

"I figured you would." Richards turned his head to call out, "Jane, would you come in here, please?"

An attractive young woman, who might have been wearing just a little too much paint, came into the room.

Richards turned his attention back to the men before him. "Before my woman went into town, I told her to write out eight bank drafts." He looked at the woman. "Did you do that?" he asked.

"Of course I did, honey. Don't I always do what you ask?" She handed the eight pieces of paper to Richards.

"You can cash them at the bank in Bury before you leave, if you would like. There's five hundred dollars apiece here. Once the job is completed, I'll give you the rest of the money."

CHAPTER 5

New York

Sally Reynolds's parents had made one last effort to talk her out of her plan, which her father had said was certainly ill conceived, if not insane. Gaining no ground with her, he had asked her to go to New York to discuss her plans with his sister, Sally's Aunt Mildred.

She spent three days in New York, enjoying the city, shopping, visiting the museum, and attending the Broadway presentation of *Little Nell and the Marchioness*.

"I've had a wonderful time with you, Aunt Mildred. You have been most gracious."

"Why, thank you, dear. But I believe you said you had something you wanted to discuss with me. Would it be your idea about going west to teach school?"

"Yes!" Sally replied with a gasp. "But how did you know that?"

"I got a letter from John telling me about it. He wants me to try to talk some sense into you."

"And are you going to try?"

"Yes."

"I see."

Mildred smiled and put her hand across the table. "I'm going to tell you to go where your heart tells you to go."

"What? Oh, Aunt Mildred, I thought . . . that is, I was afraid . . ."

"I know what you thought, dear. You thought I was going to try to talk you out of it. May I share a secret with you?"

"Yes, of course!"

"There was a time when, more than anything else in the world, I wanted to move to San Francisco to see what was on the other side of this country. I didn't go, because my older brother, your father, talked me out of it. I've wondered about that decision for my entire life. I know now that I should have gone. I don't want you to spend the rest of your life wondering. Go, Sally. Follow your heart while you are still young. If you find that you don't like it, you can always come back home, like the prodigal son or, in this case, the prodigal daughter," she added with a chuckle.

"I'm going to do it!" Sally said, a broad smile spreading across her face.

"Do you have any idea where you'll wind up?"

"I sent some letters out, and the only place that responded was a town in Idaho Territory called Bury."

Bury, Idaho Territory

Sally Reynolds had been on the train for seven days since her mother, in tears, and her father, with a stern expression on his face, had come down to the depot in Keene to see her off. Though the trip had been long, it had not been all that tiring, because Sally had the convenience of a private compartment on the Pullman car.

The Pullman car arrangements had been made by her father as a "going away" gift.

"Father, how is it going to look for a schoolteacher to step down from a Pullman car when she arrives for her first teaching job?" she had asked.

"If you feel self-conscious about it, walk through the train to one of the day cars before you get off," her father had suggested.

Sally had smiled. "Yes, that is quite devious, but I like it."

And now, with the train standing in the station at Bury, she did just that: she walked through the cars from the Pullman to a day car to make her exit.

Nobody met her at the train, but she hadn't expected anyone to do so. After leaving her luggage at the depot to be picked up later, she started down the boardwalk toward the address that was on the acceptance letter she held in her hand.

Bury was a bustling settlement, with horses tied at hitch rails and wagons and buggies parked along the street. People hurried here and there along the boardwalks and across the wide, dusty street.

Sally had gone only a short distance when she heard and felt the concussion of something whizzing by her very fast. Concurrent with her hearing the report of a gunshot, a bullet crashed through one of the square panes of the big glass window in the building she was walking past.

Actually, it was two gunshots, one right on top of the other, and as she looked out into the street, she saw two men facing each other, with smoking guns in their hands. She stared at them in shock for a moment. Then one of the men clasped his hands over his stomach, took a couple of staggering steps, and fell.

As she stood there, mesmerized by the scene, she felt

someone grab her, looked around, and saw that it was a very attractive and expensively dressed woman.

"Miss, you had better come in here and off the street! Quickly!"

Sally followed the woman into one of the buildings fronting the street.

"Isn't it over now?" Sally asked. "I saw that poor man fall."

"There's likely to be more shooting. Clay Holden is the man who was just shot, and he has a brother," the pretty woman said. "I expect Jeb will be coming out into the street shortly, wanting revenge."

"Heavens," Sally said. "Does this sort of thing go on often?"

"Fairly often."

True to the pretty lady's prediction, a second man came out into the street, firing his pistol as he did so. The two men continued to shoot at each other until the second man—Sally assumed it was Jeb—went down, as well. The first man put his gun back in the holster, then started toward a nearby saloon as several others rushed forward to congratulate him.

"It's over now," the pretty lady said.

"I . . . I've never seen anyone get shot," Sally said. "But to see two men shot in just a few minutes is, well, I must say, quite a dramatic welcome to Bury," Sally said.

"Just arrived?"

"Yes. By train a few minutes ago."

"Have you come to work at the Pink House?"

"The Pink House?"

"For Miss Flora."

"I don't know who Miss Flora is," Sally said. She

smiled. "My name is Sally Reynolds, and I'm the new schoolteacher."

"A schoolteacher, are you? Well, Miss Reynolds, it's good to meet you. I'm Janey Garner."

"Do you work at the Pink House?"

"No. I'm a business manager for the PSR," Janey replied.

"PSR?"

"It's a ranch, the Potter, Stratton, and Richards. Only it's not just a ranch. It's a huge ranch."

"A lady ranch manager? That's most impressive. You must be as intelligent as you are beautiful."

Janey laughed and extended her hand. "Sally, I think you and I are going to wind up being very good friends."

"Miss Garner—"

"Janey," Janey interrupted.

"Janey, do you know how to get to this address?" Sally held out the acceptance letter so Janey could see the address.

"Sure, come on. I'll take you," Janey said.

She accompanied Sally to a small white building that was next door to the schoolhouse.

"This is the place," Janey said. She paused, then added, "It would be better if I didn't go in."

"I understand you have other things to do," Sally said. "Thank you for showing me where to go."

"Other things to do," Janey said with an enigmatic smile. "Yes, well, welcome to Bury."

When Sally stepped into the building, she saw a thin, pinched-face woman wearing steel-rimmed glasses, a long black cord stretching from the glasses to a pin on the bodice of her dress. Her mostly gray hair was combed back into a severe bun.

"Miss, I think you are in the wrong place," the woman said, her voice thin and aloof.

"Oh, I'm sorry. I was told this was the place," Sally said. She looked at the letter. "Could you tell me where I might find Miss Olivia Peabody?"

"I'm Olivia Peabody. Why on earth would you be looking for me?"

"I'm Sally Reynolds. I was told to report to you when I reached Bury."

"You? You are Sally Reynolds?"

"Yes."

"Where did you attend school?" There was a challenging tone to the question, which Sally couldn't understand.

"Mary Woodson Normal College," Sally said. "I assure you, it is quite a good school."

The stern expression on Miss Peabody's face was replaced with a smile. "Yes, of course it is, dear. Please forgive me for questioning you in such a way, but I needed to be sure that you are who you say you are. Especially since you arrived in the company of . . . that woman." She sniffed. "I saw both of you through the window."

"That woman was quite nice to me. Not only did she lead me here for my appointment, but she also just about saved my life."

"Saved your life? In what way? I don't understand."

Sally told the school principal about the shooting in the middle of the street.

"Yes, I'm afraid that such things are only too common in Bury. And as long as the man Miss Garner works for is allowed to run roughshod over the town, and as long as Flora Yancey maintains that awful Pink House, I'm afraid the gunfights in the streets will continue."

"Heavens, is there no law in Bury?"

"Not unless you count Sheriff Reese and Deputy Rogers as representatives of the law, and I'm afraid they forfeited that distinction when they took their first bribe from Mr. Josh Richards and company."

Olivia Peabody's entire demeanor changed then, and she extended her hand. "Welcome to the Bury Public School. Come with me, and I'll show you around."

CHAPTER 6

Now that Smoke had a wife and baby to support, he had given up the search for Richards and the other two men. He planned to sell another string of horses this spring, and he had promised Nicole that sometime this summer, he would take her and the baby to Denver. He was a horse dealer now, pure and simple. He still wore his gun, but it was more an act of habit than of necessity, and it was his sincere hope that he wouldn't ever have to use it again.

Nicole had asked recently how long it would be before they went to Denver. She had never been to Denver and was excited over the prospect of a visit there.

"Don't get me wrong," she'd said. "I truly love it here, but being from Boston, I find that sometimes I miss being in a city. And out here, Denver is the closest I'm likely to come to a city."

"Well, I've never been to Boston, so I don't know how big it is," Smoke said. "But Denver's pretty big."

Smoke knew that being all alone, so far from anyone else, was probably hard on her, though she had never mouthed so much as one complaint. She seemed perfectly satisfied and happy with her little mountain home, her husband, and her child.

Preacher, meanwhile, had gone on one of his occasional journeys to, as he said, meet his Maker. It was Preacher's way though he had yet to meet anyone, much less his Maker. He had told them that he thought it was foolish to name a baby after an old man, but both Smoke and Nicole knew that Preacher was pleased by it.

"The kid knows me," Preacher had said. "You see the way his face gets all lit up ever' time I come over and he sees me?"

"Of course he knows you, Preacher," Nicole said. "He thinks you are part of the family. And why shouldn't he think that? You *are* a part of the family."

"You think maybe when the kid gets old enough that, uh, maybe he could call me Gran'pa? I mean, I know I'm not his real gran'pa but . . ."

"Oh, but you are his grandpa," Nicole said. "In every way that counts, you are little Art's grandpa."

Blodgett, Colorado

"Smoke Jensen has to be in that valley, somewhere southwest of here. Everything points in that direction," Felter said to the other bounty hunters he was with.

"Do you remember that old Indian we talked to?" Canning asked. "He said Smoke Jensen had a fortune in gold hid out in his house."

"Yeah, I know he said that, but what I wonder is, If he does have all that money, why's he livin' out here, away from ever'thing? Hell, you'd think he would live in some-place big, like Denver or Kansas City or some such place, wouldn't you?" Stoner asked.

"Yeah, but don't forget that same Injun said somethin' about a blond-haired woman that was the only white woman down in that valley. 'N you might mind that Richards told us that Jensen had took hisself a wife. To my way of thinkin', that blond-haired woman the Indian was talkin' about has to be Jensen's woman, be she is his actual wife or just a woman he's a-livin' with," Canning said.

"More'n likely," Poker said.

"That bein' the case, it might be that he's savin' the money so as to build 'im up a ranch, like that 'n that Richards, Potter, 'n Stratton has got 'em."

"Could be," Poker said.

Austin, who called himself Kid Austin, grinned. "You boys can have the gunfighter. I'm goin' to get me a taste of that yeller-haired woman of his'n. I'd like to have me a white woman for a change."

"I tell you what, Austin, you can rape all the squaws you take a mind to," the bounty hunter named Grissom told him. "There don't nobody give a damn about them anyhow. But iffen you was to do somethin' like that to a white woman, what's goin' to happen is, you're goin' to wind up gettin' yourself hung."

Kid Austin's grin spread across his unshaven face. "Not if I don't leave her alive to tell no tales, I won't."

"What about the kid?" Poker asked. "Richards said that Jensen's woman had whelped."

"We'll kill the kid, too. Hell, it don't make no never mind to me. Besides which, we don't want to leave no young'un around to grow up and get mean, then come lookin' for us when we're old men, do we?" Canning said.

To a man, the bounty hunters agreed that made sense. They would pleasure themselves with the woman. Then they would kill her and the kid.

* * *

It had just turned April and was unseasonably warm when the thunderstorm hit. The storm scattered Smoke's small herd of breeding horses, and it also ran off their milk cow.

"I have to get those horses back, or we'll have to start all over," Smoke said.

"And the cow," Nicole said. "Don't forget the cow."

"And the cow," Smoke added, smiling, before he kissed both Nicole and the baby good-bye.

Smoke saddled Seven, then mounted and rode away. Less than a hundred yards away from the cabin, he turned and looked back. Nicole was standing just out front, holding the baby. Smoke lifted his arm to wave, and Nicole waved back. As Smoke rode on, he had a sudden feeling of foreboding, and he stopped and sat in his saddle for a moment as he considered going back.

"Why am I sitting here, Seven? This isn't gathering the horses, and the milk cow isn't going to find me."

Smoke pressed his knees against Seven's sides, and the horse moved on.

Over the next few days, Smoke located the horses: sometimes it was one at a time, and other times he would find two or three together. As he found them, he herded them into a closed canyon, intending to keep them there until all were gathered. Then he would take them back.

Nicole was outside hanging up clothes, mostly little Art's diapers, when she saw the eight riders come down from Peebles's Ridge and start out across the pastureland.

The house Smoke had built for them was so isolated that it was unusual for anyone to pass by. But for *eight* riders?

Smoke had taught Nicole to be very cautious, and there was something about the men that made her feel uncomfortable. After picking up the clothes basket, she hurried inside, then closed the door. There was a rifle standing in the corner, and she picked it up, jacked a round into the chamber, then stepped up to the window.

"You, inside!" one of the men called out. "You ain't bein' very friendly to some men that's just ridin' by."

"What do you want?" Nicole called back.

"We seen you got a waterin' trough there, 'n we're just a-wantin' to water our horses, is all."

"You just passed over a creek. Why didn't you water them there?"

"You're Jensen's woman, ain't ya?"

"Who wants to know?"

"We know you're Jensen's woman. If you give us the gold, we'll pass you on by. Iffen you don't give us the gold, we'll come in there 'n kill you 'n that kid of your'n both."

Smoke had taught Nicole how to shoot, and she aimed the rifle at the man who was doing all the talking and pulled the trigger. She saw a little fountain of blood spray from the man's chest as the impact of the bullet knocked him backward, over the flank of the horse he had been sitting on.

"Damn! She kilt Stoner!"

It was the fourth day out and Smoke had gathered all the horses when he thought he heard gunfire, though the sound was so quiet that he couldn't be sure. Then, though he couldn't explain how he knew, he realized that something was dreadfully wrong, and leaving the horses and the cow, he urged Seven into a gallop. Nicole was in danger, and he had to get home!

Back at the cabin Stoner lay dead, and another bounty hunter was nursing a painful bullet wound in his arm. Felter, Canning, Grissom, and Kid Austin were now in the cabin, and a wounded Nicole lay barely conscious and naked on the floor. The baby was crying.

"Shut that kid up!" Felter ordered as he dropped his trousers and lowered himself over Nicole.

The baby's cries sounded muffled. Then they stopped. Canning took the blanket away from the baby's face, then looked down at the little body, satisfied with his work.

As the bounty hunters had their way with Nicole, mercifully, she died.

"Wait a minute," Grissom said, holding out his hand. "There's somethin' that ain't right. I'm goin' to have a look outside."

Grissom stepped through the front door, then, sensing someone close, drew his pistol.

"I'm over here," Smoke said quietly.

Grissom spun toward the sound of the voice and saw a man standing by the corner of the cabin.

"Jensen!" Grissom shouted. That was the last thing he said before Smoke fired and the bullet plunged into Grissom's heart, killing him instantly.

Hearing the warning and the gunshot, Felter came out the front door, guns blazing, and he shot toward the corner of the cabin. But Smoke was gone.

"He went around behind the house!" Felter shouted.

As Smoke reached the back of the house, he saw some-one coming from the outhouse; and shooting twice, he dropped him before he could even pull his pants up. Kid Austin was behind the house, but when he heard the gun-fire near the outhouse, he turned and tried to get back into the house.

Smoke shot him in the cheek of his buttock, and Austin passed out from the pain. Smoke ran to the woodpile and took cover there as wild and ineffective gunfire came from men in the house. The gunfire stopped, and there was a long moment of silence. Then someone shouted from the cabin.

"Here's your boy!"

Smoke looked around the edge of the woodpile and saw a small body that had been tossed outside.

It was Art, and he was obviously dead.

Smoke fought to control himself, and he worried about Nicole. He hadn't heard her voice, and he felt certain that if she was still alive, she would have protested the baby being thrown outside.

Less than a moment later, his belief that she might al-ready be dead was confirmed by someone inside the cabin.

"You wonderin' 'bout your woman, Jensen?" a mocking voice called from inside the cabin. "We got 'er in here. We kilt 'er. Course, we had our way with 'er a'fore we kilt 'er. 'N you know what? She got to likin' what we was doin' to 'er 'n kept beggin' for more, till we got plumb wore out 'n had to kill 'er."

When Smoke had dismounted earlier, he had carried with him a Sharps buffalo rifle. This rifle could drop a one-ton buffalo from six hundred yards. It could also shoot through a wall. Through an opening in the woodpile,

Smoke could see the back of the cabin, and he saw someone move to the window for a quick glance outside. He saw, too, that the man moved to the left of the window after he had had his look-see.

Smoke put the buffalo rifle into a chink in the logs, and pulled the trigger.

"Hell's bells!" he heard someone shout from inside. "He kilt him right through the wall of the house!"

Felter and Canning ran out through the front door of the house.

"Let's clumb up on our horses 'n git," Felter said.

"Poker'n Clark's still back in the cabin, 'n Poker's 's been shot. We can't leave them," Canning said.

"You can stay with 'em if you want, but I'm gettin' the hell outta here."

Kid Austin, bleeding from the painful wound in his butt, managed to get mounted, and he, too, rode away.

"Damn. Austin 'n Canning's left!" Poker said as he peered through a window. "We got to get outta here!"

"You go," Clark said. "I'm goin' to kill that ignorant shoo fly and collect the reward myself."

Poker went out the front, mounted his horse, and caught up with the others.

"Hey!" Clark shouted through the back door. "There's only you 'n me now. You're out there behind that woodpile, all alone, 'n I'm in here with your wife. 'Course she's dead. I can look over 'n see her naked body. You got nobody. No, wait, I forgot. You got your kid with you, don't you?"

Smoke slid the Sharps' barrel through a gap between two of the logs in the woodpile so it was visible from inside the cabin. Leaving the rifle there, he rolled and lit a cigarette. Took a deep puff and blew the smoke out.

"Damn. I got to hand it to you. You're one cool character to just sit back 'n enjoy yourself a cigarette like that."

"Why don't you come out 'n have a smoke with me?" Smoke called back. "Then we can get down to business."

"You go ahead 'n have your smoke," Clark said. "I can wait."

Smoke rolled a second cigarette, put the burning cigarette on a log in a way that allowed smoke to curl up above the woodpile, then laid the second cigarette against the first, so that when the first burned down, it would light the second one.

Smoke knew the layout of the property better than any man alive, and he knew he could slip away, keep the woodpile between himself and the cabin until he got below the hill then, using the hill as cover, move quickly until he was on the windowless side of the cabin. He did just that, and when he moved up to the cabin, he heard Clark, who was still talking to the woodpile. The rifle barrel and the cigarette smoke had him convinced that Smoke was still there.

"Damn, what did you do? Light up another cigarette? It ain't goin' to do you no good, you know. I got water 'n food in here, 'n you ain't got nothin' out there. Oh, wait." Clark giggled. "You got your cigarettes."

Smoke moved around to the front door, which had been left open when the others ran. Looking in, he saw Nicole's mutilated body lying in a pool of blood, and the anger rose like bile in his throat. Clark, who was at the back door, was still talking to the woodpile.

"Damn, that cigarette smells good," Clark called out. "Makes me wish I had one, but that ain't no problem. After I kill you, I'll just take your'ns."

Smoke raised his pistol and aimed it at the back of Clark's head. He had never shot anyone in the back of the head before, but if there was ever anyone who deserved to be shot in the back of the head, it was this man.

His finger began to tighten on the trigger. Then he eased off the pressure. He was going to kill Clark, but he had just figured out a better way to do it.

Fifteen minutes later, with the inhuman screams of Clark filling the air behind him, Smoke gently carried Nicole's body up to the top of the small hill beside the house. This was Nicole's favorite place, because from here, there was a magnificent view of the nearby mountains. After laying her down, he returned for little Art's body, then carried him up the hill and laid him next to his mama.

Clark's inhuman screams continued as Smoke dug two graves. Then, with the graves covered, he came back to the cabin and set it afire. He also burned the barn.

"Don't leave me like this!" Clark begged. "You ain't human! This ain't no fittin' way for a man to die!"

Smoke rode away, paying no attention to the cries of the man who, covered with honey, was staked out on a huge red-harvester-ant hill.

CHAPTER 7

On board the Leopoldina, at sea

Smoke and Hemingford were sharing a table in the salon, and when Smoke got to the part of the story where Nicole and the baby were murdered, he stopped and sat there without speaking for a long moment. Then, to cover his silence, he took a swallow from the beer he was drinking.

"What about the ones who got away?" Hemingford asked. "Felter and the other two. You did take care of them, didn't you?"

Smoke nodded. "Yes, but by the time I caught up with them, they were holed up in an old silver mining camp, and there were fifteen of them. I killed every damn one of them."

"Fifteen," Hemingford said. He nodded. "I've heard everything from five to fifty were at the mining camp that day. It's good to get the right number from the horse's mouth."

"Fifteen," Smoke repeated. "Then, with Nicole and little

Art gone, I decided there wasn't anything to keep me from going after Richards, Potter, and Stratton."

"They're the ones who hired the bounty hunters who killed Nicole and the baby?"

"Yes. And they were also the ones who killed my father, so I had more than one reason to go after them."

"They were in Bury, Idaho, I believe," Hemingford said.

"Yes."

Bury, Idaho

The town of Bury had a bank; a large mercantile store; a weekly newspaper, the *Bury Chronicle*; several saloons; a café; and the Tiger Hotel. There were a few ranches around, but the largest ranch, the PSR, was owned by three men: Wiley Potter, Muley Stratton, and Josh Richards.

There were some in the town who resented the presence of the three men, believing that they had too much influence over the community and the surrounding area. And, indeed, they did, not only because of their wealth, but also because the local law—Sheriff Reese and Deputy Rogers—were on the take, controlled by Richards and the others.

Potter, Stratton, and Richards were the three men who had hired Felter and the others to kill Smoke. It had not been their intention to have Smoke's wife and child killed, but they felt no particular remorse over it. But if they felt no remorse, they did feel fear.

"The story that's goin' around is that Jenson killed not only the eight men we hired but twenty others besides," Potter said.

"I heard it was forty men," Stratton said.

"I don't believe he killed any forty men, or even twenty men, all by himself," Richards said.

"Yeah, well, it don't really matter just how many of 'em it was that he did kill," Stratton said. "We know for a fact that he killed every one of 'em. And you know damn well that the varmint is goin' to be a-comin' after us now, so the question is, what are we goin' to do about it?"

"That's why we're paying Reese and Rogers," Richards said.

"Surely you don't think Reese and Rogers can handle Smoke Jensen, do you?" Potter asked.

"No, but they can put out reward posters, dead or alive, and if the reward is for enough money, every bounty hunter this side of the Mississippi River will be after him."

Potter and Stratton smiled at the idea Richards had presented to them.

"Yeah," Potter said. "Yeah, that'll work. There ain't no question about it, Josh. You're the smartest one of the bunch."

Denver, Colorado

Marshal Holloway looked at the wanted poster Smoke showed him.

WANTED
DEAD OR ALIVE

**The Outlaw and Murderer
SMOKE JENSEN**

$10,000 REWARD

CONTACT: Sheriff Reece, *Bury, Idaho Territory*

"Where did you get this?" Marshal Holloway asked. The marshal had known Preacher for a long time, and he went by the belief that any friend of Preacher's was a friend of his, as well. Smoke knew that, which was why he had come to see Holloway.

"There are quite a few of them around."

Smoke had told Holloway the whole story, which was a risk, but he had a hunch he could trust the lawman. Holloway confirmed that now by saying, "Don't worry about it, Smoke. I'll get these pulled."

"No, don't pull them. Leave them out there," Smoke said.

"What?" Marshal Holloway replied. "Why in heaven's name would you want to do that?"

"As you can see, the reward is being posted by the sheriff of Bury, Idaho. I've never been there, but that tells me where Potter, Stratton, and Richards are. I know they are behind this, and they've either lied to the sheriff, or what's more likely is that they have him on their payroll. Either way, I want to play this out, so don't do anything to stop it."

"Ten thousand dollars is a lot of money, Smoke. You'll have every bounty hunter in the West looking for you. And not only that, but this much money will bring on people who've never thought about bounty hunting before."

"Including Buck West," Smoke said.

"Who?"

Smoke smiled. "Buck West. That's who I'm going to be calling myself for a while. I'm going to Bury, where I'll be joining the hunt for Smoke Jensen."

"Smoke, you're crazy as a loon. Did anyone ever tell you that?" Marshal Holloway asked with a little laugh.

Smoke chuckled, as well. "Some have told me a few

times. Preacher has told me that more times than I can count."

"You should listen to that old coot more," Marshal Holloway said. "All right, if that's the way you want it, I won't do anything to call them in." Marshal Holloway took a sheet of paper from his desk, wrote something on it, then gave it to Smoke. "But if you get picked up by a legitimate officer of the law, show him this."

To whom it may concern,
Kirby "Smoke" Jensen is a deputy US marshal
who is working under cover on a case for me.
If you have questions, contact, by telegraph,
Uriah Holloway, United States Marshal, Denver,
Colorado.

Smoke read the note, then folded it and put it in his pocket. "Thanks, Marshal."

"I just hope that if the time comes, you aren't shot before you can show the note."

"I'll try not to be," Smoke said with an easy smile.

Bury, Idaho

Sally had the children working on phonemes, and she wrote on the blackboard:

LESSON FIVE

The cat and the rat ran.
Ann sat, and Nat ran.
A rat ran at Nat.
Can Ann fan the lad?
The man and the lad.

The man has a cap.
The lad has a fan.
Has Ann a hat?

"Now, who can read this for me?" she asked, turning away from the board.

Half a dozen hands went up, the children eager to be the one called on to read.

At the end of the school day, Sally was wiping off the blackboard when Janey came into the classroom.

"The cook at the Pink House did a pot roast with potatoes, carrots, and onions, and Miss Flora has invited us for dinner."

"So, the schoolmarm has been invited to have dinner in a house of prostitution," Sally said, wiping the chalk from her hands. She smiled. "Why not? The 'good' ladies of the town haven't exactly welcomed me with open arms."

Janey laughed. "That's because you don't fit their idea of what a schoolmarm is supposed to look like. You're supposed to be an old, fat, plain-looking woman. Instead, you are young and beautiful, and the 'good' ladies of the town think you are after their husbands."

"Why, that is utter nonsense!" Sally said.

"Of course it is, but what does common sense have to do with anything?"

Flora Yancey had been in town for over four years now, having arrived as a member of a theater group. The owner of the repertoire company for which Flora worked lost all the box-office receipts in an after-show poker game. Then, rather than face his troupe with the disgrace of his betrayal, he made an attempt to recover the money at the point of a gun. That attempt failed, and he was shot dead. He now lay buried in the Bury Cemetery, under a marker which read:

HERE LIES MCKINLEY HALL
A THESPIAN OF RENOWN

HE TOOK HIS FINAL CURTAIN CALL
WHEN ONE SLUG FROM A .44 PUT HIM DOWN

Disgruntled and betrayed, the rest of the theater company left town, but Flora, seeing potential business opportunities in Bury, stayed. She was a beautiful woman, and her role in the theater had inflamed the fantasies of many men. She knew that she had only to play upon those fantasies to become a very successful prostitute. There was a rumor that she had once been the mistress of Emperor Franz Joseph of Austria. "No," someone had once said. "It was Prince Leopold of Belgium." Whenever questioned as to whether or not the rumors were true and, if so, just which crowned head had she been with, Flora always replied by saying, "A lady never informs upon the indiscretions of gentlemen of station."

She knew that such rumors fed the fantasies of men who wanted to "do it with a woman who had done it with a prince," so she did nothing to dispel the rumors.

When Flora made enough money, she built the Pink House and hired only the most attractive women she could find. She then went into semiretirement, preferring to manage the affairs of "her girls" over providing her personal services to the customers.

As soon as Sally and Janey arrived at the Pink House, Sara Sue, one of the "doves" who worked for Flora, approached Sally with a paper.

"Sally, will you grade my paper?" Sara Sue asked.

"Yes, of course I will," Sally replied.

The paper was the result of an assignment Sally had given Sara Sue and four other girls who were students in the classes Sally conducted at the Pink House.

"Sally, it's very sweet of you to give lessons to my girls," Flora said. "And even sweeter that you treat my girls and me as if we are your friends. You're very different from most of the 'good' people of the town, in that you aren't judgmental."

"I treat you and the others as my friends because you are my friends." Sally smiled broadly. "Besides, how else could I enjoy Martha's cooking? That roast beef smells absolutely scrumptious."

As soon as Smoke arrived in town, he went directly to the livery, where he made arrangements to board the midnight-black stallion he now rode. The horse had unusual, yellow-green eyes that reminded Smoke of a wolf's eyes. His personality was reminiscent of a wolf's, as well, with a wild, untamed streak a mile wide.

The stallion's previous owner had lost patience with the animal and tried to beat him with a board. That had proved to be a fatal mistake, as the stallion went after the man with flashing, steel-shod hooves.

Smoke had come along a short time later and bought the stallion from the man's widow, who wasn't exactly overcome with grief.

"Man who'll take a board to an animal ain't what you'd call easy to live with," the woman had said as she took Smoke's money. "So I can't really blame the critter."

Smoke didn't have an ounce of such cruelty in his body.

The stallion seemed to sense that about him, because they took to each other right away. Smoke learned to respect the animal's feelings and moods, and before long, the stallion was gentle and loyal—at least where Smoke was concerned. Anybody else who came messing around with him was liable to regret it.

Smoke named the stallion Drifter, and with this new mount, he turned his Appaloosa, Seven, loose in a beautiful, isolated valley to enjoy a well-deserved retirement. Smoke figured he would come back there someday to check on his old friend and trail partner. By then, Seven would probably have himself a whole harem of mustangs!

The hostler in the livery stable let out a low whistle of admiration when he saw Drifter.

"That's a mighty nice-lookin' piece of horseflesh, mister," he told Smoke.

"Give him oats at least once a day while I'm here," Smoke said.

"That'll be a quarter a day extra."

"Drifter is worth it," Smoke said. "You'll want to be a mite careful around him, too."

"One-man horse, eh?"

"That's right. He'll tolerate you, though. I told him to, and he listens to me."

The liveryman grinned and said, "Well, I appreciate that, Mister . . . ?"

"West, Buck West," Smoke said as he lifted the saddle from Drifter's back.

"What's brung you into town, Mr. West?"

"Ten thousand dollars," Smoke said.

The liveryman's eyes widened. "Damn, you're one o' them bounty hunters, aren't you?"

"You mean there are more?"

"Yeah, a bunch more."

"I'm surprised that a town no bigger than this one could put up such a large reward."

"Town hell," the liveryman said derisively. "That ain't the town's money that's got put up for the reward. No, sir, that money will be comin' from Potter, Stratton, 'n Richards."

Although Smoke had suspected that the three men lived here, this was his first confirmation.

"Who are they?"

"They're s'posed to be ranchers, on account of they've got 'em a pretty good-sized ranch outside of town. But they're more'n ranchers, seein' as they got their hand into purt' near ever'thing."

After taking his rifle and saddlebags, Smoke started toward the largest building in town, identified by the sign out front as the Tiger Hotel. On the boardwalk ahead of him, he saw a beautiful young woman. He crossed over to the opposite side of the street so he could get a better look at her without her knowing that she was being observed. He saw her push open the gate on a white picket fence and walk up onto the porch of a small house. Upon going inside, she disappeared from view.

Walking a little farther down the street, Smoke came to the sheriff's office. When he stepped inside, Smoke saw two men, identified by the stars they wore on their shirts as the sheriff and his deputy.

"Sheriff, I'm Buck West. Here in town to be huntin' for Smoke Jensen."

"Who ain't huntin' 'im?" Sheriff Reese replied. "I wouldn't mind findin' 'im myself. Ten thousand dollars sounds awfully good to me."

"But you're a law officer. You aren't eligible, are you?"

"Don't tell me you ain't smart enough to figure out for yourself that the law don't have nothin' to do with this reward. This here is a private reward for some private purpose, which I don't know nothin' about."

"Hmm. If that's the case, how will I get my money once I kill Smoke Jensen?"

"It's more'n likely he'll kill you," Sheriff Reese said.

"Hey, West," the deputy said, speaking for the first time. "That woman I seen you eyeballin' just a'fore you come in here? Her name is Sally Reynolds. She's a schoolteacher here, 'n she's my woman, so you stay away from 'er."

"I don't have any plans," Smoke replied.

"You don't have any plans for what?"

"I don't have any plans to meet her or to stay away from her."

"You know what I think? I think you're all talk," Rogers said. "So I'll tell you again to stay away from 'er. I got my eyes on her. Besides, she likes me."

"So that pretty lady is a schoolteacher, huh? And I believe you said her name was Sally Reynolds? Well, that's good to know. Thanks for telling me."

CHAPTER 8

As Smoke left the sheriff's office, a grand-looking carriage rolled down the street. The curtains weren't drawn closed on the carriage, and the woman passenger glanced out toward him. The glance turned into a stare, and the woman held the stare until the carriage passed on by.

Janey wondered who the man was, and more than that, she wondered why she felt that there was something familiar about him. It wasn't a recent familiarity; she was sure of that. He wasn't a local person; she was sure of that, as well.

Smoke was experiencing the same sense of déjà vu that the woman in the carriage was. Though in Smoke's case, the feeling was even stronger.

In the hotel Smoke bathed and shaved. Then, after getting dressed, he buckled his gun belt around his waist and tied down the low-riding pistol. That done, he stepped out onto the boardwalk, looked carefully all around him, as was his habit, then headed for the café, choosing that over the hotel dining room.

When he took his seat inside, he saw that he was but one table over from Miss Sally Reynolds. Also, because the normal lunch hour was over, they were the only two customers in the cafe. He smiled at her.

"Pleasant day," Smoke said.

"Very," Sally replied. "And now that school is out for the summer, it's especially so."

"I regret that I don't have more formal education," he said. "The War between the States put a halt to that."

"It's never too late to learn, sir."

"You're a schoolteacher." Smoke's remark wasn't a question; it was a statement.

"Yes, I am. And you . . . ?"

"I'm what they call a drifter, I'm afraid."

"Oh, I think *adventurer* would be a more adequate term than *drifter*," the young woman said, meeting his gaze.

Smoke chuckled. "Adventurer? Yes, I'll take that. What grades do you teach?"

"Sixth, seventh, and eighth. Why do you wear a gun?"

"Force of habit, I suppose."

"I sometimes think that many of the men who wear guns do so for show, without adequate skill to handle them. But I don't get that impression about you."

"What makes you think that?"

"I don't know. It's just a feeling I have. Are you skilled with a pistol, sir?"

"Some say that I am."

The conversation waned as the waitress brought their lunches, and before the conversation could resume, Deputy Rogers entered the café, sat down at the counter, and ordered coffee. Seeing Sally and Smoke close together, albeit at different tables, vexed him, and he showed his irritation by glaring at them.

"Will you be in Bury long?" Sally asked Smoke.

"All depends, ma'am."

"Lady of your quality shouldn't be talking to no bounty hunter, Ms. Reynolds," Rogers said. "It ain't fittin'."

"Mr. Rogers," Sally said, "the gentleman and I are merely exchanging pleasantries over lunch, and I'll not be told by anyone who I can and who I cannot speak to, whether you wear a lawman's badge or not."

Rogers flushed, placed his coffee mug on the counter, and abruptly left the café.

"I'm afraid, Miss Reynolds, that Deputy Rogers doesn't like me very much," Smoke said.

"Why?" Sally asked bluntly.

"I imagine it is because I make him feel somewhat insecure."

"Very interesting statement from a man who professes to have little formal education, Mr. . . ." She paused and chuckled. "I seem to be at a disadvantage here. You know my name, but I don't know yours."

"It's West, ma'am. Buck West."

"Western names are very quaint. Is Buck your actual first name?"

"No, ma'am, but it might as well be, since I've been called that pretty much my whole life."

"Are you really a bounty hunter, like the deputy said?"

"Bounty hunter, cowhand, gun-hand, trapper . . . whatever I can make a living at." Smoke didn't really want to talk about that with Sally Reynolds. "I'm guessing you're from east of the Mississippi River, ma'am?"

"New Hampshire. But schoolteachers are paid better out here than they are back home."

"I reckon I've heard of New Hampshire. Sort of know where it is. Must be a lot more civilized back there than it is out here."

"To say the least, Mr. West." She laughed. "And also much duller."

If she stayed around Bury, Smoke thought, she really would feel that way—because things hadn't even started to get lively yet in this neck of the woods.

"Would you take a walk with me, Miss Reynolds?" Smoke blurted. "I hope you don't think I'm being too forward."

She looked a little surprised by the request—Smoke was a little surprised at himself for making it—but she smiled and said, "I would love to walk with you, Mr. West."

As they strolled along the street, Sally opened the parasol she carried to protect her from the sun.

"Do you ride, Miss Reynolds?" Smoke asked.

"Back in New Hampshire, I rode frequently. But I have yet to see a sidesaddle in Bury."

"They're not too common a sight out here."

"You mentioned several occupations. Which line of employment are you currently pursuing?"

"I'm looking for a killer named Smoke Jensen," Smoke said. "Ten-thousand-dollar reward for him."

"I've seen the wanted posters. That's quite a sum of money. What did this man Jensen do to justify such a large reward?"

"Killed a lot of people, ma'am. He's a fast gun for hire, or so I'm told."

"Faster than you?"

Smoke had to chuckle at the blunt question. "I sure hope not," he said.

At that moment, a group of cowboys galloped into town, whooping and hollering as they spurred their horses. They pulled their mounts to a sliding halt in front of one of the saloons, raising a considerable cloud of dust in the process.

Without thinking about what he was doing, Smoke grasped Sally's arm, firmly but gently, and pulled her into a doorway in the building they were passing. He turned his body so it shielded her from the dust and any flying dirt clods the horses had kicked up.

When the dust had settled some, he moved aside so she could step back out onto the boardwalk.

"Those riders are from the PSR Ranch," Sally said. "Ruffians, from what I've seen of them."

"PSR?" Smoke repeated, even though he already knew exactly what the initials stood for.

"Potter, Stratton, Richards. The men who own it. It's the biggest ranch in the state, people claim."

The recessed doorway where they had taken shelter from the dust opened into a dress shop. It swung back now, and an attractive woman emerged onto the boardwalk. She greeted Sally pleasantly enough, by name, but gave Smoke only a cool glance and then walked on without looking back.

Sally said, "That's the, ah, lady-friend of Mr. Richards, one of the owners of that ranch we were just discussing. Her name is Jane."

Smoke didn't have to be told that. He realized the woman was the same one he had noticed in the carriage earlier, and now that he had seen her close-up, he knew why she had seemed familiar.

He had just laid eyes on his sister for the first time in almost ten years.

* * *

By the time Janey returned home, realization had come to her with a shock. The reason she had reacted with such curiosity over the man she had seen on the street was that *he was her brother*!

She knew that, for some reason, Richards and the other two were terrified of Smoke Jensen, but even though the last name was Jensen, she had never connected "Smoke" with "Kirby." She didn't know when or why he had taken the name "Smoke," but she was sure he was keeping his identity a secret from Richards and the others. He wouldn't just ride into town and announce who he really was.

Should she tell them?

She was going to have to ponder on that for a while.

Not surprisingly, it didn't take long for trouble to erupt. A couple of Richards's gun-hands got proddy with Smoke and forced him to kill them in a gunfight, right in front of Sally. There were plenty of other witnesses to that act of self-defense, so Sheriff Reese couldn't arrest Smoke for the killings. But he didn't waste any time running to his real boss, Josh Richards, to tell the rancher what the young bounty hunter calling himself Buck West had done. That got Richards's attention and ensured that he would be keeping a close eye on West.

The best way to do that was to hire him. After all, West had killed two of Richards's men. It was only fitting that he replace them. And if he was that good, maybe someday Buck West would get his wish and he'd have his chance to kill Smoke Jensen.

Smoke wasn't the only newcomer in the area. One or two at a time, a gathering of old-time mountain men was taking place in the hills near town. Old friends of Preacher, they were, and Smoke recognized them as kindred spirits of his friend and mentor when he ran into some of them. He met Dupre, Graybull, and Beartooth, as well as the diminutive former college professor Audie and the little man's friend Nighthawk, a towering, mostly silent Crow warrior.

Sally Reynolds proved to be a considerable distraction for Smoke, causing him to put aside his quest for the time being, although he certainly didn't forget about it.

It was hard to think too much about vengeance and killing, though, when he was busy having meals with the beautiful Miss Reynolds and taking walks with her. Under those circumstances, time slipped by with surprising ease.

Like a thunderstorm forming on a hot summer afternoon, however, a sense of impending violence thickened around Bury. The final showdown could not be put off forever.

A couple of months after he arrived in Bury, Smoke took Sally for a stroll through the town and out to Canyon Creek. The casual friendship that had resulted from their first meeting had developed, at least in Smoke's mind, far beyond that. He had thought that after Nicole, he would never feel that way about another woman, and though at first, he had felt somewhat guilty about it, he knew that Nicole would want him to go on living, and perhaps even to find someone else.

That meant it was time to tell Sally the truth.

"I reckon there's something you need to know about me, Miss Sally," he began, although he would have rather just enjoyed the scenery and the company. The shade trees and the sun-dappled water of the creek were beautiful, and Sally was even prettier.

She laughed and said, "What I need to know is how I'm

going to get you to stop calling me Miss Sally. Just Sally is fine, thank you. And you're Buck."

"Actually . . . I'm not."

Now she frowned at him in confusion and said, "I don't know what you mean."

"I'm Smoke Jensen."

"The . . . the gunfighter and outlaw on those wanted posters?"

"Those posters are a lie," Smoke said. "Sheriff Reese put them out because he works for the Big Three."

"So do you, or so I've heard," Sally said. "I never really knew whether or not to believe that. You . . . you don't seem like the sort to work for men like that."

"That's because I don't really work for them." Smoke drew in a breath. "But I do intend to kill them."

It all poured out of him then, as they sat on the grassy creek bank. He told her how Richards, Potter, Stratton, and several other men had been responsible for his brother Luke's death during the last days of the Civil War, as well as the theft of a fortune in Confederate gold. His voice threatened to break a little as he described his father's death at the hands of those men, as Emmett Jensen sought vengeance for his older son's murder. He kept his emotions under control, but only barely, as he explained how gunmen hired by the Big Three had killed his wife and infant son.

For her part, Sally had to struggle to contain the growing horror she felt as she listened to Smoke tell his story. She absolutely believed everything he said. There was no question in her mind—or her heart—about whether he was telling the truth.

Finally she said, "And to think that those . . . those

monsters pay my salary. I shall tender my resignation immediately, of course."

"I don't want you to do that," Smoke said.

"But I'm quite fond of you, Buck. I mean, Smoke. In fact . . . Well, you might kiss me."

She didn't have to tell him twice.

They were wrapped up in each other's arms when a voice said from behind them, "Plumb sickenin'! Great big growedup man a-moonin' and a-sparkin' like some green kid. Puredee disgustin'!"

Smoke whirled, his hands ready to grab the butts of his guns, but he froze with his mouth hanging open in surprise.

"Flies is bad this time o' year," the scrawny, grizzled hombre in buckskins said with a grin. "Best shut your mouth, boy."

Preacher was back.

Smoke hadn't seen the old mountain man in so many months he was convinced that Preacher had finally wandered off and died, as he kept threatening to do. Clearly, that wasn't the case, because he was standing there on the creek bank, big as life and twice as dirty. Smoke whooped, hugged him, and pounded him on the back. It was a joyous reunion, made even better when Smoke introduced Preacher and Sally, who took to each other right away.

"Preacher, what are you doing here, anyway?" Smoke asked.

"You didn't figure I was gonna let you take on Richards 'n his men all by yourself, did you? I got Lobo, Grizzly, Chopper, 'n a couple others come out here with me. We're all camped just outside of town with them other fellas who been driftin' in since I put out the word there was gonna be big doin's here. I figure that no matter how many men Richards 'n the others throw at us, we ought to be able to handle 'em, 'n that'll leave you free to go after thems that kilt your pa."

"What makes you think Richards will throw a bunch of men at me?"

"They hired the men that kilt Nicole 'n little Art, didn't they? All right, you done kilt all of them, but what makes you think they won't hire nobody else? Besides which, I've been pokin' aroun', 'n it turns out that them three has hired 'em most near a whole army of about fifteen or so to protect 'em. 'N if you go after Richards, Potter, 'n Stratton, them gunmen they has hired will all be a-comin' after you. 'N passin' yourself off as Buck West ain't goin' to do nothin' for you, neither."

"Yeah, there've been a couple who have recognized me, so I already know that using that name won't work for me. But as to having Richards and the other two hiring their own private army, I guess I hadn't thought of that," Smoke said.

Preacher grinned. "Yeah, well, sometimes you go off half-cocked 'n don't think things through like you ought to. But it don't matter iffen you ain't never thought nothin' about them three, on account of I have. You go ahead 'n take care of them three rattlesnakes that kilt your pa 'n hired them as what killed Nicole 'n little Art. You can leave the army to me 'n them other old-timers. We'll take care of them boys for you."

"I'll do that, but I intend to help you and the others deal with the army first."

"There ain't goin' to be no need for you to have to do nothin' but takin' care of them three."

"That may be so, but I plan to be with you, anyway."

"All right, if that's the way you're a-lookin' at it. Now

you 'n your girlfriend can go on back to sparkin'. Me 'n the other 'ns will be camped just outta town on account of it's too crowded in town."

Smoke and Sally watched Preacher walk away. Sally chuckled.

"What are you laughing at?" Smoke asked, his expression making it clear he was just curious, not offended by her amusement.

Sally shook her head. "Never in my entire life have I heard one conversation with so many grammatical errors."

"Well, you'll have to take it easy with Preacher. He can read, write, and cipher some, but that's about the extent of his education, and he taught himself that."

"Oh, don't get me wrong, Smoke. I consider it artistry, pure artistry."

Once that discussion was out of the way, there were more revelations still to be made, such as the fact that Janey, Josh Richards's mistress and the business manager of the PSR Ranch, was actually his sister.

"I had no idea she was up here, and even less of an idea that she was the mistress of one of the three men I'm looking for. But I don't hold this against her. She was just a young girl when she wound up on her own, and I mean all on her own. I was a lot luckier. I didn't have to go through what she did, and I had Pa until he was killed, and Preacher here, too."

"Smoke, I'm glad you don't hold Janey's history against her," Sally said. "I know that your sister doesn't have the best reputation, but I consider her to be a friend, and not just a casual friend. And I hope it doesn't cause you to think less of me when I tell you that I am also friends with Flora Yancey, who is the madam at the Pink House. I am also friends with all the soiled doves who work for her.

And while I pass no judgment on them, there are people in this town who pass judgment on me because I have such friends," she added.

"Sally, I can't think of anything you could possibly do that would cause me to think any less of you."

Smoke had never made a more truthful statement in his life.

Just as Preacher had predicted, Richards, Potter, and Stratton had hired a veritable army of gunfighters. But Smoke, Preacher, and the mountain men who had come to help were more than the match for them, killing most of the mercenaries and sending the rest of them fleeing. After the shoot-out, Smoke knew there was nothing to prevent him from completing the promise he had made at his father's grave. He had found the men who killed his father, and he planned to hold them to account.

First, though, he fulfilled another promise. He burned Bury to the ground.

The honest citizens, and there were some, had been warned already to leave town. None of them owned the businesses they operated, since Bury belonged to the Big Three, lock, stock, and barrel. The townspeople would be able to start over elsewhere without having to work for thieves and murderers. Miss Flora and her girls were already gone, having fled earlier before the shooting started.

At approximately the same time, a plan put in motion by Smoke to set Richards, Stratton, and Potter against each other almost bore fruit, as some of the gunmen working for them split into different factions and shot holes in each other. Before they could wipe each other out, though, the three men realized what was going on and called a halt to the hostilities.

United again, and knowing that Smoke would be coming after them, they lit a shuck.

Janey's heart slugged heavily in her chest as she stepped out onto the porch of the PSR Ranch house. The bodies of dead gunhands littered the ground in front of the house. The guards Josh Richards had left behind to protect her. That was a joke! All of them were shot to doll rags.

And sitting there on horseback were the men who had killed them. A more disreputable-looking bunch of men, Janey had never seen in her life. They were all old, too. Old as the hills. Or the mountains.

Except her brother, who was riding a big, mean-looking black stallion.

"Hello, Kirby," she said. "Now what?"

"How much money do you have in the house, sis?" he asked as he leaned on the saddle horn.

She laughed humorlessly. "Are you going to rob me?"

"You know better than that."

"Quite a bit, I guess," she replied with a shrug. "Yeah. Lots of money in the house."

"Can you ride astride?"

That drew another laugh from her. "Kid, I've ridden more things astride than I care to think about."

At least he had the good grace to look a little uncomfortable as he said, "Get what you can carry and clear out. I don't care where you go, just go. I don't ever want to see you again."

"You always could screw up every plan I made," she said bitterly.

"Don't you even care what Richards and his friends did to our pa and brother?"

"Hell, no!" Janey burst out, unable to control herself any longer. "I left all that behind a long time ago."

Smoke sighed and said, "I guess Pa was right, Janey. He said you were trash."

"Rich trash, brother. Doesn't that bother you?"

"Money rich, that's all. If you think that's enough, I feel sorry for you."

"Then that makes you a fool, Kirby. And I don't need your damn pity!"

He shrugged and told her, "One hour. That's all the time I'm giving you. Pack up and clear out."

When she rode away, she didn't look back, but she knew a column of black smoke began to rise into the sky behind her. Her brother was burning the PSR Ranch house, just as he had burned Bury.

By this time, Richards, Potter, and Stratton were on their way back to the ranch. They saw the black smoke and knew what had happened. Harried, harrassed, and shot up in a series of skirmishes with the old mountain men, their trail had just about run out.

All that was left was the showdown.

Smoke stood on the porch of an abandoned store in an old ghost town, watching the riders come toward him. Preacher and the others had driven them to him, skirmishing but not trying to wipe out the Big Three and the hired gun-wolves they had left.

"You sure you don't want us to kill the low-down

varmints?" Preacher had asked earlier. He patted the stock of his long-barreled rifle as he spoke. "It'd be a plumb pleasin' chore."

"No, just chouse them toward that old ghost town," Smoke had said. "I can't think of a more fitting place for a showdown. I appreciate everything you and the other boys have done so far, Preacher, but it's my job, and mine alone, to put an end to this."

"All right," the old mountain man had said with grudging acceptance. "But we'll be up on that hill yonder, overlookin' the town, and if we see Richards and the rest o' them startin' to ride away . . ."

"Then you'll know I've failed, and it'll be up to you and the others to avenge Nicole and little Arthur."

Preacher had jerked his grizzled head in a nod. "We'll sure do it," he promised. "You can bet a hat on that."

Now, as Smoke stood on the porch, he had twin .44s holstered at his waist, a Henry rifle in his right hand, and a double-barreled coach gun in his left. He waited until he was sure the men had seen him, then drifted back into the building like one of the proverbial ghosts that haunted deserted settlements like this.

It was a good place to end the struggle. Death in a dead place . . .

Through a dusty, cracked window, he saw his enemies split into several groups. Some charged down the hill into town while others circled to attack from other directions.

Smoke had stashed Drifter in an old stable where the stallion would be out of danger, he hoped. He had taken off his spurs and hung them from the saddle horn, knowing that he would be needing to move fast and quiet and not wanting the jingle of their rowels to give him away.

As soon as he was out of sight, he ducked out the back

of the store and ran along an alley, leaving the coach gun and the rifle in different spots along the way so they would be handy when he needed them later.

Then he heard one of the hired gun-wolves stomping around in what had been a saloon and stepped inside to meet him.

The man saw him and looked shocked that Smoke would confront him so openly. He yelled, "Draw!" and clawed out his revolvers.

Smoke waited until the gun barrels were coming level before his hands flashed down, then up, and then were filled with flame-spitting .44s. Two slugs smashed into the gunnie's chest and knocked him backward before he could even cock his weapons.

"In the saloon!" a man yelled outside.

All the glass in the building's front window had long since been knocked out. A man leaped through it, brandishing a pistol, but just as his boots hit the warped floorboards, a slug from Smoke's .44 knocked him back out through the window. He crawled away, whimpering from the pain of his bullet-broken arm.

"Smoke Jensen! You ain't got the sand to face me, you—"

Another bullet from Smoke cut off the obscene tirade from the gunman in the street who was challenging him. He didn't have time to mess with the hombre.

A bullet flew in from somewhere and hit the side of the window, chewing splinters from the wood that stung Smoke's cheek as he swung away. He ran out the back to the alley again, where another gunnie waited for him with a revolver in each hand.

The man didn't get off a shot with either weapon before twin hammerblows of lead slammed into his chest and knocked him to the ground. His dying breath rattled from his throat as Smoke stood over him, thumbing fresh rounds into his cylinders.

Smoke pouched his own irons, picked up the dead man's guns, and stuck them behind his belt. He hurried along the alley. A man loomed up in a doorway and actually got a shot off at him. The bullet burned Smoke's shoulder. He palmed out both Colts and blasted a shot from each gun. One bullet ripped into the man's throat, the other struck him just above the nose. He had drawn first blood on Smoke, but he paid for it with his life.

As Smoke reached the corner of the building, he caught a glimpse of someone running toward him and dropped to one knee. His right-hand gun roared. The slug shattered the hip of the running man and dropped him howling and cursing into the dirt. Smoke recognized Rogers, the crooked deputy from back in Bury. He left Rogers lying there and cut through to another building.

He'd been spotted again, though. Sheriff Reese was mounted and spurred his horse onto the boardwalk, then forced the animal to smash right through the old, rotten door. Smoke swung up his guns but didn't have to fire because Reese's mount, wild-eyed and panic-stricken, lost its footing and fell, pinning the sheriff to the floor and crushing his chest. Reese screamed in agony as blood gurgled from his mouth.

Smoke left him there and headed back out.

The old ghost town was a madhouse of gunsmoke and flying lead and the cries of dying men. Guided by instinct and cold nerve, Smoke fought like perhaps no man had ever fought in the West before that fateful day, darting and spinning, hearing bullets whine past his head, triggering again and again, seeking shelter only to reload. At some point, a bullet nicked his right ear. He wasn't really aware of the injury until he felt the hot trickle of blood down the side of his neck. As a doorway filled with men intent on killing him, he snatched up the shotgun he had left earlier and let them have both barrels. The buckshot shredded flesh and scattered dead and dying men.

Deputy Rogers, wounded but still in the fight, got another shot at Smoke and drilled a slug through his left leg. As Smoke fell to the boardwalk, he got off a shot of his own that bored through Rogers's brain and ended his lawless career.

A bullet lanced into Smoke's side from behind as he struggled back to his feet. He managed to stay upright as the impact spun him halfway around. That was all right; he had to turn, anyway, to kill the man who had just wounded him.

He limped into a building and reloaded the coach gun. Spurs jingled in the alley behind the building. Smoke slipped closer, listened for the telltale sound, then fired through the thin wall. The charge blew a fist-sized hole through the wood and also through the gunhawk who had been crouched just outside, breathing heavily.

As the echoes of the shotgun blast faded, a man shouted outside, calling for his friends. No one answered, and Smoke knew why.

That was the last of the hired guns out there.

Smoke fetched the rifle he had laid aside before and knelt at the front window. The gunman was still yelling, sounding more desperate with every plea for the others to answer him. He was in an empty storefront across the street, Smoke could tell from his voice.

Snugging the rifle butt against his shoulder, Smoke emptied all fifteen rounds in the repeater into the storefront's wall, firing as fast as he could work the rifle's lever between rounds.

The gunman staggered out, clutching the bleeding wounds in his chest and belly, and pitched forward into the street. He died facedown in the dirt.

Smoke lowered the rifle, set it aside, and went to the door. He cracked it open and shouted, "Richards! Potter! Stratton! Holster your guns and step out into the street. Face me if you've got the nerve, you snakes!"

The words echoed against the hills for a moment, mingling with the smells of blood and gunsmoke in the hot, still summer air.

Three figures moved into view at the end of the block. Smoke knew them all. He had seen them in his dreams often enough, and in those dreams he was killing them, avenging the deaths of his loved ones.

He stepped out to face them. He had barely gotten squared away with them when Stratton screamed a curse at him and yelled, "You ruined it all!" as he clawed at his .44.

Smoke drew and fired before Stratton cleared leather. At the same time, Potter grabbed for his pistol. Smoke shot him dead, just like Stratton. The two men had died in less than the blink of an eye.

Josh Richards stood slightly to one side, smiling faintly. He hadn't made a try for his gun, content, no doubt, to let Potter and Stratton make the attempt first. Who knew, there was a chance that one of them might have gotten lucky . . .

"You ready to die, Richards?" Smoke asked.

"As ready as I'll ever be, I suppose." Richards's voice was steady, and so were his hands. With what sounded like genuine interest, he asked, "Janey gone? Or did you kill her, too, when you burned the ranch?"

"She took your money and pulled out." Smoke paused. "She was my sister."

Richards actually laughed. "I know. There toward the end, she broke down and told me. Damnedest thing, her showing up here and getting involved with me, not seeing you for years, but all this time you've been after me." He shook his head, then said, "What happens to all our holdings?"

"The fellas who've been working your mines can have them. Your range and your stock will go to decent, honest punchers and homesteaders. Maybe this part of the country will actually be fit to live in . . . once the stink from you and the others wears off."

A puzzled frown creased Richards's forehead. "You mean . . . you did all *this*?" He waved a hand at the carnage surrounding them. "For *nothing*?"

"I did it for my pa, my brother, my wife, and my baby son."

"But it won't bring them back!"

"No," Smoke said. "It won't. But it still needs doin'."

Richards drew in a long breath, blew it out. "I wish I'd never heard the name Jensen."

"You'll never hear it again."

Richards must have figured he'd never have a better chance. His hand darted, snake-quick, to his gun. He made the draw, even got off a shot, but he hurried it and the bullet kicked up dirt at Smoke's feet.

Smoke shot him in the right shoulder. Richards cried out as the impact spun him halfway around and his Colt flew out of his hand. He grabbed for his left-hand gun. Smoke shot him again, this time in the left side of the chest. Richards staggered to the side. His hand shook as he lifted the left-hand gun. He got his thumb over the hammer and managed to cock it before Smoke's third shot punched into his belly. Richards doubled over and sat down hard in the bloody, dusty street.

He looked up at Smoke and opened his mouth to try to say something. Blood came out instead. Thickly, he got out the words, "You'll . . . meet . . ."

He toppled over, dead. Smoke never did find out who Josh Richards wanted him to meet.

CHAPTER 9

On board the Leopoldina

"Well, now, that is a story for the ages," Ernest Hemingford said. "It has a bit of everything. Tragedy, comedy—"

"Preacher could be pretty humorous, all right . . . as long as you didn't cross him," Smoke said.

Hemingford went on. "Romance, adventure, greed, hatred, vengeance . . . and a true hero. You have guts, sir, and by that I mean grace under pressure." Hemingford held up his drink. "Here, let's drink a toast to that."

Smoke lifted his own glass to Hemingford's, and the two men drank.

"I have my own confession to make," Hemingford said. "I have said that I am going to Paris to write stories for the *Toronto Star*. And that is true, but I am also motivated by the fact that in Europe, one can escape Prohibition. That ill-conceived law is an affront to civility. It is an attack upon the ability to magnify the good things in life and to modify life's great tragedies, to deal with heartbreaks and sorrow. Alcohol is the ointment of conversation, a contemplative beverage that one can enjoy with friends. One can only wonder how much longer it will be before America discontinues that draconian experiment."

Now it was Smoke's turn to laugh. "I must say, I've never heard a more eloquent opposition to Prohibition. Do you think the Volstead Act will be repealed?"

"My boy, I can promise you that it will be," Hemingford said with assurance as he lifted his glass to his lips.

"What is that you're drinking?" Smoke asked.

"This is a Gibson, my friend," Hemingford replied, holding his glass out for Smoke's inspection. "It is best when served with the garnish of extremely chilled Spanish cocktail onions. You should try it. The taste is cool and clean, and it will make you feel civilized."

"Occasionally, I will drink whiskey, but primarily, I'm a beer drinker," Smoke replied. "And being civilized isn't something I've been accused of too often in my life."

"Now that I think about it, I suppose a delicate drink like a Gibson in a place like . . . oh, let's call it the Red Bull Saloon in some Wild West town . . . would be a little out of place."

"A little," Smoke agreed with a chuckle.

"Say, our wives seem to have drifted off while we were talking," Hemingford asked. "Where did they go?"

"I'm sure they'll be back along in a minute." Smoke looked toward the entrance to the Observation Bar. "Oh, wait, there's Sally now. Don't see your wife, though."

"Hadley's probably returned to our stateroom. She knows how I get caught up in talking if I think it might lead to a good story. Speaking of which, in order to make *your* story complete, I would also very much like to talk with her and hear all about how the two of you got married and everything that's happened to you since. Have you any objections to my interviewing her?"

"It's been a mighty busy life," Smoke said with a smile. "You might have to sail around the world several times to cover all of it. I don't have any objections to you talking to her, but she's the one you need to ask."

"Indeed, and so I shall," Hemingford said.

"Hello," Sally said, greeting Smoke and Hemingford with a warm smile as she approached their table. Both Smoke and Hemingford stood and remained motionless until Sally was seated.

"Daughter, we need to talk. I need your input for the story I'm writing."

"Daughter?" Sally replied with a laugh. "Mr. Hemingford, I'm more than twice your age."

"Ah, but it was you who bestowed upon me the sobriquet of Papa. And as such, I shall think of some women, at least those for whom I feel some affection, as daughter."

"All right, *Papa*. What do we need to talk about?"

"In the story Smoke has told me, you were doubly displaced, first from a home of elegance and sophistication back East, then, after the wedding, from Bury. You embarked upon what had to be for you a life-changing journey. If you would, I would like for you to tell me some of your story."

"All right," Sally agreed. "Where should I start?"

"Smoke took me up to the end of his vendetta against *Messrs*. Richards, Stratton, and Potter. Why don't you pick it up from there?"

Sally's Story

Sally sat in the train station waiting room while Smoke arranged for their baggage and their horses to be unloaded.

Drifter and the horse he had recently bought for Sally, as well as two pack animals, had arrived in Cheyenne on the same train as Smoke and Sally, riding in the stock car. They were changing trains here, from the Union Pacific to the Denver Pacific, for the last leg of their journey by rail, and there would be a short layover.

As she sat there, she was alone with her thoughts for the first time since the wedding.

Sally, what have you gotten yourself into? she asked herself. *You have married a man you've known for just over a month. Not only that, he is one of the best-known men in the West, and what is he known for? For being someone who is fast and deadly with a gun. Why did you do this?*

The practical side of her knew that marrying someone so quickly after meeting him was an impetuous act, but she also thought of her aunt Mildred's admonition to "go where your heart tells you where to go." And her heart had definitely led to this man who had so recently come into her life and now so completely filled it.

She was also aware of the mantle she must now wear as the wife of someone as well known as Smoke Jensen. Smoke's fight against overwhelming odds had not only enabled him to extract revenge from the men who had killed his father, but had also enhanced his widespread recognition for his expertise with a gun, and his willingness to use it in defense of what was right.

As a result, Sally was embarking upon a new and even more challenging chapter of her life. Having given up her teaching job and the friends she had made in Bury, she was prepared in every way to be the wife of a true man of the West.

"Well, hello there, missy," someone said to Sally, interrupting her reverie.

Looking up, Sally saw not only the man who had addressed her but another, as well. The two men, wearing the rough, dusty attire of cowboys, were staring at her with expressions that could be described only as leering.

Sally looked away from them and coolly pretended that they weren't there.

"Now, don't be like that, little lady," the man said. "You know you'll be talkin' to me 'n Johnny here soon as you get to whichever saloon it is that you're a-goin' to be a percentage girl at."

"Yeah," Johnny said. "And me 'n Pete's goin' to follow you to find out which one it is. Then all we'll have to do is buy you a couple of drinks, and you'll be ready enough to take us up to your room, so you may as well start by bein' nice to us now. 'Cause who else does whores have to be nice to iffen it ain't the men that comes to visit 'em?"

Sally saw that they weren't going to go away, so she would have to respond to their crude comments.

"You gentlemen . . . and under the circumstances, I use the term *gentlemen* with some reservation . . . seem to be laboring under the misconception that I am a lady of the evening. And while I pass no judgment on such women, I assure you I am not one of them," Sally said, speaking for the first time.

"What did she just say?" Johnny asked.

"I don't know, but whoo-ee, don't she talk purty, though?" Pete said.

"Come on now, missy, don't be like that," Johnny said. "Hey, Pete. We got some time a'fore the boss gets here on the train. Why don't me 'n you take the little lady here over to the saloon 'n buy her a drink?"

"Yeah," Pete replied. "What about it, little lady? Whyn't you come across the street 'n have a drink with us?"

"Oh, I don't think my husband would like that," Sally replied.

"Hey, Pete. She says she has a husband," Johnny said. "What kind of husband do you reckon she has?"

"If she really does have a husband, it's more'n likely some store clerk who'd pee in his pants iffen someone said boo to him," Pete replied with a laugh.

"Why don't one of you men say boo to me and see if I really will pee in my pants?"

Startled by the voice behind them, the two men turned to see a taller than average man standing there, with shoulders as broad as an ax handle and a smile that could be described only as mocking.

"Who . . . who are you?" Pete asked.

Even though there were two of them against one, there was something about the self-confident demeanor of the man who had just spoken to them that left Pete feeling a little uneasy. The look in the fella's eyes plumb gave him the fantods.

"I'm the little lady's store clerk husband," Smoke said.

Smiling brightly, Sally said, "Hello, dear. You've arrived just in time. These two men have graciously offered to buy me a drink, and it seems they aren't willing to accept my refusal. Gentlemen, I would like you to meet my husband . . . Smoke Jensen."

"Smoke Jensen?" Pete said in a voice that cracked with fear.

"That's my name. And you are?"

"Uh, listen here, Mr. Jensen, we didn't know nothin' 'bout this here woman, uh, lady bein' your wife," Johnny said hastily. "We was just foolin', is all. I sure hope you 'n your wife don't take it none too serious."

"Let me see if I can understand this," Smoke said. "You are apologizing only because the lady happens to be my wife, but if it had been any other lady, you would have continued with your rude comments."

"No, we, uh . . . Look, Mr. Jensen, we was just waitin' to meet our boss, who's comin' in on the train, 'n it'd prob'ly be best if we waited for 'im outside. I hope you 'n the little lady here have a real good trip."

Johnny and Pete hurried off. They were practically running by the time they went through the depot's door. Sally could no longer hold back the laughter.

"Oh, Smoke, now look what you have done. You scared poor Pete and Johnny. Don't you feel bad about that?"

"No, not really. Do you?"

"Not a bit," Sally said as, with a big smile, she took Smoke's arm.

On the train to Denver, Sally was soothed by the rhythm of the wheels as they clacked over the rail joints. She had learned a trick on the long trip from Keene, New Hampshire, back out west again. A friendly conductor had told her to count the number of joints they passed over for a period of twenty seconds, and that would give her the speed at which they were traveling. After taking a pocket watch from her purse, she looked at the sweep hand monitoring seconds and began counting. They were doing twenty-eight miles per hour.

After putting the watch away, she looked through the window at the magnificent scenery sliding by outside. The closest mountains had a profuse growth of aspen, which made them green. Beyond that they were blue; then finally, the most distant mountains were a deep purple.

She glanced over at Smoke, who was napping beside her, and thought about the totally unexpected turn her life had taken. Getting married had not been a part of her grand scheme, at least not yet. Although she had never actually given marriage much thought, if she had been asked about it, she would have answered that she planned to teach for a few more years, while enjoying the ambiance of the West. Then, when her adventurous experiment was over, she would return to New York or New Hampshire or some such place, where she would settle down into another teaching job. Then marriage, if it came, would be to a businessman or a lawyer or a doctor, someone who was secure not only in his profession but also with his position in metropolitan society.

Falling in love with Smoke Jensen had changed all that, and though it was nothing she had planned, she knew that it had been a very right thing to do. As she continued to gaze at Smoke, she smiled.

As it happened, Smoke opened his eyes to catch her smiling at him. He returned the smile.

"What are you smiling about?" he asked.

"You."

"Me?"

Sally reached for Smoke's hand. "Yes, you," she repeated. "Never in my life would I have imagined myself on a train, married to someone I had known but such a short time. But I love you, Smoke, and I don't think I could be any happier than I am right now, going home with you."

"Home," Smoke said, with a self-conscious chuckle. "Uh, we haven't actually talked about that yet, have we? You do understand, don't you, that I don't actually have a home, as such? To be honest with you, Sally, I don't have a house or anyplace to live."

"What about where you and Nicole were living?"

"I was homesteading that land, and when I left, I gave it up. It doesn't belong to me anymore."

"Where have you been living?" Sally asked.

"In the Uncompahgre," Smoke answered.

"The Uncompahgre?"

"It's a range of mountains. There's a valley there I've seen, and it's one of the most beautiful places I've ever laid eyes on. I was thinking . . . that would be a good place for a young couple to live."

Sally squeezed his hand. "Darling, as long as I am with you, I have no problem with where we live. If you choose to sleep on the ground, under the stars, I will be fine with it."

Smoke chuckled. "You haven't slept on the open ground as often as I have, though I admit that sometimes it does have its appeal. However, I promise you that we will have a place to live soon, because the winters can get awfully cold."

Sally leaned into him. "We can always snuggle if it gets too cold."

"Yeah," Smoke said, smiling and putting his arm around her. "We can always snuggle."

Sally leaned into him. She realized that such an open display of affection might be off-putting to some of the others, but she didn't care what anyone else in the car thought. She was enjoying the close contact.

"We'll have to find someplace to get settled in soon after we get there." Smoke was quiet for a long moment. "That valley I mentioned has plenty of grassland for horses, and cattle, too. Five miles long and every bit as wide as that. It'd make a mighty fine ranch." He nodded slowly.

"Some of the mountains around it look like sugarloaves. I was thinking I might call the valley the Sugarloaf."

"And that would be the name of our ranch, as well?" Sally guessed.

Smoke grinned at her. "If you're sure you're willing to set out on an adventure like that."

"I don't mind at all!" Sally said quickly. "After all, I came west for an adventure, and what could be more adventurous than starting a ranch with an authentic mountain man?"

"Sally, I'm not sure you quite understand just how much 'adventure' you'll see, married to me."

Sally lifted Smoke's hand to her lips and kissed it. "As long as I'm with you," she said.

CHAPTER 10

"Denver! We're coming into Denver," the conductor called as he came through the day car in which Smoke and Sally were riding.

Although Denver was small by the standards of the cities Sally was familiar with back East, it was considerably larger than anywhere she had been since coming west. She examined the city as the train began slowing for its approach to the depot. Instead of a single dirt street, she saw brick avenues and horse-drawn trolleys moving up and down those avenues on rails that had been laid just for the horse cars.

There was a sense of familiarity to seeing four-and five-story brick buildings rather than the weathered gray whipsawed boards of the small structures that faced each other across the main street of Bury.

As the train drew closer to the depot, several people in the car stood and reached overhead for their luggage. Smoke and Sally had checked their bags through, including the horses. And because there was no need for them to get anything from the overhead bin, they were able to remain seated until the train came to a complete stop.

After they stepped down from the car, Smoke left Sally to claim their bags while he saw to the horses. There was a stable near the depot, and he made arrangement to board the horses there. Then he and Sally checked in to the Mountain View Hotel.

At dinner that evening, several people stopped by the table to chat with them.

"My, I had no idea you were so popular," Sally said with a big smile.

"It's not me that's drawing them over here. Nobody knows me unless they've seen my picture on one of those phony wanted posters that crooked Sheriff Reese put out. Everyone likes talking to a beautiful woman, though."

"You don't need to keep up the flattery," Sally said. "You won me over the first day we met."

When Sally awakened the next morning, she felt a sense of contentment unlike anything she had ever experienced before. She stretched, smiled, then glanced over toward Smoke.

He wasn't there!

Confused and a little frightened, Sally sat up in bed and looked around the room but didn't see him. She was about to get dressed and go downstairs to see if she could find him when the door opened. Startled, Sally pulled the sheet up, but her concern left when she saw Smoke coming through the door and carrying a tray.

"Oh, you're awake," he said. "I was hoping to be back before you woke up, because I wanted to surprise you with breakfast in bed."

Sally chuckled. "Well, I'm still in bed, and you did surprise me," she said.

Smoke set the tray down on the bedside table. Sally looked at what he had brought up.

"I got pancakes and sausage, bacon and eggs, biscuits and toast, and some fresh fruit because I didn't know what you might want."

"Smoke, surely you don't expect me to eat all of this?"

"Eat what you can," Smoke said. "I have something to take care of, so I'm going out again. But I promise to be back within the hour."

Sally ate what she could, feeling terribly guilty about leaving so much of it on the plates.

"Well, he said to eat what I can, and this is all I can eat," Sally said aloud.

On board the Leopoldina, at sea

"You were a brave young lady to set out on such a . . . What did you call it? An adventure?" Hemingford said.

"As I look back on it, I suppose it was. But it was . . ." Sally stopped in midsentence, then chuckled. "I was going to say it was love at first sight, that is, if you believe in such a thing."

"Oh, but I do believe in it," Hemingford said. "I was at a party in Chicago when a girl came in and sat by herself on a sofa. She was very pretty. I remember that it was raining outside, and she had rain-freshened skin. Her hair was the color of burnished copper, and a bit of it fell over her forehead. She extended her lower lip, blew out some air to push the hair back as she tossed her head, and at that moment, I fell in love with her."

"Hadley," Sally said. It wasn't a question.

"Yes."

Smoke joined them then. "How is it going?" he asked.

"Splendidly," Sally replied with a smile. "We were just talking about our first loves."

"No, we were talking about love at first sight, and indeed, when I saw Hadley, it was love at first sight, but she wasn't my first love. My first love was Agnes von Kurowsky, a nurse in the American Red Cross. Agnes took care of me when I was wounded by an Austrian mortar."

"You were in the war?" Smoke asked.

"Yes, but I was never a shooter. I was always a shootee." Hemingford's laughter was mocking and self-deprecating. "Do you know what I was doing when I was wounded? I was passing out chocolate candy bars to a group of Italian soldiers."

"But you were there," Smoke said.

"Yes, I was there, and I wound up having pieces of shrapnel picked out of my derriere." Hemingford smiled. "Or perhaps I should say Agnes picked them out. I was eighteen and naive, and she was twenty and worldly. How could I not have fallen in love with her? But eventually, she spurned me, and now here I am with a new love, a new wife, and a new life ahead of me."

As Hemingford interviewed Smoke or Sally or both of them, he had two blue-backed notebooks, two pencils, and a small pencil sharpener. He had picked up the sharpener and begun sharpening one of his pencils when Smoke interrupted with a question.

"Do you carry that sharpener with you all the time?"

"Yes."

"Why don't you use a pocketknife?"

"A pocketknife is too wasteful, and you don't get the perfect symmetry at the point that you do with a sharpener." Hemingford held out the pencil he had just finished sharpening. "Writing is more than putting words on paper.

Writing is a liturgy that joins man to idea, and it is the means of bringing to life that idea. For that, you need a pencil." Again, he held it out. "And because the pencil is a part of this ritual, it must be treated with as much respect as the cup on an altar."

Smoke smiled.

"You find humor in this, do you, Mr. Jensen?"

"On the contrary, Mr. Hemingford. I find comfort in the knowledge that my story will be told with truth and passion."

"Truth and passion," Hemingford repeated. "That is an excellent observation."

"I know you and Sally spoke of love at first sight, but other than that, how did the session go?" Smoke asked.

"It went very well," Hemingford replied. "Sally should write something of her own, perhaps a book, someday."

"I've always thought that myself," Sally said.

"Sally took the story as far as Denver. Suppose you pick it up from there," Hemingford said.

"All right," Smoke agreed.

Smoke couldn't think of anything better than riding the high country with this lovely, intelligent woman at his side. He had known tragedy and hardship in his life, but there were plenty of times—like looking over at Sally right now—when he felt like he was the luckiest son of a gun on the face of the earth.

They were riding south by southwest from Denver. Sally asked, "Is there a town in this valley of yours?"

"It's not mine yet," Smoke said. "But I intend to file on it. When I was there, there was no town anywhere around, but I've heard that some little no-name settlement has sprung up not far from the Sugarloaf. It's probably not much more than a wide spot in the trail."

"How far is it?" Sally asked. "This . . . Sugarloaf, I mean."

"We'll get there sometime tomorrow."

"Will we spend the night out on the ground?"

"Would you be willing to do that, knowing there are snakes and wolves and mountain lions about?" Smoke asked.

"I wouldn't want to do it by myself, but I'd be fine with it as long as you're with me."

Smoke chuckled. "There may be times when we have to do that, but tonight we'll stay at Barnes's Crossing."

"Barnes's Crossing?"

"Barnes's Crossing is a stagecoach relay station about halfway between here and where we're going. Preacher and I stopped there a couple of times a few years ago. And even though it is principally a place for stagecoach passengers, they also have sleeping rooms for folks who are just passing through," Smoke said.

Lunch was on the trail: jerky, pan-fried bread, and coffee. Sally enjoyed it more than she thought she would. She was also enjoying the ride, though the knowledge that it wouldn't be more than a couple of days made it less foreboding.

They arrived at the Barnes's Crossing relay station late in the afternoon, and Smoke was greeted effusively by Jim Barnes, the station manager. Smoke introduced his new wife with a great deal of pride.

"Will you be here for supper?" Barnes asked.

"Yes, and to stay the night, if you have room."

"The coach is due in about an hour," Barnes said. "I don't know how many passengers it'll be carrying, but we'll make room for you. If they have to, Abe 'n Moody can stay in the stable tonight."

"Oh, I wouldn't want to put anyone out," Sally said.

Barnes chuckled. "You won't be puttin' no one out, Miz Jensen. Them boys have spent many a night there. They've got a couple of bunks out there that sleeps real good. Smoke, Moody will take care of your horses. Let me go get Ma, so's your mizzus can meet mine."

"You won't be puttin' no one out," Smoke said quietly after Barnes had walked away. With a smile, he turned to Sally. "That's a double negative. He should have said, 'You won't be putting *anyone* out.'"

"Yes! Oh, Smoke, I'm proud of you for that," Sally said. "I suppose you *have* been paying attention since we met."

"Now and then," Smoke said with a smile.

A year earlier Sally would have been amused by the small scattering of buildings staring at each other across the single dirt road that had the audacity to call itself a town. But that year had been spent in Bury, a town not much larger than this little no-name settlement Smoke had mentioned, and she had developed an affinity for such places.

A building that housed a store and a saloon stood to the right. Diagonally across from that structure were a blacksmith shop, a couple of corrals, a barn, and another store. Set back a ways were a handful of crude cabins.

"I can see why the place doesn't have a name," Sally said quietly as she and Smoke rode through. "What would you call it?"

"Hellhole?" Smoke suggested with a smile. "Dirtville?" He gestured at their surroundings. "If you just look at the landscape hereabouts, though, you can see how someday this might be a really nice little town. Everybody and everything have to start somewhere, I reckon."

"That's actually rather profound, Mr. Jensen."

"Why, thank you, Mrs. Jensen." Smoke grinned.

They rode on, leaving the tiny settlement behind. Smoke looked relieved when they had done so. Sally noticed that and said, "Is something bothering you, Smoke?"

"A time or two back there, I felt like somebody was watching us. I don't think it amounts to anything, mind you.

"Out here on the frontier, any stranger riding through is interesting. But I felt the same thing in Salcedo, and in Denver before that." He looked over at her solemnly as they kept their horses moving at a steady pace. "Could be some of those old wanted posters are still floating around, Sally. And it's possible not every bounty hunter in these parts has heard that they were fake.'

"You're afraid someone might come after you."

"Not afraid for myself—"

"But afraid for me," she finished for him.

Smoke shrugged. "The thought weighs on my mind sometimes."

"I wish you wouldn't let it. I knew when I married you that there might be trouble waiting for us now and then. I can accept that risk, if it means being with you."

"You can accept it," he said. "I don't know if I can."

"Why, Smoke Jensen!" she exclaimed. "Are you already talking about divorcing me?"

"What! Good grief, no. Never. I guess what I'm trying to say is that if we settle down in that valley, I want to put everything in the past behind us. I plan on hanging up my guns, Sally. I don't want to ever be anything except a rancher . . . and your husband."

She looked at him for a long moment, then said, "That's very sweet, Smoke, and I hope it works out that way. I genuinely do. But putting aside who we are . . . that's not an easy thing to do."

"Worth it, though," he insisted. "For us."

"There will always be an us, Smoke, no matter what happens."

He reached over, caught hold of her hand, squeezed it. And they rode on.

The sun was almost touching the peaks on the western horizon when they reined in at the head of the valley. Sally saw what Smoke meant about some of the mountains looking like sugarloaves. The snow on their crests just added to the impression. The lower slopes were covered thickly with pines, and the broad meadows in the valley itself had lush carpets of grass. Sparkling streams threaded their way here and there.

"Oh, Smoke," Sally said with awe in her voice. "It's beautiful. Just like you said. I don't know if I've ever seen a lovelier place." She looked over at him. "Are you *sure* this can be our home?"

"I'm pretty sure nobody's ever filed on it. I intend to do so, just as soon as I can." He leaned forward in the saddle and pointed. "See that creek yonder? Follow it with your eyes to where it makes that big S-bend to the west. There's a place there that'll be perfect for our house. Plenty of room for barns and corrals, too, and a good garden patch. We're pretty high up here, but vegetables will still grow, I reckon. And we'll never run out of good water."

Sally drew in a deep breath and let it out in a long sigh. "Home," she said. "The Sugarloaf."

"Home," Smoke repeated, and he sounded like a man who couldn't believe his incredible luck.

"You're going to teach me to shoot?"

"Yes. It's important," Smoke said.

Sally looked both amused and a little bit nervous as she said, "Well, I must say that it will certainly be interesting . . . a schoolteacher from Keene, New Hampshire, learning to shoot a pistol. But why do you say it's important?"

"Sally, I've made a lot of friends in my life, but I have made just as many enemies. And some of those enemies wouldn't think twice about trying to get to me through you, just like they did with . . ." Smoke stopped in mid-sentence and closed his eyes.

Sally knew that he was thinking about Nicole, so she let him have his moment.

"So," he said after the moment had passed, "you're going to learn to draw and shoot. I'm going to teach you the same way my pa taught me. By the time I'm finished with you, I guarantee you will be able to defend yourself against almost anyone who might come after you."

"*Almost* anyone?" Sally asked with a whimsical smile.

"Don't worry. If you run into someone you can't handle, I'll pick up the slack," Smoke replied, his smile matching her own.

"All right," Sally agreed. "I might well be the only member of the Keene, New Hampshire, Women's Club ever to fire a pistol, but I'm willing to learn if you are willing to teach."

"That's my girl," Smoke said.

"Yes," Sally said. "Yes, I am."

They were standing in front of the house Smoke had started to build. He had laid it all out, marking it with sticks and string, consulting with Sally about what would go best where, and once they were settled on that, he'd begun felling trees and hauling rocks to build the foundation and walls. It would have a real plank floor, he'd promised her, not just rough puncheons. And the windows would have real glass in them, not at first, no, but in time.

There was nothing like hard work, mountain air, good solid food, and nights spent in the arms of a beautiful woman to make the time pass. Days, weeks, months went by. The walls rose. Getting the roof on by himself would have been difficult, but Sally was right there beside him, willing to work hard and do anything he asked of her. By the time the nights began getting chilly, the house was closed in and they had a bed that Smoke had made, as he made the rest of their furniture.

They took the time for Sally to practice with the pistol he had bought for her in Denver without her knowing, too, which she wore in a gun belt he had shortened to fit her trim hips.

"Let's see what I've got to work with," Smoke said when they began their first lesson. He pointed to a nearby aspen tree. "Take a shot at that tree for me."

"I . . . I don't even know where to start."

"You do know which end of the gun the bullets come from, don't you?"

Sally laughed. "Yes, of course I do."

"Well?" Smoke said "That's a start."

Smoke lifted Sally's arm, showed her how to thumb the hammer back and to line up the gunsight with the target.

"Now, you don't want to pull the trigger."

"What do you mean. How is the gun going to shoot unless I pull the trigger?"

"Here's the thing," Smoke said. "If you pull the trigger, you'll pull the gun off target. Best way is to squeeze the trigger, and in order to do that, all you have to do is make a fist while your hand is wrapped around the gun. But I have to warn you, the gun will kick back against your hand as you fire. At first, that might surprise you a bit, but once you're used to it, it might even help you concentrate. Are you aiming at the tree?"

"Yes."

"All right. Let's see what you can do."

Sally raised the pistol to eye level and fired. Her bullet missed.

"It's a start," Smoke said.

After six weeks of shooting, Sally had made a lot of progress, so much so that Smoke was sure it was time to advance his instruction.

"Do you see that little branch sticking out there?" Smoke asked.

"Yes. You want me to shoot it off?"

"If you can."

Confidently, Sally raised the pistol, sighted down the barrel, then, closing her hand into a fist, squeezed rather than pulled the trigger.

Part of the branch was snapped off, and with a self-satisfied smile, Sally turned to her husband.

"What did you think of that?" she asked, holstering the pistol.

"You aimed, didn't you?"

"What? Yes, of course I did."

"Why?"

"Why? Because I wanted to hit what I was shooting at, that's why. If you don't mind my saying so, Smoke, that seems like a very strange question for you to ask." Sally's exasperation was evident in her voice.

"Shoot at it again, but don't aim this time."

"What do you mean, don't aim? I don't understand. How am I going to hit it if I don't aim?"

"Just know that you're going to hit it."

"What?"

"Let me show you what I'm talking about." Smoke pulled his own pistol and shot at the part of the branch that was left. He didn't raise the pistol to eye level and aim; he just pulled the trigger, and another piece of the branch was shot away.

"How did you do that without aiming?"

"I told you, I just knew that I was going to do it."

"I don't understand what that means."

"It's something my pa taught me, and I've found that it has worked very well, so now I'm going to teach you," he said as he put his pistol back in the holster. "There's no sense in drawing really fast if you have to stop and aim. You have to draw, aim, and shoot all at the same time. And in order to do that, you have to know that you're going to hit the target. Now, you try it."

Sally pulled the pistol from her holster and, without lifting it, pulled the trigger. She missed.

"Turn yourself at an angle, so that you aren't directly facing the target." Smoke positioned Sally accordingly. "Now, don't turn your body, but look at the target by turning your head back toward it."

Sally followed the instructions.

"Bring the pistol up to eye level and aim at the target, just as you did before, but don't shoot. Good. Now close your eyes and lower your pistol so that it is pointing straight down. Now, with your eyes closed, aim at it again."

"What do you mean, with my eyes closed, aim at it again? How am I going to do that if my eyes are closed?"

"Trust me, you'll catch on. With your eyes still closed, put the picture in your mind of what you just saw when you were aiming at the target. Now, I want you to bring your arm back up, all the while thinking about where the target is. When you think you have it lined up, tell me."

Sally did as Smoke asked, bringing the gun up with her eyes closed and aiming at the target she was imagining.

"Pull the trigger, but don't open your eyes."

Sally did so.

"Now open your eyes and look."

When Sally opened her eyes, she saw that she hadn't hit the small branch she was shooting at, but she had hit the tree trunk. It was a miss, but it was a very close miss.

"I almost hit it!" she said excitedly.

"That was pretty good. Now, spread your feet apart about the width of your shoulders. Keep your legs straight, but not stiff."

"All right," Sally said, complying with Smoke's instructions.

"Now, again, put your pistol back in the holster, and then look at your target by turning your head and eyes slightly without moving from the neck down. When you know exactly where the target is, pull the pistol from the holster, but don't raise the gun to eye level. Shoot it as soon as your arm comes level."

"Should I try a quick draw?"

"No. That comes later. First, learn to shoot. Then learn to draw. Now, pull the gun and shoot it."

Sally pulled the pistol and fired as soon as it came level. She had no idea where the bullet went.

By the end of that day of practice, Sally learned to

"know that she was going to hit the target," and she did so at least half the time. Within two more weeks, she could draw, cock the pistol, fire, and hit the target, doing it all with a speed that nearly matched Smoke's.

"Sally," Smoke said, "you are fast enough and you can shoot well enough that I have the confidence that you can deal with anyone. There's only one thing left, and I can't teach you that. You'll have to handle that on your own."

"I know what you're talking about," Sally said.

"Do you?"

"I can shoot tree limbs, pine cones, and tin cans. But can I actually shoot a person?"

"Yes, that is exactly what I'm talking about. The average person, when it comes to actually shooting someone else, realizes that they are about to take the life of another human being, and that is such an awesome thing that they have to stop to think about it. Now, it may be that they think about it for only a second, but that's too long. Sally, if you really do get into a shooting episode with another person, you can't afford to think about it. And when you shoot someone, you must shoot to kill, not to wound. If you shoot to wound, you are likely to get killed. Do you understand all of that?"

"Smoke, you speak of no hesitation and shooting to kill. Do you know what you are telling me?"

"Yes, I'm telling you what you must know to survive. If you ever get into a situation where you are confronting someone who is pointing a gun at you, you have to understand that he is willing to kill you. And for you, that means it's going to come down to a case of kill or be killed. Can you do that, Sally?"

"I . . . I really don't know. I suppose that if I had to, I could."

"There is no supposing to it," Smoke said. "It is kill . . . or be killed." Smoke smiled. "And I don't want you to be killed."

"Kill or be killed," Sally said. She returned Smoke's smile. "I don't want to be killed, either."

He believed her. If she could actually follow through with that intention, she would be all right.

When he was satisfied with her gun handling, they moved on to practicing with Smoke's Henry rifle. Not surprisingly, she was an excellent shot with it, too, although the rifle was harder for her to handle because it was heavier.

"I won't have to worry about you if trouble comes a-calling," Smoke told her with a grin. "You can shoot the eye out of a gnat a hundred yards."

"You're exaggerating."

"Maybe just a mite," he admitted.

Despite his joshing, he was very glad she had taken to shooting. He had never forgotten what had happened to Nicole and little Arthur when he left them alone, and he knew he never would forget. Now that the house was in good shape, he needed to get started on some corrals. Once those were done, he could round up some of the mustangs that ran wild in the area and begin the job of taming them. But to do that, he would need to be away from home at times, and he knew he would worry about leaving Sally alone. Less so, though, after teaching her how to shoot.

CHAPTER 11

For the next two and a half years, Smoke Jensen kept the vow he made to himself. He lived a life of peace as a rancher and as Sally's husband. His horse herd grew, and he built up a good-sized herd of cattle, too. He had filed on the valley and gotten title to it. Other folks moved into the area and started spreads, but the Sugarloaf Ranch was known to be one of the best, if not *the* best. The little no-name settlement continued to grow as the region developed. People started calling it Fontana, although Smoke didn't know why.

He didn't go there very often.

Why would he, when he had Sally at home?

That was the other part of his vow, to be a good husband to Sally, and he liked to think he had fulfilled that, too. They were still very much in love. No kids had come along so far, but Smoke figured that was just a matter of time.

Part and parcel of his contentment was the fact that he hadn't been forced to fire his guns in anger in all that time. Not that he had hung up his Colts. He still wore them part of the time, and he always carried a rifle when he was riding the range because there were lobo wolves and mountain lions in these parts. But luck had been with him and he hadn't had to face another man with a gun in his hand and end the hombre's life.

Then, on a beautiful spring morning, something inside Smoke Jensen told him that was all about to change . . .

Many miles to the north, four men were waiting for a stagecoach. One of them, Jack Slade, was tall and broad shouldered. He wore his dark hair closely cropped, and he had a well-trimmed mustache that didn't extend beyond the outer edge of his mouth. Slade had a strong jawline, and most women found him handsome, until they saw him up close.

Slade's eyes were a deep brown, but it wasn't the color of his eyes that caught their attention. The eyes had to be described in terms of something more than color. There was a hardness to them, and in certain light they were almost orange, and one might get the idea they were windows into the fires of Hell.

At the moment, Slade was standing on top of a ridge, looking south down the road. The other three, Ian Dolan, Marv Cooley, and Milt Wolcott, were behind him, standing beside their horses, with the reins in their hand.

"Hey, Slade, how much money do you think there will be on that stagecoach?" Dolan asked.

"How much money do you have now?" Slade replied.

"About forty cents."

"Forty cents? Well, I don't know how much money will be on the stage, but it's a lead-pipe cinch that it will be more money than you have now, so what difference does it make?"

"What difference does it make? We're about to hold up

a stagecoach, 'n that's what you might call a dangerous thing to do. I'd like to think there was enough money for it to be worth doin' it."

"You don't have to do it, Ian. You can stay back here 'n let me, Slade, 'n Wolcott do it, 'n you won't be in no danger a'tall," Cooley said.

"Yeah, 'n with you out of it, it'll be more money for me 'n Marv 'n Slade to have," Wolcott added.

"You fellers can't get rid of me that easy. I'll be right with you, 'n I'll get my share of money, don't you be worryin' none about that."

"Here comes the stagecoach," Slade said. He smiled. "Boys, it's got a shotgun guard. That means that it's more'n likely carryin' a money shipment."

"Marv, what you goin' to do with your money?" Wolcott asked.

"I'm going to invest it wisely," Cooley answered.

"What?" Wolcott and Dolan had the same reaction.

"What are you plannin' on investin' in?" Wolcott asked.

Cooley laughed. "In whiskey and women."

The others joined him in laughing.

"Get mounted," Slade said. "We'll wait for 'em on the other side of the bend in the road. They won't even know we're here till it's too late."

There had been no vote about who would be the leader of the gang, but Jack Slade had assumed the position. Jack Slade was known as one of the fastest and deadliest gunmen in the West, so his assumption of leadership was not questioned by any of the other three.

All four of the men were experienced outlaws, and all four knew how to use their gun. But Slade was not only exceptionally skilled in the employment of his pistol. Unlike most men, even most outlaws, Slade had never experienced even the slightest moment of hesitancy before he killed. He could kill a man with no more thought than he would have in stepping on a bug, and he had done so many times.

The four men mounted, then rode down the back side of the ridge and out onto the road, where they waited. The coach was still out of sight around the bend, but they could hear it approach.

"What about the shotgun guard?" Dolan asked.

"I'll take care of him first thing," Slade said, pulling a rifle from the saddle sheath. He jacked a shell into the chamber as he waited.

Bart Thomas was driving the coach, and Sid Kellogg was sitting beside him with the butt of a double-barreled coach gun propped against his denim-clad thigh.

"You know what I'm goin' to do soon as we get to the way station?" Kellogg asked.

"Let me guess. You're goin' to take a leak," Thomas said.

Kellogg laughed. "Yeah, well, that, too. But then I'm goin' to get me a piece of pie. Ma Barnes makes the best pie of any relay station, 'n I'm goin' to get me a big ole piece of apple pie 'n a glass of milk."

"Milk? Not coffee?" Thomas asked.

"Yeah, with apple pie, I like—" Kellogg stopped in midsentence as the coach rounded the bend. There were four mounted horsemen on the road in front of them. "Now, just what do you think them fellers want?" he asked.

"I don't know, but I don't like the looks of—"

That was as far as Thomas got before he saw one of the four men raise a rifle to his shoulder. Thomas saw the puff of smoke, heard the shot, then a surprised grunt of pain from Kellogg.

"Damn, Bart. I've been shot," Kellogg gasped. He sounded as amazed as he did pained. The shotgun fell out of his hand, bounced off the edge of the floorboards, and was left behind. The next moment Kellogg toppled over the side of the coach and onto the road.

"Sid, Sid!" Thomas called, stopping the coach.

"Get your hands up, driver!" the man with the rifle shouted.

"Don't shoot, don't shoot!" Thomas said, putting his hands up.

The four riders approached him, all four of them now with drawn pistols.

"You're a smart hombre," one of the men said. "Let's see just how smart you are. Toss down the money box."

"What are you talkin' about, mister?" Thomas asked, his voice breaking in fear. "We ain't got no money box."

"You want to join your friend down here on the ground? 'Cause you're goin' to do just that if you don't throw down that money box," the road agent said gruffly.

"There ain't no money box, 'cause we ain't carryin' no money! If you don't believe me, come up here 'n look for yourself." Thomas was literally shouting now.

Slade glanced over at Dolan and nodded. "Check it out."

Dolan climbed up onto the driver's box next to the frightened Thomas and made a thorough perusal. "The driver's tellin' the truth," Dolan said in a disgusted tone. "There ain't no money box here. Nothin' but the mail sack."

"All right, we'll take it," Slade said. "You folks in the coach, come on out of there!"

Three men climbed down. One was tall, thin, gray

headed, and wrinkled with age. The second man struggled to exit, because he had a rather large stomach. The third was bald and wore glasses.

"Soon as you three fellers contribute to this little fund I've got goin', you can climb back in the stage and be on your way," Slade said.

"What fund?" the bald one asked.

"Why, the whiskey and whore fund," Slade said. The other three outlaws laughed at his joke.

The three men turned out their pockets and handed all the money they were carrying to the outlaws.

"What about you, driver? We'll take your money, too," Slade said.

"I don't carry no money with me. Why should I? I can eat 'n sleep for free at the relay stations." He paused, then added, "Same with Sid," when he saw one of them going through his friend's pockets.

"He's tellin' the truth. There ain't no money on him," Cooley said.

"Let's go," Slade ordered.

As the outlaws rode away, Thomas jumped down to check on Kellogg.

"Sid, Sid!"

He expected Kellogg to be dead, but the guard's chest still rose and fell despite the spreading bloodstain on his shirt.

"I'm shot bad, Bart," Kellogg said in a strained voice.

"Hang on. We're goin' to get you somewhere safe," Thomas said.

"Damn, Bart. I think I peed in my pants," Kellogg said.

Thomas looked over at the three passengers. "Help me get 'im in the coach. There's a relay station only a couple miles away."

He was afraid it was going to be too late for Sid Kellogg by the time they got there, but they had to try.

"It's gold, Sally," Smoke said to his wife, the simple words weighted with portent.

"Around here? I didn't think there was any gold to be found in these parts."

Smoke smiled slightly to himself at Sally's use of the term "these parts." New Englander or not, living in the West was rubbing off on her.

"I knew it was here," he told her. "Found a shelf of it years ago, when I was first passing through with Preacher. But I'm not a miner and never have been, so I just let it lay. I'm hearing rumors of it from all around now, though, from the friendly Indians and the other ranchers. Once word starts to get around, with every day that passes it'll spread more, and before you know it gold-hunters will flock in from all over. Fontana will become a boomtown."

He said the word like it tasted bad in his mouth.

"That's bad enough," Smoke went on, "but it's not the worst of it." He drew in a breath. "Tilden Franklin."

One name popped up over and over again along the main street of Fontana: the Franklin Mercantile, the Franklin Livery, the Franklin Feed and Seed Store, the Franklin Café, and the Franklin Apothecary. Somewhat surprisingly, the most prominent drinking and gambling establishment in the settlement was known as the Blue Dog Saloon.

But Tilden Franklin owned it, too, along with the Circle TF Ranch outside of town.

The only major business in Fontana that Franklin didn't own was the bank, which belonged to a man named Fred Malone. At one time, in the old days, Malone had been a trapper. Preacher was acquainted with him and called him "Big Cat" Malone, but the old mountain man was the only one who used that nickname.

"Franklin has his sights set on owning everything in this part of the state," Smoke continued. "I know good and well he wants the Sugarloaf."

Franklin wanted more than just his ranch, Smoke thought. On the rare occasions when he and Sally had been in Fontana and had passed the businessman on the street, he had seen the way Franklin eyed Sally. The man's lust had been open enough that it was all Smoke could do not to smash a fist into his face.

Sally seemed unaware of it, though, and since Smoke didn't want to upset her, he had kept a tight rein on his temper. It hadn't always been easy, but the effort had been eased by a hunch that someday Franklin would go too far and Smoke would be justified in taking action against him.

Now, however, it looked like greed for gold was going to prompt that, rather than Franklin's desire for Sally.

"What are you going to do?" Sally asked.

"Thought I'd ride into town and try to get a better sense of what's going on, what moves Franklin might make."

"If there's gold here in the valley, he'll want to take it." Smoke nodded and said grimly, "I know. But he won't succeed."

Sally sighed. "The peaceful days are over, aren't they?"

"I'm afraid they might be," Smoke said.

Smoke had found his Appaloosa, Seven, and brought the stallion and some of the mares and foals Seven was running with back to the Sugarloaf. One of those foals had grown into the fine mount Smoke was riding today as he moved at a deliberate pace along Fontana's main street. He reined to a stop in front of a neat frame building with a sign on it that read LAMBERT'S CAFÉ.

Tilden Franklin didn't have anything to do with Lambert's, so Smoke always ate there when he was in town. It was the middle of the day, so he went inside for lunch.

He was halfway through his meal when a tall, gangly man with a cadaverous face and gray eyes set deep in their sockets walked over to the table. The expression on his face was austere.

"I see you're back," the man said.

"What do you want, Franklin?" Smoke asked.

"I want to know what you are going to do about your horses."

"Why are you interested?"

"I'd like to buy them."

"I suppose we could work something out. How many do you want?"

"I want all of them."

Smoke shook his head. "I can't sell all of them. I need to keep several breeder mares and a few stallions."

"That won't do. I want all of them or none at all."

"Well, then, this discussion is pretty much closed, isn't it?"

"You may wonder why I've offered to buy them," Franklin said.

"No, not particularly. I guess maybe you need mounts for your ranch."

"I need no more horses. I made the offer out of goodwill, because your horses are already on my ranch, eating my grass."

"I don't think so," Smoke said bluntly. "They're on

Sugarloaf range, unless some of them have strayed over onto Fred Malone's spread. And Mr. Malone doesn't mind, because some of his cattle graze on my range at times." He smiled, but there was no real friendliness in the expression. "You see, Mr. Malone and I figure it's best to be good neighbors."

"Yes, well, as you know, Malone's range is right next to my own on the other side, and your horses and his cattle are getting fat on my grass. I won't tolerate that, so you can consider this a friendly warning."

"A friendly warning? Franklin, you've never done a friendly thing in your life."

"You have been warned," Franklin said gruffly before he turned and walked away.

Smoke watched the man go, knowing full well now that his instincts had been right.

Trouble was on the way, riding a fast horse.

After leaving the restaurant, Tilden Franklin stopped by the office of Lloyd Briggs, the justice of the peace. Franklin owned the justice of the peace, in that Franklin was responsible for him getting his position.

Lloyd Briggs wasn't without some qualifications; he was an educated man who had actually passed the bar. He had a background in criminal law, but in New Madrid, Missouri, he had been run out of town because he'd managed to get free, on a technicality, a man who had raped and murdered a fourteen-year-old girl.

That reputation had followed Briggs for the next few years, so that nobody had wanted anything to do with him. So, unable to practice his profession anymore, Briggs had had a brief run as an outlaw. Then, turning state's evidence against some of the men he had ridden with, he had been granted a full pardon by the governor of Kansas.

Now, thanks to Tilden Franklin, he was back in the law practice again, but as a justice of the peace rather than an attorney.

"I have a feeling that Smoke Jensen is going to cause me some trouble," Franklin said.

Briggs, who was tall and thin, with a prominent Adam's apple, took the ever-present cigar from his mouth and examined the end of it before he spoke.

"What you need is someone who can hold him in check."

"Yeah, well, I've got a veritable army on my payroll."

"No, you can't send an entire army after him, not without incurring trouble with the law."

"You are the law," Franklin said.

Briggs shook his head. "No, I'm a justice of the peace, liable to the state supreme court. What you need is someone who is as good with a gun as Smoke Jensen. Hire such a man and I will appoint him as an officer of the court. That way any confrontation that may develop between the two men will be covered by the law, and the law will be on the side of the special officer of the court I will appoint."

"I don't have any idea who that might be," Franklin said. "As far as I know, there isn't anyone as good as Smoke Jensen."

"Lucas McCabe," Briggs said.

"McCabe," Franklin said. He smiled. "Yes, I've heard of him. He might be as good as Jensen, at that."

Briggs put the cigar back in his mouth and took a few puffs before he responded. "Anything that may develop between McCabe and Jensen will be beyond your purview.

If he succeeds, the benefit of such a situation will accrue to you. If he fails, you'll be none the worse."

"Yeah," Franklin replied. "And if he is killed, well, better him than me."

"If you would like, I'll contact McCabe and ask him to come to Fontana to accept an appointment."

"You think he will come?"

Briggs smiled. "Lucas McCabe is a smart man. He knows well the advantages of being a law officer 'on the take,' as it were. Yes, I am quite sure he will come."

Ten miles from the relay station, Jack Slade divided the money between them.

"Forty-six dollars? We done this for forty-six dollars?" Ian Dolan asked, the tone of his voice indicating his frustration. "That means we only get eleven dollars 'n fifty cents apiece. What the hell, Slade? I thought you said the stage would be carryin' a money shipment."

"I thought it was, else why would they have a shotgun guard ridin' with 'em? Anyhow, you don't have to take your share of the money if you don't want it," Jack Slade replied.

"No, I'll take my eleven dollars, all right," Dolan said.

"And fifty cents," Wolcott added.

"Yeah, and fifty cents."

"Slade, you said that if we joined up with you, we'd make a lot of money. Well, eleven dollars 'n fifty cents ain't a hell of a lot of money," Wolcott complained.

"Wolcott, if you think you can do better on your own, well, you just go out 'n do it," Slade said.

"No, uh, I don't want to leave. I was just sayin' that I

wish we could come up with somethin' that would pay us more'n we got from this holdup."

"Anyhow, this was mostly just a practice to see how we can all work together," Slade said. "That way when somethin' good comes along, we'll be ready for it."

"Whyn't we rob us a bank? We know there's money there," Marv Cooley suggested.

CHAPTER 12

On board the Leopoldina, at sea

Ernest Hemingford frowned slightly as he said, "I'm relying on memory here, but I don't believe this story you're telling me matches up in every detail with the legends I've heard about you. When I was a boy, I used to see dime novels that had been written about you."

"Those dime novel writers weren't hired because they always stuck exactly to the truth," Smoke pointed out with a smile. "They were just paid to be good yarn-spinners. But most of what they scribbled was the truth. Just not one hundred percent factual. There's a difference between 'truth' and 'fact.'"

Hemingford clapped his hands quietly. "Very good, Smoke. Very good indeed. One of the first things a writer must learn is to realize that in writing, there is a difference between 'truth,' as in an honest portrayal, but with nuances in tone and tint. Facts, on the other hand, are exact portrayals of events, sometimes with tone and tint, but more often, it is nothing more than unvarnished truth."

"Yes. I've never heard it explained better," Smoke said.

"Well, Smoke, I live by words. I would be a poor writer

if I didn't have a grasp of the difference between truth and fact, now wouldn't I? So what you are telling me is some of the stories I've read about you have the essence of truth but not hard fact. You, on the other hand, are providing me with a factual account of some of the events in the saga of your life."

Smoke smiled. "Well, yes, but I do hope it has the essence of—how did you say it?—tone and tint."

"Believe me, Smoke, the story you are telling me, though differing in some minor details of the earlier accounts I have read of your life, does not hold back on the promise of provocative prose."

"Promise of provocative prose," Smoke repeated. He chuckled. "It's too bad Sally isn't here right now. She would appreciate your alliteration."

"She would have enjoyed it, to be sure," Hemingford said. "I'm just glad to see that it wasn't wasted on you. Now, please, go on with the story."

Summit County, Colorado

Preacher had a cabin some miles north and a little west of Fontana. From time to time during his years as a wandering fur trapper, he had decided to settle down for a spell and would build himself a cabin, only to abandon it when the restlessness came over him again. They were sturdily built and usually still standing whenever he got back that way.

Knowing that Smoke had established the Sugarloaf not far away, Preacher figured it wouldn't hurt anything to be in the vicinity. Life never stayed boring around that younker for too long, although here lately it hadn't showed any signs of getting exciting. That was bound to change sooner or later, so Preacher stayed put . . . for now.

This was one of those cabins he had built for himself many years before the town of Fontana was born. At that time there was nothing within one hundred miles of where he had chosen to live.

Preacher was still a boy when he ran away from home, and little more than a boy when he had taken part in the Battle of New Orleans during the War of 1812. He came west soon after that war had ended and, in doing so, became one of the earliest of the breed of mountain men who had opened the West and earned their living by trapping and selling beaver pelts. It wasn't too long after he arrived that he picked up the name Preacher, a name he identified with more than he did his given name of Arthur. The name came about because once, when he was captured by Indians, he "preached" a nonstop sermon for almost six hours. The Indians, thinking that he was crazy and believing it bad to harm such a person, let him go. Other mountain men, hearing of his ploy to escape the Indians, began calling him Preacher, and the name had stuck with him ever since.

By now Preacher had lived in the mountains for more than half a century, during which time he had become acquainted with, and made friends of, Kit Carson, Grizzly Adams, Jim Baker, Big Cat Malone, and James Beckwourth. He used to meet such men during the Rendezvous, an almost fair-like event that drew merchants, beer peddlers, charlatans, and prostitutes, as well as every fur trapper within two hundred miles of where the Rendezvous was being held. At the conclusion of the Rendezvous, the fur trappers, already referred to as mountain men, returned to the high lonesome.

When Preacher first built his cabin, he was one hundred miles from his nearest neighbor and four hundred miles from the nearest town. Forty years after he arrived, Denver was settled, and now Fontana was just over ten miles away, a town close enough to visit, though he did so only when it was absolutely necessary to replenish his supplies of coffee, flour, cornmeal, sugar, beans, and bacon, all viands of civilization that he had become accustomed to.

"Preacher, you old son of a gun, how are you getting along?"

Preacher had been lying on the bunk in his cabin one day when he heard a familiar voice, and with a smile, he hurried out to greet Big Cat Malone.

Years earlier, Preacher and Big Cat Malone had wintered together. The next year Malone had gone out on his own, but the two men had remained friends after that, even though for the next several years they'd seen each other only at Rendezvous

Then Malone had traded his buckskins for denim and his black powder rifle for a pickaxe. After four years of prospecting, Malone had found a very productive vein of gold and was now one of the richest men in all of Colorado.

"Big Cat!" Preacher greeted warmly. "Come on in. Your chair is still at the table. What do you say we have a drink?"

"That's fine by me," Malone said. "But I brought us a real bottle of whiskey. We can drink like civilized folk. I'm goin' by my given name now. I'm not Big Cat anymore. I'm Fred Malone."

Preacher laughed. "Who are you kidding? You might have struck it rich 'n live in some fine house, but you ain't never goin' to be plumb civilized, 'n you're always goin' to be Big Cat to me. If you hadn't a-wanted that name, you wouldn't a-kilt that mountain lion with your bare hands, 'n there wouldn't nobody have ever called you Big Cat."

"Preacher, you can call me anything you want. Just because I own a hundred thousand acres of grassland and a bank, and there's not one out of ten people who knows anything about my time in the mountains, doesn't mean I've forgotten any of my old friends."

"Also, you've got yourself a good family," Preacher said. "But how they manage to put up with an old mountain goat like you, I'll never know."

"Don't forget, I wasn't a mountain man when I met Lauren. By then I was an up-and-coming businessman. And now we're no different from any other family out here."

"Except that you're richer than just 'bout all the other families out here put together. How's that daughter of your'n doin'? How old is she now? Twelve? Thirteen?"

"Sue Ellen is seventeen, and she gets prettier every day," Malone said proudly. "I already have to hold the boys off with a shotgun."

"I imagine she's got a pretty good head on her shoulders. Pretty, young girls learn just real quick how to handle boys."

"Yeah, you're right. And I do trust her." Malone changed the subject. "I reckon Smoke Jensen is the reason you're back in these parts?"

"You've heard about me and Smoke bein' friends?"

"More than that," Malone said. "He's told me about the time he spent with you. We've met numerous times in Fontana. He has money in my bank, and his range butts up next to mine. I'd like to think that we're friends." Malone took a cigar from his vest pocket, put it in his mouth, and said around it, "I wouldn't want to have Smoke Jensen for an enemy."

"Only a plumb fool'd want that," Preacher said.

"Unfortunately, you know as well as I do, Preacher . . . if there's one thing this world has plenty of, it's fools."

The same day that Smoke was in Fontana, having his unpleasant conversation with Tilden Franklin in Lambert's Café, Fred Malone was in Denver, speaking with William Jackson Palmer, who was the president of the Denver and Rio Grande Railroad. Palmer was rather unprepossessing in appearance, a small man with a receding hairline. His accomplishments were much more than his appearance. For his actions as a brigadier general in the Union army during the Civil War, Palmer had received the Medal of Honor. He was a civil engineer with a long history in the railroad business, having helped build the Kansas Pacific Railroad. He had also introduced to the United States the practice of burning coal rather than wood in locomotives.

"Fred," Palmer greeted. "To what do I owe the pleasure of a meeting with one of the wealthiest men in Colorado?"

"I'm wantin' to build me a railroad, Bill, so I thought I'd come to Denver to talk about it with the most successful railroad builder I know."

"How many railroad builders do you know?"

"Well, fact is, you're the only one I know, but you are the most successful one."

Palmer laughed out loud. "You know what? I'll take that as a compliment. Where do you plan to build this railroad?"

"I'm going to build it from Denver to Fontana. The

thing is, we ain't got us no railroad down in southwest Colorado, so what I'm aimin' to do is to build one for us."

Malone didn't say anything about the rumors of a gold strike he had heard. He wanted to keep that to himself for the time being. But if those rumors turned out to be true, a railroad would be a very lucrative enterprise to own.

"How are you planning to finance this railroad?"

"You mean where 'm I gettin' the money? I figure I can get most of it from my own self," Malone said. "'N what I can't come up with on my own, I'll borrow from the bank." Malone chuckled. "I own the bank, so I don't reckon I'll have much trouble in gettin' the bank to give me a loan."

"If you would be interested, I would like to go into partnership with you on the railroad you plan to build. It never hurts to have an extra source of funds, and I would be perfectly fine with being your junior partner."

Malone flashed a broad smile, then stuck out his hand. "Actually, I was comin' around to askin' you if you'd like to do somethin' like that. You saved us a whole lot of palaverin'."

"I know just the man to head up the construction crew," Palmer said. "His name is Frank Magee, and he was one of the leading engineers in the building of the Denver and Rio Grande."

"Do you think a feller like that would work for me?" Malone asked.

"Let's put it this way. I know he would work for us."

"Good. You hire him, then."

"Fred, we may have a problem that you haven't considered," Palmer said.

"What problem would that be?"

"Tilden Franklin. How is he going to take it with you building a railroad and he being no part of it?"

"He prob'ly ain't goin' to take it all that good," Malone said.

"Do you think we should invite him?" Palmer asked.

"No," Malone said emphatically. "I can't put my finger on it, Bill, but I've got enough of the old mountain man left in me that I just smell something wrong about Franklin."

"Do you think he might be a problem for us?"

"He might try 'n be a problem, but I got me someone in mind who could take care of that problem for us just real quick."

CHAPTER 13

Trail Back was the name of the large ranch belonging to Fred "Big Cat" Malone. It bordered the Sugarloaf at the far end of the valley, and as Tilden Franklin had mentioned to Smoke in Fontana, the Circle TF was on the far side of Trail Back. Taken together, the three spreads covered a vast swath of territory. Smoke had no doubt that Franklin had his eye on the other two ranches, especially now with rumors of a gold strike flying. Franklin's offer to buy all of Smoke's horse herd was just the first step in a takeover attempt.

His refusal to sell must have frustrated Franklin, Smoke knew—but it wouldn't cause the man to back off.

Smoke wasn't surprised when one of the cowboys from the Trail Back rode over to the Sugarloaf one day soon after Smoke's visit to Fontana and delivered an invitation for him and Sally to join the Malone family for dinner. Smoke was out on the range when the puncher found him. That evening he told Sally that Malone had invited them to dinner.

"I said I would check with you, but I gave a tentative yes."

Sally chuckled. "Tentative?"

"We can always back out of it if you want to."

"No, I welcome the opportunity," Sally replied enthusiastically. "The Malones have been good neighbors to us. You can tell Mr. Malone that your tentative yes is a definite yes."

"As far as he is concerned, it's already a definite yes. It was tentative only in my mind, and if you had said no, I would have backed out."

Now it was Sally's time to laugh. "You can be a devious one, Smoke. I'll have to remember that."

Trail Back Ranch

Because Sally wanted to dress for the occasion, it would have been awkward to ride a horse, so they took the buckboard. The residence at Trail Back was a large white two-story house with Corinthian columns framing the front porch. When they arrived, a little white dog came running out to meet them.

"Well, hello, you cute thing, you," Sally said, greeting the little dog.

"Charley, don't you be bothering those nice people now, you hear me? Get on back into the house," said an exceptionally pretty young woman, stepping out onto the porch.

Charley, acquiescing to her demand, gave up his own personal welcome and ran back to the house as ordered.

"Welcome to Trail Back. And I'm sorry about the dog bothering you."

"Nonsense. The dog was no bother," Sally said. "My, don't you look lovely today, Sue Ellen?"

Sue Ellen blushed. "Thank you, Mrs. Jensen. I'm so glad you could come. Lula Belle has prepared the most wonderful dinner for us. Come on in. Mama is waiting in the foyer, and Papa and Preacher are in the library."

Smoke laughed. "Preacher in a library? Now, there's something I never thought I would see."

Sue Ellen led them into the house, where they were met by Lauren Malone.

"I have been so looking forward to this," Lauren said, smiling and taking Sally's hands into her own. "Smoke, why don't you go on into the library? Fred and Preacher are waiting for you there. Sally, we'll let the men talk, and we can visit until dinner is ready."

"Yes, that sounds wonderful." Sally graciously accepted the offer, though, in truth, she would rather have gone into the library with Smoke to participate in the men's conversation. Lauren took her to the keeping room, where the cook and housekeeper Lula Belle poured a cup of hot tea for them all, including Sue Ellen, who had accompanied them.

"Oh, you've no idea how welcome this is," Sally said, taking her cup. "I love tea, but Smoke isn't that fond of it, so we seldom have it." She held out her cup. "To friends," she said.

"To friends," Lauren and Sue Ellen repeated.

"So, Sally, how is married life treating you these days?" Lauren asked.

"Oh, I'm very happy with it," Sally replied. "I must say, though, that married life came along quite unexpectedly. It had been my plan to stay out here but a few years to learn and enjoy the West, all the while supporting myself as a schoolteacher. But I met a handsome young paladin, and my world got turned upside down."

"Paladin?" Sue Ellen asked.

"A knight and a hero in Charlemagne's court," Sally said. "A bit of romantic hyperbole on my part, to be sure, but I can't think of any better way to describe Smoke."

"Oh, what a wonderful new word to learn!" Sue Ellen said enthusiastically. "And yes, Mr. Jensen is a knight and a hero. You are, too. Well, actually, you would be a heroine."

Sally laughed. "Why would you say such a thing?"

"Because you are a schoolteacher, and I consider schoolteachers to be heroes and heroines."

"How sweet of you to say so."

"Will you ever go back to teaching?" Lauren asked.

"Oh, I think it's too early to know whether I will or not. I do enjoy teaching, though."

"I want to be a schoolteacher, just like you," Sue Ellen said.

"Well, it is a wonderful profession," Sally replied. "I don't regret one moment of it."

"And yet you gave it up to marry Smoke Jensen," Lauren said.

Sally smiled. "Yes, as much as I loved teaching, I found that I loved Smoke even more."

"How do you keep yourself busy if you aren't teaching?" Lauren asked. "I mean, other than housework."

Sally thought of the many hours she still put in practicing with a pistol and rifle, and how she also never hesitated to pull on trousers, fork a horse, and help Smoke on the range when she needed to. She smiled. "Oh, I've found a few things to do."

Back in the library, Preacher and Fred Malone greeted Smoke with hearty handshakes and a glass of brandy.

"Sally still practicin' her shootin'?" Preacher asked.

"She can shoot a flea off a steer from a hundred yards," Smoke said.

Preacher laughed. "If that's the case, I don't expect anyone is going to mess with her."

"That's the whole purpose," Smoke said. He got serious. "Preacher, you know that I have made a lot of enemies in my life, and as soon as they learn about Sally, she's likely to become a target. It happened with Nicole. And I'll be honest with you, I don't think I could take it if it happened again. So, if someone comes around and I'm not there, I want Sally to be able to take care of herself."

"I ain't got me no doubt a'tall but that she'll be able to do just that," Preacher said.

"Smoke, I'm glad you accepted my invitation to dinner tonight," Malone said. "I want to run an idea by you."

"What idea would that be?" Smoke asked.

"Railroad."

"What?"

"Railroad," Malone repeated. "I'm going to build a railroad from Denver to here."

"By *here*, are you talking about Fontana?"

"Yes, though I intend to extend the railroad beyond that. I'm going to bring it all the way to Cimarrona Creek. That way every rancher and farmer in this whole area will have access to the railroad."

"That's pretty ambitious," Smoke said.

"Well, we'll have to lay tracks across Slumgullion Gulch and through the Pettibone Pass. Ambitious? I suppose so, but what can I say? I'm an ambitious person," Malone said.

"I can go along with that. I'm pretty ambitious, too," Smoke replied.

"Good, because if you help me get this railroad built, I'll give you title to thirty thousand acres of good grassland. Add that to what you already have, and you'll be the owner of the best ranch in Colorado, bar none!"

Smoke frowned in thought for a long moment, then shook his head.

"Big Cat, what you are proposing sounds great, and I wish I could take you up on it, but I can't, because I'm too honest a person to take advantage of you."

"Why do you say that?" Malone asked, surprised that Smoke had turned him down.

"Well, because I'm not an engineer, and I know absolutely nothing about building a railroad. Short of swinging a sledgehammer as the track is laid, I don't know what I could do. And I'm sure you aren't telling me you would make such a generous arrangement for a section hand," Smoke replied.

"Frank Magee," Malone said. He smiled. "Frank was one of the lead engineers in building the Denver and Rio Grande. He will be in charge of laying the track. I want you to be in charge of everything else."

"Besides laying the track, what exactly is everything else?"

"Anything that isn't the actual laying of track," Malone said with an enigmatic smile.

Smoke wasn't sure what the banker meant by that, but a troubled feeling stirred inside him. Rumors of gold being found in the area were already going to stir things up. Throw in the prospect of a railroad being built, too . . .

With all of that going on, this part of the state might well become a powder keg ready to blow sky-high.

* * *

"This isn't the way home," Sally said later that same day, as Smoke drove away from Trai Back.

"I know," Smoke said. "But I want to show you something."

"All right," Sally said, taking Smoke's arm in her two hands.

Smoke chuckled. "You aren't going to ask me what?"

"Sweetheart, whatever it is, I want to see it just because you want to show it to me."

After a drive of about an hour, they stopped on a small rise to enjoy the scenery.

"What do you think?" Smoke asked.

"I think this is the most beautiful vista I have ever seen," Sally said. She crossed her arms over her chest. "Thank you for bringing me here to enjoy it. This is still part of Mr. Malone's ranch, isn't it?"

"For now," Smoke said. "He's offered to deed thirty thousand acres of it, contiguous with the Sugarloaf, over to me, to be added to our range."

"Oh!" Sally said. "That's wonderful, but . . . why would he do that?"

"Because he has a job he wants me to do," Smoke replied as he gazed off into the distance, seeing not just the land but what it might hold in the future. "And I've agreed to do it."

Brown Spur, Colorado

Lucas McCabe was in the Pigsty Saloon, standing at the bar, with his hands wrapped around a beer mug. Earlier this morning he had received a letter from Lloyd Briggs. In the letter Briggs said that he was a justice of the peace in the town of Fontana. At first, McCabe hadn't believed that, but while checking a few sources, he'd learned that Briggs's claim was true. He was, as he claimed, a justice of the peace.

McCabe found that interesting, because a few years ago, McCabe and Briggs had pulled a few jobs together, and McCabe was having a hard time believing that Briggs had gone from being an outlaw to being a justice of the peace.

In addition to his claim of being a justice of the peace, Briggs made a most interesting offer. McCabe pulled the letter out and read the paragraph that he found most significant.

If you would come to Fontana, I will appoint you a special officer of the court. As such, you will have police powers, meaning you can arrest anyone you want and can close your eyes to anyone you want. In addition, you will be in a position to take advantage of lucrative opportunities. And, as an additional incentive, your previous record will be expunged (as mine has been).

I must tell you, however, that your principal adversary in keeping the peace in the endeavor you are about to undertake—indeed, if you accept this offer—will be no less than Smoke Jensen. There are some who claim that Smoke Jensen is the greatest gunfighter alive today, if not of all time. I'm not ready to concede that, and I don't think you are, either. If, however, the thought that you might have to encounter Jensen fills you with dread and self-doubt, I will understand if you decide to pass on this offer.

The more McCabe thought of Briggs's offer, the more interesting it sounded. Lucas McCabe was good with a gun—some said he was the best—and McCabe had enough arrogance and self-confidence to believe that.

McCabe didn't notch his pistol handle, as many did. He didn't have to. He was perfectly aware of how many men he had killed. The number now was thirteen.

And it hadn't escaped him that thirteen was an unlucky number. He wasn't prepared to shoot someone down in cold blood just so he could get past that number, but he wished fourteen would come soon. He put the letter away and, with both hands wrapped around the mug, stared down at the receding head on his beer. If he accepted Briggs's offer to become a law officer, he was certain the opportunity would come soon.

"Lucas McCabe, this is the day you die!"

The loud declaration not only interrupted McCabe's reverie, but it also halted all conversation in the Pigsty Saloon as the patrons turned to see who had issued the challenge.

Lucas McCabe remained standing at the bar, with both of his hands gripping the mug of beer he was drinking. He was aware of the quick movement of others in the bar, but he remained in place. Some saw him smile and were amazed at his quiet courage. Not one of the saloon patrons was aware that he was thinking of the number fourteen, nor would they understand the significance of his thought if they did know.

"Did you hear me, McCabe?"

With a sigh, McCabe turned toward the man who had called out to him. His challenger was standing just inside the batwing doors. The man in the door was small, with a scar that started at the corner of his left eye, then slashed down like a purple streak of lightning across his cheek before hooking under the corner of his mouth.

"You would be Deke Crowley?" McCabe asked.

The little man's lips spread into a sinister smile. "You've heard of me?"

"Yeah, I've heard of you."

"I've heard of you, too. You're supposed to be good. Real good."

"Is that what you've heard?" McCabe asked.

"Yeah. I've heard some say you're better 'n me."

"Then you know that if we do this thing, I might kill you."

"I'm willin' to take that chance," Crowley said.

"Why?"

The sinister smile grew a little broader. "Let's just say I'd like to be known as the man that kilt Lucas McCabe."

McCabe didn't know if he was fast enough to deal with this fool or not, so he decided not to take a chance. Without saying another word or calling Crowley out, McCabe made a grab for his pistol. McCabe was fast, and he made a quick, clean draw, but even before he was able to bring the gun up, he heard the crash of gunfire and saw the muzzle flash, concurrent with a blow to his chest like a kick from a mule.

"Thirteen," McCabe gasped. "Thirteen?" That was all he said before he fell, dead before he hit the floor.

"Damn!" somebody said. "I didn't think there was nobody who could beat McCabe."

"Thirteen," one of the other patrons said. "Now, what in the hell do you think he meant by that?"

"Gentlemen!" the owner of the saloon called. "Step up to the bar! Drinks are on the house!"

The saloon owner, Cyrus Bean, thought it would be well worth it to buy drinks for the house. He knew that his customers would tell everyone they knew about what they had seen here today, and his business would grow as a result of so many wanting to come see where Lucas McCabe, previously thought to be unbeatable, was killed by Deke Crowley.

He had also figured out a way to make a little money from this.

A little more than a hundred miles away, four men came riding into the little town of Mitchell. They didn't raise too much attention, because when they arrived in town, they arrived one at a time. One of the citizens commented to another that it seemed a bit unusual for four perfect strangers to show up in town in a single day.

It was even stranger that all four of the riders just happened to wind up in front of the bank. That was when Deputy Michael Glenn stopped his rounds to pay particular attention to them. Three of the men went into the bank. The fourth man remained mounted, holding the reins of the other three horses.

Deputy Glenn was less than half a block from the town marshal's office, and by now the four strangers had gotten his full attention.

"Marshal, I think maybe you should take a look at this," the deputy said after sticking his head just inside the door.

Marshal Dan McGill, who had been playing a game of solitaire, didn't question his deputy's summons. He stood up, leaving the cards on his desk, grabbed his hat, and stepped outside.

"What is it, Mike?"

"I don't know. Maybe it ain't nothin', but it looked a mite peculiar to me. I mean, with three men goin' inside the bank 'n one stayin' outside, mounted 'n holdin' the reins of the other three horses. 'N what makes it even more peculiar is them four men didn't even come into town together."

"I'll be damned! The bank is being robb—" That was as far as Marshal McGill got before they heard shots, then saw three men come running out of the bank building, one of them carrying a cloth bag and all three of them holding pistols.

"It's Jack Slade!" Glenn shouted.

Both Marshal McGill and his deputy had their pistols in hand.

"Slade, you and your men hold it right there!" McGill shouted, extending his pistol.

Jack Slade's gun was still in the holster, but he drew so fast that later, some would insist that he had had his gun in hand all along. Slade fired twice, the gunshots so close together that some would report it as one shot. Both Marshal McGill and Deputy Glenn went down with fatal gunshot wounds.

The four men made their getaway.

Jack Slade, Ian Dolan, Marv Cooley, and Milt Wolcott rode hard and fast until they were several miles from town. Then they stopped at a stream to water and rest their horses.

"How much did we get, Jack?" Dolan asked, rubbing his hands in anticipation.

Slade had tied the bag to the saddle horn, and now he took it down and emptied it. Several packets of bound bills came out. Two of the packets were composed of twenty-dollar bills, and there were three packets of ten-dollar bills, three of five-dollar bills, and six packets of ones.

"Count it, count it!" Dolan said, rubbing his hands together again.

Slade began counting as the others watched. When he was through with the count, he looked over at the others, his face spread into a huge grin.

"It comes to eight thousand five hundred dollars!"

"How much is that for each of us?" Cooley asked.

"I don't know," Slade said. "I haven't ciphered it out yet. Give me a minute."

Slade scratched some numbers in the dirt, worked for a moment, then smiled. "Boys, this here ciphers out to two thousand one hunnert 'n twenty-five dollars apiece. How about it, Dolan? This is a little better than the ten dollars we got for the stagecoach robbery, don't you think?"

"Yeah, it sure as hell is."

"Where's the best place to go to spend it?" Wolcott asked.

"How 'bout Dixon Switch?" Dolan suggested. "That's far enough from Mitchell, they won't nobody there know nothin' about us."

"Dixon Switch? Where's Dixon Switch?" Cooley asked.

"It's just south of Denver, on the Denver and Rio Grande Railroad. 'N bein' that it's actual on the railroad tracks, it's got more saloons than any town that size that ain't on the tracks. 'N that means more women."

Slade nodded. "That sounds all right to me."

Summit County, Colorado

Malone had given Smoke a map of the proposed railroad, and when Smoke and Sally got back to the ranch house, he began examining it. The proposed railroad would start at Denver, continue on through Fontana, and end at Sierra Cimarrona Creek, seven miles east of the Sugarloaf.

"End of track," he said.

"What?" Sally asked.

Smoke pointed to the spot on the map. "The new railroad would end here. This would be the perfect place for a town to be built. I need to talk to a few businessmen and see if I couldn't get them interested in coming to end of track. That way we, and the other ranchers in the area, wouldn't have to go as far as Fontana when we needed something, like a store, a blacksmith, a place for boots and saddles."

"A dress shop, a nice restaurant, perhaps?" Sally added.

"Why not?"

"But who are you going to get to move here?"

"Anybody who's tired of dealing with Tilden Franklin and his heavy-handed ways," Smoke said.

CHAPTER 14

Fontana, Colorado

"Are you telling me that Fred Malone is building a railroad?" Tilden Franklin asked.

"He is indeed," Haywood Arden said with a huge smile. Arden was the owner and publisher of the Fontana *Sunburst*. "I've heard that he's already hired Frank Magee, and Magee is hiring track workers."

"And he plans for it to come here?"

"Yes, sir, it'll run from Denver to Cimarrona Creek, which is about one hundred miles." Arden smiled. "If that is so, then the tracks will have to come right through Fontana. I reckon you know what that means."

"Yeah, I know."

"It means Fontana will be growing. Why, I wouldn't be surprised if we didn't experience one hundred percent growth within the next year."

"I wonder how long it'll take him to build it?"

"He should average a good five miles a day," Arden said. "At that rate, I'd say about a month and a half, maybe two months, since he has to go through a couple of passes."

"Good. That gives me enough time," Franklin replied.

Arden looked at Franklin with a questioning expression on his face. "Enough time for what?"

"Enough time," Franklin replied, as if the cryptic answer was all that was needed.

When Franklin returned to his ranch, he had some thinking to do. A railroad from Denver to the town of Fontana would be very good for business. But it would be even better business for whoever owned the railroad. As Arden had said, Fontana was primed to explode with growth, especially if the rumors of gold proved to be true.

Franklin was peeved that it was Malone who was building the railroad, and not him. The truth was, Franklin had considered building it, but he had delayed his plans because it was going to be so expensive.

He grinned. On the other hand, if Malone got a good start on the railroad, then was unable to continue for one reason or another, Franklin could step in and take advantage of what Malone had already done. That would make him owner of the new railroad, as well as all the rangeland and all the gold that would come with it.

He would just have to see to it that Malone ran into a lot of difficulty along the way.

"Smoke Jensen?" Franklin said, repeating the name that Sheriff Colby had said

"Yeah, he's going to be a troubleshooter for Malone."

"What kind of troubleshooter?"

"I expect when problems of one kind or another come up, he'll take care of 'em. For example, if, for some reason, somebody with a gun wants to make problems for the railroad, well, I expect he'll take care of that, too."

Franklin thought about his conversation with Colby as he sat brooding in his office. He hadn't thought about Malone hiring someone like Smoke Jensen. Franklin had already made some plans to delay and interfere with the railroad, not enough to destroy what had already been put down, but just enough to frustrate Malone into quitting. Franklin would be able to buy him out then, though he realized that Smoke Jensen might pose a problem.

Franklin smiled. "But problems are made to be fixed."

"What for did Mr. Franklin send for a gunman?" Tay asked Pearlie.

Tay was one of the twelve men to whom Franklin was paying fighting wages. Franklin had two separate outfits working for him. One group was made up of legitimate cowboys who were working his ranch. The other group consisted of men who were particularly skilled with weapons. These were men whose wages were twice as high as those received by the working cowboys. They called themselves, half in jest, "the Demons," and Wes Fontaine, who went by the name of Pearlie, was the foreman of the group.

"I expect it's because Mr. Franklin has a special job for him," Pearlie replied.

"Mr. Franklin will prob'ly be payin' him lots of money, won't he?"

"I expect he will pay him a lot of money."

"That don't make no sense a'tall. I'm as good with a gun as anyone else. Hell, I could do whatever it is he's wantin' done."

"That's just it. You don't know what it is he's wantin' done. I reckon Mr. Franklin knows what he's doin'," Pearlie said.

"Dead?" Franklin said. "What do you mean, McCabe is dead?"

"I mean that all body functions have ceased. His heart has stopped, his breathing has stopped, and his blood flow has—"

"I know what the hell dead is, Briggs," Franklin said. "How did he die?"

"He was killed in a gunfight with Deke Crowley."

"Deke Crowley, you say?"

"Yes. I've heard that he is very good."

Franklin nodded. "That's good to know."

Brown Spur, Colorado

Gene Welsh was the undertaker, and anyone killed in Brown Spur would come to him. Normally, he would have buried McCabe as he did any other transient, at minimum pay from the county, and as cheaply as possible. But Cyrus Bean had come to him with an idea on how to make money.

"I'll give you the idea, if you will agree to an even split."

"I don't know what your proposal is, but if it has anything to do with the body, I'll be out the expense of burying him."

"You'll get money from the county."

"Not even enough to embalm him."

"For what I have planned, he'll have to be embalmed," Bean said. "All right. An even split after your expenses."

"Wait, I know what you have planned. You're going to find someplace where a reward is being offered, 'n you plan to take his body there."

"Nope." A big smile spread across Bean's face. "We're goin' to charge folks to come look at him."

SEE THE BODY OF THE GUNFIGHTER
LUCAS MCCABE
KILLED IN A FAIR GUNFIGHT
BY
DEKE CROWLEY
50 CENTS A VIEW

Gene Welsh stood by the open casket in his mortuary, collecting fifty cents apiece from the people who were standing in line to get a look at Lucas McCabe in death. He was trying to maintain a professional expression of the solemnity that the event warranted, but that was difficult for him to do, because he had already made one hundred dollars above what it would cost him. And the money was still coming in, because the line stretched halfway down the block, as the morbidly curious waited for the privilege of spending thirty seconds staring down at the deceased gunfighter.

Welsh had prepared the body for viewing, using rouge to keep him looking as natural as possible. He had enhanced the bullet hole that was just over McCabe's heart, enlarging it with red wax so that the actual entry wound appeared to have blood around it.

"I tell you," Thurman Rosco said. "I seen McCabe take on Peter Pizen 'n Wally Simmons over in Frisco, 'n McCabe kilt both of 'em. I ain't never seen no one that fast. I never woulda thought anyone could beat 'im, but Crowley done it fair and square."

"Is Crowley still in town?" someone asked.

"I reckon he is. I seen 'im in the Pigsty Saloon just a few minutes ago. He's sittin' there at a table all by his own self, 'n when somebody comes to talk to 'im, why, he don't say more'n a couple of words."

"You'd think he'd be talkin' up a storm, wouldn't you? I mean, after him killin' McCabe like he done. That's goin' to make Crowley famous."

"What do you mean, it's goin' to make 'im famous? Hell, he already was famous."

"Yeah, I reckon he was. But this here killin' of McCabe is goin' to make 'im even more famous."

"I wonder if McCabe coulda took Jack Slade in a gunfight?"

"I don't know. From what I've heard, Slade is faster than McCabe, though there won't nobody ever know that, seein' as McCabe up 'n got hisself kilt, like he done."

"Next," Welsh called.

"Me 'n Thurman is here together. Can we both go in at the same time?"

"I don't care, long as you both pay the fifty cents."

The two men stepped into the visitation room, where family and friends could say a final good-bye to their loved ones. In this case, however, the only ones viewing the remains had paid to do so.

"He don't look all that tough now, does he?" Thurman said.

"No, he don't."

* * *

Over in the Pigsty Saloon, Crowley was nursing a beer. He would prefer a few whiskeys, but he knew that if someone was going to challenge him to make a name for themselves, now would be a good time for them to do it. That was why he was staying sober, and that was why he was discouraging anyone from talking to him.

"Mr. Crowley?" a young man said, approaching his table. The young man was wearing a white shirt and cotton trousers. He wasn't armed.

"Go away."

"Telegram for you, sir," the young man said, holding out a yellow envelope.

"Telegram? For me?"

"Yes, sir."

"I'll be damned. I ain't never got me no telegram in my entire life." Crowley had intended to send the young man away, but curiosity got the best of him and he reached for the missive.

The young man gave him the telegram, then remained standing by the table.

"What are you still standin' there for?"

"It is customary to provide the one who delivers the telegram with a gratuity," the young man said.

"With a what?"

"A tip, sir, as thanks for delivering the telegram."

"I didn't ask for the telegram. You just brung it to me. Go away."

"Yes, sir," the young man said before, with a look of chagrin on his face, he turned away from the table and left the room.

Crowley opened the envelope.

IF YOU ARE INTERESTED IN MAKING A
LOT OF MONEY COME TO FONTANA AND
SEE ME STOP
LLOYD BRIGGS

Crowley wondered what he meant by "a lot of money."
And where the hell was Fontana? And who the hell was
Lloyd Briggs?

Denver, Colorado

Smoke had come to Denver with Fred "Big Cat"
Malone, riding in Malone's private stagecoach. Unlike the
commercial stagecoaches, which had hard benches de-
signed to accommodate the greatest number of people,
Malone's coach, which was painted a royal blue, had four
well-cushioned seats. It was only marginally faster than a
commercial coach, however, so it took them two and a half
days to make the trip.

When Smoke and Malone stepped out of the coach,
they were greeted by William Palmer, the president of the
D&RG. There was another man with Palmer.

"Fred, this is Frank Magee," Palmer said, introducing
the man with him. "He is the construction engineer I told
you about."

"It's good to meet you, Mr. Magee. This is Smoke
Jensen. He'll be working with you as a troubleshooter."

"Smoke Jensen?" Magee said, a look of curiosity on his
face. "Are you *the*, I mean?"

"Yes," Smoke said, answering Magee's uncompleted
question. There was a disarming grin on Smoke's face as
he extended his hand.

"I, uh, am very pleased to meet you, Mr. Jensen."

"If we're going to work together, Frank, I would prefer to be called Smoke."

"Yes, sir, Smoke it is."

"It looks like you had an elegant ride," Palmer said. "How long did it take you to get here?"

"A little over two days," Malone replied.

Palmer smiled. "After the railroad is completed, that same trip will take only a few hours."

"Well, then, let's get it built," Malone said. "Where do we start?"

"Frank, you want to show the man what his money has bought so far?" Palmer suggested.

"The first allotment of supplies is stacked up back here," Magee said, leading Smoke and Malone to another part of the yard. Here, several iron rails, wooden barrels filled with spikes, and crossties occupied a rather substantial area of the train yard.

"That's a lot of railing and crossties," Malone said. "How far will this take us?"

"We have six hundred seventy rails laid out here. That's good for ten miles. But we have only ten thousand crossties, and that will take us about three miles," Magee said. "We'll begin by taking our material out by wagon, but after two or three days, we should have ten to fifteen miles of track laid, and then we'll start bringing out the new rails, crossties, and spikes by train. Everything will go a little faster then, providing we don't have any trouble."

"Well, if you do have trouble, take it up with Smoke here," Malone said with a broad smile. "He's our trouble-shooter."

CHAPTER 15

Dixon Switch, Colorado

Even before there was a town called Dixon Switch, there was a small shack alongside the tracks. This was the residence of the switchman, whose job it was to switch the track in order to send the trains to their proper destination, according to the schedule. The switchman's name was Ed Dixon, and the switch became known as Dixon's Switch. A few structures grew up alongside the switch track: a trading store, a saloon, some houses, a railroad depot, a shoe store, another saloon, an apothecary, another saloon, a hotel and restaurant, a bank, more houses, more saloons, and more businesses. The new town became known as Dixon Switch. Once incorporated, Dixon Switch was a busy and fully functioning town, with a city hall, a court, and a city marshal's office and jail. It was a surprise to no one that Ed Dixon became the first mayor of the town bearing his name.

Slade and the others stopped just outside of town.

"You know, it might be a good idea if we hid most of the money before we go into town. If somebody was to find out that each one of us has a couple thousand dollars, it could raise some suspicion," Slade said.

"Yeah, you might be right," Cooley said. "Where can we hide it?"

"We'll bury it," Slade suggested.

The sky was threatening rain when Slade and the others rode into town. Their arrival raised no particular attention, though the four men did come in together.

"Hey, you think anyone in town will recognize us?" Wolcott asked.

"They won't recognize me for sure, 'cause I ain't never been here before," Slade said. "Dolan, you was the one that was wantin' us to come here. You ever done anythin' here that would make 'em remember you?"

"No, I ain't been here but one time, 'n I just stopped into the saloon for a beer, and to have a look at some of the whores. Onliest thing is, I didn't have no money, so I couldn't have none of 'em, and as I recollect, there didn't nobody even speak to me, neither."

"Well, hell, Ian, who'd want to speak to you, anyway?" Cooley asked, and the others laughed.

"It ain't that I want to be all that popular, but from time to time, I'd kinda like to talk to some woman or somethin'."

"You can get all the talkin' you want from the percentage girls by payin' 'em," Cooley said.

"Yeah, but the thing is, at the time I just barely had me enough money to buy me a beer, 'n I didn't have no money for women a'tall," Dolan said.

"Well, by damn, we got us enough now!" Wolcott said.

"Yeah!" Dolan said. "I'll bet they'll talk to us now."

"Let's spend some of it," Cooley suggested.

After dismounting in front of the Cow Bell Saloon, the

four men went inside, then stepped up to the bar, where they were greeted by the bartender.

"What'll it be, gents?"

"Whiskey," Dolan said. "'N leave the bottle."

"That'll cost you a buck and a half."

Dolan put the money down, then turned his back to the bar and looked out over the saloon floor. There were at least four percentage girls working. Two of them were sitting at two tables, talking to patrons; the other two were walking around. Wolcott called out to them.

"Why don't you girls come over here 'n keep us company?" He pulled some money out of his pocket, holding up a dollar bill.

The two girls who weren't engaged smiled and responded to the summons.

"Give these ladies whatever they want," Wolcott said.

"Well, now, honey, do all four of you have money or just you?" one of the two girls asked as they approached the bar.

"We all four have money," Slade said. "We was just paid out for our last job."

"They's four of us here. You reckon you can get them other two to come over?" Dolan asked.

"Cindy might come over," one of the girls said. "But there's no way Julie's goin' to. She's in love with Felker."

As predicted, Cindy responded to the invitation, while Julie remained at the table with Felker.

"Damn. They's four of us 'n only three of you," Wolcott complained.

"That'll work out all right," Slade said. He had been studying a card game or, more accurately, he had been studying a specific player. "I'm going to see if I can get into a card game."

"What's the matter with him?" Cindy asked. "Don't he like girls?"

"He likes girls, all right," Dolan said. "Onliest thing is, he likes playin' cards a lot."

While Dolan, Wolcott, and Cooley drank with the three bar girls, Slade found an open seat in the game he had been studying.

"Jack Slade." The player who spoke was Case Dockins.

"Hello, Dockins."

Case Dockins, like Jack Slade, had built a reputation as a gunfighter. As it became known throughout the saloon that two of the deadliest gunfighters in the country were engaged in a card game, tension gradually began to grow.

The relative tranquility of the saloon lasted less than half an hour before it was broken.

"Dockins, I seen you pull that ace from out'n your sleeve," Slade said in a cold, expressionless voice.

Case Dockins had not pulled an ace from his sleeve, and what was more, he knew that Slade knew that he hadn't. He had been waiting for the challenge from the gunfighter, and he knew that it had just been issued.

"If this is to be a test between us, Slade, why didn't you just say so? Why the lie about me cheating? Some people might actually believe you, and it might make it harder for me to find games to play in."

"You don't have to worry about finding any games to play in, because after today there won't be any more games for you."

Neither man had raised his voice or made a direct challenge, but the other two cardplayers, who were close enough to judge the tenor of their voices, knew that this was going to end in a shooting, so they got up and moved away, leaving their cards and chips on the table.

"Where do you want to do it?" Slade asked.

"In the street? Out front?" Dockins replied.

"There's goin' to be a shoot-out in the street!" someone yelled, running toward the batwing door.

His shout galvanized all the other saloon patrons, so that within moments the establishment emptied, except for Dolan, Cooley, and Wolcott, and the girls who were with them.

"That man is your friend, isn't he?" Cindy asked. "You came in with him."

"Yeah," Dolan said. "He's our friend." The bartender had gone out front with all the others, leaving a bottle on the bar. Dolan reached for the bottle and refilled his glass. "But he'll be back in, in a minute."

"But what if he . . . ?" Cindy started to ask.

"He ain't goin' to get kilt, if that's what you're askin'. He'll be the one doin' the killin'."

"You're sure of that?"

"Yeah, I'm sure. How much will it cost me to go upstairs with you?"

"I . . . I can't do anything like that now," Cindy insisted. "Not when somebody's goin' to get killed just outside the door."

"Case Dockins a friend of your'n?" Dolan asked.

"No, he isn't a friend."

"Then why are you a-worryin'?"

The street in front of the Cow Bell Saloon was crowded now, and not only with the saloon patrons. Citizens of the town, having heard about the upcoming confrontation, had come pouring out of stores and shops all up and down Dixon Street.

"Case Dockins 'n Jack Slade," one of the men on the

boardwalk said. "Damn, this is somethin' we'll be talkin' about for a long time."

"Ten dollars says that Dockins is the one that'll walk away," someone nearby said.

"Uh-uh. I'm bettin' on Dockins, too."

"All right. I'll bet on Slade, if you give me odds."

"Two to one," the first man said. "Ten, against your five."

A few other bets were placed between those who lined both sides of the street, waiting on the show to begin.

The two men who were about to provide the drama, Slade and Dockins, walked out into the middle of the street with studied indifference. One of them was but a moment away from eternity, but which one?

"How we goin' to do this, Slade?" Dockins asked.

"You, over there," Slade called out to someone who was wearing a badge. "You the town marshal?"

"I'm a deputy," the young man answered nervously. He knew it was probably his job to stop this fight, but he wanted to see this as much as anyone else did. Besides, he was too frightened to actually interfere with it.

"Good. I'm glad we got the law here. That way when it's all over with, you can say that it was all on the up-'n-up. Now, how 'bout you gettin' out there in the middle of the street 'n standin' where me 'n him can both see you?"

"I, uh, don't want to interfere with nothin'," the deputy replied.

"You ain't goin' to be interferin'," Slade said. "You're goin' to be helpin' us. Now, get out there in the middle of the street, like I told you to."

"But if any shootin' starts, I could be hit by a stray bullet," the deputy said.

"Don't you be worryin' none about no stray bullet,"

Slade said. "If you don't get out there in the middle of the street, like I told you, the bullet that hits you won't be no stray."

With his heart in his throat, the deputy stepped out into the middle of the street, following Slade's directions, and kept going until he was standing halfway between Slade and Dockins, but off to one side.

"Now, you stand there 'n hold your arm up in the air," Slade said. "When you bring your arm down, me 'n Dockins will commence a-shootin' at one another. That all right with you, Dockins?"

"Yeah," Dockins said, showing no nervousness. "Hey, Slade, I see Harold Denman standin' over there. He's the editor of the *Dixon Switch News*. You got 'ny last words for 'im?"

"Nah, I'll talk to 'im when this is over. Deputy, get your arm up."

Because the bar girls had abandoned Dolan, Cooley, and Wolcott, the three men stepped outside to watch the show.

The deputy stood there with his arm raised, knowing that when he brought his arm down, one or possibly both of the men would be killed. That meant that in a way, he would be responsible for their death. He held his arm up for a long time, so long that Slade got irritated.

"Damn it, Deputy. Bring your arm down!" Slade shouted, looking over toward the deputy.

Dockins, seeing that Slade was distracted, started his draw. Slade wasn't looking directly at Dockins, but he saw him in his peripheral vision and started his own draw. Slade was faster, and he fired an instant before Dockins did. Slade's bullet plunged into Dockins's chest just before he was able to pull the trigger to his own gun.

Dockins's shot went straight down into the street in front of him, and he fell forward, following the bullet into the dirt.

Someone said, "I ain't never seen nothin' that fast!"

"I'll tell you this," one of the others said. "That Jack Slade is 'bout the fastest man with a gun that they is."

"No, I seen Deke Crowley once, 'n he's faster," another said.

"There ain't no way Deke Crowley is faster than Slade. Hell, Slade is even faster 'n Smoke Jensen."

"Uh-uh, there ain't nobody faster 'n Smoke Jensen," another said.

"Are you kidding me? You seen how fast Slade was. Smoke Jensen wouldn't have a chance."

"Lord, wouldn't you love to see them two go ag'in each other, though?"

"Yes, sir, I would truly love to see that. Fact is, I'd pay to see it."

From the *Dixon Switch News:*

Showdown in Streets
Of Dixon Switch.

One Man Hurled Into Eternity.

Two men skilled in the art of death faced each other on Dixon Street on the eighth instant. Little is known of the reason for the deadly encounter, though it may have been for naught but to establish who could employ their weapon quicker and shoot straighter.

This encounter between Jack Slade and Case Dockins ended with Dockins lying dead in the dirt and Jack Slade putting one more notch on his gun handle, giving him, perhaps, the title of the fastest gun in the West.

Fontana, Colorado

When the man came into his office without so much as a knock on the door, Briggs looked up in irritation.

"How dare you come into my office without so much as a fare-thee-well?" Briggs said, the tone of his voice indicating his irritation.

"Is your name Briggs?"

"I am Judge Briggs, yes."

"You're a judge?"

"I am."

"Your telegram didn't say nothin' 'bout you bein' a judge."

"My telegram? Wait, are you Deke Crowley?"

"Yeah."

Briggs winced a little. He would have thought that Crowley would show a little more respect to a sitting judge.

"Your telegram said I could make a lot of money."

"Yes, you can, if you are willing to do what is asked of you."

"Yeah, well, what is it that I'm supposed to do?"

"Hold up your right hand."

"What?" Crowley asked, totally confused by the strange request.

"Hold up your right hand. I'm about to make you a deputy sheriff."

"Look here, Briggs, maybe I ain't the smartest man you ever seed, but I'm smart enough to know that deputy sheriffs don't make a lot of money. Your telegram didn't say nothin' 'bout you needin' a deputy sheriff. All it said was I could make a lot of money."

"And so you can," Briggs replied with a smile. "The only reason I'm making you a deputy sheriff is so you will have the authority of the badge when you do whatever Mr. Franklin asks you to do."

"Who is Franklin?"

"He is the one who will pay you a lot of money."

When Franklin came down the stairs, he was startled to see a man standing in his foyer. He wasn't a very big man. In fact, if Franklin had to guess, he would say that the man was barely five feet tall. But there was something about him, perhaps the disfiguring scar on his face or the deep-set eyes.

No, Franklin decided. It was the apparent arrogance of the man that seemed to make him bigger than his size.

"Who are you? What are you doing in my house?" Franklin asked.

"The name is Deke Crowley. You sent for me," the little man answered in a sibilant voice.

"You're the gunfighter? You?" Franklin asked.

"Yeah."

"I thought you would be . . ."

"Bigger?"

"Well, yes."

"How big do you have to be to kill a man?"

"Yes, you do have a point."

CHAPTER 16

Tilden Franklin had taken the first step in causing problems for Malone.

Malone planned to bring the railroad through Fontana, because the businesses, ranchers, and farmers around Fontana would provide a revenue stream. Without that revenue stream, the railroad would not be able to sustain itself.

All Franklin had to do was deny Malone that revenue stream, and he could do that by preventing the railroad from coming to Fontana.

Some of the businessmen of Fontana, those who weren't obligated to him, might take issue with his stopping the railroad from coming to town, but that was why he was paying fighting wages to ten of his men. And if someone like Smoke Jensen made too much trouble, that was why he had just hired Crowley at two hundred dollars a month, which was more than twice as much as he was paying Pearlie.

The first step Franklin took in his plan to stop the railroad was to visit the newspaper office.

"What do you mean, you want to keep the railroad from coming through Fontana?" asked Haywood Arden, the owner and publisher of the *Fontana Sunburst*. "Excuse me, Mr. Franklin, but that just makes no sense at all. Why, with the railroad coming to town, we would grow exponentially. New stores, new businesses, and people . . . Why, we'll get lots and lots of new people. If there actually is gold in the area, that would lead to a boom, but it might be of limited duration. A railroad would mean that Fontana flourished from now on!"

"And that is exactly what I don't want," Franklin said. "Right now, I control this town. I own most of the businesses, and I hold the mortgages on most of those I don't own. I control the people. If the town gets too big, there will undoubtedly be people that I can't control, and businesses that will be in competition with me."

"Competition is good for the town," Arden said.

"A newspaper is good for the town, as well, wouldn't you agree, Mr. Arden?"

"Yes, of course a newspaper is good for the town," Arden said, beaming proudly.

"And cleverly written articles in a newspaper can have a great influence on a town's attitude," Franklin said.

"A town's attitude?" Arden replied. He wasn't sure where Franklin was going with this rather pointed discussion.

"Yes, for example, if you wrote an article suggesting that the town would be better off without the railroad, why, I'm sure that the resistance of the people would be great enough to prevent the railroad from coming through."

"Perhaps that is true, but why would I write such an article? As I told you, I feel that a railroad would be an absolute boon to our community."

"You will write such an article, Mr. Arden, because I'm asking you to do so," Franklin said pointedly. "And I don't think I need to point out to you that I have enough equity in your newspaper to have some influence on what stories you print."

"Mr. Franklin, may I remind you that the right to report news or circulate opinion without censorship from the government was considered important enough by the Founding Fathers of the United States to make freedom of the press as one of the rights guaranteed by its enshrinement into the First Amendment of the Constitution?"

Franklin chuckled. "Mr. Arden, I'm afraid that you don't understand the situation here. It isn't the government that you need to worry about. It's me. You will either print the story I tell you to print or I will take over your newspaper and give it to someone who will do as I say. Now, what will it be, Mr. Arden? Will you still be owner and publisher of the *Sunburst* tomorrow?"

When Franklin left, Arden sat down behind his desk, thinking about the conversation that had just taken place. If he did the story that Franklin wanted, it would be the total antithesis of all that he believed in, all that he stood for. On the other hand, if he didn't do the story, he would lose the newspaper.

Arden sat there for a long moment, fighting with himself. Finally, he made his decision and, after rising from his chair, went to the type trays and began putting type into the sticks to set the article he didn't want to write. An hour later the first copy came off the press, and he read through the story.

APPROACHING RAILROAD.

By now, every citizen of Fontana is aware that a railroad is to be constructed that would connect Fontana with Denver. There are some who might laud this development, and indeed, the thought of measuring travel by hours, instead of days, has some appeal.

But I ask you to give this a second thought. We, the citizens of Fontana, are rightly proud of our little town. Here neighbor *knows* neighbor, and we live in peace and tranquility. We are a self-sufficient community, with stores to serve our every need, nice restaurants, and saloons where gentlemen can meet to share a convivial drink.

In short, dear citizens of Fontana, we have re-created here a veritable Garden of Eden. But just as an invading serpent disrupted the blissfulness of the Garden of Eden, the railroad, which one could liken to a mechanical serpent, would, when it comes to our fair town, destroy the peace and tranquility that we now *enjoy*.

The railroad will inevitably bring with it uncouth workers who have no sense of propriety and who would disturb our community with their drunkenness and *debauchery*. So, too, could we expect the arrival of gamblers, harlots, pickpockets, and ruffians, who would make our peaceful streets unsafe for women and children.

So that our fair community not be destroyed in such a way, this newspaper is calling upon the mayor and the city council to pass an ordinance that would deny the railroad entry into Fontana.

Haywood Arden attended the meeting of the city council. It wasn't unusual for him to attend the meetings; as the owner and publisher of the newspaper, it was his job to keep the citizenry apprised of the business of the city council.

"Gentlemen," Mayor Osgood said, "I'm sure that all of you have read Mr. Arden's editorial by now." Osgood looked toward Arden. "And I, for one, would like to congratulate him on a brilliant observation."

"But, Mr. Mayor, wouldn't the railroad be good for business?" Howard McGill asked. McGill managed the McGill Feed and Seed Company.

"Perhaps, but at what cost?" Mayor Osgood asked. "You read Mr. Arden's editorial. I'm sure you agree that he did an excellent job of pointing out the perils of too rapid a growth. I propose that this council pass an ordinance forbidding Malone's railroad from coming into our town."

"That won't do any good, Mayor," Roy Beck said. Beck was the town blacksmith. "All Malone has to do is build a depot just outside the town limits, and the railroad would still be here."

"That may be so," Osgood replied. "But at least we will have a public declaration of our opposition to this . . ." He paused in midsentence, then, with a smile, appropriated a term from Arden's editorial. "Mechanical serpent."

The mayor's proposal was voted on and passed with unanimous consent.

Arden had not said a word during the meeting, and he left the city hall with a feeling of self-loathing for having caved to Franklin.

Half an hour later, Arden was standing at the bar in the Blue Dog Saloon. He pushed his glass across the bar.

"I'll have another drink."

"That's your fifth drink, Haywood, *mon ami*. I've never seen you drink this much," Louis Longmont said.

Longmont was Louisiana French, one of *les Acadiens*, more commonly referred to as Cajuns, and his speech was often interspersed with French and Cajun patois. And though Tilden Franklin owned the saloon, Longmont, as the manager, often tended bar, not because he was required to, but because he wanted to, and he was doing so now.

"Is something wrong?" he asked as he slid the full glass back toward Arden.

Arden held the glass out, not in a toast, but in a symbolic gesture. "Louis, my friend, you see before you a broken and dispirited man. I am the Benedict Arnold of my profession, I have committed treason against honest journalism, against my town, and I am a traitor to myself. I forfeited my soul upon the altar of greed, for I was too frightened to stand up to the devil."

Arden put a coda to his long self-condemning dissertation by tossing down his drink, then holding the glass out for another.

"If I understand you, Haywood, and I believe that I do, you are telling me that you don't believe what you wrote in that article."

"Please, fill the glass again," Arden said without a direct response.

"Franklin made you do it," Longmont said.

"What makes you say that?"

"Let's say that I know from personal experience, because *beaucoup d'entre nous portent le joug de l'oppression de Franklin*."

"I heard the words *beaucoup* and *oppression*," Arden said. "Are you saying that . . ."

"Many of us wear the yoke of Franklin's oppression, myself included," Longmont said, translating his French.

"Did you read the paper today?" Smoke asked.

"Yes," Sally replied. "I must say that I'm surprised that Mr. Arden would take such a stand. Who wouldn't want the railroad?"

"Since nothing happens in Fontana that Franklin isn't aware of, I'm sure that he is behind this in some way."

"As many businesses as he owns, and with cattle he must get to market, you would think that he, more than anyone else, would be supportive of the railroad."

"Who knows what goes on in that sick mind of his?" Smoke smiled. "Sally, I have a great idea!"

"What?"

"End of track."

"What?"

"We're going to build a town at end of track. If Fontana doesn't want us, we don't want them. We'll build our own town."

Sally laughed. "Build our own town? You have to have people to have a town. Where are you going to get the people?"

"Why, from Fontana, of course. I know there are enough people who want to get away from Franklin to make a town. They can come to our new town and own their own business."

"Smoke, you are absolutely the most intriguing person I have ever known."

"Thank you, I think. I mean, that is good, isn't it?"

"Oh, yes, that's good. That's very good," Sally said. "Oh, you know what we should do now?"

"What?"

"We should draw a map of the town, put in streets and name them. Since you are building the town, I think the main street should be Jensen Avenue."

"We can name one of the streets Jensen, but the main street should be Malone Street."

"No," Sally replied.

"Big Cat is building the railroad. You don't think we should name a street after him?"

"It should be called Malone Avenue," Sally said. She smiled. "That sounds more dignified than street."

CHAPTER 17

Circle TF Ranch

"Hey, Pearlie, did you know that Franklin has hired himself a gunfighter?"

"Yes," Pearlie said. "Deke Crowley."

"Have you ever heard of him?"

"I've heard of him."

"I reckon he'll be ridin' with the Demons. What do you plan to do with him?"

"He won't be one of the Demons. Mr. Franklin plans to use him for something else."

"Use him how?"

"I don't know," Pearlie admitted.

"Hmm. That's kind of strange, ain't it?"

"I suppose so, but if you ask me, there ain't a lot that goes on around here that ain't kind of strange."

"Yeah, I guess that's right, when you think about it. Hey, Pearlie, what do you say we go into town tonight?" Ray Perkins asked.

"It depends," Pearlie replied.

"Depends on what?"

"On whether or not you get so drunk, I'd have to bring you back home."

"Ha! How do you know it won't be you getting so drunk that I'll have to bring *you* back home?"

Pearlie stared at Perkins without answering him.

"All right, all right. I ain't never seen you drunk, but that don't mean you can't get drunk," Perkins insisted.

"Anyone can get drunk," Pearlie replied. "It isn't whether or not you can. It's whether or not you will. I can tell you for a fact that I won't get drunk."

"Yeah, well, you're right. I know you won't get drunk. But I don't plan to get drunk, neither, so what do you say about me 'n you goin' into town tonight?"

"Yeah," Pearlie said. "I'll go into town with you."

A short time later, as Pearlie and Perkins were saddling their horses, Pearlie was aware of the unfriendly gaze of some of the other cowboys who worked on the Circle TF. Technically, Pearlie knew, they were real cowboys; they were the only ones who actually worked with the cattle. Pearlie and the Demons drew twice the wages of the average cowboy. That was because Pearlie and the twelve men who made up the Demons were drawing what was called "fighting wages."

"I am a very wealthy man," Franklin had explained to Pearlie when he hired him. "There are those who resent my wealth and position, and they will do whatever they can to attack me, either personally or indirectly, by stealing some of my cattle. It will be your job to protect me and my property."

Pearlie knew that there were people in town who didn't like Franklin. Actually, that was an understatement. There were people who hated Franklin, and the more brazen ones liked to take it out on those who worked for the Circle TF, so Pearlie had decided that his job wasn't only to look out for Franklin, but also to look out for anyone who rode for the brand.

When Pearlie and Perkins stepped into the Blue Dog that evening, they were greeted by a couple of the percentage girls. One of the girls, who called herself Delight, put her arm through Pearlie's arm and smiled up at him.

"Hello, Pearlie, you handsome devil, you," Delight said. "Won't you come over to my table and have a drink with me?"

"I'd be glad to have a drink with a pretty girl like you," Pearlie replied, and he and Perkins, each with a girl on his arm, found an empty table. Perkins and Sara Sue were at another table. Pearlie knew that Perkins wanted the privacy so he could negotiate with Sara Sue to go upstairs; that was the main reason Perkins had wanted to come into town. That would take a while, for as Perkins had explained once, "Even if it's a whore, you can't come right out 'n ask her to go to bed with you. That ain't polite. You've got to sort of work 'em into it, so's that they want to go upstairs as bad as you do."

Pearlie glanced over toward Perkins and Sara Sue and smiled, as Perkins was "working" on her.

"Pearlie?" Delight said, calling his attention away from Perkins's table.

"Oh, I'm sorry. I was sort of lookin' around 'n not paying attention to you," Pearlie said.

Delight chuckled. "You don't have to apologize for nothin' like that. I was just wantin' to ask you, why does a nice fella like you work for someone like Tilden Franklin?"

"I take it by your comment that you don't particularly like Mr. Franklin."

"No, I don't like him. I don't like the way he lords it over everyone. He acts like he is king of the walk."

Pearlie chuckled. "Well, Delight, around here I would say that he is king of the walk, wouldn't you?"

"Hey, you!" someone shouted toward Pearlie's table.

At first Pearlie paid no attention to the shout, which he wasn't sure had even been directed at him.

"You!" the loudmouth said again. "Look at me when I'm talkin'."

"Are you talkin' to me, mister?" Pearlie asked.

"No, I ain't talkin' to you, you prairie rat. I'm talkin' to that whore you're a-sittin' with."

"Do you know him?" Pearlie asked Delight.

"Yes, I know him. His name is Purvis Depro, and he's the meanest man I've ever met. None of the girls will have anything to do with him, because he likes to beat on us."

Depro came over to the table and looked down at Delight. "I told you no more'n an hour ago that I'd be comin' back. Now, what are you sittin' with him for?"

"It's my job to visit with the gentlemen who come here," Delight replied, the tone of her voice apprehensive.

"Yeah, well, you've been nice long enough," Depro said. "Now finish your drink. Then come upstairs with me."

"Please go away," Delight said. "I told you, I am with this gentleman now."

"Gentleman?" Depro replied mockingly. "If this prairie rat is a gentleman, I'm the king of Prussia. Now, I'm tellin' you to come upstairs with me, or I'll knock the hell out of you." Depro reached down and grabbed her by the arm.

"Ow! Let me go. You're hurting me!" Delight said.

"Let her go, Depro," Pearlie said harshly.

Depro released his grip on Delight's arm and turned to Pearlie. "What did you say to me?"

"I told you to let her go."

Without a word of warning, Depro went for his gun. He had the element of surprise, as Pearlie certainly wasn't expecting him to draw; and he also had the advantage of standing, while Pearlie was still sitting in his chair.

"Draw, you coward!" Depro shouted, as he was already drawing his own pistol.

Because Pearlie hadn't expected anything like this, he didn't start his own draw until Depro's gun had cleared the holster, but even so, Pearlie drew and fired just as Depro managed to bring his own pistol to bear. Pearlie's shot hit Depro right where the second button of his shirt fastened. Depro's gun fell, unfired, as he slapped his hand over the hole in his chest, then looked down at the wound as blood spilled through his fingers. He pitched forward.

Delight let out a sharp cry of alarm and jumped up from her chair just as Depro crashed into the table.

"Are you all right?" Pearlie asked Delight. Pearlie had risen to his feet and was still holding the smoking gun in his hand.

"Yes, I . . . I think so," Delight replied.

"Perkins?" Pearlie called over to the man who had come to town with him. Perkins and Sara Sue, like every other person in the Blue Dog, were standing now.

"Yeah?" Perkins answered.

"I reckon you'd better go get the sheriff. I'll need to stay here."

"Yeah, all right," Perkins replied.

"You was in the right. I seen it!" one of the other customers called out.

"Yeah, me, too!"

Perkins came back no more than a few minutes later, with Sheriff Colby following close behind. Colby walked over to stare down at Depro, whose sightless eyes were still open. Depro's gun lay on the floor beside him.

"Pearlie was just sittin' there, mindin' his own business, when Depro drawed on 'im," Perkins said.

"Are you tellin' me that Depro drawed first, 'n Pearlie was sittin' down, but he still beat 'im?"

"Perkins's tellin' you like it is, Sheriff," one of the saloon patrons said.

"What about you, Longmont?" Colby asked.

"I'm afraid I didn't see it, Sheriff," Longmont replied. "But I have no reason to doubt what everyone else is saying."

"You work for Tilden Franklin, don't you?" Sheriff Colby asked Pearlie.

"Yes, I do."

"Well, you can tell Mr. Franklin that he don't have to worry 'bout nothin', seein' as ever'body says it was self-defense."

"Thank you, Sheriff."

"You killed Purvis Depro?" Franklin asked after Pearlie and Perkins returned to the ranch.

"Yes, sir. I'm sorry if it's going to cause you any trouble," Pearlie said contritely.

"Trouble? Hell, no, it isn't going to cause any trouble at all!" Franklin said, almost as if he was elated by the news. "You know, Depro tried to sell his services to me. That was before I hired you, and he wanted considerably more money. I'll be honest with you, Pearlie. There have been times when I wondered if I made the right decision in hiring you over him. I mean, you don't seem to have the kind of instinct you would think somebody doing a job like yours should have. But with this little episode in town today, I must say that you have justified my choosing you. In fact, I'm going to give you a one-hundred-dollar bonus for killing him."

Pearlie raised his arm, with the palm of his hand facing Franklin. "No, sir, there ain't no need in you adoin' anything like that. I feel bad enough about killin' Depro as it is, but I had no choice. I do have a choice in whether or not I take any money for shootin' 'im, though. And I choose not to take it."

Franklin chuckled. "Yes, sir, hiring you as the head of my security force may just well be the best hire I have ever made."

Smoke and Sally came into Fontana together, but once they got there, they each went their separate ways, agreeing to meet for supper at Lambert's Café, choosing it because it wasn't owned by Franklin. Sally stopped first at the mercantile and Smoke checked in at the feed and seed store.

"We got some good oats in from Denver," Howard McGill said. "I can have 'em delivered out to you, if you'd like."

"You can?"

"Yes, sir."

"I've sort of gotten the idea that Franklin would just as soon not do any business with me."

"Yeah, well, I owe Franklin a lot of money, so I reckon I am obligated to him somewhat. But I don't plan on him telling me who I can and who I can't do business with."

"Good. That's good to hear," Smoke replied. "Now, tell me, how do you feel about the railroad coming into town?"

McGill paused, then looked around before he answered.

And even though there was no one close, he lowered his voice.

"I think it would have been a really good thing to have the railroad come to town, 'n I wish Mr. Malone all the luck in the world gettin' it done."

"Apparently, not everyone in town agrees with you," Smoke replied.

"You're talkin' 'bout that newspaper article 'n the city council ordnance, ain't you?"

"Both the newspaper and the city council made it very clear that they are opposed to the railroad," Smoke said.

McGill shook his head. "Uh-uh. No they ain't, neither. I know for a fact that Haywood Arden would like to see the railroad come to town. He told me so his own self, 'n he said he just wrote that article 'cause Franklin said he would take the newspaper away from him if he didn't write it that way."

"The city council?"

"Same thing. Ever'one that's on the city council is there on account of Franklin put 'em there. 'N they either work for 'im or else he's loaned them lots of money, so's that they could wind up losin' their business if they don't go along with just about anything he wants."

"What about you, Howard? You are independent enough to sell me oats for my horses. Are you independent enough to say you support the railroad?"

"Mr. Jensen, I . . ." McGill stopped in midsentence, obviously searching for just the right thing to say. "I can do some things that, even if he don't particular like me doin' 'em, I can most get away with it, on account of most of the time he won't never know nothin' about it. Like me takin' the oats out to your place 'n such. But for some reason that there can't nobody understand why, he is most particular about not wantin' no railroad to come in here, so folks like me—I mean ones that's beholdin' to 'im— has to pick whatever it might be that we can do without him findin' out. Most likely, Franklin won't even know that I sold you rolled oats for your horses."

Smoke smiled and nodded. "I appreciate that, Howard. I really do. Now, let me ask you something. If you could relocate somewhere else, without it costing you too much, would you do it?"

"Yes, sir, I would do it in a heartbeat," McGill said. "But where would I go? There's only one other town in the county, 'n they've already got a feed 'n seed store. 'N the truth is, it would be like that no matter where I'd go. Things ain't all that good here, but at least I don't have no competition."

"So, competition is what you would be concerned about, is that it?"

"That's it, all right."

"Well, we'll just have to find you a place you can relocate to where there won't be any competition."

"Ha. Lots of luck with that one," McGill replied.

"I may have just the place in mind, if you are courageous enough to try it."

"Yeah? Well, I'll tell you this. If there was even the slightest possibility that I could get shed of Franklin 'n take a chance on a-goin' some'ers else, I'd do it in a heartbeat, just like I said."

Smoke smiled. "You just keep that thought in mind," he said without being any more specific.

From McGill's Feed and Seed Store, Smoke walked down to the newspaper office. He had been in enough newspaper offices, so the smell of press lubricating oil, ink, and newsprint was familiar to him. He saw Haywood

Arden cleaning the press. Arden looked up at him as he came inside.

"Mr. Smoke Jensen," Arden said. "What can I do for you?"

"Do you own that press outright?" Smoke asked. "Or do you owe Franklin for it?"

Arden got a perplexed, almost annoyed look by the question.

"May I ask why you are asking me that?"

"If you owned the land, and if you had enough of a loan to build your own office on that land so that you owed Franklin nothing, would you take that opportunity?"

"Did someone tell you that I regret selling out to Franklin by writing that article against the railroad?"

"Well, do you?"

"Yes, as a matter of fact, I do. But to answer your question, even if I did own my own land and building, it wouldn't matter. Franklin has so much control over the businesses in town that he could convince them not to advertise with me. And without advertising, I would be reduced to trying to make a living selling the newspaper at two cents a copy. I sell about two hundred fifty copies per week, which breaks down to five dollars a week. The lowest-paid cowboys make more than that, and that is with found. Also, I've got a wife that depends on me."

"But just so that I understand, if you could publish your own paper somewhere else, where you could sell advertising and not be dependent upon Franklin, you would do it?"

"What do you have in mind, Mr. Jensen?"

"I'm not ready to say yet."

"Whatever it is, if it is some way for me to publish the paper on my own, the answer is yes, I would do it."

CHAPTER 18

Denver, Colorado

There was a lot of activity at the marshaling yard in Denver as steel rails, crossties, steel spikes, transoms, and other elements of construction were off-loaded from freight cars and loaded into wagons. There were at least two dozen mule team–pulled wagons standing by to receive the cargo.

Fred Malone had rented office space in the Denver and Rio Grande Railroad Depot, and he and Frank Magee were going over the construction details when Smoke arrived.

"Smoke," Malone said by way of greeting. "What are you doing here?" He chuckled. "That didn't sound right, did it? That made it sound like you weren't welcome. But what I mean is, I won't really have any use for you until the railroad construction actually begins."

"Are you still planning on taking the railroad to Fontana?" Smoke asked.

Malone nodded. "You're talking about the newspaper article and the action of the city council, aren't you? Well, the answer is yes. If I don't connect to Fontana, there would be no business to support the railroad. I have to go through Fontana."

Smoke smiled. "Not if there was another town for you to go to."

"What do you mean?"

"Let me show you something," Smoke said. After taking a folded piece of paper from his shirt pocket, he spread it out on Malone's desk. At first, it looked like no more than a series of crossed double lines, but upon further examination, it looked like a map. It was obvious that the double lines were streets, as each of the streets was named.

"What is that?" Malone asked. "That looks like the map of a town."

"It is the map of a town."

"What town?"

"The town we are going to build where the track ends at Sierra Cimarrona Creek," Smoke said with a big smile. "With this town, you won't need Fontana."

"You forget one thing," Malone said. "You can't have a town without people."

"And maybe you've forgotten how much most of the people in Fontana dislike Franklin. I've already spoken to some of them. We'll get a good start on the town by bringing in people from Fontana. And the railroad will provide that attraction."

A big smile spread across Malone's face. "Damn!" he said. "Damn, that is a good idea! We'll build our own town." The smile left his face, to be replaced by an expression of concern. "How will we start?"

"You own the land there on the Sierra Cimarrona, don't you?"

"Yes, I do."

"Would you be willing to set aside two thousand acres? We could divide those acres up into commercial and residential lots and give them free to anyone who would relocate there, not only from Fontana, but from all over. If someone agrees to start a business, we could give him a lot for his business and a lot for his house. The land on the other side of the creek, as well as the land outside your specific holdings, is available for homesteading. I could see a few ranches and farms moving into the area."

"I've got an idea," Malone said. "I'll relocate the bank there. That way those who are banking with me in Fontana will have to migrate out to our new town if they want to continue to do business with the First Malone and Trust."

"First Malone and Trust Bank," Smoke said. "Yeah, I like that. It has a real classy sound to it. And you're right. It will cause people to have to transfer their business."

"When do we start?" Malone asked.

"I've already started, and I'll continue to suggest to people from Fontana that they ought to come over to our new town."

Circle TF Ranch

"What do you mean, he's planning on starting his own town?" Franklin asked.

"He's been askin' around," Tay said. "They's some, I've heard, has already said they would leave Fontana 'n go to where his new town is goin' to be."

Tay was one of the men who worked under Pearlie, though grudgingly. He was convinced that he would be a better foreman of the men who were drawing fighting wages than Pearlie, and he thought that bringing this information to Franklin might improve his position.

"And just where is this new town that he's building?" Franklin asked.

"That's just it. There ain't none of it been built yet, so there ain't no place it is now."

"None of it has been built?"

"No, sir."

"That's good to know," Franklin said. "Have you seen Crowley this morning?"

"Yeah. After breakfast he went back into the bunkhouse 'n is a-lyin' on his bed," Tay said.

Tay provided the information in a tone of voice that he thought would cause Franklin to be irritated with Crowley. As he did Pearlie, Tay considered Crowley to be competition for him in positioning himself in Franklin's hierarchy.

"If you would, please, ask him to come see me."

"There ain't really no need to be wakin' 'im up, as I can see," Tay said. "Whatever it is you're a-wantin' done, I'm right sure I can do it for you."

"Send Crowley over to see me," Franklin repeated with an impatient note in his voice.

Going along with the boss's wishes would be the wise thing to do, Tay decided for now.

"What do you want?" Crowley asked a few minutes later, after he had sauntered arrogantly into Franklin's office in the ranch house.

Franklin suppressed the irritation he felt at the gunman's tone and said, "When I hired you, I told you that there might come a time when I wanted to take advantage of your particular . . . uh, skill. That time has come."

"Who do you want me to kill?"

"How do you know I want you to kill someone?"

"You said you wanted to use my skill. Killin' people is my skill."

"All right. I want you to kill Smoke Jensen."

"Smoke Jensen?"

"Have you ever heard of him?"

"Yeah, I've heard of 'im. Who ain't heard of 'im? I know this, though. A man like Smoke Jensen, as fast as he is, is goin' to take a lot of killin'."

"Are you up to the job?"

"What?"

"Are you fast enough?" Franklin asked, somewhat surprised by Crowley's hesitancy.

"Why do you want him dead?" Crowley asked.

"I have my reasons," Franklin replied. "Is it important for you to know my reasons?"

Crowley shrugged. "No, it ain't all that important to me. I'll tell you this, though. The two hunnert dollars a month you're a-payin' me now ain't enough for me to go up ag'in someone like Smoke Jensen."

"How about five thousand dollars? Is that important enough to you?"

Crowley gasped. "Five thousand dollars? Wait a minute. Are you tellin' me you would actual give me five thousand dollars to kill Jensen?"

"I think that the man who is fast enough to kill Lucas McCabe deserves such a payment to kill Smoke Jensen, don't you?"

Crowley smiled, the scar tissue causing his mouth to be even more misshapen.

"Yeah, I'd say so. When do I get the money?" Crowley asked.

"I'll give you five thousand dollars as soon as the job is done," Franklin said. "You've got my word on that."

"There ain't really no need for you to give me your word," Crowley said.

"Oh? And why is that?"

"'Cause once I kill Jensen, iffen you don't give me the money, then I'll kill you."

CHAPTER 19

Smoke had a few more people he wanted to talk to before he met Sally at Lambert's Café for dinner.

Smoke talked to Earl Montgomery about moving his barbershop to the new town, and also to Dennis White about moving his apothecary. After receiving positive answers from them, he decided that his next stop was the Blue Dog Saloon. The Blue Dog was relatively quiet when Smoke pushed through the batwing doors that afternoon. Three cowboys were sharing a table in the back corner, Delight and Sara Sue were sitting at a table by themselves, and one customer stood at the far end of the bar, staring down into his mug of beer. Louis Longmont was polishing glasses, though Smoke got the idea that he was doing this just to have something to do.

"Smoke Jensen," Longmont greeted with a welcoming smile. "You'll be wanting a beer?"

"Yes."

Smoke waited until the beer was put before him before he said what was on his mind.

"Louis, how would you like to run your own saloon?"

"How did you know?"

"How did I know what?"

"How did you know I'll be opening my own saloon soon, just across the street from this one?"

"I didn't know that, but that might work out even for the better."

"What do you mean?"

"How would you like to have a new saloon, bigger than this one, in another town?"

"I agree that I have considered the idea of leaving Fontana, but my thoughts have never gone beyond that. For example, I have no idea where I might go, or where I would get the money to buy the lot and build such a place."

"I'll tell you where you might go," Smoke said. And for the next few minutes, Smoke shared with Louis Longmont his idea of building a new town, and the more he spoke, the more intrigued Longmont became.

"*Oui*, that would make me a *père fondateur* of the town, wouldn't it?"

"That would make you a what?"

"One of the founding fathers," Longmont said, translating.

Smoke chuckled. "I guess you could say that."

"It is an exciting idea. I'll do it! I won't open my saloon here, then," Longmont said.

"No, go ahead and open a saloon here. In the long run, that might help, because you can get some regular customers who might follow you over to the new town."

"You might be right," Longmont said. He looked up then, just as Monte Carson came into the saloon.

"This new town you're building," Longmont said. "It's going to need some law, isn't it?"

"I expect it will."

Longmont nodded toward Carson. "Then that's the man you need to talk to."

"He's Colby's deputy, isn't he?"

"*Oui*, but do not hold that against him. Monte Carson is nothing like Colby. Carson is a gunman, but he is also a man of honor." Longmont smiled. "The same could be said of us, could it not?"

Smoke couldn't argue with that. He knew that Longmont had a reputation as both a gambler and a fast gun, and he had wondered how such a man wound up tending bar in a town like Fontana. He didn't figure it was his place to ask, though.

"All right, I'll talk to him. What's his drink?" Smoke asked.

"Beer. Same as you."

"Give him a beer, on me, and ask him to come over to that table for a little visit."

Smoke walked over to a nearby table and watched as Monte Carson accepted the beer, then turned toward him. Smoke nodded, signaling him to come over.

"Thanks for the beer," Carson said as he took a seat. "What's the catch?"

"Let me ask you something," Smoke said. "Did you ever think you would be wearing a badge?"

"You've heard of me, haven't you?" Carson said. "I mean, before this place."

"I've heard of you," Smoke said.

Carson smiled and nodded. "I admit I've spent a little time on the outlaw trail, but I walked away from all that. I've been pretty much on the straight and narrow since then."

Smoke chuckled. "Pretty much?"

Carson's smile broadened. "Maybe just a little more than pretty much."

"How long have you been a deputy?"

"Better than a year now."

"That's experience enough. How would you like to be sheriff?" Smoke asked. He had sized up Monte Carson pretty quickly, he knew, but he was a man who trusted his judgment, especially when it came to another man's character.

Carson shook his head. "Franklin pretty much determines who is going to be sheriff here, and right now his man is Colby. And even though I'm willing to be a deputy, I'm not sure I would want to be sheriff here. The cost is too high."

"The cost?" Smoke said.

"I would never want to be that beholden to Tilden Franklin."

A broad smile spread across Smoke's face. "I was hoping you would say that."

"Hey, you!" someone shouted. The man with the loud mouth had just stepped into the saloon, and he pointed to Smoke. "Are you the one they call Smoke Jensen?"

The man was considerably shorter than average, and he had deep-set eyes and a scar on his left cheek that hooked down to disfigure his mouth. He was also pointing a gun at Smoke.

"Yes, I'm Smoke Jensen. And unless I miss my guess, you would be Deke Crowley."

The man stretched his mouth into what might have been a smile, though the smile was somewhat distorted. "You've heard of me, huh?"

"I heard you killed Lucas McCabe."

"Yeah. Yeah, I did. And a few others besides."

"Why did you kill McCabe?"

"To see if I could kill 'im. And it turns out that I could."

"And is that why you're here now? To see if you can kill me?"

"That's part of the reason," Crowley said. He smirked. "I got other reasons."

Smoke figured Crowley meant he was being paid to kill him, and he had a pretty good idea who might have done such a thing.

Monte Carson spoke up, saying, "I don't think you can kill him, but if you do, I'll kill you."

Crowley stood there for a long moment, the center of attention of everyone in the room. His eyes cut back and forth between Smoke and Carson, and for the first time, a hint of uncertainty showed in them. In the quiet that prevailed, the only audible sound was the ticktock of the clock that stood against the wall.

Finally, Crowley said, "I know you, Carson, and I ain't facin' odds like that, not for no five thousand dollars." He put his pistol in his holster, then turned and walked out of the saloon. His exit was greeted with a collective sigh.

Smoke turned to see Carson just putting away his pistol. He had drawn it while all of Crowley's attention was focused on Smoke.

"Damn," Carson said. "I thought for a minute there, my sheriffin' days might be over before they even started."

Suddenly, Crowley came rushing back in through the batwing doors, his pistol in his hand and pointing toward Smoke, who still had his attention on Carson.

"Draw, Jensen!" Crowley shouted even as he pulled the trigger.

The .44 slug from Crowley's gun plunged into a supporting post inches away from Smoke. Smoke responded by drawing and shooting in one fast and graceful move.

Crowley, realizing that he had missed with his first shot, pulled the hammer back for another try. The bullet smashing into the center of his chest prevented him from getting off a second shot. His gun sagged as he swayed a little, then the revolver slipped from nerveless fingers and thudded to the floor.

Crowley followed it a split second later.

For a long moment, there was a *tableau vivant*, as a silent and motionless group of people stood fixated upon the results of the scene that had just played out before them.

Then one of the saloon patrons whooped and said, "Damn if I ain't never seen nothin' like that before!"

CHAPTER 20

Smoke, who was still holding the pistol, slid it back into his holster.

"Smoke, how about another beer, on me this time?" Monte Carson asked.

"Thank you, Monte, but Sally came into town with me, and I promised to meet her for supper at six. That's only five minutes from now. Oh, I guess I should wait for the sheriff, so I can explain what just happened here."

"No need for that," Carson said. He smiled. "I'm the deputy, after all. I'll just tell him what happened. That ought to be official enough."

"All right. Thanks," Smoke said. "If he needs to talk to me, I'll be at Lambert's Café." He started to leave, then paused and added, "Might've been nice if Crowley had come right out and said who offered to pay him five thousand dollars for killing me . . . but I reckon we don't have to think too hard to figure out who that was."

The little grimace that crossed Carson's face told Smoke that the deputy knew who he was talking about—and agreed with the conclusion.

By now the shooting in the saloon had drawn a few

more people, and they were standing around Crowley, looking down at his body with morbid curiosity. Without another word, Smoke stepped around the little gathering and started toward the restaurant to meet Sally.

"I've already got us a table," Sally said when Smoke showed up. She smiled. "It's in the back corner, so you can have your back to the wall. I know how you prefer that."

"Good, good. You learn fast," Smoke replied with a broad grin.

"I've already ordered our supper, but I asked them to hold it until you joined me."

"What did you order? Not some real fancy thing, was it?"

"I don't know. It depends on how fancy the steak is," Sally replied with a smile.

"How was your time in town?"

"Oh, I enjoyed it," Sally said. "I bought some material so I can make some curtains."

As they were enjoying their dinner a few minutes later, Smoke looked up to see Monte Carson and Sheriff Colby come into the restaurant.

"There's Sheriff Colby," Sally said. "He's perusing the room, as if he is looking for someone."

"That would be me, I expect," Smoke said.

"Why would he be looking for you?"

"It might have something to do with a little flare-up I had over in the saloon a little while ago."

Smoke held up his hand, getting Carson's attention. Carson saw the signal. Then the two lawmen made their way between the tables and through the room.

"Hello, Carson, Sheriff Colby," Smoke said, acknowledging them both with a nod of his head.

"Beg your pardon for interrupting your meal, ma'am," Carson said to Sally. Then to Smoke, he added, "Sheriff

Colby decided that since there was a killing, he probably should have a few words with you."

"A killing?" Sally asked.

"The fella seemed determined to have it wind up that way," Smoke said.

"How many more men have you killed, Jensen?" Sheriff Colby demanded.

"Only as many as I needed to."

"Well, for the peace and tranquility of the town, let's hope it won't be necessary for you to kill many more."

"That's my hope, as well. What about this business with Crowley? Will you need a statement or anything from me?"

"No," Sheriff Colby said after a moment's hesitation. He didn't sound as if he liked it as he went on, "I've got all the information I need from my deputy here. It appears that it was justifiable homicide by means of self-defense. I've already entered it that way. No need to be botherin' Judge Briggs about it."

Smoke looked at Carson. "Thanks, Deputy. I appreciate that."

"He was certainly upset about there being a killing in his town," Sally commented when Colby and Carson were gone.

"Maybe," Smoke said. "And maybe he was just upset about which one wound up dead."

As soon as Sheriff Colby left the restaurant, he rode out to the Circle TF Ranch. Now he was in Franklin's office. He had taken off his hat and was standing just across the desk from Franklin.

"You say Jensen killed him?" Franklin asked. His cadaverous face was set in a scowl.

"Yeah, deader 'n a doornail," Colby replied.

"Damn and blast." Then, surprisingly, Franklin smiled. "Wait a minute. This might work out better, after all. Briggs made Crowley a deputy, didn't he?"

"Crowley was a deputy?" Colby replied in surprise. "He warn't my deputy."

"No, he was a deputy of the court, and Jensen was resisting arrest. You could arrest him for that, and for killing an officer of the law."

Colby shook his head. "That won't work. First of all, according to Carson, Crowley never identified hisself as no deputy of the court, 'n second, he never tried to arrest Jensen. He came in, threatened Jensen, then pretended to leave the saloon. Then he busted back in and just commenced a-shootin', 'n there was enough people what seen the fight to testify that it was self-defense. We could never make the charge stick."

"There must be something else he could be charged with. The man's a notorious gunman!"

"Maybe, but he's been leadin' a law-abiding life ever since he came to these parts. Why, he didn't even let on that he's really Smoke Jensen for a long time."

Franklin glared at him for several seconds, then said coldly, "All right, get out. If I need you for something you can actually do, I'll send for you."

With a surly look on his face, Colby turned around and walked out of the room.

After the sheriff left, Franklin sent for Pearlie. Though he called himself Pearlie, Franklin didn't know his real name—or care what it was. What was important was that he was incredibly fast with a gun and had left lead in a string of men. Exactly how many Pearlie had killed, nobody knew, and Pearlie wasn't the kind of man to brag about it.

"I have just been told that Smoke Jensen killed the new man I just hired," Franklin told Pearlie. "Though it isn't clear just how it was done. I thought Crowley would be the match of Jensen."

"No, sir, that ain't nothin' like what I would think. Jensen is faster than anyone you could hire or even think about hirin'."

"Is he faster than you?"

"I know I damn sure don't want to go up against him," Pearlie replied.

"Yes, well, if we play our cards right, you won't have to. Right now, I have two things to worry about. The new railroad and this new town. We must stop the railroad from being built."

"I don't know why you don't want the railroad to come here," Pearlie said. "I would think it would be a good thing."

"You aren't being paid to think," Franklin said gruffly. "You are being paid to do exactly what I tell you to do. And I'm paying you very well."

"Yeah, you are," Pearlie agreed. "So what exactly do you want me to do? I'm not going to kill any of the railroad workers or anything like that."

"Why not? You've killed before. Hell, you just killed Purvis Depro. I wouldn't think you would be all that squeamish about killing."

"I've killed in the past," Pearlie admitted. "But the only time I've ever killed anyone was when they were trying to kill me."

"How do you think you would do against Smoke Jensen?"

"Smoke Jensen? I don't know. He's awfully good. In fact, they say he's the best, 'n I ain't got no reason to doubt that. I told you, Mr. Franklin, I wouldn't want to go up against him unless it was a life-or-death situation."

"It may come to that. It did with Deke Crowley," Franklin said. He made a dismissive grunt. "He told me he was better than Jensen. That's why I hired him. But it turns out the fool wasn't as good, and now he's dead."

"Yeah, I heard that Deke Crowley got hisself killed, but I didn't have no idea why he went up against Jensen." Pearlie frowned. "Are you sayin' you hired Deke Crowley to kill Smoke Jensen?"

"I was going to give him a thousand dollars if he got the job done. He didn't, and the money is still there for whoever can do it. You, for example." Franklin was keeping secret the fact that he had offered five thousand. He didn't have to pay it after all, and there was no sense in making the offer known now.

"Mr. Franklin, I'm not going to go up against Smoke Jensen," Pearlie stated bluntly. "I told you, I'm not going to kill anyone for you unless I wind up in a situation where it's kill or be killed. And if I was to get into it with Jensen, there ain't no doubt in my mind but that I'd be the one gettin' killed."

"All right, all right. We'll worry about Jensen later. They've laid thirty miles of track, and they've got the ties, rails, and spikes brought up to extend the track, but they're building a trestle across Slumgullion Gulch," Franklin said. "Seems to me that if you were to take some men with you, you could destroy the trestle right after it is finished, say, just as a train is crossing. That would certainly slow them down some."

"All right. We'll take care of the trestle," Pearlie said.

What Pearlie didn't say was that he had no intention of doing it while a train was crossing.

End of track

It had been a fairly easy construction so far. No tunnels had been necessary; two creeks had to be crossed, but they weren't very large and were easily bridged.

Slumgullion Gulch was another matter. Here a very high trestle had to be built, and the forward progress of laying the rails came to a temporary but complete halt.

It was just after supper on the day the trestle was completed and a short stretch of track laid on the far side. The workers, who had spent the day in hard labor, were enjoying a well-earned rest. More than a dozen tents had been erected, including a mess tent where the men gathered to eat. The mess tent was empty now, except for the cook and his helper, who were cleaning up from the recent meal.

Frank Magee was taking inventory of the construction material on hand and figured that he had about ten miles of rails, as well as enough crossties and spikes for the next advance.

He called O'Malley and Lee Cho to his tent to talk about the next day. O'Malley was the head of the Irish work gang, while Cho headed up the Chinese workers.

"What do you need, boss?" O'Malley asked.

"Have you made the final check on the trestle?"

"Oh, yeah. It's ready," O'Malley answered.

"Good. Start loading the material on the train. We'll

take it to the other side tonight so we'll be ready to start work on new track first thing in the morning."

"Yes, sir."

"The trestle is up," Pearlie said. "Blow it up."

"Not yet. There ain't no train on it yet," Tay said.

"We're not going to blow it up while a train is goin' acrost it," Pearlie said.

"Franklin said to wait till there was a train on it. That way it would cost 'em a train."

"It could also kill the train and work crews," Pearlie said. "More'n likely twenty to twenty-five men will be on the train when it crosses."

Tay smiled. "Well, yeah, that's the whole point of it, don't you see? Iffen we kill ever'body that's on the train, why, that would stop the tracklayin' once 'n for all."

"We ain't a-goin' to kill any innocent men," Pearlie insisted.

"When did you get so all-fired holy on us?"

"I'm in charge, Tay. And I say we ain't goin' to take no chance on killin' all the men who might be on the train. Conner, Ramsey, Jones, get your dynamite ready and go blow it now."

"All right," Conner said. "Come on, boys. Let's get them charges laid."

Just then the engine blew its whistle, and looking in that direction, Pearlie saw the train starting toward the trestle.

"No, hold it!" he shouted. "It's too late. The train's started."

"So, what do we do now?" Conner asked.

"I say we blow it up while the train is a-crossin'," Tay said.

Pearlie pulled his pistol and pointed it at Tay. "And I say we ain't goin' to do that."

"So, it's like I said. What do we do now?" Conner asked. "I mean, if we don't blow up the trestle, that means they'll get the rails, crossties, 'n spikes acrost the gulch, 'n then they can start in a-workin' on the other side."

"We're goin' back to Fontana," Pearlie said.

"Franklin ain't a-goin' to like that," Tay said.

"You let me worry about that."

Realizing that the trestle would be a prime target of anyone who wanted to sabotage the building of the railroad, Smoke stayed at the construction site until the trestle was completed. He waited until the train crossed the gulch and until the rails, crossties, and spikes were off-loaded on the other side. Once that was finished, he decided to return and give a firsthand report to Malone.

When Pearlie and the others returned to Fontana, they stopped in the Blue Dog for a drink. It was there that Tay announced his intention to report to Franklin.

"I plan to tell 'im that we coulda stopped the railroad right in its tracks, only you was too weakhearted to kill a bunch of railroad workers, which some of 'em was Chinese, anyway, 'n it don't count if all you do is kill a bunch o' Chinamen."

"You go ahead and tell Mr. Franklin anything you want to tell him," Pearlie said. "I ain't goin' to try 'n talk you out of it."

"You know that if I do tell 'im, he'll more'n likely fire you," Tay said.

"No, he won't," Pearlie said.

"What do you mean, he won't fire you? He sure as hell will."

"He won't fire me, on account of I quit."

"Since when do you quit?"

"Since now," Pearlie said.

CHAPTER 21

After Smoke returned to Fontana, he stopped in front of the Blue Dog Saloon, looped the reins around the hitching rail, then stepped up onto the porch. He could hear the piano and laughter and conversation from the saloon patrons, and putting his hands on the batwing door before pushing it open, he looked inside. The saloon was full, and he started to go in, then changed his mind. He decided to walk down to the bank instead, because Malone had an office there, and Smoke was fairly certain he would be there, even at this hour.

Inside the saloon, Conner had seen Smoke step up to the door, then change his mind and turn away.

"I wonder why he didn't come in?" Conner asked.

"Why who didn't come in?" Perkins asked.

"Smoke Jensen. He come up to the door, looked in, and then he turned around 'n went away," Conner said.

"Well, hell, Conner, I can tell you why he didn't come in. It's easy enough to figure out," Tay said.

"It is? Well, I sure haven't figured it out," Conner replied. "So if you know, tell me."

Tay drained the rest of his glass of whiskey, then drew the back of his hand over his mouth before he answered.

"The reason he didn't come in is 'cause he seen me."

"Wait a minute. You're saying he didn't come in, 'cause he seen you?" Conner asked. "Why the hell would seein' you keep 'im from comin' in?"

"On account of he's a-scairt of me, that's why. He knows that if me 'n him was to ever have us a face-off, I'd wind up killin' 'im."

"Tay, I wouldn't be goin' around sayin' things like that if I was you," Pearlie said. "Word might get back to 'im, 'n you sure as hell don't want that to happen."

"Yeah, I do want it to happen. 'N I ain't just sayin' he's a-scairt of me. I know he is, on account of I've run into him before. No, sir, I can tell you for sure that Smoke Jensen don't want nothin' to do with me. 'N iffin I was to kill 'im, I'd get that thousand dollars Mr. Franklin was goin' to pay Crowley, 'n Mr. Franklin wouldn't have no trouble at all stoppin' that railroad," Tay said. He looked at Pearlie. "'N once I kill 'im, why, it's more'n likely that Mr. Franklin would put me in charge."

"You don't have to kill nobody, Tay. Far as I'm concerned, you're in charge now. I've done quit, remember?"

"You mean you was serious when you said that?"

"Yeah, I was serious. I was real serious. That means he'll prob'ly put you in charge, anyway. So you don't have to kill Jensen or, what's more'n likely, get your own self kilt."

"Yeah, well, I'm goin' to kill Jensen no matter what. That would make me as famous as he is, and to tell the truth, I think it's mostly just talk about him, anyhow."

Tay started telling all the others how he was going to kill Smoke Jensen, and everyone began to flock around him, asking how and when he was going to do it. To a degree, just making the announcement that he planned to kill Smoke Jensen brought him a little fame. And though the fame was premature, it was not an unwelcome situation.

After a few more drinks, the men who called themselves the Demons left the saloon. Pearlie stayed behind, staring into his half-drunk beer as he thought about Tay's arrogant insistence that he was better than Smoke Jensen.

Pearlie was very good with a gun, which was why Franklin had put him in charge of the men who were drawing fighting wages. But as good as Pearlie was, he knew he wasn't as good as Smoke Jensen, and for someone to survive in a world where confrontations often developed into gunplay, it was important to know your limits.

Instead of going to the bank, Smoke paused when he saw a saloon across the street from the Blue Dog. The new saloon wasn't as large as the Blue Dog, and while the Blue Dog was painted white, with blue trim, the new saloon was constructed of unpainted sunbaked wood. Attached to the false front was a rather crudely painted sign that read LONGMONT'S SALOON.

Smoke stepped up to the batwings and looked over them. The saloon was narrow but went back a good ways, with the bar running along the right-hand side of the room. A few men stood in front of it, some of them with a foot propped on the customary brass railing. The tables, only a handful of them, were empty. The place wasn't doing a booming business yet, but Smoke knew it hadn't been open long.

Louis Longmont stood behind the bar, polishing glasses. He was better dressed tonight than he had been when he was working in the Blue Dog. The dapper black suit looked more like the sort of garb he'd been accustomed to wearing when he was working as a professional gambler.

Smoke pushed the batwings aside and walked into the saloon.

"I see that you did what you said you were going to do," Smoke said to Longmont when he stepped up to the hardwood. "You've started your new saloon."

"Yes, but this one is temporary only, because I intend to move out to this new town you mentioned," Longmont replied. Then, with an ominous tone to his voice, he added, "Uh-oh."

"What is it?"

"I don't know. Maybe something, maybe nothing. Do you see that fellow who just came in?"

Smoke looked toward the recent entry. "Yes, I do. Who is he? And why did you say uh-oh?"

"His name is Pearlie."

"Pearlie?"

"That's the only name I know him by. Anyway, he works for Franklin, and when I say he works for Franklin, I don't mean he rides for the brand. He is one of Franklin's bunch of gunfighters. As a matter of fact, he's the head of them, from what I've heard."

When Pearlie saw that he had been seen and recognized, he walked over to Longmont and the man he knew was Smoke Jensen.

"Mr. Jensen?"

To Smoke's surprise, Pearlie had addressed him cordially.

"Yes?"

"We have a rider, that is, Mr. Franklin has a rider, by the name of Tay."

"Tay? Marcus Tay? I've heard of him. His name used

to be Carter, until he killed someone in Arkansas and had to change his name."

"He says that he intends to kill you, which is why I've come here to warn you."

"You said he rides for Franklin," Longmont said. "Don't you mean he rides for you? I've heard that you are the head of Franklin's gunfighters."

"I was foreman of the Demons, but I ain't no more," Pearlie said.

"Why is that?" Smoke asked.

"Franklin was wantin' me to do some things I didn't want to do, so I quit," was Pearlie's answer.

"You say Carter, that is, Tay, plans to kill me?" Smoke asked.

"Yes, sir. At least that's what he's been tellin' ever'one for the past few days. Fact is, he's over at the Blue Dog talkin' about it now."

"Do me a favor, will you, Pearlie?"

"Yes, sir, I'll be glad to. What is it you want me to do?"

"I want you to go back over to the Blue Dog and tell him you saw me in here."

Pearlie frowned as if he didn't know if that was a good idea, but he said, "Yes, sir," and walked back out of the saloon.

"What do you know about that man?" Smoke asked Longmont after Pearlie had left.

"I know it will sound strange, seeing as he was the leader of Franklin's *armée personnelle*, but I think he is basically a good man. I used to see him when I was still working at the Blue Dog. He would come in with the others, but he wasn't like them. He didn't aggravate the women. He never tried to pick a fight. He was quiet and tended to keep to himself."

"He said he quit Franklin."

"*Oui*, he did say that. And I'm sure that is true."

"Jensen! Smoke Jensen!" a voice called from outside.

"That would be Marcus Tay," Smoke said. "Or Carter, as he used to be known."

"I've seen him shoot before, Smoke. He is fast, very fast."

"No one is faster than me, Louis," Smoke said. From most, such a comment would be arrogant. From Smoke, it was simply a matter of quiet confidence.

Smoke and Longmont both stepped out into the street.

"Well, you come out," Tay said. "I didn't think you would."

"Is this a challenge, Carter?"

Tay blinked. "I wasn't sure you'd remember."

"I remember."

"You didn't get ever'body," Tay said.

"What do you mean?"

"I was there, you know. At that cabin of your'n."

"Were you?"

"Yeah. 'N your wife . . . What was her name? Nicole? Yeah, that was it. Nicole. She was just real good. Tell me, is this here wife you got now just as good? 'Cause after I kill you, I plan to have her."

Smoke didn't know if the man who was now calling himself Tay had been part of that group who had raped and murdered Nicole, or if Tay was just trying to make him angry and careless.

"You're a fool, Carter," Smoke said. "I hope you have enough money in your pockets to bury you, otherwise you'll more than likely get tossed into John Loomis's pigpen."

"Draw, you dirty dog!" Tay shouted, going for his gun.

Smoke had his gun up and shooting even before Tay was able to clear leather. The single slug struck Tay in the chest and knocked him backward. Once down, he struggled up onto one elbow and looked at Smoke through eyes that were already glazing over.

"You . . . you devil! You've . . . you've kilt me."

"Yes, I have," Smoke answered calmly.

Tay fell back and let out a death rattle, then quit breathing.

Several of the other Franklin gunnies had watched the fight and were now in complete shock over how quickly Smoke had been able to draw and fire.

"Tie him across his saddle and take him back to Franklin," Smoke said. "Unless one of you want to try me."

The gunmen looked at each other but said nothing. After a moment, Pearlie spoke.

"You heard Mr. Jensen," Pearlie said. "Get Tay throw'd over his saddle 'n take him out to the Circle TF."

"You ain't the head of us no more, Pearlie," one of the men said.

"Let's do it," Perkins said, starting toward Tay's body.

Smoke waited until the others had ridden off before he spoke again.

"Pearlie, how much was Franklin paying you?"

"Sixty a month."

"I'd like you to come work for me. I'll pay you thirty and found."

"All right," Pearlie said, with a big smile. "I'll take the job."

"Will you stand by me and my wife if it comes to it?"

"Till I soak up so much lead, I can't stand."

"You're hired, Pearlie."

CHAPTER 22

Cimarrona Creek

"This is where we will build our town," Smoke said as he and Sally stood on the bank of the swiftly moving creek.

"Oh, listen to it," Sally said. "It's almost as if it were singing to us."

True to Sally's comment, the rushing sound of the creek seemed to provide a bass note, while the tinkling of the water provided a soprano overtone.

"We need to name the town," Smoke said. "Louis Longmont said he would move his saloon here as soon I named the town. And I think the others who have said they would come here would come quicker if there was a saloon here."

"I think we should name it after you," Sally said. "We can call it Jensenville. Or maybe just Jensen."

"No, I don't think I would like that," Smoke said with a slow shake of his head. "We've already named one of the streets after me, and I'm not at all comfortable with that. But I sure don't want the town named after me, which means we'll have to come up with something else."

"Colorado City? Cimarrona, after the creek? Mountainville?" Sally suggested.

"I don't know. Cimarrona, maybe," Smoke replied.

"Oh, Smoke, look at that huge rock over there," Sally said as she pointed to a massive outcropping that overlooked the creek. "Isn't it magnificent?"

"It probably rolled down from the Uncompahgre Mountains," Smoke said. "I'm sure glad it's already here. A rock that size rolling through the town would play hell with any buildings that might be here."

"That rock didn't just roll down any hill," Sally said. "It's been here since the Proterozoic Eon."

"The what?"

"Proterozoic Eon. It's a scientific term describing different eras in the geological history of Earth, in this case, while the earth's crust was forming."

"Damn, Sally. How do you know stuff like that? You're the smartest person I've ever known."

"Smoke, I'm no smarter than you. In fact, I doubt if I am as smart. I'm knowledgeable, because I have the ability to maintain information I have previously absorbed. Being 'smart' is having a strong cognitive ability, and Smoke, I've never met anyone with more cognitive skills than you."

Smoke laughed. "Well, I'm smart enough to know that that was a compliment."

Sally returned his smile and gave him a quick kiss on the lips.

"Big Rock," Sally said.

"It sure is, no matter how it got here."

"No," Sally said. "I mean the name of the town. We'll call it Big Rock."

"Yeah!" Smoke said. "Yeah, I like that. I mean, if Arkansas can have a Little Rock, why can't we have a Big Rock?"

* * *

After Marcus Tay was killed, Ray Perkins became the leader of the Demons, and a couple of weeks after he assumed that position, he saw four riders approaching the Circle TF Ranch. He went into the ranch office to report the information to Franklin.

"Four riders, you say?"

"Yes, sir."

Franklin smiled. "Good. I've been expecting them."

Franklin and Perkins stepped outside just as the four riders rode up to the ranch house. Although there were four riders, only one dismounted and walked up to Franklin. He had closely cropped dark hair and a well-trimmed mustache.

"Are you Franklin?" the man asked.

"I am."

"I'm Jack Slade."

"It's good of you to answer my request to come work for me," Franklin said.

Jack Slade shook his head, then held his hand out toward the three men who had arrived with him. "We'll sell you our guns, but these men work for me, and I don't work for anyone."

"Your guns are all I want. I want Jensen and a couple more men killed."

"I want ten thousand dollars for Jensen. Who else do you want killed?"

"Frank Magee. He is the new railroad construction engineer. Oh, and Pearlie."

"Pearlie who?"

"I believe his last name is Fontaine, but he never uses it. He was working for me as head of my, let's call it security people, and he deserted his post. I'm not sure but what he didn't warn Jensen about Crowley and Tay. Tay, for sure."

"Five thousand for him and a thousand for anyone else." Slade smiled. "I believe that adds up to sixteen thousand dollars . . . assuming you don't think of anybody else you want killed."

"All right. That's expensive, but it will be worth it to get rid of Jensen's meddling and stop the railroad."

"How many men are you paying fighting wages to?" Slade asked.

"I don't know the exact number." Franklin nodded toward Perkins. "Perkins, here, is the head of them now, unless you want that job as well."

"No, I don't want to be the boss of 'em, as long as we can work together." Slade looked at Perkins. "We'll have a talk later." He waved a hand at the three mounted men who had come with him. "You fellas climb down 'n come meet the man who's goin' to pay us," he said.

The three gun-wolves dismounted and walked over to join Slade. Unlike Slade, who was particular in his appearance, Ian Dolan, Marv Cooley, and Milt Wolcott were scruffy looking. None of the three was wearing a beard, but neither were any of them clean-shaven.

Franklin frowned in thought and said, "It might be that I'll want you to kill several of the Chinamen and a few of the Micks who are working on the construction of the railroad, as well."

Slade nodded. "Bein' Chinks and Micks, they won't cost you as much."

After listening in on the conversation between Slade and Franklin, Perkins returned to the Demons' bunkhouse.

"Who are those four men who just arrived?" Conner asked.

"Jack Slade is one of them."

"Jack Slade? What does Franklin want with Jack Slade?"

"He wants him to do a lot of killin'," Perkins said. "And one of the people he wants killed is Pearlie."

Pearlie was leading his horse out of the barn at the Sugarloaf, ready to get started on his new job working on the ranch with Smoke, who had left earlier with Sally on some errand he hadn't explained. Before they had ridden off, though, he had given Pearlie his assignment for the day. It was Pearlie's task today to check the southern pastures and make sure none of the stock had gotten themselves into trouble.

He stopped short when he saw a rider approaching. The man on horseback wasn't coming toward the ranch at a hell-for-leather pace, so he didn't seem to be bringing trouble with him, but Pearlie knew that sometimes appearances could be deceiving.

Without being too obvious about it, Pearlie shifted his hand closer to the butt of his holstered gun as he recognized the rider.

"Perkins, what are you doing here?" Pearlie called. "If you've come to raise hell, you've come to the wrong place."

Perkins held out his right hand in the universal gesture of peace to show Pearlie that he had no intention of making trouble.

"No, it's nothing like that, I swear," Perkins said. "I've just come here to warn you."

"Warn me?" Pearlie replied, his voice still challenging. "Warn me about what?"

"Pearlie, Franklin has hired Jack Slade. He wants Slade to kill you and Jensen, as well as a bunch of the Chinamen and Irish who are working on the railroad."

"What about the Demons? Are they goin' along with it? I mean, I can't see Conner or Springer or Coats or Loomis or Sharkey going along with something like that. Actually, I can't see any of them going along with that."

Perkins smiled. "They ain't goin' along with it," he said. "Fact is, there ain't none of us goin' along with it. They've all done quit Franklin 'n rode off, ever' damn one of 'em. 'N I'm leavin', too."

"You mean Franklin doesn't have paid gunfighters with him now?" Pearlie asked.

"Well, yeah, he's got Slade and the three men who came with him, remember. 'N I heard Slade tellin' Franklin he would round up a bunch of men to take our place."

"Yeah, I can see that he probably would do something like that," Pearlie said. He sighed. "But if it actually comes to shooting, it's good to know that I won't be shooting at people like Smitty or Luly or the others I've sat at the supper table with."

"I'll be ridin' on now, Pearlie," Perkins said. "If you was smart, you'd ride on, too. You ain't got no stake in this."

"I gave my word," Pearlie said. "I told Smoke Jensen I'd stand by 'im, 'n I intend to do just that."

Perkins, who had not dismounted, leaned down from the saddle and extended his hand.

"I consider you a friend, Pearlie. I couldn't have ridden off without at least warnin' you. I wish you luck."

"Thanks," Pearlie said, shaking Perkins's hand.

Pearlie watched Perkins ride away, thankful for his visit,

not only because of the warning, but also because if it came to a shooting war, it would not involve any of the men Pearlie had once led.

Smoke and Sally came back that afternoon.

"We've been to Big Rock, Pearlie," Smoke said. "Anything happen while we were gone?"

"Big Rock?" Pearlie repeated with a puzzled frown.

"I told you I was building a town, didn't I? We'll be calling it Big Rock."

"You mean like Little Rock, only Big Rock?"

Smoke laughed. "What did I tell you, Sally? I knew people would make that connection."

"You'll see why we are calling it Big Rock when you see this huge, lovely rock there from the Proterozoic Eon," Sally said.

"What?"

"That means it didn't roll down a mountain. It's always been there," Smoke explained.

"Very good, Smoke," Sally said with a complimentary smile.

Pearlie said, "Smoke, have you ever heard of a man by the name of Jack Slade?"

"Yeah, I've heard of him," Smoke said. His expression was solemn. He had a pretty good idea where Pearlie was going with this conversation.

"Do you think you could beat him?" Pearlie asked.

The blunt question put a look of concern on Sally's face.

"Pearlie, I know that you are pretty good with a gun yourself," Smoke said, "and I also know that you have been in a few gunfights of your own. Have you ever gone into a gunfight thinking you could *not* beat the other man?"

"No, I ain't," Pearlie said. "Truth is, if you ain't got it in you that you can beat the feller you're up ag'in, that's the best way there is to get yourself kilt."

"Exactly," Smoke said. "Then that should answer your question as to whether or not I could beat Jack Slade. Yes, I can beat him. Now, why do you ask?"

"'Cause Franklin has hired Jack Slade to kill you " Pearlie was quiet for a moment. "'N to kill me."

CHAPTER 23

From the *Fontana Sunburst:*

NEW TOWN BEING BUILT.

From the beginning of time, there has been a fascination with the origin of things: the birth of a child, the blooming of a flower, the opening of a new business. Now a fifteen-mile ride northwest, until one reaches Cimarrona Creek, will give the interested explorer a look at the town of Big Rock while yet in its embryonic stage.

Big Rock is the brainchild of Kirby Jensen, known throughout the West as Smoke Jensen. The new town will provide ranchers, farmers, miners, and travelers with all the conveniences to be offered by a flourishing settlement. Already there are plans for a restaurant, a mercantile store, a leather goods store, a blacksmith shop, and an apothecary, and Fred Malone has announced his intention to move the Malone Bank to Big Rock.

In addition, there will be a depot for the

Mountain and Pacific Railroad, which will put travelers within a week's travel of any city in America. Readers may remember that this paper published an editorial in opposition to the railroad coming to Fontana, and our city council voted to deny the Mountain and Pacific entry. This paper now regrets that shortsighted approach and is very much in support of the railroad coming to Big Rock.

Final Issue.

I hereby give notice to the readers of the SUNBURST that this will be the final edition. My wife and I have worked together to bring to the citizens of Fontana a newspaper that would provide news and information, and we appreciate the loyal support of our readers.

However, I must report that too often, I have betrayed the sacred duty of the journalist and allowed outside influences to dictate what I could and could not publish. I am surrendering ownership of the SUNBURST to Tilden Franklin, who has held me his financial hostage for far too long. I will soon begin publication of a new newspaper in a new town. I hope that within no more than two weeks, the BIG ROCK BULLETIN will make its debut.

HT Ranch

"How dare that prairie rat stab me in the back like that!" Franklin shouted angrily when he read the latest and, according to the paper itself, the last issue of the *Fontana*

Sunburst. He crumpled the paper and then slammed it down on his desk. "I've loaned him money. I've kept his newspaper going. And now he's going to help start a new town? There is no need for a new town. Fontana has everything anyone would ever need."

"I've got a suggestion," Slade said. "We stop the town from being built."

Franklin shook his head. "No, there are only four of you, now that all the others have deserted like rats from a sinking ship, and I want the railroad stopped. That's more important. If we can bankrupt the railroad, I can move in and take over."

"We can do both," Slade said. "All I have to do is recruit a few more people."

"How much is that going to cost me?"

"Just fighting wages, same thing you were paying before."

Franklin smiled and nodded. "All right," he said. "Yes, we could stop the railroad and the town at the same time if we had enough men. And because Smoke Jensen is all alone, there will be damn little, if anything, he can do about it." He looked up at the gunman. "Recruit the men, Mr. Slade. Whatever you need, as long as that railroad is stopped . . . and Smoke Jensen dies."

That very day Slade sent out Dolan, Cooley, and Wolcott to recruit men to create a new cadre of fighting men. Over the next several days, the new recruits began arriving in twos and threes or sometimes alone.

Curtis, Simpson, and Percy arrived together. They came up from Texas, where they had killed a rancher and his wife. Marshal and Duncan were next. They had robbed a remote trading post and killed the owner and two customers who happened to be in the store at the time.

Jonas Bardsley arrived alone. Of all the new recruits, Bardsley was the best known and, arguably, the evilest of the bunch. Nobody knew how many men Bardsley had killed; some said it could be as many as twenty. Bardsley's reputation was not because he was a good gunfighter, for the truth was, he had never actually been tested. His reputation was purely and simply because he was a killer. He killed without compunction, and he had killed all his victims from a particular point of advantage: either from afar, by rifle, or by shooting them in the back, or in any way that allowed him to catch his adversaries by surprise.

Drake and Cummings were from New Mexico, Boyce and Stryker came up from Arizona Territory, Jones was from the Nations, and Rowe and Edmonson were from right there in Colorado. By the time Slade finished his recruiting, he had sixteen men under him, including in that count his original three of Dolan, Cooley, and Wolcott.

Fontana, Colorado

Sally was in Baker's Grocery Store, which was still located in Fontana, though Baker had already announced his intention to close his store there and build a new one in Big Rock.

"That's quite a lot of groceries, Mrs. Jensen," Don Baker said.

"I'm taking the groceries to the new town site. We've got quite a few people working out there now, and all that work builds up quite an appetite."

Baker chuckled. "Yes, ma'am, I suppose it does."

"Mrs. Jensen!" a young woman called.

Looking toward the person who had hailed her, Sally saw Malone's pretty teenage daughter, Sue Ellen.

"Sue Ellen, how nice to see you," Sally said.

"What are you doing in town?"

"I've come to pick up groceries for the men working at the new town site."

"You're going to Big Rock?"

"I am indeed," Sally replied.

"Oh, Mrs. Jensen, could I ride out with you? I've just been dying to go see it."

"You're sure your mother won't mind?"

"I came into town with Lula Belle," Sue Ellen said. "I'll send word back to Mama by her. If Mama knows that I'm with you and not just wandering around, bothering people, she won't mind at all. Oh, how will we be going? Are you riding out?"

"No. I brought the buckboard, because I'll have to be taking the groceries there."

"Good," Sue Ellen said. "Because I came into town with Lula Belle by buckboard. You won't mind taking me home later, will you? Because without Lula Belle, I won't have a way back."

"No, of course not. I won't mind at all."

Sally and Sue Ellen did not notice the tall, dark-haired customer with the well trimmed mustache who was standing nearby. He was close enough to overhear their conversation, and when they left, he saw them climb into Sally's buckboard and head for the Big Rock town site. Jack Slade crossed the street and stepped into the Blue Dog Saloon, where he saw Ian Dolan, Marv Cooley, and Milt Wolcott drinking beer and flirting with the percentage girls.

"I have a job for you," he said.

"What kind of job?" Dolan asked.

"A real easy job," Slade replied as a smile spread across his face.

Big Rock town site

Smoke, Pearlie, and Louis Longmont began laying out the streets. Three would run east and west. These three streets were named Malone Avenue, Center Street, and Jensen Street. Center would be the town's main street. Like Smoke, Fred Malone preferred not to have the town's main street named after him and thought Center Street was more appropriate for that. The four streets running north and south would be Tanner, Ranney, Sikes, and Lanning Street. The grid was thus established.

Norman Lambert, called "Hog Jaw" by his friends, was the first to begin construction at the new town site and was building his restaurant on the corner of Malone Avenue and Tanner Street.

Don Baker was the second to start building, and he had arrived in a wagon loaded with the material he would need. He would build a mercantile, called the Big Rock Mercantile, on Malone Avenue. White's Apothecary, Trammell's Butcher Shop, Murchison's Leather Store, and Beck's Blacksmith Shop would be next.

Because Big Rock was being built on two thousand acres Malone owned, he had agreed to make free land available to anyone who would build a business or a house there. In most cases, land was acquired for business and residential use by the same person. Unofficially, the population of Big Rock was already at forty-five, because some had moved into tents to be close to the construction.

The new town of Big Rock was alive with activity and

the sound of hammers and saws at work. Sally was going to deliver all the groceries to Hog Jaw Lambert, who had offered to cook for everyone in return for them helping him with his restaurant and house.

"I don't know which is more exciting," Sally said as she and Sue Ellen arrived at the building site with provisions for Lambert. "Starting a new house or building a town."

"I would think it is building a new town," Sue Ellen said. "I've seen houses being built, but I've never seen a whole town being built!"

"You know what? I think you may be right."

"Oh, we'll need a school!" Sue Ellen said.

"Indeed, we will need a new school, but I'm way ahead of you," Sally replied. "I already have the location picked out and the plans. It will be on Malone Avenue, and the first school will be a one-room school that will teach children from the first grade to the eighth grade. After that, they will have to go to Denver to attend high school. At least until we're able to expand the school."

"Who will you get to teach?" Sue Ellen asked.

"I'll be teaching at the beginning. We'll acquire teachers as soon as the town is large enough to afford them."

"I know," Sue Ellen said with a broad grin. "I'll go away to college and learn to be a schoolteacher. Then I'll come back here and teach in a school that is being built on a street with my name."

"By then I should be in a position to hire you," Sally said.

Dolan, Cooley, and Wolcott were waiting about two miles east of Big Rock.

"Are you sure they'll be comin' thisaway?" Wolcott asked.

"They have to come this way. This is the only road they is a-comin' from where they're buildin' the town," Dolan said.

"This ain't no road," Cooley said.

"It ain't no real road yet, but you can see that lots of wagons has come this way, so it's the same as a road."

"Slade said there would be a woman drivin' the buckboard that the Malone girl's goin' to be in. What'll we do about the woman?" Wolcott asked.

"We'll shoot her," Dolan said.

"I don't like the idea of shootin' a woman," Wolcott said.

"Me neither," Cooley added.

"Yeah, but here's the thing. We don't have no other choice. Slade wants us to take the girl, 'n we can't just take her 'n leave the woman behind. She'd see which way we went, 'n if she didn't recognize us, well, she could for sure tell what we look like, seein' as we won't be wearin' no mask or nothin'."

"How much longer do you reckon it'll be before they come through here?" Cooley asked.

"I don't know, but what else have you got to do?" Dolan asked.

"I could be drinkin' beer."

"All right, you go on back 'n have yourself a beer. Me 'n Milt will just split the three hunnert dollars betwixt us."

"No, now, there ain't no need for you all to be a-doin' somethin' like that. I ain't a-goin' nowhere. I'll be right here with you two when the woman 'n the girl come along."

Back in the town that was being built—called Big Rock by everyone now—Hog Jaw Lambert held out a pan and began beating on it with a large spoon. The result was a loud clanging noise, which Lambert augmented by calling out.

"Come 'n get it, boys! I got food here waitin' on you!"

"You said, 'Come and get it, boys.' But we aren't boys, so does that mean we don't get to eat with the rest of you?" Sue Ellen asked.

"Darlin', the two of you are standin' right here. I don't yell at ladies. I just invite them in a real nice voice. Would you two ladies like to join us?"

Sally laughed. "Now, how could we refuse an invitation so politely extended? Sue Ellen and I would be honored to join you and the others."

"Yes," Sue Ellen said. "We would be honored to join you." The meal Lambert had prepared consisted of bacon, fried potatoes, beans from airtight cans, and rolls. The rolls weren't laid out but were kept in a big pan.

"Hey, Hog Jaw, you plannin' on eatin' all them rolls yourself?" someone called out to him.

"I didn't have no place to put 'em. Here you go," Lambert said, tossing a roll to him.

"Hey, you know what?" Haywood Arden called out to him. "Once you get your restaurant built, this is what you ought to do. You ought to throw your rolls at them. I'll even give you your first advertisement in my newspaper for free. Lambert's, home of the thrown rolls."

"Throwed," Lambert said.

"What?"

"Throwed rolls. It sounds better."

Sally said, "That's not the least bit gramatically correct."

"Certainly not, Mrs. Jensen," Arden said, "but Mr. Lambert has a point. In advertising, you want something catchy that's easy for your customers to remember." He nodded. "Throwed rolls *does* sound better. Although it's going to grate on my editorial nerves to put that in print!"

"You'll do it, though, won't you?" Lambert asked.

"The customer, as they say, is always right, and that's true in the newspaper business as well as any other."

After having lunch with all the people who were building the town, Sally asked Sue Ellen if she would like to see where the school would be built.

"Oh, yes," Sue Ellen replied enthusiastically.

Sally took Sue Ellen to the corner of Malone Avenue and Sikes Street, though there was actually no difference between the "streets" and the rest of the ground. The streets could be located, though, because there were stakes on each side of the proposed streets to indicate where they would be.

"We'll start with a one-room school, because I'll be the only teacher, and I don't know how many students there will be. But as the town grows, and the need develops, we can always enlarge the school . . ."

"And hire more teachers," Sue Ellen added.

"Yes," Sally agreed with a smile. "And hire more teachers."

"I'll be the first one you hire," Sue Ellen insisted.

"You just might be," Sally said. "Oh, my goodness, look at the time. I had better get you back home, before your mother starts worrying about you."

"Mama won't be worried about me as long as she knows I'm with you," Sue Ellen said.

"Yes, well, I wouldn't want to lose that trust, so I need to be getting you home."

"All right, and thanks for bringing me here. It's so exciting to see a new town being built," Sue Ellen said as the two climbed into the buckboard.

* * *

About two miles east of the new town site, Dolan, Cooley, and Wolcott were still waiting. Wolcott dismounted and walked over to the side of the road and began urinating.

"Wolcott, what the hell are you doin'?" Cooley asked.

"What's it look like I'm doin'? I'm takin' a leak."

"You can't do that! There's women comin'."

Wolcott laughed as he buttoned up his pants and remounted. "That's funny," he said. "We're goin' to kill the woman, 'n we're goin' to take the Malone girl prisoner. Why the hell should I be worryin' 'bout peein' in front of 'em?"

"Here comes the buckboard," Dolan said.

"I've just been thinking," Sue Ellen said. "When I start teaching, I'm going to move to Big Rock and find a place to live."

"You won't have to find a place," Sally said. "The school will furnish you with an apartment free, as part of your compensation."

"Compensation," Sue Ellen said. "That's a real official-sounding word. I like that."

"Hmm, I wonder what that's about?" Sally asked when she saw the three mounted men ahead of them.

"Maybe they're just out for a ride," Sue Ellen suggested.

Sally shook her head. "No, I don't think so. We don't even have any roads yet. It seems highly unlikely they would be out here by coincidence. I think they are after us."

"Why?"

"I don't know why," Sally said. "But we're about to find out."

Sally was carrying a pistol with her, as she always did when she was riding anywhere. That was by Smoke's request. She reached down to the pistol, which lay on the seat beside her, under the folds of her dress. Quietly she cocked it when one of the three riders held up his hand to stop them.

"What do you want?" Sally asked.

"We want the little lady to come with us," the man said.

"And just why should we come with you?"

The man laughed. "It's just the little lady that'll be comin' with us to the Circle TF Ranch, not you. You'll be stayin' here." He paused for a moment, then added, "Forever. Take care of her, boys!"

The three men raised their pistols, but before they could fire, Sally jerked the gun up and, remembering all the hours she had put into shooting at targets without aiming, did just that. She pulled the trigger three times, one on top of the other, the shots coming out in one continuous roar, and all three men were knocked out of their saddles.

Sue Ellen let out a little sharp shout of surprise and fear, and Sally reached over to put her hand on Sue Ellen's arm.

"It's all right, honey," she said. "These men will give us no more trouble."

She hoped that was right. The three would-be kidnappers all looked dead or at least badly wounded enough that they were no longer a threat, but Sally wasn't just about to wait around to find out if that was true. With a shout, she slapped the reins against the backs of the two horses hitched to the buckboard and sent them bolting forward in a run.

"Hang on!" she called to Sue Ellen.

CHAPTER 24

When Sally brought the buckboard to a stop in front of the Malone house, Lauren came out to meet them with a smile on her face, blissfully unaware of the trouble.

"Lula Belle told me that you had gone out to the site of the new town," she said. "Did you have a nice time?"

"Oh, Mama, the awfullest thing happened!" Sue Ellen practically wailed. "Some men wanted to . . . to kidnap me."

Lauren's eyes widened in shock. "Kidnap you?" she gasped. "What men? Where did this happen?"

She looked around hurriedly, as if fearful that the would-be kidnappers might be right behind Sally and Sue Ellen.

"Between here and Big Rock," Sally explained. "And I don't think you have to worry about these particular men anymore."

The implication of those words didn't seem to sink in on Lauren. "What happened? I mean, how did you get away?"

"I killed them," Sally said.

"Oh, my dear!" Lauren said, putting her hand over her mouth.

"At least, I'm pretty sure I did," Sally added calmly. "We didn't stay there to check."

"Miz Sally didn't have any choice, Mama," Sue Ellen said. "They were going to kill her and take me. That's what they said. And all three of them had guns."

"Are you all right? I mean, neither of you were hurt, were you?"

"No, we weren't hurt, thanks to Miz Sally."

Looking very shaken, Lauren said, "Come into the house, both of you. I just made some hot tea and, Sally, I know how you like tea."

"Thank you, Lauren," Sally said. "But I think I had better go to town and report this."

"Yes, of course," Lauren said. "Sally, thank you for saving my daughter's life, and there is no doubt in my mind that you did. I will be eternally grateful."

"I'm just glad that I was able to prevent them from doing any harm."

Lauren put an arm around her daughter's still-trembling shoulders and led her into the house while Sally drove away.

Circle TF Ranch

The Circle TF Ranch had two bunkhouses, one for the actual working cowboys and another for the men who were drawing fighting wages. Unlike the Demons, the new gun-wolves who had answered Jack Slade's summons had no name, and they identified themselves more as riders for Slade than riders for the Circle TF. Slade lived in the bunkhouse with the men who were drawing fighting wages, but because he was their chief, he had a private room. An hour earlier, Slade had sent Dolan, Cooley, and Wolcott out to snatch the Malone girl. It was a simple enough job, and they should have been back by now.

Stepping out into the bunkhouse's main room, he saw some of the men playing cards. Drake was there, as well, but he wasn't playing. He was kibitzing.

"Ha!" Drake said when some of the men groaned as Bardsley showed his hand and dragged in the pot. "I knowed ole Jonas here was bluffin', but I didn't think he'd get away with it."

"Has anyone seen Dolan, Cooley, or Wolcott?" Slade asked.

"I ain't seen 'em, Jack. Not since you sent 'em out to do whatever it was you sent 'em to do," Drake replied.

"You know where the Malone house is?" Slade asked.

"Yeah, I know."

"Do me a favor 'n ride out that way 'n see if you run acrost 'em."

"Sure," Drake said.

Half an hour later, Drake saw some buzzards circling about a quarter of a mile in front of him.

"Damn, that don't look good," Drake said to himself. "No, sir, that don't look good a'tall."

After another couple of minutes, Drake spotted the three horses Dolan, Cooley, and Wolcott had been riding. They were just standing there alongside the trail, cropping idly at the grass and waiting for directions as to what they should do next. Then, as Drake drew closer, he saw three men on the ground, and he stopped, drew his pistol, and looked around. He could see little but grass and low-lying sage. There were some trees not too far away, but they were spaced widely enough apart that Drake didn't think any bushwhackers were lurking there. Slapping his legs against the sides of his horse, he hurried toward the bodies. Then, after pulling his mount to a stop, he swung down from the saddle for a closer look.

Dolan, Cooley, and Wolcott had guns in their hands and bullet holes in their chests. And all three were dead.

Fontana, Colorado

Sally had kept the team at a rapid trot as she drove from Trail Back into Fontana, and she didn't slow once she reached town. The buckboard moved at such a rapid pace as she drove down the main street that the wheels were sending up rooster tails of dust behind her. She stopped in front of the sheriff's office, then hopped down even before the dust had cleared. She was wrapping the reins around the hitching rail when Deputy Monte Carson stepped out of the sheriff's office.

"Here, Mrs. Jensen, what are you doing driving so fast? Is something wrong?"

"I killed them, Deputy Carson!" Sally had been able to remain calm and coolheaded while she had Sue Ellen with her, since she hadn't known if more trouble would crop up and she felt responsible for the girl's safety. Since leaving Sue Ellen at Trail Back, though, the aftereffects of the violent encounter were starting to soak in on her. "I killed all three of them!"

"You killed who?" Carson asked, staring.

"Some men. I don't know who they were."

"I expect maybe you need to come in, so we can talk about it."

Carson held the door open for Sally, and when she stepped into the sheriff's office, he held a chair for her.

"I've never killed anyone before," Sally said as she sank down wearily in the chair.

"Well, if you've just killed three men, my guess would be that the sons of . . . I mean the varmints needed killin'," Carson said. "Excuse my language, ma'am."

"What's all this about killing someone?" Sheriff Colby asked, looking up from behind his desk.

"I killed them, Sheriff," Sally said in a low, hesitant voice.

"Who did you kill?"

"I . . . I don't know their names. I'd never seen them before, but I know they were sent by Franklin."

"How do you know they were sent by Franklin?"

"Because one of them said they would be taking Sue Ellen with them out to the Circle TF Ranch. And since Franklin owns the ranch, I figure that means he is the one behind it."

"I wouldn't put it past him to do something like that," Carson said. "He is one evil son of a . . . uh, one evil man," he said, checking his language again before Sally.

"Tell me what happened," Sheriff Colby said. He didn't look pleased about any of this.

Sally told the sheriff how she and Sue Ellen had been driving back home when they were accosted by three men. "They wanted to kidnap Sue Ellen for some reason," she said. "And they said they were going to kill me, so I shot them."

"Were they armed?" the sheriff asked.

"Yes, sir, and all three had guns in their hands, pointed toward us."

"Wait a minute. I don't understand," Sheriff Colby said.

"If all three of them already had guns in their hands, how is it that you were able to shoot them?"

"I acted ahead of their reflex action," Sally explained.

"Their reflex action?"

"Yes, as soon as you perceive danger, your brain has to react by telling you what to do, whether it is run or fight. It takes some time for that to happen. For example, if you are holding a gun in your hand, your brain has to tell your finger to pull the trigger, and that takes a finite amount of time. I had already begun my sequence, so I was able to shoot all three of them before they could react."

"I don't have no idea a'tall what you're talking about, but I reckon I'd better ride out where it happened 'n see if maybe I don't know 'em," Sheriff Colby said.

"You'll find them about halfway between where they are building Big Rock and the Trail Back Ranch."

"Thanks," Colby said.

Circle TF Ranch

"All three of them are dead?" Slade asked when Drake told the gunfighter what he had found.

"Yep, deader 'n a coornail, just lyin' out there in the middle of the road."

"What road? There ain't no roads out there."

"It's goin' to be a road soon enough, what with all the wagons runnin' back 'n forth over it."

"How were they killed?" Slade asked.

"They was shot, ever' damn one of 'em. 'N they all three was shot right 'n the middle of their chest. Whoever it was doin' the shootin' sure as hell knowed what he was a-doin', 'cause all three of 'em had their guns out, but they was kilt, anyway."

"Jensen. It had to be Jensen," Slade said. "Nobody else could do something like that. Come with me. I want to tell Franklin about it."

Drake followed Slade to the ranch office. Though all the men who worked on the ranch, the cowboys and the fighting men alike, knocked on the door before they entered the office, Slade didn't. He assumed a position of such importance that he believed he had the right to just step in anytime he wished, and that was what he did now. Drake, with some hesitation, went in behind him.

"Yes, Slade? What do you want?" Franklin asked. Although he had never specifically told Slade he should knock, it always irritated him the way Slade took it on himself to enter in such a fashion, and that irritation was reflected in Franklin's tone of voice and the scowl on his gaunt face.

"Them three men I sent out to snatch the Malone girl for you?" Slade said.

"Yes, what about them?"

"They're dead. All three of 'em."

"Dead?" Franklin sat back in the chair behind the desk, almost as if he'd been struck. "How the hell did that happen? All they were supposed to do is take the girl."

"And kill the Jensen woman," Slade said. "Here's what I think happened. I think it was more'n likely that they met up with Smoke Jensen, 'n when he seen what they was about, he killed them."

"All three of them? But how could that be? They had him outnumbered three to one."

"If no more'n three men was to come after me, I could kill 'em. 'N I figure that Smoke Jensen is damn near as good as me, so I ain't got no doubt in my mind but what he was able to kill all three of 'em."

"Yeah, you're probably right about it being Smoke Jensen. He's the only one who is good enough to shoot like that," Franklin said.

"Except for me," Slade put in.

"Yes, except for you," Franklin conceded. "But the question is, what is he doing here? I thought he was out at end of track, managing the building of the railroad."

"Maybe buildin' the town is more important to him than buildin' the railroad," Drake suggested.

"That's another thing," Franklin said. "I don't like it that they're building a new town, either."

"It's mostly Smoke Jensen that's buildin' it."

"I don't care who he is. I'm paying you to take care of things like that, and right now that pretty much means taking care of Jensen," Franklin said.

"Oh, I'll take care of him, all right," Slade said. "Dolan, Cooley, and Wolcott, those men he killed? They was all pards of mine, so it's kinda personal with me now. I figure to make Jensen pay for what he done."

Their conversation was interrupted by a knock on the office door, and Franklin nodded toward Drake by way of telling him to open the door.

"Boss?" Jonas Bardsley said, coming into the ranch office. "The sheriff's here, 'n he wants to see you."

"Sheriff Colby wants to see me?" Franklin asked.

"Yes, sir, that's what he said. He said he wanted to see Tilden Franklin."

"Slade, you, Drake, and Bardsley go out the back door. There's no need for him to see any of you here."

"He's done seen me," Bardsley said.

"Perhaps so, but at this point, you could be no more than one of my cowhands, and I would just as soon have him believe that. Just do what I say."

"You heard the man, Bardsley. Let's get out of here," Slade said.

Franklin waited until the three men who were drawing fighting wages had left his office. Then he opened the door and looked out front. Sheriff Colby was standing near a sapling.

"Come on in, Sheriff."

"Are we alone?" Colby asked.

"We're alone."

Colby stepped into the office with Franklin.

"What have you got for me?" Franklin asked.

"Would you like to know who it was that kilt your three men?"

"Hell, I know who it was. It was Smoke Jensen."

Colby smiled and shook his head. "No, it wasn't him."

"It wasn't? Then who the hell was it?"

"It was his wife."

"What? His wife?"

Colby nodded and said, "Yep, it was Sally Jensen what did the deed."

"I'll be damned," Franklin said. "Who would have thought a woman could shoot like that?"

"Yeah, well, you have to figure it like this," Sheriff Colby said. "Sally Jensen ain't just an ordinary woman. She's Smoke Jensen's wife, 'n you have to know that he's learned her to shoot real good."

"So, what do we do now?" Franklin said.

"You let me take care of that."

Colby sounded confident enough, but Franklin gave him a hard look and said, "You had better not let me down, Sheriff. I've been disappointed enough lately . . . and I don't like the feeling."

CHAPTER 25

End of track

Sally rode her mare out to end of track, arriving about suppertime. There were more than a dozen campfires with groups of men gathered around each, many of them Chinese. At one of the fires, she saw Smoke with Fred Malone and another man she didn't recognize. Smoke saw her about as quickly as she had seen him, and he stood and walked out to greet her. He was smiling, but there was a look of concern in his eyes, as well.

"Sally, what are you doing here?" he asked as she dismounted. "Not that I'm not happy to see you."

"Oh, Smoke," Sally said, throwing her arms around him and placing her head on his chest.

He instinctively returned the embrace and patted her on the back in a comforting fashion. "Sweetheart, what is it? What's wrong?"

Sally leaned back and told Smoke about the incident with the three men.

Smoke tightened his arms around her and drew her close to him, because he knew that she needed it. And, if truth be told, he needed it, as well. Thank God he had taught her to shoot, or he could have had another tragedy on his hands, as with Nicole.

"And you think they were after Sue Ellen?"

"That's who they said they were after. They said that they intended to take her and kill me. Oh, Smoke, I've never had to shoot anyone before. But I remembered what you told me when you talked about how to react in a 'kill or be killed' situation."

"I am so glad you remembered that lesson."

"But I feel so awful. You've done this before. Does it ever get any easier?"

"It's never easy to take a human life," Smoke said. "But it does get easier to recognize the need for doing it. Come, let's talk to Big Cat. Then I'll introduce you to Frank Magee."

"Mrs. Jensen," Malone said, standing to greet her when she approached the campfire. Magee stood, as well.

"Frank, this is Sally, my wife," Smoke said. "Sally, Mr. Magee is the engineer in charge of building this railroad. He is the one who determines exactly where the track is to go, and not one rail is laid without his approval."

"My, that is a most demanding and responsible job," Sally said.

"I was told by Palmer that he is the best there is, and after seeing him work, I agree with that," Malone said.

Sally and Magee exchanged greetings, then Sally turned to address Fred Malone.

"Before I tell you what I came out here to tell, I want you to know that Sue Ellen is fine. She is safe at home with Lauren."

"What? Sally, why do you even have to tell me such a thing?"

Sally explained to Malone what had happened. The banker looked more and more shaken as the story came out. His normally ruddy face was pale in the firelight by the time Sally finished.

"Thank God you were with her," Malone said fervently. He turned to Smoke. "Smoke, I need to go home. I'd like to leave first thing in the morning, and if you don't mind, I'd like you to go with me."

"Of course I'll go with you."

"Oh, and as far as sleeping accommodations go, we've got an empty boxcar now. You and Sally can sleep there."

"Thanks," Smoke said.

On their way back to Trail Back Ranch the next morning, Smoke, Sally, and Fred Malone stopped by Smoke and Sally's ranch. Pearlie was there and had been taking care of things in Smoke's absence.

"I have something else I want you to do," Smoke told the former hired gun.

"All right," Pearlie said without argument. "You're the boss man. One of the fellas who used to work for Franklin—I mean as a regular cowhand, not one of the fightin' crew—drifted in yesterday and was wonderin' if you might be lookin' for fellas to ride for you. I told him to hang around until you got back. His name's Dewey, and I reckon he'd be a good hombre to look after things here for a spell."

"If you trust him, Pearlie, then so do I." Smoke nodded slowly. "If you know any more good cowhands who are looking for work, then after this is all over you can hunt them up. Sally and I have been taking care of the chores ourselves for the past couple of years, but with all the changes going on in these parts, I have a hunch the Sugarloaf is going to need a real crew before too much longer."

Pearlie grinned and said, "I got that same hunch. I'll go tell Dewey he's ridin' for the brand, then I'll take care of whatever else it is you want me to do."

At a brisk pace, it took them no more than half an hour to cover the distance between the Jensen ranch and Trail Back. Sue Ellen met them on the front porch when they arrived.

"Sue Ellen, sweetheart!" Malone said, dismounting and going quickly to embrace his daughter. "Are you all right?"

"I'm fine, Papa," Sue Ellen said. She looked toward Sally and smiled. "Thanks to Miz Sally."

"Yes, she told us about the confrontation you had."

"Papa, why do you think they wanted to snatch me?"

"They were trying to get to me through you, sweetheart," Malone answered. "They know that if they held you captive, I would do anything to get you back safely."

"Oh," Sue Ellen said, with a little cry. Her face contorted in fear as she lifted her hand to her mouth.

"But you needn't worry about it, because we aren't going to let anything happen to you."

"How do you intend to prevent it from happening?" Lauren asked, having come out onto the porch to join them.

"We're going to stop it two ways," Smoke said. "The first thing we're going to do is leave Pearlie here, while I go after whoever is behind all this. Pearlie's a good man and won't let anything happen."

"Ma'am," Pearlie said to Lauren with a polite nod as he pinched the brim of his black hat. He nodded to Sue Ellen as well and added, "Miss. I give you my word I won't allow no varmints anywhere near you."

Despite his rough appearance and reputation as a gunman, both women appeared to be comforted by Pearlie's pledge.

Sally said to Smoke, "I'm going with you."

"Shouldn't you stay here to look after Sue Ellen?" Smoke asked.

She replied with a wry smile, "Why, Smoke, are you suggesting Pearlie isn't capable enough to leave here by himself?"

"No, I'm not saying that. I'm . . ." Smoke paused in mid-sentence and returned Sally's smile. "You win," he said. "Sally, you come with me."

Smoke and Sally rode into Fontana. It had been their intention to go to the sheriff's office, but it was dinnertime by the time they arrived. As they rode down the street, they saw that several of the businesses were either closed or had signs up announcing their imminent closing.

"It looks like our choices as to where we might eat are somewhat limited," Smoke said. "Lambert's and the City Pig have already moved to Big Rock."

"I want to see the sheriff, though," Sally said. "I told him what happened, but I want you to talk to him, as well."

"All right. We'll go see the sheriff, and then we'll try to find us a place to eat."

Smoke and Sally rode down to the sheriff's office, dismounted, tied their horses at the hitch rail, then went inside. There they were met, not by Sheriff Colby, but by Deputy Monte Carson.

"Hello, Monte," Smoke greeted.

"Hello, Smoke, Sally. You haven't encountered anyone else on the road, have you? I mean, you haven't had to—"

"No," Sally said, speaking before Carson could finish his question. "Just the three I told you about. Is the sheriff in town? I wanted Smoke to talk to him."

"No, I haven't seen Colby in quite a while," Carson answered. "Not since right after you were here yesterday, in fact." He shook his head. "I can't figure out where he might've gotten off to, but I've been trying to hold down the fort."

"We're about to have dinner," Smoke said. "Would you like to join us?"

"Where are you going to eat?"

Smoke chuckled. "I don't know. I was sort of hoping you would have an idea."

"Louis Longmont hasn't completely moved to Big Rock yet," Carson said. "And his place, even though it is primarily a saloon, puts out a pretty good meal." He looked toward Sally. "And it is a decent enough place that a woman can go in without causing talk."

"What do you think, Sally?"

"Sounds fine to me," Sally said.

Smoke, Sally, and Carson left the sheriff's office, then walked down the street toward Longmont's Saloon.

"This entire town is dying," Carson said, pointing to the CLOSED and CLOSING SOON signs. "Everyone seems to be moving to Big Rock."

"Well, I'm glad our little town is growing," Smoke said. "But it wasn't my intention to kill Fontana."

"Believe me, Smoke, if this town were to dry up and blow away, it would be no great loss. It isn't a free town, anyway, not as long as Tilden Franklin has his hold over it. What he doesn't own outright, he holds the mortgage on, so it might as well be his property."

The three were greeted by Louis Longmont as soon as they stepped inside the saloon.

"Monsieur et Madame Jensen, et la loi locale. A quoi doisje l'honneur de votre visite?"

"Merci pour votre salutation chaleureuse, M. Longmont."

"Ah, quelle charmante dame, et vous parlez français."

"Oui. Le français est une belle langue."

"What in the world was all that?" Carson asked as he stared at Longmont and Sally.

"The lovely lady and I were exchanging greetings in French," Longmont said. "And how beautiful it sounded on her lips."

"You didn't say anything you didn't want us to hear, did you?" Carson asked.

Longmont smiled. "We will repeat it in English."

"With your accent, how will we know it's in English?" Carson teased.

"I will begin," Longmont said. "Mr. and Mrs. Jensen, and the local law. To what do I owe the honor of your visit?"

"Thank you for your warm greeting, Mr. Longmont," Sally replied.

"Oh, what a lovely lady, and you speak French."

"Yes. French is a beautiful language."

"I didn't know your wife spoke French," Carson said to Smoke.

"Oh, Sally is just full of surprises," Smoke answered. "I wouldn't be surprised if she knows two or three more languages."

"Louis, we've come for dinner. What is on your menu for tonight?" Sally asked.

"For an appetizer, a tart made of Roquefort cheese and caramelized onion, followed by a nice tomato bisque and chicken cooked in a wine sauce."

"Oh, what a lovely-sounding dinner," Sally said. "I do hope you continue with this menu once you are relocated to Big Rock."

"But of course, except that it will be even better," Longmont promised.

Monte Carson looked around at their rough surroundings and said, "Fancy-sounding food like that in a place like this. When you were bartending at the Blue Dog, I never would've expected such from you, Longmont."

"Madame Jensen is not the only one full of surprises, *n'est-ce pas?*"

"Yeah, whatever you say, I reckon."

Haywood Arden came into the saloon then, and seeing Smoke, Sally, and Carson talking with Longmont, he came over to join them.

"What are you doing back in town, Haywood? I thought you and your lovely wife had moved to Big Rock," Longmont said.

"I have come to talk to you, Louis," the newspaper publisher replied.

"What do you mean, you came to talk to me?"

"I just wanted to make certain that you aren't going to move the location for your saloon. Right now, it is next door to my newspaper office."

"Right next to your newspaper office? What's the matter? You don't want to be that far away from a drink?" Carson teased.

"It's just I have found that the best place to gather news is in a saloon," Arden replied.

"And get a drink?" Carson asked.

"Well, where else would one go to get a drink?" Arden replied. "One would hardly be able to get a drink at Roy Beck's blacksmith shop, now would one?"

"I guess you've got me on that one," Carson replied with a chuckle.

"Say, Mr. Arden, that was a fine article you wrote in your newspaper about the new town," Smoke said.

"Yes, it was," Longmont agreed. "It was much better than the article you wrote about the railroad."

"I'm sorry about the railroad article," Arden said. "But, as I hinted in this last article I wrote, I was intimidated into writing it. I regret now having succumbed to Franklin's pressure, and never again will I besmirch the free press in such a way."

"You know, Louis, Mr. Arden does have a point," Smoke said. "Your saloon would make a fine addition to Big Rock." He turned to the deputy. "How soon do you want to come over, Monte? We've already started building a sheriff's office for you."

"How soon do you want me over there?"

"That's up to you," Smoke replied. "Any time is fine, once you think you can leave Fontana in Sheriff Colby's hands."

"Since I don't know where Sheriff Colby's hands are right now—or the rest of him, neither—I'd best stay on here for the time being." Carson nodded slowly and added, "But I've got to admit, being the sheriff of Big Rock has a mighty nice ring to it."

CHAPTER 26

After dinner, Smoke, Sally, and Monte Carson returned to the sheriff's office. When they went inside, they saw Sheriff Colby sitting at his desk.

"Hello, Sheriff," Smoke said.

"Hi, Sheriff. Where've you been?" Carson asked.

Colby glared at Carson. "I'm the sheriff. You're the deputy. It ain't none of your business where I've been."

"I suppose you're right about that," Carson said without losing his temper. "I'll have to remember that, now that I'm a sheriff."

"What do you mean, now that you are a sheriff?"

"Smoke offered me the job of being sheriff over in Big Rock, and I've taken him up on it."

"There is no Big Rock," Colby said. "You'll be the sheriff of a town that don't even exist."

"Oh, but we soon will exist," Smoke said. "I've called a meeting of the citizens of Big Rock, and we'll be filing incorporation papers soon. By the time the railroad reaches Big Rock, I believe it will be a well-established town, perhaps with a population that is even larger than Fontana's."

"What do you want, Jensen?" Colby asked with a scowl. "Why are you in my office?"

"I was wondering if you had any information on the three men my wife encountered between Big Rock and Trail Back yesterday."

"You're talking about the three men your wife killed?"

"I don't know that I would put it exactly like that," Smoke replied, surprised not only by the sheriff's reply but also by the tone of his voice.

"You are the one who killed them, aren't you, Mrs. Jensen?"

"Well, yes, but I had no choice," Sally said. "I had to kill them."

"What do you want to know about them?" Colby asked.

"Do you know who they were?" Smoke asked.

"No, not yet. That's where I've been today, trying to find out who they were and exactly what happened."

"What do you mean by exactly what happened, Sheriff? I told you exactly what happened," Sally said.

"You also told me you're the one who killed them. I'm an officer of the law, Miz Jensen. When somebody comes to tell me they've kilt someone, it's my job to find out ever'thing about it that I can. I'm sure you can understand that most of the time when someone kills someone else, they lie about it."

"I assure you, Sheriff, I am not lying."

"You won't mind if I do a little more investigatin' on it, though, will you?"

"Of course I won't mind. That's the reason my husband and I have come to see you, to request that you do a thorough investigation."

"We'll expect you to find out the identity of the three men, who sent them, and why they wanted to kidnap

Sue Ellen Malone. Because if you won't find out, I will," Smoke said.

"What do you mean, you'll find out? What right do you have to meddle in my investigation?"

"I am a deputy US marshal," Smoke replied.

"Well, you ain't a deputy US marshal here. I'm the sheriff of Fontana."

"Sheriff, I have police authority anywhere in Colorado or anywhere in Wyoming, or anywhere in Alabama, for that matter. As I said, I am a deputy *US* marshal, and that gives me jurisdiction anywhere in the entire country." Smoke emphasized *US*.

Sheriff Colby was a little taken aback by Smoke's response. "Yes, well, I guess that's right. But I do expect you to keep me informed as to what you find out in your investigation. Oh, and, uh, I'll let you know what I'm finding out, too."

"Yes," Judge Briggs said. "As a deputy United States marshal, Mr. Jensen's authority isn't constrained by location."

"I'm afraid that's going to cause Franklin some problems," Colby replied.

Briggs opened a drawer in his desk, took out a bottle of whiskey and, without offering any of it to Colby, raised the bottle to his lips and took several deep swallows. His Adam's apple bobbed up and down.

"Of course," he said when he finally lowered the bottle. Then he swiped the back of his hand across his mouth before he continued, "If we can give Jensen enough to worry about, he may become distracted enough that he won't have time to deal with Mr. Franklin."

"What do you mean, if we give him enough to worry about? What can we do to worry him?"

Briggs smiled. "I can issue a warrant, charging his wife with murder."

Big Rock

Everyone who had moved to Big Rock, and even those who had yet to do so but who intended to, had gathered on the street in front of the sheriff's office. Smoke had called them together with the intention of getting their approval for incorporating the settlement into an actual town, and even though women were not allowed to vote, they were present for the meeting, as well.

Smoke stood on the porch of the new sheriff's office and looked out over the gathering. There were at least 150 people present, certainly enough to start a new town.

"Folks, it is my intention to go to the county seat at Red Cliff and file the incorporation papers that will be necessary to make Big Rock a town. And I have called all of you together because I will need the support from a majority of you before I can approach the county judge."

"Why should we bother with all that?" Baker asked. "I mean, if we are a town, won't that mean that the county and state government will be tellin' us what we can and can't do?"

Smoke chuckled. "As long as we are in the county and the state, they can tell us what we can and can't do, anyway. But if we are incorporated, we'll have some self-government, which means we'll have a little more say-so in our own affairs."

"It also means we can be taxed for our property, too, doesn't it?" Vernon Mathis asked.

"Yes," Smoke agreed. "But a town can't function without a source of income."

"Smoke is right," Carson said. "If you are going to have a sheriff here, or even a town marshal, you are going to have to pay for it."

"I say we should incorporate," Louis Longmont said. "If I'm going to open a saloon here, I shall certainly want the protection of a sheriff."

"Well, I'll tell you this," one of the others said. "I sure as hell don't want a town without a saloon."

The others laughed, but then they voted, and there was overwhelming approval for incorporation. Smoke agreed to take the petition to Red Cliff.

The town of Red Cliff, the county seat, was slightly larger than Fontana, which was the only other incorporated municipality in Summit County.

Sally had come with Smoke, and they dismounted in front of the log building that served as the county court-house, then went inside. The courthouse had offices for the mayor, the county sheriff, and the circuit judge.

"Somethin' I can do for you?" the sheriff asked when Smoke and Sally stepped inside.

"We would like to see the judge," Smoke said.

"What for?"

"Because we have business with him."

"I'm Sheriff Walker. If you want to see the judge, you have to come through me. Who are you?" There was a challenging arrogance to the sheriff's demeanor.

"All right, Sheriff, if that's the way you do things here. My name is Smoke Jensen, and I would like to speak with the judge."

"You're . . . you're Smoke Jensen?" The challenge and the arrogance were gone.

"Yes, and if the judge isn't too busy, we would like to see him."

"Yes, sir, he isn't busy at all. It's just that I'm s'posed to tell 'im before I let anyone in to see him. I hope you don't take nothin' wrong about it."

"Not at all," Smoke said with a smile.

The sheriff stepped into another room, and a moment later he and another man came out. The second man was dignified-looking, trim, clean-shaven, and with white hair.

"Mr. Jensen?" the white-haired man said, extending his hand. "I'm Judge Martin Fielding. I assume you are here to see me about your wife."

Smoke got a confused look on his face, and when he looked over at Sally, he saw that she was just as confused as he was.

"No, I'm here to incorporate a new town," Smoke said.

"You would be talking about the town they are building at what will be the terminus of the Mountain and Pacific Railroad?"

"Yes. Why did you think I was here about my wife?"

"It will be good to have another town in Summit County. There are only two towns in the entire county now, and I have a feeling that Fontana won't be around much longer."

"Judge Fielding, what did you mean when you asked if I was here about my wife?"

"Well, I, uh, assumed that you were here to talk about the murder warrant that has been issued for your wife," Judge Fielding said.

"What murder warrant?" Smoke literally shouted as

Sally clutched his arm, just as surprised as he was. "What are you talking about?"

"Judge Briggs in Fontana has issued a warrant on Mrs. Smoke Jensen for the murder of Ian Dolan, Marv Cooley, and Milt Wolcott. Did you, uh, kill those men, Mrs. Jensen?"

"I suppose so," Sally said.

"You suppose so? Mrs. Jensen, that's a rather strange answer, isn't it? Did you or did you not kill those three men?"

"I shot and killed three men in self-defense," Sally said. "My response to your question is because I didn't know their names."

"And I didn't know Fontana had a judge," Smoke said.

"Actually, Briggs is a justice of the peace, assigned to Fontana."

"Are you also a justice of the peace?"

"No, I'm a circuit judge with jurisdiction over the entire county." He chuckled. "At the moment that is Red Cliff and Fontana. Once we get your town incorporated, however, I'll have three towns."

"Your Honor, could you, by mandamus, hold in abeyance the warrant issued by Mr. Briggs?" Sally asked.

"Hold in abeyance by mandamus? Oh, my, are you a lawyer, Mrs. Jensen?"

"I'm not a lawyer, Your Honor, but I am relatively well read."

"Yes, I would say that you are. I'll tell you what I can do. If you would surrender yourself to my court, I can grant you release upon your own recognizance."

"Thank you, Your Honor." Sally lifted her chin and went on in a formal tone, "I hereby surrender myself to your court."

Judge Fielding wrote out a certificate of release and handed it to Sally. "If Sheriff Walker or Sheriff Colby or Deputy Carson attempts to serve the warrant, show them this."

"Thank you," Sally said.

"You do understand that you will still have to stand trial, don't you?" Fielding asked.

"We want to stand trial," Sally said.

"We do?" Smoke asked.

"Yes," Sally said. "Once we get this over with, it can never be brought up again."

"The young lady is right," Fielding said. "It's called double jeopardy."

"Whose court will we be tried in?" Sally asked.

Judge Fielding grimaced slightly and said, "Oh, well, I'm afraid that you will be tried in Judge Briggs's court."

CHAPTER 27

"We are officially a town," Smoke told the others when he returned to Big Rock.

Cheers filled the air as those who had gathered to hear the news waved their hats in the air and slapped each other on the back.

Just as Smoke and Sally took leave of those who were busy building homes and businesses in Big Rock, they happened to run into Monte Carson.

"Monte," Smoke greeted him. "Or should I say Sheriff Carson?"

Carson smiled. "You've got the town incorporated." It wasn't a question; it was an affirmation.

"We do, and your tenure as sheriff officially begins as soon as you resign from your present post as deputy."

"Which will be today," Carson promised.

"Monte, can Sally and I talk to you about something?"

"Yes, of course. Come on into my fancy new office," Carson replied with a wide smile.

Smoke and Sally followed the new sheriff into his office, and he pointed toward the jail cell.

"Look there, my own jail cell," he said. "I can hardly wait until I put someone in there."

"You almost didn't have to wait at all," Sally said.

"What do you mean?"

"I could have been your first prisoner. Your first customer, so to speak."

Carson shook his head and said, "Miz Sally, I don't have the slightest idea what you are talking about."

Smoke told Carson about the warrant Briggs had issued.

"That sidewinder!" Carson said, striking his fist into his open palm. "Excuse the language, ma'am."

"Do you know Briggs very well?" Smoke asked. "Do you have any idea why he would do such a thing?"

"Franklin," Carson said without a second's hesitation. "Briggs won't put on his boots without Franklin's permission, and if he did this, you can bet your bottom dollar that Franklin is behind it."

"It stands to reason," Sally said. "Those men, Dolan, Cooley, and Wolcott, said they were going to take Sue Ellen to the Circle TF."

The front door banged open, and Sheriff Colby barged in. "All right, Carson, if you really are a sheriff, I've got a warrant you can serve if you happen to see . . ." Colby stopped in midsentence and stared at Smoke and Sally. "You!" he said to Sally. "What are you doing here?"

"I have just surrendered myself to Sheriff Carson," Sally said. "I am the one you have the warrant for, aren't I?"

"Yes, but see here, I'm the one that's s'posed to serve the warrant. You ain't Carson's prisoner. You're my prisoner, 'n you're comin' back to Fontana with me."

"She's going nowhere with you, Colby," Smoke said.

"I . . . I don't want no trouble with you, Jensen. I've got a job to do, is all."

"I've been released on my own recognizance," Sally said, showing the bond to Sheriff Colby.

Colby looked at it. "That don't mean nothin'. That ain't Briggs's name there."

"No, it is Judge Fielding's name," Smoke said. "He is the one who granted a certificate of release to my wife."

"But he can't do that. He ain't the one who issued the warrant," Colby insisted.

"You do realize that Judge Fielding's position as a judge of the circuit court is higher than Briggs's position as a justice of the peace, don't you?" Smoke asked.

"Briggs is the one who's goin' to hold the trial, 'n it's goin' to be in Fontana," Colby insisted.

"I'll come to Fontana," Sally said. "Trust me, Sheriff, I want this farce to be over with."

From the *Big Rock Bulletin:*

MRS. SMOKE JENSEN
To Be Tried for Murder.

In what has to be the biggest miscarriage of justice in the history of Colorado, both while it was a territory and since it achieved statehood, Mrs. Sally Jensen has been put in a position where her very life is at stake.

Mrs. Jensen killed three men who had accosted her at gunpoint, with the intention of killing her and kidnapping Miss Sue Ellen Malone. This writer does not understand why a trial is even necessary, as it was obviously justifiable homicide, by right of self-defense.

Mrs. Jensen's performance on that day should be lauded as an act of heroism, not an act of murder. This newspaper is going on record as declaring this trial to be illegal, and should she be convicted, the newspaper will lead the appeal campaign for judicial correction of the misdeed.

Haywood Arden's newspaper article resonated not only with the new residents of Big Rock, but also with those who, though they remained in Fontana, were still subscribers to Arden's journalistic endeavors. Most were stirred by curiosity, and many by a sense of perceived injustice, and a few, for one reason or another, wished to see Sally found guilty.

One of the people who learned that Sally was to be tried was their old friend Preacher.

"What are you lettin' yourself get tried for?" Preacher asked. "You know they ain't goin' to be fair to you."

Preacher was at the Jensen ranch house on the Sugarloaf, having learned of the upcoming trial when he went into Fontana to buy some Arbuckles' coffee.

"I think it has reached the point where I have no choice," Sally said. "A warrant has been issued on me, and I see no other way to deal with it."

"If you was to ask me, we'd do just like we done it 'n Bury. We'd just kill ever' piece of dirt that was wantin' you to be tried."

"Preacher, has it occurred to you that the reason I'm in trouble in the first place is that I killed someone?" Sally asked.

"Hell, yes, it occurred to me. Fact is, the way I heared it, you didn't just shoot someone. You kilt three someones.

'N if they was doin' what I've been told they was doin', why, them sorry snakes in the grass needed to be kilt."

"There's a lot to what you're saying, Preacher," Smoke said. "The three men Sally shot, Ian Dolan, Marv Cooley, and Milt Wolcott, are wanted in three states. Instead of being tried, she should be given a reward."

"When is it that you're a-goin' into town?" Preacher asked.

"We're going now," Smoke said.

"I'm comin' with you," Preacher insisted, walking over to the corner to pick up his buffalo rifle.

"Uh-uh," Smoke said, shaking his head, with a smile. "You can come with us, but that buffalo rifle stays here."

"All right," Preacher agreed. "But there may come a time in all this that you'll be a-wishin' I had my rifle with me."

The three, accompanied by the new sheriff of Big Rock, started out on the ride to Fontana, with Preacher still insisting that he should have brought his rifle with him.

When they rode into town, they were struck by the number of people they saw in the street and on the porches and boardwalks in front of the buildings.

"There's Louis Longmont," Smoke said.

"And there's Mr. Murchison and Mr. Lambert," Sally pointed out.

"Looks like ever'body in the whole county is here," Preacher said. He chuckled. "'Course, there ain't that many people in Summit County."

"Look over there," Carson said. "Colby, Briggs, and Tilden Franklin."

"You didn't expect Franklin to miss this show, did you?" Smoke asked.

Never in the history of Fontana had there been so many gathered for any occasion as were gathered for the trial of Sally Jensen. And although Fontana had lost almost half of its population, the size of the crowd was augmented by the fact that nearly everyone from Big Rock, most of whom were former residents of Fontana, had come to town just for the trial.

Tilden Franklin, Judge Lloyd Briggs, and Sheriff Emanuel Colby were standing in front of the Fontana sheriff's office, which was also the only municipal building in town.

"There she is," Colby told the two men with him as he pointed toward Sally, Smoke, and Preacher.

"They brought that old man into town with them," Franklin said.

"Do you know him, Mr. Franklin?" Briggs asked. "The old man, I mean."

"Yes, I know him. He's one of the original settlers in the Uncompahgre. Hell, in all of Colorado. He's a cantankerous old scoundrel. They call him Preacher."

"Look at all them people that's a-comin' into town," Colby said. "They're most likely comin' for the trial, 'n there ain't no way in hell we can get 'em all into this here buildin'."

"You may hold the trial in the Blue Dog Saloon," Franklin said.

"You're sayin' we should use the saloon?"

"Why not? It's the biggest building in town."

"It's too bad we don't have a prosecuting attorney," Briggs said. "As it is, we will merely present the charges. But I've been told that the Jensen woman intends to defend herself, so it should be no problem to get our jury to convict her. Have either of you ever seen a woman hanged before?"

"No, I ain't never seen no woman hung," Colby said.

"I was present when Mary Surratt went to the gallows," Franklin said.

"Who's that?" Colby asked.

"She was part of the Lincoln assassination conspirators. And I figure if the United States government can hang a woman, we can. By the way, don't worry about not having a prosecutor. I've hired Jason Freeze to act as our prosecutor."

"You have hired Jason Freeze?" Briggs asked. "Are you talking about that lawyer from Denver?"

"Yes."

"Damn, Mr. Franklin. Jason Freeze is the best lawyer in the state. Some say he's the best lawyer west of the Mississippi River. And you say you have hired him to act as the prosecutor?"

"I have."

"How in the hell did you ever convince someone like Jason Freeze to come to a tiny town like Fontana and to take part in a trial no bigger than this?"

"Judge Briggs, it has been my observation that you can get just about anyone to do anything if you are willing to pay them enough," Franklin said. "And in this case, I am willing to pay enough to get the job done."

Even though the Blue Dog was the biggest building in town, it wasn't large enough to accommodate all who wanted to come to the trial. In addition to Sheriff Monte Carson, Louis Longmont and Hog Jaw Lambert were among those who came over from Big Rock, and Big Cat Malone, his wife, Lauren, and their daughter, Sue Ellen, were also present. Sue Ellen, of course, was a material witness, and her parents had come to provide her with moral support.

A surprise visitor to the trial was the circuit judge Martin Fielding.

"Look here, Judge, this is my trial," Briggs said. "You've got no business here interfering."

"Don't get all out of sorts, Briggs," Judge Fielding said. He took in all the others who were coming into the saloon. "I'm just part of the gallery."

"All right," Briggs said. "As long as you're just here watching, and you recognize my authority to conduct the trial."

"I'm perfectly willing to do that, Briggs, as long as you realize that the findings in your court are subject to appeal. And if that should happen, then it will come under my jurisdiction."

CHAPTER 28

Pearlie Fontaine was sitting at a table in the newly built bunkhouse. He was playing solitaire, which was fitting, because he was the only one on the premises of Sugarloaf.

"Sugarloaf." He chuckled as he said the name aloud, because he had never heard of a ranch being called such a thing.

The reason Pearlie was alone was that Smoke and Miz Sally had gone to Fontana for Miz Sally's trial. There were three other cowboys who would normally be here, but they, too, had gone to Fontana to be present at the trial.

"If them town varmints wind up sayin' Miz Sally is guilty, they're goin' to play hell puttin' her in jail," Charley Cooper had said earlier. "You know damn well Smoke ain't goin' to let 'em do that, 'n I'll be right there with Smoke."

"Me, too," the other two men had added.

Pearlie had wanted to go into town, as well, but Smoke had asked him to stay behind and "keep an eye on the place," and that was what he was doing. Although his eyes weren't "on the place" as much as they were on the cards spread out on the table in front of him.

"Damn, I need a red ten," he said aloud.

Pearlie was so engrossed with his game that he had no idea the ranch was under the observation of two men.

"You sure there ain't goin' to be nobody here?" Miller asked.

"Slade said there wouldn't be nobody," Boyce said. "He said they'd more'n likely all be in town today, on account of the woman is bein' tried for murder."

"You reckon they'll hang her?" Miller asked. "I ain't never seen no woman get herself hung."

The two men had just ridden up, and now they were sitting in their saddles on a small ridge, looking down at the place. They were mounted on Circle TF horses today, having left their regular horses in one of the corrals back at Franklin's ranch.

"It sure don't look like there's anybody there," Miller said.

"Slade said there wouldn't be nobody here," Boyce said. "That sure is a purty house Jensen has built," Boyce said. "Seems like a shame to burn it."

"You heard what Slade said. He wants us to burn the whole damn place down. House, bunkhouse, barn, all of it."

"That sure is a big house. I don't know if we got us enough coal oil to set it on fire," Boyce said.

"How much coal oil does it take just to get it started? The house is all made out of wood, so all you got to do is get it started."

"Well, come on. We might as well get a-burnin'," Boyce said.

Inside the bunkhouse, Pearlie had just turned up the ten of hearts in his shuffling of the cards and triumphantly laid it on the jack of clubs. He heard horses approaching, and thinking it might be some of the other cowboys, or maybe even Smoke and Sally, he got up from the table and walked over to the door to look outside.

It wasn't Smoke and Sally; it wasn't even any of the other Sugarloaf hands. He had no idea who these two men were, but when he saw one of the men dismount, then start walking toward the corner of the house, carrying a can of coal oil, he knew they were up to no good.

After going back into the bunkhouse, Pearlie grabbed his rifle, jacked a round into the chamber, then stepped outside again.

"You men, hold it right there!" Pearlie shouted, lifting the rifle to his shoulder.

The mounted intruder shouted out, "We ain't alone!" He pulled his own gun and triggered a shot toward Pearlie. The bullet hit the doorframe right beside Pearlie, throwing splinters in the air, and Pearlie returned fire, his bullet knocking the man from the saddle.

"Boyce!" shouted the man who was standing at the corner of the house. He set down his can of coal oil and pulled his own pistol.

Pearlie levered another round into the chamber of his Winchester. "Drop it!" he called out to the man who was standing at the corner of the house.

Miller responded to the call by shooting at Pearlie. Pearlie returned fire.

Miller missed; Pearlie didn't.

Pearlie stood just outside the bunkhouse. The air was perfumed by the acrid smell of gunpowder. There was no smell of smoke, though, so he was certain that the man who had the can of coal oil had been unable to complete his loathsome task.

Pearlie waited for a minute or two to make sure these

men were the only marauders, and when he was sure he
was alone, he ventured out to check on them. The man
he had shot off the horse was dead. The man by the corner
of the house was still alive, but barely.

"You the one that shot me?" the man gasped.

"Yeah."

"Damn. Slade told us there wouldn't be no one here.
The lyin' buzzard."

"Why did you come to try to burn the house down?"
Pearlie asked.

"On account of that's what he wanted."

"Who wanted? Slade?"

"Yeah, it was Slade." Miller took a couple more rattling
breaths. Then the gasping stopped.

"I know Slade didn't do this on his own. It was Franklin,
wasn't it? I know it was Franklin, because I used to work
for the lowlife." Even before Pearlie finished the question,
he realized that the man he was talking to would be unable
to answer. He, like the other would-be arsonist, was dead.

He wasn't sure what he should do with them. He didn't
want to leave them lying here like this.

One of the two horses the men had been riding whick-
ered. Pearlie looked at it and saw that both of the animals
bore Circle TF brands on their hides. That gave him an
idea.

"I'm goin' to send you two boys back where you come
from," he said. "Someone over at the Circle TF will take
care of you."

He put each of the two men belly down over a saddle.
He didn't know if he got the right man with the right horse,
but truth to tell, it didn't really matter. Using their own
ropes, he tied them securely enough that they would stay
in the saddle, and then he gave each of the horses a slap

on the rump. Just as he thought they would, the two horses took off at a trot.

Pearlie saw that the horses were headed in the direction of the Circle TF Ranch, and he nodded in satisfaction.

On board the Leopoldina, at sea

Hemingford held up the bottle of whiskey that sat on the table between him and Smoke. He turned it so Smoke could clearly see the label.

"Twenty-five-year-old Glenlivet, distilled in Ballindalloch, in Moray, Scotland. I intend to visit the place while I am in Europe." He poured some into Smoke's glass. "Not since you suckled the milk from your mother's breast have you imbibed anything so satisfying."

Smoke chuckled. "I wouldn't be so sure. I've had a cool beer after a week of parching in the desert. This will have to go some to beat that."

Hemingford lifted the glass to his mouth, took a swallow, then smacked his lips in appreciation.

"Let's get back to your story. It looks to me like, in the scheme of things, it was a good thing you left Pearlie behind. Had you not done so, I have no doubt but that you would have lost your house," Hemingford said.

Smoke chuckled. "Would you believe I raised his salary after that?"

"Yes, one would think that would be the thing to do," Hemingford said.

"But to be honest, until that incident where he saved our home, I guess I considered Pearlie as little more than another hired hand. He, and sometime later, Calvin Woods, became almost like family. No, they were more than 'almost.' They *were* family. Still are, in fact."

"Sally was tried for the righteous shooting of the three men who accosted her and Sue Ellen. What about Pearlie? Was he tried for killing the two men who came to burn your house?"

"No. After Pearlie sent the two bodies back to Franklin's ranch, they couldn't accuse Pearlie of the shooting without admitting that they knew the two men had been at my house."

"What about the trial with Sally? You left off just before the trial began."

"I did, didn't I?" Smoke chuckled. "It was something to behold."

Fontana, Colorado

Tables and chairs were arranged in the Blue Dog Saloon to enable it to serve as a courtroom. The saloon was filled to capacity, and several who couldn't find a chair were actually sitting on the bar, while many were standing around the edge of the room. Others were on the second-floor balcony, where some were sitting on the floor with their legs poked between the spindles of the railing. That allowed an additional line of people to stand behind them so they could also follow the proceedings of the "court." This kind of creative accommodation allowed at least two hundred people to be in a room that had never even had a hundred occupants before.

Smoke and Sally were sitting at a table that was in front and on the left side, while Jason Freeze sat alone at the front table that was on the right.

There was a constant buzz of conversation until Sheriff Colby, who was acting as the bailiff, stepped out in front and held both arms up.

"Ever'one, shut up your talkin' 'n be quiet now, 'cause

if you don't, you'll get throwed out of here. This here court is about to get goin', with Judge Briggs doin' the judgin'. Thems of you what's got seats, stand up now, while the judge comes into the room."

Lloyd Briggs was already in the room, but he was standing near the piano, out of sight, and now he walked up to the table that would be serving as his "bench," sat down, then banged his gavel against the table.

"Take your seats, and order in the court," he said. "Bailiff, for what purpose is this court assembled?"

"This court is here to find Sally Jensen guilty of murderin' Ian Dolan, Marv Cooley, and Milt Wolcott, so's she can legally be hung."

"Your Honor, I object to the preemptive statement of the bailiff in publishing the purpose of this trial," Sally said.

"Objection sustained," Briggs said. "Colby, you know better than to say something like that."

"Sorry," Colby muttered.

"Is the prosecutor present?" Briggs asked.

Jason Freeze stood. "I am, Your Honor, Jason Freeze, duly appointed to the position of prosecutor for this trial."

"Is counsel for defense present?"

Sally stood. "Your Honor, I will be acting as pro se in my defense."

"You'll be doing what?"

"I will be acting as my own defense counsel."

"Mrs. Jensen, I didn't say anything about your objection a moment ago, because it was a correct objection, but I had no idea you would be representing yourself. Are you a lawyer?"

"No, Your Honor, I'm not."

Briggs shook his head. "Then you are not qualified to represent yourself."

"The Sixth Amendment of the United States Constitution grants me that right, and precedence has been established that the competency standard for waiving the right to counsel at trial is no higher than the general competency standard for standing trial. That is because there is no reason to believe that the decision to waive counsel requires an appreciably higher level of mental functioning than the decision to waive other constitutional rights."

"Look here, Judge Fielding, is that right? Can she really do this?" Briggs asked.

"She has every right to do it," Judge Fielding replied. "And it is incumbent upon you not only to allow this, but also to advise her of her right to exercise peremptory challenges, to make evidentiary objections, to cross-examine prosecution witnesses, to subpoena her own witnesses, and to testify, or to refuse to testify."

"All right. You can serve as your own counsel," Briggs said in a disgruntled tone.

"Your Honor, I waive the right to be told of rights and obligations of counsel, as I just heard them enumerated by Judge Fielding."

"All right, all right," Briggs said, waving his hand. "Bailiff, select the jury."

Colby began seating the jury, which consisted of men who worked on the Circle TF Ranch, as well as businessmen from Fontana who had a pecuniary obligation to Tilden Franklin.

Sally expertly reshaped the jury using preemptive removal as well as removal for cause. By the time the final jury was empaneled Haywood Arden, Norman Lambert, one of the cowboys who rode for the Sugarloaf, and three of the cowboys who rode for Trail Back were on the jury. Sally was satisfied.

CHAPTER 29

Again, Briggs banged his gavel on the table. "With the jury seated and the court in order, Prosecutor, I charge you with making your case."

Jason Freeze stood, and though he walked over to the jury, he positioned himself in such a way so as to be addressing the gallery as much as he was addressing the jury.

"Be sober, be vigilant, because your adversary, the devil, walks about like a roaring lion, seeking whom he may devour. That, my friends is from First Peter, chapter five, verse eight." He pointed at Sally. "With apologies to St. Peter, I am going to make a slight amendment to his admonition, so that it would read, 'walks about like a beautiful woman, seeking whom she may devour.'"

Freeze made a dramatic pause and stared at Sally in an attempt to intimidate her. Sally smiled back at him, and he cleared his throat and turned away from her.

"I am told that the seventh day of this month was a beautiful day, with the sun in a clear blue sky, and a gentle breeze that ameliorated the natural heat of a July morning. Three fine young men, Ian Dolan, Marv Cooley, and Milt Wolcott, went out, as friends will do, to take a ride together, to enjoy that beautiful day. Their hearts, no doubt, beat a little faster with the joy they felt over being with friends on such a magnificent day. But tragically, these good men, brothers in the soul, if not in the flesh, would be dead before nightfall."

Freeze paused for a moment to let the heartrending words sink in.

"Where were these three musketeers going? And yes, I call them musketeers, because Athos, Porthos, and Aramis of the story had no closer relationship than Dolan, Cooley, and Wolcott. Well, they might have been going fishing, or they may have been out just enjoying the ride, though it is more likely they were coming right here, to this place, to enjoy convivial conversation and a beer."

Freeze smiled. "You have heard the old adage that some see half a glass of water and will say that it is half empty, and some will see it is half full. But it was said by friends of Ian Dolan that given such a choice to make, he would pour out the half-full or half-empty glass of water and fill it with beer."

The gallery laughed.

The smile left Freeze's face, and again, he assumed a demeanor of sadness, before continuing. "But, woefully, as it turned out, our three musketeers encountered Sally Jensen on the road. How did they handle this encounter? Well, they were young, virile men who had unexpectedly come in contact with a beautiful young woman, and not just one beautiful young woman, but two beautiful young women, as Sue Ellen Malone was riding in the buckboard with Sally Jensen.

"I have no doubt but that they behaved in a flirtatious manner. I am sure that they, as young men are wont to do, made what may have been considered a few ribald, perhaps even untoward remarks. This is the nature of young men, and young women have traditionally treated such an advance in two ways. Either they have participated in the flirtatious behavior or they have told the man in no uncertain terms that they don't appreciate such talk."

Freeze paused for a long moment. Then he pointed at Sally and said in a rather loud voice, "As a rule they do not, as this woman did, kill someone in retaliation for an innocent flirtation!"

Freeze stood for a long moment to allow his last, damning comment to resonate, and then he took his seat.

"Counsel for defense," Judge Briggs said.

Sally got to her feet and walked over to address the jury.

"I don't know if you have ever seen a woman lawyer before. Well, there are a few. Arabella Mansfield and Myra Brandfield are a couple that come to mind. I'm not a lawyer, but I'm sure you heard in the trial preliminaries how it is that I am perfectly qualified to act in my own defense."

Sally smiled disarmingly at the jury, and then she looked back toward Freeze.

"Of course, when I made the decision to represent myself, I had no idea that I would, literally, be pleading for my life against such a formidable opponent. You may wonder why such a well-known and powerful lawyer would come to the small town of Fontana to act as prosecutor in this case. The answer is, he was brought here by a citizen who, though he has no standing, paid an exorbitant fee to Mr. Freeze to prosecute this case.

"What do I mean by standing? Well, *standing* is a legal term used in connection with any court trial, and to establish that standing, one must meet the requirement of Article III of the United States Constitution. Mr. Franklin does not meet that requirement. The law is very clear. It is not enough merely to be a citizen concerned about the case. A party must actually suffer some injury to have standing. Mr. Franklin does not have standing. The lawyer he bought cannot legally act as prosecutor in this case."

"Objection, Your Honor!" Freeze called out. "I am offering my service to the court pro bono. The fact that I have a non-court-related pecuniary relationship with Mr. Franklin has no bearing on this case."

"Objection sustained. Mr. Freeze may continue as prosecuting attorney," Briggs said. "Mrs. Jensen, you may continue with your opening remarks."

Sally smiled at Freeze and nodded her head ever so slightly before turning back to the jury.

"That's all right. Spirited women have stood up to such men before, powerful men like Jason Freeze, or in the case of Tilden Franklin . . ." She paused for a long moment, then added, "Evil men."

There was a gasp from the gallery but no outburst.

"Your Honor, this concludes my opening. I will give a more thorough defense during the course of the trial."

"Very well. You may be seated. Mr. Prosecutor, call your first witness."

Freeze called a series of witnesses, men who had known Dolan, Cooley, and Wolcott at the Circle TF Ranch.

"They was good ole boys, if you ask me," Drake said.

Drake's comments were typical, but after cross-examining several of the witnesses and finding her cross-examination nonproductive, Sally passed on any further cross-examination until Jack Slade took the stand. Pearlie had reminded her about Slade the very day he came to work for Franklin.

"Slade is as bad as they come, Miz Sally," Pearlie had told her. "He's a cattle thief, a bank robber, and a gunman.

He's sold his gun all over Colorado, Wyoming, Idaho. To tell you the truth, I don't know how it is that he ain't been hung long before now."

Sally kept that conversation in mind as Freeze examined his witness. Slade was wearing a dark jacket and a white shirt with a dark red cravat. He had a nervous habit of running his finger over his well-trimmed mustache as he was listening to the questions.

"Mr. Slade, I'll ask you as I have asked all the others. How well did you know these three men?"

"I knew 'em a lot better 'n any of the others."

"The truth is, when you arrived to take your employment at the Circle TF Ranch, Dolan, Cooley, and Wolcott came with you. Is that correct?"

"Yeah, that's right. Me 'n them three boys was pards from 'way back. We done lots o' jobs together a'fore we come here to take on this here job for Mr. Franklin. We was just real good friends, we was."

"Did you see Dolan, Cooley, and Wolcott before they left on that fateful morning?"

Slade looked confused by the question. "What kind o' mornin'?"

"On the day they were killed," Freeze clarified. "Did you see them just before they left?"

"Oh, yeah, they wanted me to go with 'em. They was comin' here, to the Blue Dog, to have a couple o' beers. I told 'em I couldn't come, 'cause I had some work to do. I wish now that I had come. If I had, I don't think she could've killed them. They was just ordinary boys 'n wasn't lookin' for her to pull a gun 'n shoot 'em dead like she done, for no reason."

"Your witness," Freeze said as he took his seat.

"Mr. Slade, when you said that you and the decedents

had done some jobs together, were some of those jobs of a nature that would be beyond the parameters of the law?"

"Objection, Your Honor. Mr. Slade is a witness, not a defendant," Freeze called.

"Objection sustained."

"Mr. Slade, what kind of work do you do for Mr. Franklin?"

"I'm sort of a foreman, like."

"You tend cattle?"

"Yeah. That's what you do on a ranch, ain't it?"

"Mr. Slade, what's an acorn calf?"

"An acorn calf? I don't know what you mean."

"It's a weak or runty calf. What's a chopper?"

When Slade still couldn't answer, Sally did. "It's the cowboy who cuts out the cattle during a roundup." She paused. "You don't know any of those terms, because the truth is, your job at the Circle TF Ranch has nothing to do with tending cattle, does it?"

"There's other things to do on a ranch besides tendin' cattle."

"What exactly are these 'other things' that you do for Mr. Franklin?"

"Well, you might say I keep 'im safe, sorta."

"You keep him safe? And how do you do that?"

"I just make sure that if there's anyone that wants to kill Mr. Franklin, well, I'll stop 'em."

"By killing them?"

"Yeah, if I have to."

"How many men have you killed, Mr. Slade?"

"Objection!" Freeze called.

"Your Honor, I'm being accused of murder by a man who is known to be a gunman. I think the court has a right to know how many men Jack Slade has killed."

"The objection is—" Briggs started to say, but Fielding finished the sentence for him.

"Overruled."

"How many men have you killed, Mr. Slade?" Sally repeated.

"I don't know," Slade replied. "I've killed quite a few, I guess."

"Quite a few. Have you killed so many men that you don't even know how many it is?"

"I've killed twenty-three," Slade said.

"You have killed twenty-three, and you haven't been hanged for murder, and you haven't been put into prison. Why is that, Mr. Slade? How is it that you have killed so many men, and yet you haven't been prosecuted for murder?"

"On account of 'cause they wasn't murders!" Slade insisted. "Ever'one I killed was tryin' to kill me."

"So what you are saying, then, is that if someone is forced to kill in an act of self-defense that it isn't murder?"

"Yeah," Slade said.

"And if it is justifiable by an act of self-defense, then the perpetrator of that act should receive no punishment from the state."

"Yeah," Slade replied resolutely. "They shouldn't get no punishment from the state."

"No further questions, Your Honor."

After Slade was dismissed, Sally was given the opportunity to call her own witnesses. The first person she called was Sue Ellen Malone.

The young woman described in vivid detail what had happened that day, how the three men, with guns drawn, had accosted them, with the intention of kidnapping her and killing Sally.

"Were you frightened, Sue Ellen?"

"Frightened? Yes, I was scared to death!"

"Why?"

"Because I thought they were going to kill you and kidnap me."

"Thank you. I have no further questions."

In his cross-examination, Freeze was unable to shake her testimony, especially as to the fact that the three men were already holding guns in their hands when Sally shot them.

Sally's next witness was Monte Carson.

"Sheriff Carson, I have no wish to put you on the spot, but it is generally known that you have been engaged in life-or-death gunfights. Is that true?"

"It is," Carson replied.

"If you are put into a position where you must use your gun against someone who is armed, and who has every intention of using that gun against you, how do you deal with the natural inclination against killing another human being?"

"You have but one choice if you want to come out of that encounter alive," Carson said solemnly. "You must set aside any compunctions you have about shooting another person, because in these situations, it becomes a case of kill or be killed."

Sally's next witness was Louis Longmont. Like Carson, Louis Longmont had a reputation of having used his gun in self-defense. When asked what was the most important thing that one must keep in mind when engaged in a life-or-death gun battle, Louis said substantially the same thing Carson had said. One must set aside any hesitancy about taking the life of another human being, because it would be a situation of kill or be killed.

Sally called Smoke Jensen to the stand.

"May I call you Smoke, Mr. Jensen?" Sally asked with a smile.

"Yeah, sure. That's better than some of the things you've called me," Smoke replied.

The gallery laughed out loud, and Briggs had to use his gavel to restore order.

"Smoke, just so that everyone knows, what is our relationship?"

"We are married," Smoke said. "You are my wife."

"I'm not your first wife, am I?"

"No. I was married before."

"And her name was Nicole?"

"Yes."

"What happened to Nicole?"

"Some gunmen came to the house and killed her," Smoke said quietly, somberly.

"And what action have you taken so that such a thing won't happen to me?"

Smoke smiled. "I've taught you to shoot."

"Based upon what you know of my acumen with a handheld firearm, do you believe that if I had my hand on a pistol and that pistol was hidden beneath the folds of my dress, I could raise that pistol and shoot three men who already had their guns in hand?"

"Oh, yeah, they wouldn't be expecting it. You could do that real easy."

"So, your knowledge of my ability would allow you to substantiate the story told by Sue Ellen?"

"Yes, without a doubt."

"Your witness, Mr. Freeze."

Under questioning by Freeze, Smoke went into some detail as to how he had trained Sally to shoot, and insisted again that she had the capability of dealing with the three men she had encountered exactly as Sue Ellen had testified.

Freeze, realizing too late that he had hurt his own case by this line of questioning, dismissed the witness.

Sally then took the stand, subjecting herself to cross-examination. And, as Sue Ellen had before, Sally did not deviate from her testimony.

"Jack Slade admitted that he has killed men," Sally told the jury in summation. "He insists that they were not murders, because the shootings were in self-defense. And, indeed, those killings that we know about must have been in self-defense, because otherwise he would have been hanged or would be in prison now. But he is here with us. Anyone who kills another person in self-defense is not guilty of murder, because such a killing is justifiable homicide.

"I would like to call to your attention the fact that in this case, there was only one factual witness. By that I mean that there was only one person, besides me, who actually saw what happened. You might say that my testimony was self-serving, but you can't say that of Sue Ellen's. She is under no peril from this trial, and yet Sue Ellen Malone's testimony and my own were exactly the same. Prosecution could produce no witness who, by actual observation, could contradict our testimony. You must find me not guilty."

Freeze, perhaps realizing that he had no sustainable case, made an appeal to the jury that was long on histrionics and short on fact. It was more than just short on fact: he had no facts at all.

Despite the six Franklin people on the jury, the jury found Sally innocent.

CHAPTER 30

Johnny Kincaid, the foreman of the Circle TF Ranch, was a legitimate cowhand. He knew that Franklin wasn't always honest in his dealings, and he knew that Jack Slade and the men with him were all gunmen, though he wasn't exactly sure why Franklin had need of such people.

As far as Kincaid knew, Franklin didn't have a long rope, because he had never seen cattle or horses that had been acquired by any way that wasn't illegal. And more importantly, Kincaid had never been asked to do anything that was illegal.

He knew that the three men who had been killed weren't cowboys working for him but were gunmen working for Jack Slade. Right now, there was a trial going on as to how they had been killed, though the story was they had been killed by a woman.

Kincaid didn't like Dolan, Cooley, or Wolcott, and the truth was, he didn't think their being killed was any great loss. He wished he had been able to go in for the trial, but he didn't think it would be right for him to go in if none of the cowboys who worked for him could.

At the moment, Kincaid was in the barn, separating the harnesses, when Bo James, one of the cowboys, came in.

"Hey, cow boss, there's somethin' out here you ought to see."

"I need to get these harnesses straightened out," Kincaid said.

"No, sir, you need to come see this," James said.

Kincaid shrugged, then walked outside with James.

Two horses were standing just outside the corral gate, as if asking to be allowed in. There was a body lying across the saddle of each horse. At least half a dozen men were standing there, looking at the horses and their grim load.

"Who are they?" Kincaid asked.

"Lobo Miller 'n Pete Boyce. They're Jack Slade's men."

"Then I don't see them as any great loss."

"You have to wonder how they got here, though, don't you? I mean, them bein' dead 'n all."

"Whoever killed 'em just put 'em up on the horses, 'n the horses knew the way home. Get them off the horses. There's no need for the poor animals to have to stand there like that."

"What'll we do with 'em?" James asked.

"Take 'em over 'n lay 'em out in front of Slade's bunkhouse. They're his men. Let him worry about 'em soon as he gets back."

"Here he comes now," James said. "Looks like all of 'em is comin' back now."

Slade, Drake, and the others who had gone into Fontana for the trial came riding in then. They were riding in front of and behind the carriage that was carrying Franklin. The large group raised a considerable amount of dust.

The carriage stopped in front of the big house and the driver hopped down, then came around to open the door for Franklin to exit.

"Thank you, Bertram. You may put the carriage away. I

will have no further need of it," Franklin said as he stepped down.

"Very well, sir," Bertram replied.

One thousand dollars, Franklin thought. He had paid Jason Freeze, supposedly the best lawyer in Colorado, to prosecute the case, and he had been beaten by a woman who wasn't even a lawyer.

Franklin was still fuming over the outcome of the trial when Jack Slade stepped into his office.

"I've got somethin' to tell you, boss," Slade said.

"What is it, Slade?" Franklin asked, his irritation with the outcome of the trial showing in the tone of his voice.

"It's about Boyce and Miller. They're back."

"They're back? Well, at least there's something good about today. Let the Jensens go back to find their house and all the buildings burned to the ground."

"No, sir, it ain't like that," Slade replied. "At least I don't think so, when you consider the way they come back."

"The way they came back? What are you talking about? How did they come back?"

"They come back dead, both of 'em. Kincaid said they was draped across their saddles."

"Tell me, Slade, how many men did you bring here?"

"There was sixteen of 'em," Slade said.

"Sixteen. And now five of them are dead."

"Yeah," Slade said.

"That pretty much decimates your army, doesn't it? I don't know how you expect to get anything accomplished with the men you have left."

"What is it you want done?"

"We sent three who, you assured me, were your best men to capture one young girl, but your three good men were killed by one woman. Then you sent two men to burn down Jensen's house while he was gone, and they came back dead."

Franklin stared coldly at Slade and went on, "You ask what I want? I want the railroad stopped, I want this thing they are building, and calling a town, destroyed, and I want Smoke Jensen dead!"

"I'm going to have to get more men," Slade said.

"Get them. Only this time, find some men who can draw a pistol without shooting themselves in the foot. Can you do that, Slade? Or do I have to hire someone else as captain of my personal militia?"

"I can do it," Slade said.

"Oh, and, Slade?"

"Yes, sir?"

"I've added another name to the list of who I want killed. In addition to Smoke Jensen and that traitorous devil Pearlie Fontaine, I want that woman Jensen is married to killed." Franklin scowled. "I had some thoughts about taking her for myself, but now I'd rather she was disposed of."

"You can consider it done," Slade said.

"You mean like I could consider it done that the Malone girl was kidnapped?"

"No, I'll be gettin' some more men, some really good men this time."

"Get Boyce and Miller buried," Franklin said.

"All right. I'll take 'em into town this afternoon 'n bury 'em next to Ian, Marv, and Milt."

Franklin made a dismissive wave of his hand.

"I don't care where you put the incompetent fools."

Big Rock, Colorado

When the other Sugarloaf hands returned to the ranch, they brought the news that Sally had been found not guilty in the trial and said that she and Smoke were going to Big Rock this evening to celebrate that victory with their friends. Pearlie saddled a horse and headed for the new settlement, leaving the three hands there with strict orders to keep their guns handy and their eyes open all the time. Once he'd explained about the two men who had showed up to try to burn down the place, they understood and promised they would remain vigilant.

Louis Longmont closed his saloon for business so he could hold the celebration. Pearlie found Smoke there, drew him aside, and told him what had happened.

Smoke's jaw tightened in anger. "So Jack Slade had some of his gun-wolves try to burn down my house, did he? And on Tilden Franklin's orders, no doubt."

"Smoke, ain't it just about time for a bunch of the honest folks around here to strap on guns and clean out that rat's nest at the Circle TF? Actually, it's plumb *past* time."

"I can't argue with you, Pearlie. That's exactly what I would have done a few years ago." Smoke sighed. "But we just handed Franklin another defeat today, and we did it by legal means, in a courtroom. That's what Sally wants for Colorado. That's what a lot of people want. We've got to give that a chance to happen."

"The law's all well and good, but there comes a time when a fella's got to stomp his own snakes."

"I know that," Smoke said. "And I'm not just about to forget it, either."

Monte Carson was there at Longmont's for the celebration, and so were Hog Jaw Lambert, Tim Murchison, and every other man or woman who had come to Big Rock to start a business. Fred Malone was there because he was building a bank here, but that wasn't the only reason. He was also there because Sally had kept Sue

Ellen from being kidnapped, and he was sure that had kept her from being killed.

Because Louis Longmont had closed the saloon for business, Sue Ellen was also allowed to come to the celebration.

"If I ever need a lawyer, I know exactly who to come to," Fred Malone said.

"Oh, but, Mr. Malone, I'm not a lawyer," Sally said.

"You couldn't prove that by me, little lady. I've never heard any lawyer do a better job, and you sure put that pompous ass from Denver in his place. If you aren't a lawyer, where did you learn all that?"

"Judge Fielding was kind enough to lend me some of the books from his law library."

"I'm glad you didn't get hung."

Sally laughed and put her hand to her throat. "Mr. Malone, I concur. I'm glad I didn't get hung, as well."

"Yes, well, as far as I'm concerned, that's the second time you've saved Sue Ellen, because there's no doubt in my mind that if Franklin had been able to get rid of you, that would have emboldened him enough to make another try to get her."

"I doubt that he's given up on that idea," Smoke said. "If I were you, I would keep a close eye on her."

"I won't let her go anywhere alone. I'll keep her locked up all the time."

"Papa, that would be the same as keeping me in jail!" Sue Ellen complained when she heard Malone's remarks.

"Miss Sue Ellen, anytime you want to go somewhere, I'll take you," Pearlie offered.

Sue Ellen smiled coquettishly at Pearlie. "Well, Pearlie, I just may take you up on that."

CHAPTER 31

On board the Leopoldina, at sea

Hemingford laughed. "I've always heard it said that if anyone acts as their own lawyer, they have a fool for a client. Clearly, that wasn't true in Sally's case."

"Jason Freeze had not lost a case in the previous five years," Smoke said. "I think when he left town, he was . . . What's the term that's used for soldiers from the Great War? Oh, yes, shell-shocked. I think Freeze was shell-shocked."

"Well, it's easy to see why, isn't it? I mean, a lawyer with a reputation like Freeze's getting beaten by someone without a law degree had to be about the most disheartening thing that could possibly have happened to him. I'm sure he considered Sally a lifelong enemy."

Smoke shook his head. "No, they actually became friends later."

"You don't say. Well, I have to give credit to Freeze for that. Most lawyers I've known are quite vain, and to have been defeated by someone who isn't a lawyer would, I think, be even more devastating. How did he ever manage that?"

"He was the guest speaker when Sally became the first woman to graduate from Colorado Law School in eighteen ninety-four."

"Do you mean to tell me that Sally Jensen is a lawyer?"

"She is, but she doesn't actually practice law. By that I mean she doesn't normally argue cases in court, nor does she solicit clients. For the most part, her practice is limited to taking care of Sugarloaf Incorporated."

"By being Sugarloaf Incorporated, does that mean you've gone beyond being a horse and cattle ranch?"

"By the time the Mountain and Pacific Railroad actually reached the Pacific, Sugarloaf was a major stockholder, second only to Big Cat Malone. Only, by then we had extended our track all the way to Kansas City, so the name of the railroad became the Midland and Pacific."

"So the railroad did get built. I guess that means that after the trial, Franklin dropped his opposition to the railroad."

"Yes and no," Smoke replied.

"Yes and no?" For a moment Hemingford was perplexed by the answer. Then, with a broad smile, he realized what Smoke was telling him.

"I mean, yes, the railroad was built, and no, Franklin had not dropped his opposition to the railroad."

Circle TF Ranch

"Stop the railroad," Franklin said as he pounded a scrawny fist on the desk. "I don't care what it takes. If you have to hire more men, do it."

"What about the town that's bein' built?" Slade asked. "I thought you wanted it destroyed."

"You could kill the town, and the railroad would survive. But if you stop the railroad, that will kill the town."

Slade nodded. "All right."

"Oh, and, Slade, I intend to take over the railroad, so I don't want any of the rolling stock or the track that is already laid to be destroyed."

"You do know what that means, don't you?" Slade asked.

"Yes, it means kill Malone, Magee, Jensen, and as many of the track workers as is necessary to stop it in place. Concentrate on the Chinamen. We can always get more of them."

"I'm going to need at least five more men."

Franklin gave a dismissive wave of his hand. "Do whatever it takes."

"And a thousand dollars apiece for ever'one that's ridin' with me when we do it."

"If you get the railroad stopped, it'll be worth it," Franklin said.

"Slade is out lookin' for more men," Edmonson said. "I wonder why he needs more?"

"Didn't you hear what Drake was sayin'?" Rowe asked. "He says it's 'cause we're goin' to hit them that's buildin' the railroad. 'N if we stop it from bein' built, we're goin' to get a thousand dollars apiece."

"A thousand dollars?"

"That's what Drake is tellin', 'n he says he got it direct from Slade his own self."

Edmonson and Rowe were on their way to the town they were now calling Big Rock. "Just to see what new buildin' they've started," Drake had said when he'd sent them out this morning.

"Hey, Rowe. Look over there," Edmonson said. "Ain't that Pearlie 'n that little ole Malone gal?"

"Yeah. Yeah, I think it is," Rowe replied. He smiled. "Here's a chance to make some money. I know he wants Pearlie dead, 'n I'll just bet that he's also willin' to pay somethin' for the girl."

"How do you want to do this?" Edmonson asked, willingly giving the leadership position to Rowe.

"We'll set an ambush for the low-down scum, kill him, 'n take the girl with us."

"Oh, have you ever seen a more beautiful day, Pearlie? I mean really!" Sue Ellen stretched her arms out to either side and thrust her chest forward, causing her breasts to push out against the plaid shirt she was wearing.

Pearlie and Sue Ellen were on horseback, riding between Trail Back and Big Rock at a tranquil, deliberate pace. They weren't necessarily going anywhere. Sue Ellen had wanted to get out of the house for a while, she said.

Pearlie smiled, knowing exactly what the girl was doing. She was flirting with him, and while he appreciated it, he couldn't get over the fact that she was very young and he was very old, at least in experience. As he had heard more than one gunman and rider of the dark trails comment, it wasn't the years that aged men like them. It was the roar of gunshots and the smell of powder smoke.

"It is a pretty day," Pearlie agreed.

"It's a pretty day? That's all you can say about it? Oh, my, Pearlie, you are so old!"

Pearlie laughed. She had just put into words what he had been thinking.

"We should have brought some fishing poles," Pearlie said. "We could—" Pearlie stopped in midsentence. "Sue Ellen, stop right there," he ordered.

"What? What is it?" Sue Ellen asked, instantly alert to the change of tone in Pearlie's voice.

"There are a couple of men up ahead of us."

"Where? I don't see them," Sue Ellen said.

"They don't want to be seen. That's why I'm a little worried about it."

"Oh, pooh. I don't see anything to be worried about."

"You didn't see anything to worry about when you were with Miz Sally, either, did you?"

"Oh," Sue Ellen said in a crestfallen voice, realizing then the validity of Pearlie's concern. "What should we do?"

"Let's go back," Pearlie said.

"Oh, Pearlie, do we have to?"

"Yes. We have to."

Pearlie waited while Sue Ellen turned her horse and started back toward the house. He peered at the last place in which he had seen the two men, but now he saw nothing. After staring for a while with no sign of trouble, he began to think that he was just too jumpy and had only imagined seeing them.

Then one of them showed himself, only for an instant, before disappearing quickly.

Pearlie knew then that this wasn't just an imagined danger. The two men were lying in ambush for him. Now he wondered if he should go forward and force them to expose themselves, or should he go back and keep Sue Ellen company? He decided to ride back with Sue Ellen.

* * *

"What the hell, Edmonson? He musta seen us, 'cause he's goin' back."

"Let's see if we can catch up to 'em. You know that girl's goin' to slow 'em down."

The two started after Pearlie and Sue Ellen, though they held their horses at no more than a brisk walk, which was faster than Pearlie and Sue Ellen were going. This allowed their pursuers to close the distance but without giving up the alarm of someone galloping toward them.

"Talk to me, Edmonson," Rowe said.

"What?"

"Talk to me, and then laugh. That way they'll think we're just out riding together or somethin' like that."

"What are we supposed to talk about?"

"Hell, it don't make no difference what we talk about. He can't hear us, anyway."

"Well, if he can't hear us, how will he know we're talkin'?"

"Laugh," Rowe said.

Edmonson laughed.

"Look," Sue Ellen said. "They must not be after us. They're just riding along, talking to each other."

Pearlie glanced back at them. From all appearances, they seemed to be no more than a couple of casual riders. And, as Sue Ellen had pointed out, they were having a conversation, because one of them had just laughed.

"They're not after us," Sue Ellen said. "If they were, they surely wouldn't be laughing about it."

"Yeah, I guess you're right," Pearlie said. "All right, if

you want to, we can ride down to the creek, like we started to."

Sue Ellen turned around, and the two of them resumed their leisurely ride. The two men were still coming toward them.

"You said you wanted a fishing pole," Sue Ellen said. She smiled. "Well, guess what? There's already a fishing pole there. I keep one there."

Pearlie wasn't certain when he realized there was something wrong. He didn't see anything exactly, but he just had a feeling about it.

"Sue Ellen, go back to the house!" His order was sharp, and this time Sue Ellen didn't question him. She pulled her horse around sharply and jabbed her heels into its flanks, making the animal leap ahead in a run.

"Damn it, Rowe! They're a-gettin' away!" Edmonson shouted. "Let's get after 'em!"

Now all pretense was gone, as the two men broke into a gallop. After pulling their pistols, they began shooting at Pearlie and Sue Ellen. Clouds of smoke spurted from their guns and were whipped behind them by the wind of their passage.

Pearlie dropped behind Sue Ellen and used his own body as a shield. Then, when they were in sight of the Malone house, Pearlie shouted at her.

"Keep goin'. Go all the way to the house and get inside!"

With that, Pearlie stopped, then turned around to face the two men who were chasing them. He pulled his pistol and fired at them.

"What the hell? Now *he's* shootin' at *us!*" Rowe said as

a bullet passed by so close, he could hear it pop. "I'm gettin' outta here!"

Rowe turned his horse and started galloping away in the opposite direction.

"Rowe, you yellow dog!" Edmonson shouted. Then, looking back around, he saw Pearlie coming after him. The pursuer had suddenly become the pursued, so he turned and galloped after Rowe.

Pearlie kept after them for a short while, throwing a few more rounds in their direction. They weren't aimed shots. He was just trying to hurry the varmints on their way, and it worked.

By the time he got back to Sue Ellen, he saw that she had stopped her own retreat and was waiting for him, despite the orders he had given her. He was about to reprimand her for that when, with a huge smile, she greeted him.

"You charged both of them. That's the bravest thing I've ever seen."

"Yeah, well, uh . . ." Pearlie struggled to find words. His anger evaporated in his relief that Sue Ellen was all right. "Let's get on back to the house. We'll go fishin' some other day."

CHAPTER 32

Smoke was talking to Frank Magee as they watched the tracklayers at work. Six men pulled a rail off the flatcar, two men grabbed the front end of the rail, two more men the middle, and two more men the back end of the rail. Then, moving quickly, they positioned the rail, then went back for another as the gandy dancers drove in the spikes.

"From here on, we should be able to lay at least five miles of track a day," Magee said. "We could have this railroad completed pretty soon now. Especially since we have a straight shot to Big Rock and won't have to go through Fontana."

"I have a feeling Fontana won't be around that much longer," Smoke said. "They didn't want the railroad, so they've brought this on themselves."

"Mr. Malone said that there are already as many people in Big Rock as there are in Fontana."

"Yes, and our growth is coming at the expense of Fontana, since the people who have lived and done business there are coming to Big Rock."

Smoke and Magee were having to raise their voices to speak because of the sound of hammers against the spikes, as well as the shouts of the men as they were putting the rails in position. It was a fascinating thing to watch as the twin rails gradually stretched out in front of them.

Then there was another noise on top of the sound of hammering. The new sound was that of gunshots.

Smoke saw two of the tracklayers fall and roll down the berm.

"There!" Magee said, pointing toward a group of men on horseback. The riders charged the work site with guns blazing.

Smoke pulled his pistol, but the attack was taking place at the far end of the track, and because that was at least five hundred yards away, they were out of range.

Smoke ran back to where he had left Drifter and practically vaulted into the saddle. He started toward end of track. By the time he got there, however, the shooters had already withdrawn and he had no targets. Four men were down, and at least four more men, while still on their feet, were nursing wounds.

Smoke dismounted to check on them. Three of the four men on the ground were dead, and the fourth man appeared to be seriously wounded.

Smoke ordered that the injured men be helped onto the work train, where they could be taken back to the doctor in Denver as quickly as possible.

"Did you recognize any of those raiders?" Magee asked.

"No, but I didn't have to. I know who they are."

"Franklin's men," Magee said. It wasn't a question; it was a statement.

"Yes."

"They'll be back, won't they?"

"Yes."

After the train started back toward Denver, work resumed

on laying track. Smoke began asking around, and after finding six men who had experience with guns, he called them all together.

"I've spoken to each of you, and each of you has said you would be willing to act as an armed guard against any future attacks. From now on, your new job will be to protect the tracklayers. You'll answer to Mr. Magee."

"Where will you be, Mr. Jensen?" one of the men asked.

"I'm going to cut the head off this snake," Smoke replied.

When Smoke returned to the Sugarloaf, he saw Pearlie giving instructions to the three cowboys he had hired. By the time he swung down from the saddle, Pearlie had concluded his business. After sending the men off on the tasks he had assigned them, Pearlie came over to Smoke.

"What's up, boss?" Pearlie asked. "How come you ain't . . . ?" Pearlie stopped in midsentence to correct himself. "Miz Sally says I'm not supposed to say *ain't*. How come you aren't at end of track?"

Smoke explained about the attack on the railroad workers. "They killed three innocent men, and at least one of the wounded men may die," he said. "I'm not going to let that happen anymore."

"You're going after Franklin, aren't you?"

"Yes, and I want you to go with me."

"Uh, Smoke, you know that Slade is there with Franklin, don't you? And I figure Slade has seven or eight men with him by now. Maybe as many as ten."

"We won't be going by ourselves," Smoke said. "I'm

going into town. I think I might able to gather up a couple more."

"You mean that time we were talkin' about is here?"

"It's here," Smoke said.

A grin of anticipation creased Pearlie's leathery face.

When the two men reached Big Rock, Smoke, who hadn't been here for a few weeks, was quite pleased with what he saw. There were several business buildings facing each other across Center Street. White's Apothecary was across from Lambert's Café, Nancy's Bakery faced the Big Rock Mercantile, Delmonico's Restaurant was across the street from Ed's Gunshop, and Murchison's Leather Goods was opposite Ethan's Barbershop. Longmont's Saloon was large enough to face two buildings, Ann's Dress Shop and the Bank of Big Rock; and the *Big Rock Bulletin* newspaper, as Haywood Arden had wanted, was next door to Longmont's Saloon and across the street from a partially built building, which would be the Dunn Hotel. There was an empty lot next door to the newspaper, though Moe Gates had announced his intention to build a butcher shop there. The last building on Center Street was the sheriff's office and jail. As yet, nothing had been built across the street from the jail, though at the corner, a lot was marked out for the school, which Sally had been promised would be in place before the summer was over so she could begin teaching as soon as the new school year started.

In addition to the twelve commercial buildings that were already open and doing business, at least twenty homes had been built, and more were going up. The air was filled with the sounds of hammers and saws.

"Let's start with the sheriff's office," Smoke suggested.

Monte Carson was sweeping the floor when Smoke and Pearlie stepped inside.

"Sweeping up, I see. Well, it's always good to see that a sheriff can keep himself busy," Smoke teased. Even under these grim circumstances, he hadn't completely forgotten his sense of humor.

"Yeah, I'm sweeping. What else have I got to do? I've got two new cells back there and nobody to put in them. So far everyone in town is behaving themselves, so that I don't have any business."

"Then you wouldn't mind being a temporary deputy US marshal long enough to help me take care of a little chore."

"What chore?" Carson asked. Then he waved his hand. "Forget that I asked you that question. No matter what you need me for, I'm your man."

"Good. Come along with me now. You can help me recruit a few others."

"Is there going to be any shooting involved?"

"Yes, I'm sure there will be. That isn't going to be a problem for you, is it?" Smoke said.

"No problem at all, but I've got a suggestion for our next recruit."

"Who?"

"Louis Longmont," Carson replied.

"Louis?"

"You don't know all of Louis's past, do you?" Carson asked.

"I guess I don't."

"Louis is a dead shot and has proven his courage more than once."

Smoke nodded. "All right. Let's go see him."

Longmont agreed enthusiastically to be part of the posse.

"Good. That gives us four," Smoke said.

"Smoke, if you'd like another man, I figure Ray Perkins would be a good choice," Pearlie said.

"Wait a minute," Carson said. "Perkins rides for Franklin, doesn't he?"

"Not anymore, he don't. Hell, ever'one that was a Demon has quit Franklin, which is why I don't mind goin' up against 'im, 'cause there won't be any of my friends there."

"Where is Perkins?" Smoke asked.

Pearlie smiled. "I just saw him across the street. He's one of the men that's buildin' the hotel."

Conner was also engaged in some construction in the town, and he was recruited by Perkins and Pearlie, so that, as Smoke started toward the Circle TF Ranch, he had a posse of six men, counting himself.

When they reached the ranch, they saw someone riding the fence line.

"That's Bo James," Pearlie said. "He's an actual working hand. He wasn't a Demon, 'n I'm pretty sure he's not ridin' for Slade now."

"He ain't," Perkins said. "Fact is, he was in town just the other night 'n was complainin' as how Slade 'n his bunch are a lot worse 'n we ever was."

"Pearlie, go talk to him," Smoke said. "Tell him to get all the cowboys away from the ranch, because there's going to be trouble."

"Yeah, good idea," Pearlie said. "I wouldn't want any of the regular men to get hurt."

By now Bo James had seen the six approaching men, and letting curiosity take hold of him, he started riding toward them. Recognizing Pearlie, he was a little less anxious.

"Hello, Pearlie," James said cautiously. "I never thought I'd see you around here again."

"Hello, Bo. Have you missed me?"

James chuckled. "When I compare you and the Demons to those dirt piles that's ridin' with Slade, yeah, I do miss you. All the riders for the brand miss you."

"How many are riding for the brand?"

"There's only five us actually ridin' for the brand, but Slade has eight with him."

"Eight with him or eight counting him?"

"Eight counting him. What's this all about, Pearlie?"

"I need you to go tell Johnny Kincaid to take all the actual cowboys somewhere else for a while."

"Why?"

"Because we're goin' to clean out Slade and the men with him."

"Pearlie, you sure you want to do this? Slade is a . . . Well, he's a killer. There's no other way of putting it."

"Just have Kincaid get you and the others to someplace safe."

"All right."

"And, Bo, when they're all gone, come tell me."

James nodded, then turned his horse and spurred back toward the ranch compound.

* * *

Johnny Kincaid, the actual foreman of the Circle TF, was in the ranch office talking with Franklin.

"I've got Bo James out riding fence. Bill Hanlon is working on the hay mower, and Dooley is working on harness. The thing is, Mr. Franklin, all this is just busy-work. We need to get some cattle to market, or we're goin' to run out of grazing land for them."

"That's not your worry, Kincaid," Franklin said with a dismissive wave of his hands. "I've got other things to do that are more important now."

"You mean like stopping the railroad from being built?"

"What I do with the railroad is none of your business," Franklin snapped. "Why are you concerned? I'm paying you and the men, aren't I?"

"Yes, but you're paying those lazy slobs who work for Slade a lot more."

"This conversation is over, Kincaid. And if you want to keep your job, I would suggest that you not bring this subject up again."

"Yes, sir," Kincaid said.

As Kincaid was leaving the ranch office, he saw Bo James come riding up.

"I thought I had you riding fence line," Kincaid called. "Did you find a break that needs to be repaired?"

"Where are the others?" James asked.

"They're in the barn and the machine shed. Why do you ask that?"

"We've got to get out of here, Kincaid."

"Get out of here? What do you mean? What are you talking about?"

James made a face and said, "I've got a hunch it's about to become plumb unhealthy around here, Johnny."

CHAPTER 33

Smoke and the others had dismounted, and Pearlie, at Smoke's request, drew the layout of the ranch in a bare patch of dirt.

"This is the bunkhouse where the Demons stayed, and I figure Slade and his men are there now. If we come this way"—he pointed out a position on the dirt map he had drawn—"we can get all the way up to the barn before anyone could see us."

"Here comes Bo James," Conner said.

"He's not alone," Carson said.

"That's all right," Pearlie said. "That's just Kincaid and the others. It looks like Bo got their attention, sure enough."

When the riders approached, Kincaid dismounted and walked up to Smoke and his companions. "Is it true, what James is saying? You've come to take care of Slade and the others?"

"That's right," Smoke said.

"Past time, I'd say. What about Franklin?"

"Him, too," Smoke said. "Some men attacked rail's end this morning, and three of the workers were killed. If they did it because Franklin sent them, then we intend to arrest him for murder."

"How many men attacked you?"

"There were four of them."

"So that's where they went," Kincaid said.

"That's where who went?"

"Drake, Cummings, Edmonson, and Rowe. They left last night, and when they came back in this morning, they were all giddy about something. And after they talked to Slade, he went in to talk to Franklin about something. There's no doubt in my mind but that it was about killing the track workers."

"Now you can see why we called you away. I don't want anyone who is innocent to be hurt."

Kincaid nodded. "Believe me, Mr. Jensen. There's nobody left at that ranch who is innocent."

"Where did they all go?" Slade asked.

"I don't know, but there's not a one of them that's still here. Kincaid, Bo James, ever' damn one of 'em is gone," Stryker said.

As Slade and Stryker stood out by the corral, talking, they saw Cummings galloping toward them.

"What the hell's wrong with Cummings?" Slade asked as he and Stryker turned their attention toward the man who was coming toward them at a gallop.

Cummings pulled up in front of them and shouted down his news, even as he remained in the saddle.

"They're here, Slade!" Cummings shouted.

"Who's here?"

"Jensen and Pearlie. 'N they got the new sheriff with

'em, too. Also, that saloon feller, Longmont and a few others."

"How many are there?"

"Well, sir, I counted six of 'em."

Slade smiled. "We've got 'em outnumbered. Get yourself a fresh horse, Cummings. Then lead us to 'em. Boys, we've got 'em," he said. "Stryker, you get my horse saddled. I'm going to talk to Franklin."

When Slade stepped into the ranch office a moment later, he saw Franklin standing at the window, looking out at all the commotion.

"What's going on?" Franklin asked.

"Jensen is leading a posse toward us. They'll be here within half an hour, unless we stop them."

"Do you think you will be able to stop them?" Franklin asked anxiously.

Slade's smile was confident and without humor. "They're dead meat," he said. "And this is finally going to be over."

He stepped out of the office.

Franklin stood in the window and watched Slade and his men gallop off.

Bo James, Johnny Kincaid, and the other actual working hands rode on into town, leaving Smoke and the posse to carry out their attack against the Circle TF Ranch. Using the information the cowhands had provided, Smoke led the men toward the big house compound.

Smoke saw Conner's head jerk back suddenly, with blood and brain matter exploding out the side, just an instant before he heard the rifle shot.

"It's an ambush!" Pearlie shouted.

"Dismount!" Smoke ordered.

Smoke leaped off Drifter, grabbed his rifle from the saddle holster, then gave the stallion a slap on the rump to send him to safety. Drifter didn't have to be told a second time, as he turned and galloped away.

Smoke jacked a round into the Winchester's chamber, and after checking that his men were finding cover, he looked toward the direction from which the shot had come. That was when he saw one of Slade's men raise his head to get a good look. His head was just high enough to see over the rock.

That was all the opportunity Smoke needed, and lifting the rifle to his shoulder, he squeezed the trigger and felt the familiar and satisfying kick, then saw the bullet strike his target right in the forehead. The man flew backward out of sight.

Smoke dived to the left as several bullets came his way. None of them found their mark or even came close.

For the next several minutes, the area near the Circle TF ranch house was a battlefield as guns roared and clouds of powder smoke rolled through the air. Bullets whined and whipped and buzzed like a swarm of furious hornets.

"Damn! They got Perkins!" Pearlie shouted, even as he killed one of Slade's men. He didn't know if this was the same man who had killed Perkins, but he comforted himself in thinking so.

Slade had come to the fight with eight men, confident that he would be able to take care of Smoke Jensen. But now he had only five men remaining, and he abruptly lost another one.

"Uh!" Bardsley grunted, and looking toward him, Slade saw him go down with a bullet wound in his chest.

Four men now.

Slade saw Monte Carson lift his head up from where he had taken cover.

"I've got you now!" Slade said as he lined his sights on Carson's head. Slade pulled the trigger, then heard the click as the hammer fell on an empty chamber. "Damn!"

Slade stuck his hands in his pockets, looking for ammunition, but even as he did so, he realized that his spare ammunition was in his saddlebags, and they had tethered their horses well behind them when they'd set up the ambush.

"Drake!" Slade shouted. "Got any extra ammunition?"

"No."

Slade got up but held himself in a deep crouch as he started toward the rear.

"Where are you going?" Drake shouted.

"After ammunition!"

"Slade, this ain't turnin' out right," Drake said. "Maybe we'd better get out of here!"

"We're going to stay," Slade said. "Keep shooting. I'll bring more bullets back!"

When Slade was far enough away, he was able to stand up and run faster. When he reached his horse, he stuck his hand down in one of the saddlebags to pull out another box of .44-40. Then, just as he turned to start back, he saw Drake go down. That left only two men. Only two men against at least four.

He shoved the ammunition back in the saddlebag, pulled himself onto the horse as quickly as he could, and galloped away.

* * *

"Stryker!" Cummings shouted. "Stryker, Slade is running away!"

"What?"

"Slade, he just climbed onto his horse and galloped off. The lily-livered snake is runnin' away!"

Stryker looked back and saw that Cummings was telling the truth. "Damn! We're the only ones left," Stryker said.

"What are we going to do?"

"Well, I ain't stayin' here to fight Franklin's war with just the two of us." Stryker stood up and started to run, but when he exposed himself, at least two bullets ripped through him and he went down.

Cummings realized now that he was the only one left. He tied his handkerchief to the end of his rifle, then held it up and waved it back and forth.

"I give up! Don't shoot no more. I give up!"

"Smoke, do you think this is for real, or is it a trick?" Pearlie asked.

"There's one way of finding out," Smoke replied. Smoke cupped his hands around his mouth, then shouted across the open space.

"Come on out with your hands up!"

A moment later someone came out from behind the line of rocks, holding his arms in the air. One hand was still holding the rifle, with the white handkerchief tied to the end of the barrel.

"Throw down that rifle," Smoke shouted, and the man who was surrendering tossed the rifle aside.

Smoke, Pearlie, Carson, and Longmont watched cautiously as the man walked toward them.

"I wonder if this is some kind of trick," Pearlie said.

"I don't think so. If he was surrendering on his own, anyone still back there would have shot him by now," Smoke said.

"What's your name?" Smoke asked when the man reached them.

"His name is Cummings," Longmont said. "I've seen him before."

"That's right, Cummings. Jeremiah Cummings," Cummings said.

"Why didn't the others come with you?" Carson asked.

"Others? What others? There ain't nobody left alive." Cummings made a scoffing sound. "Except for Slade. That devil run away."

Franklin heard the sound of a galloping horse, and he stepped out of his ranch office to see who it was. At first, he was surprised to see that it was Slade, but then he smiled. If Slade came back at a gallop, then he must have good news to share.

Franklin stood on the front porch, leaning against the narrow post that supported the overhanging roof.

"Well, you must have good news for me, or you wouldn't have come back the way you did," Franklin said. "Come on into the office and tell me all about it."

Slade didn't dismount. Instead he asked, "How much money do you have here?"

"What? Why would you ask such a thing?"

"Jensen's won. Everyone else is dead, and I have to get out of here. How much money do you have?"

"I see," Franklin said. "Well, I suppose I can scrape up some money for you. Let me see how much cash I have on hand . . ."

He started to turn away, but as he did, his right hand slipped under his coat and came out clutching a pistol. Continuing the turn, he moved faster now, spinning all the way around so that he faced Slade again. Slade hadn't been paying that much attention to him, underestimating Tilden Franklin as men always did when it came to any sort of physical threat. Slade was looking over his shoulder again, as if keeping an eye out for Smoke Jensen.

But he saw movement from the corner of his eye and realized too late what was going on. He tried to jerk his gun up, but the pistol in Franklin's hand cracked wickedly before Slade could raise his own gun.

The bullet drilled into his forehead and snapped his head back as it bored through his brain. In the last fading instants of life, Slade realized he had been killed by a man who didn't look dangerous enough to scare a kitten.

He might have laughed at the irony of that, Jack Slade, the deadly gunman, killed by somebody like that . . . but he was already dead when he toppled out of the saddle and crashed to the ground.

Franklin lowered his smoking pistol and stared at the corpse. So, it had come to this. No matter what he did, no matter how many men he hired to get what he wanted, Smoke Jensen was still alive, and Tilden Franklin was left alone. That meant only one course of action was left open to him.

He would just have to kill Smoke Jensen himself.

CHAPTER 34

Because they had not had time to tether their horses, it took Smoke and the others a few minutes to round them up. Fortunately, they had not gone far, possibly because Drifter went only far enough away to get out of danger and the other horses stayed with him.

When they reached the place where the outlaws had made their ambush, they saw six bodies.

"Are there any more?" Smoke asked.

"No, this is all that's left. Except of Slade, of course," Cummings said.

Slade, and Tilden Franklin . . .

"Monte, why don't you take this gentleman to jail?" Smoke suggested. "We'll help put the bodies up on their horses, and you can take them into town."

"Which town? Fontana or Big Rock? Remember, we don't have a mortician in Big Rock. We don't even have a cemetery there."

"We don't need a mortician. And these six can be the first occupants of our new cemetery," Smoke said.

After the outlaws' bodies were draped across their

saddles, Carson handcuffed Cummings and got him mounted.

"Pearlie, let's you and I go visit Slade and Franklin," Smoke suggested.

Smoke and Pearlie heard the crack of a single shot as they approached the Circle TF ranch house. They glanced at each other. Pearlie said, "What do you reckon that was about?"

"One good way to find out," Smoke said. He nudged Drifter into a slightly faster pace.

They came in sight of the house and saw a riderless horse dancing around skittishly. A man lay on the ground near the animal, unmoving. Another man—smaller, leaner, wearing a dark suit—went to the horse and grabbed its reins.

"Dadgummit, that's Franklin!" Pearlie exclaimed. "That means the other fella must be . . ."

"Jack Slade," Smoke finished as Pearlie's stunned voice trailed away. "They must have had a falling-out. Looks like Slade made the mistake of not taking Franklin seriously enough."

"Yeah, but now what's he—Blast it, Smoke, that loco devil's got Slade's rifle!" Pearlie reached for his own Winchester. "I'll take care of that before he starts throwin' lead at us."

Smoke held out a hand. "This is between me and Franklin, Pearlie. His men tried to burn down my house. Even worse, they tried to kill Sally, and when they failed, he tried to get the law to do it for him." Smoke drew in a deep breath. "And his greed came close to ruining these parts for a lot of people. We're going to settle this ourselves."

"Smoke, don't you go to underestimatin' him the way Slade did."

Smoke shook his head, said, "No chance of that," and started Drifter forward again.

He watched as Franklin awkwardly worked the lever on Slade's Winchester. The man lifted the rifle to his shoulder and tried to aim it, but the barrel waved around wildly. The rifle cracked. Smoke heard the bullet sing high overhead.

"That's all, Franklin," he called. "Drop the rifle. I'll take you back to Big Rock, and Sheriff Carson can arrest you. You'll answer for your crimes in a court of law."

Franklin lowered the rifle but didn't toss it aside. "I'm the law around here!" he shrieked at Smoke. "I have an empire here, Jensen, don't you know that? It's mine to rule!" He laughed. "Big Rock? There's no Big Rock! In a year it'll be gone, just a figment of your imagination, and Fontana will still be the center of my holdings!"

Smoke shook his head as Drifter kept walking and the distance between him and Franklin continued to close.

"Fontana's the one that will be a ghost town, if there's anything left at all," Smoke said. "It's a new day, and you might as well accept that. Save your life, what's left of it."

Franklin sneered. "Mine to rule," he said again, "and I'll rule it with that pretty wife of yours at my side. She'll be mine, too, Jensen, and she'll be in my bed while you're cold in the ground."

Smoke's jaw tightened. He was close enough now he could have blasted a handful of slugs through Franklin before the man could lift that rifle, but he wasn't going to do that. Three years of living in peace hadn't softened him . . . but it *had* changed him. Deepened his resolve to live for more than vengeance and anger. Three years of peace . . . three years with Sally . . .

Franklin's shoulders sagged suddenly. Holding the rifle with his left hand, he held it down at his side and then let go of the barrel so it fell over. "I give up," he muttered. "I'm beaten and you're close enough at last!"

He yanked the pistol from his pocket, the same one he had used to kill Jack Slade, and started to raise it while Smoke's eyes were following the falling rifle . . .

Only Smoke wasn't watching the rifle. Flame geysered from the muzzle of the Colt he held as he fired three times, the shots coming out in one deafening roll of gun-thunder. The slugs hammered into Tilden Franklin's chest and drove him back in a grisly, jittering dance. He pawed at his bloody chest and whimpered, "Mine . . . mine to rule . . ." before pitching forward on his face, not to move again.

"Six feet of it, anyway," Smoke said, but Franklin was long past hearing him.

Three months later

Almost every citizen of Big Rock, and now there were six hundred of them, turned out to watch the first scheduled passenger train run arrive at the newly built depot. As soon as the train arrived, the telegrapher at the new Western Union office flashed out the news back to Denver and Kansas City.

BIG ROCK IS NOW CONNECTED TO THE REST OF THE NATION STOP

Smoke and Sally were riding in Fred "Big Cat" Malone's special car. Malone was there, of course, as were Lauren and Sue Ellen. Sue Ellen was sitting with Pearlie, and they had been talking quietly, in their own world, ever since the train had left Denver.

Preacher was there, as well.

"I ain't never rid nothin' like this before," Preacher said.

"Why, Preacher, you've been on a train before," Sally said.

"Oh, I ain't sayin' I never rid on a train before, 'cause that wouldn't be true, 'cause I have. But I ain't never been on no train car that's all fancied up like this 'n just a few ridin' on it."

The train came to a complete halt, and Smoke stood up, then reached down for Sally.

"Uh-uh," Sally said with a broad grin. "You first, remember?"

"It doesn't seem right for me to just go off and leave you here."

"I'll be right behind you," Sally promised.

As Sally reminded him, it had been arranged that when the train stopped, Smoke and Fred Malone would step down first. As soon as they did, a band began playing, and Smoke saw two big signs spread out on the walls of the depot.

**THANK YOU, SMOKE JENSEN,
FOR BUILDING OUR TOWN.**

**THANK YOU, FRED MALONE, FOR CONNECTING OUR TOWN
TO THE REST OF THE WORLD.**

Festivities in the town took up most of the afternoon, and it was dusk by the time Smoke and Sally returned to the ranch.

"Wait," Smoke said as he brought the buckboard to a halt. "I just want to . . ."

"I know what you want. I want to look, too," Sally said.

They were on a long dedicated road that passed under an arch with wrought-iron words spelling out SUGARLOAF RANCH. In smaller words beneath those read SMOKE AND SALLY JENSEN, PROPRIETORS.

Smoke reached over to take Sally's hand. "Let's go home," he said.

On board the Leopoldina

"Wait a minute," Ernest Hemingford said. "What about the gold strike?"

"Oh, as gold strikes go, this particular one was nothing to really shout about," Smoke said. "For a while, fellas dug it out, chipped it free, and blasted it out of the rock, but the mines played out in just over a year. But with the railroad and the ranches—and a lot of good people—Big Rock was able to live on. Things like that are a lot more lasting than gold."

"That is a fine story, Smoke, and it will take many fine words to capture it," Hemingford said. "What is the population of Big Rock now?"

"A little over five thousand," Smoke said.

"What a great size, just large enough to provide for all the citizens' needs, but small enough for everyone to be good neighbors to each other."

"I like it there," Smoke agreed.

"Oh, there is one thing that has been bothering me. What ever happened between Pearlie and Sue Ellen? From your story, it's obvious that they were attracted to each other."

"They were, but Sue Ellen went off to college, and

Pearlie felt that he would be a hindrance to her, so they parted as good friends, but it never went beyond that."

"Did Sue Ellen become a teacher?"

Smoke chuckled. "You might say that. She's an English professor at Washington University in St. Louis."

"Good for her."

"Ernest, don't write the story," Smoke said.

"Oh, I can't not write this story," Hemingford insisted. "I'm a writer, and this thing has taken hold of me."

"All right, you can write the story, but I ask that you don't publish it."

"Why not? Smoke, as I said, it is a wonderful story, and you are an American icon."

"I wouldn't say that. I reckon most people have forgotten about Smoke Jensen by now, and that doesn't bother me a bit. My life has been calm and pleasant for the past few years, and I am enjoying that. I'm enjoying it very much. This book, if published, might just start it all over again. I know it is asking a lot of you, but I beg you, let me have some privacy for what remains of my life."

For a long moment, Hemingford didn't respond, then he said, "I'm going to write the story, Smoke, because I can't not write it. But I suppose, if it means that much to you, I'll never publish it."

Smoke leaned back in the chair where he was sitting, crossed his long legs at the ankles, and said, "Don't worry, Ernest. You'll find plenty of other things to write about. You said you were in the Great War. You could always write about that. And since you'll be in Paris, you can write about that." He smiled. "Just remember to write what's true . . . even if you have to make some of it up."

Keep reading for a special excerpt….

Chapter 1

John Zachary walked into the post office in Springfield, Missouri, hoping a letter he had been waiting for might have arrived. The postmaster, Sam Gunter, answered his question before John had a chance to ask. "Howdy, John. That letter you've been looking for came yesterday." He went over to a box that held all the mail for the farms out James Bridge Road and sorted through it until he came to the one letter addressed to John Zachary. "Must be important," Gunter remarked, hoping John might share the content.

"Much obliged, Sam," Zachary replied. "Yeah, it's kinda important—some information a fellow is sendin' me about growin' better corn." That was not entirely untrue, but he wasn't ready to tell Sam, or anyone else he knew in town what he had in mind to do. And as if on cue, Sam then brought up one of the main reasons.

"You know, if you're gonna be in town later this evening, the mayor's holding a meeting to discuss the future of our town, what with there being more and more talk about the possibility of the southern states seceding from the Union. A lot of us think it'd be a good idea to know where everybody stands if it comes to war."

"I reckon I already know where I stand," John said. "I won't be at the meetin', but you can tell the mayor I stand for the Union and against war. So I sure hope it doesn't come to that."

"I suspect that's where most of us stand," Sam allowed. "But there's liable to be some trouble in Greene County 'cause there's lots of folks with southern ties."

"You may be right, Sam." John said and started walking toward the door. "Well, I'd best be gettin' back. Emmett's waitin' for me at Simpson's."

"Tell him about the meeting," Sam said.

"I will. I'll tell him," John assured him. He left the post office and went directly to Simpson's General Merchandise where his friend, Emmett Braxton, was waiting with the wagon. The two men had been best friends since their school days and for the past five years had worked to raise crops on adjoining farms. When he reached the store, Emmett was sitting on the wagon seat, waiting for him. John's son, Johnny, and Emmett's son, Skeeter, were chasing each other around and around the wagon. Seeing the boys playing caused John to think, *I don't want their future to promise nothing more than to be sent off to fight a war as soon as they're old enough.*

"Did you get your letter?" Emmett asked.

"Yep," John answered, holding the letter up for him to see.

"Ain'tcha gonna open it?"

"Yep," John answered again. "You drive the horses and I'll read it on the way home." He called the boys then. "Hop on, boys. We're headin' home."

"It looks like a helluva letter," Emmett commented. "How many pages is that?"

"A lot," John answered, already reading and not bothering to stop and count the pages.

Emmett pulled the empty envelope out of John's hand and read, "From Mr. Clayton Scofield. Is that the fellow that leads the wagon train? The wagon master, I guess you call him."

"Yeah, he's the guide." After reading the first three pages, John started informing his friend of the contents. "Boy, he didn't leave anything out. It's all right here in this letter, everything you need to make the trip; how to equip your wagon, what supplies and how much of 'em you need to take you through, how far you go each day, and everything else."

Emmett shook his head, marveling at his friend's excitement over the prospect of traveling in a wagon all the way across the continent to Oregon country. He couldn't really say John was making a bad decision. He couldn't blame him for leaving his poorly producing farm here for land in the fertile Willamette Valley the emigrants talked about. He wondered if he shouldn't pack up his family and go with him. John had talked so enthusiastically about it for the last couple of months, it was hard not to catch some of his excitement. He wouldn't admit it to anyone, but sometimes he felt a little resentment for the fact that John didn't consult him about the wisdom of dumping everything here they had worked so hard to build before making a final decision. But they were best friends, so he had to wish him well.

They stopped at Emmett's farm first and unloaded his purchases. "Why don't you and Sarah and the kids come on over to the house with me?" John suggested. "We can all tell Marcy she can start gettin' ready 'cause we're goin' to Oregon for sure."

"I don't know, John," Emmett said. "You and Marcy might wanna do some serious talkin', or something."

"Nonsense," Sarah commented in her typically blunt fashion, "we'll go and help you get excited." She paused and gazed at a grinning John Zachary, then added, "It may be too late for that, judging by that silly expression on your face." So, Sarah, Skeeter, and Lou Ann scrambled up on the wagon with Johnny behind John and Emmett, and they continued on to the Zachary farm.

"Evenin', Marcy," Sarah sang out when the wagon pulled up by the back door and Marcy came outside to meet them. "John invited us all to come to dinner, so I hope you're cookin' something good."

"I'll just pour another quart or two of water in the soup and that'll have to do," Marcy answered, accustomed to Sarah's japing. "What is the occasion for this visit?"

"We've come to help you celebrate," Sarah replied. "John got that letter you were waitin' for."

Marcy's eyes lit up in excitement upon hearing that news. She looked at once toward her husband. "The letter came?" He answered with a nod and a grin. "Well, hallelujah," she declared, "I guess we're goin' to Oregon!" She took hold of Sarah's arm. "Well, come on in the house. It's cold out here."

When he saw John deliberating over whether or not to unhitch the horses, Emmett said, "Come on, I'll help you unhitch. We'll just walk back home. Those two women get to gabbin' and there ain't no tellin' how long we'll be here. No sense in lettin' your horses stand hitched up." It was not a long walk back to their house, anyway. It was just a matter of cutting across a cornfield that separated the two homesteads. When they returned to the house, they found the two wives chattering away about the adventure of the cross-country trip and the new life to be anticipated in that faraway land of Oregon. They also noticed that Marcy had seen fit to bring out one of the apple cider jugs for the celebration.

While the women were shuffling through the pages of Clayton Scofield's instructions and recommendations, and the kids were chasing all over the house, only Emmett had concerns about his friend's decision. While he forced a smile to stay in place on his face, he was troubled by his own indecision during the months before when John talked about it so much. He now found himself regretting his hesitancy and thinking that maybe he should have followed John's lead once more. When his wife noticed his seeming lack of enthusiasm, she asked, "What's wrong, hon?"

He looked at her and shook his head, then spoke softly, so no one else would hear, "I don't know. I think maybe it woulda been smart if we had signed up to go with 'em."

"Maybe you should take a look at this letter and see all the things you would need and what you'd have to do to our wagon, and how long that trip would be," she suggested. When he showed no incentive to do so, she asked Marcy for the first few pages, since she had already read them. She handed the pages to Emmett. "Might as well see what you're missin'."

Emmett shrugged and started reading the first page. It started out: *Dear Mr. Zachary, I'm happy to hear that you and your family, and the Braxton family, have decided to join our train, leaving Independence, Missouri on April 1, 1860.* That was as far as he got before he looked up to find all conversation stopped and all eyes upon him, faces waiting expectantly. He looked at his wife, who was grinning from ear to ear. He looked at John then, whose smile was equal to that of Sarah's. "You son of a gun. You signed me up, too."

"Hell, I knew you'd wanna go. It just takes you longer to realize what's best for you. And I knew—hell, we all knew—you wouldn't let me ride off without you."

Emmett's grin was now wider than anybody's. "I oughta let you go out there by yourself and see how you make it without me to keep you straight. Gimme the rest of that letter. There's a heck of a lot to do between now and April first." He paused then when he remembered. "'Course, I'll have to talk this over with Sarah first. She might not wanna make a trip like that."

"Shoot," John scoffed, "she's the one who told me to put your name on my letter."

The drop-in visit from the Braxtons turned out to be an all-day affair that lasted well into suppertime and the sudden demise of two fat chickens that ended up in the pot. Corn bread to go with the chicken required a good portion of the cornmeal just purchased at Simpson's that morning as well. It would be the first of many days the two families would work to prepare for the journey of their lives. Paying strict attention to the letter from Scofield, the two men fixed their wagons just as he recommended and followed the specified guidelines for quantities of food and provisions. Over the two-month time before the first of April, they sold their farms and furniture. Selling the furniture was the hardest part, but there was no room in the wagons for anything beyond clothes to wear and things necessary to eat and prepare meals. Sometimes it was difficult to believe they could accomplish everything that had to be done. However, three days prior to April first found the two families driving their wagons into the town of Independence, hoping their decision was a sensible one. They had made an appointment to meet Mr. Scofield on the morning of the twenty-eighth, at the Henry House Hotel to finalize any agreements and pay any advance charges.

CHAPTER 2

While the Braxtons and the Zacharys were bedding their families down for the night, the man they had come to meet was passing his time in a card game in The Gateway Saloon. "I swear, sonny, I know I've had a helluva lot to drink since I sat down at this table, but I don't reckon I could get drunk enough to where I couldn't see that card come off the bottom of the deck. I ain't sore enough to wanna shoot you for cheatin', but that's the reason I've just throwed my cards in the last few times it's your deal."

"What the hell are you talkin' about?" The young gambler exclaimed. "You'd best watch who you're callin' a cheat, old man. I don't take that offa nobody."

"Like I said," Scofield responded, "ain't no use gettin' your feathers ruffled. I'm just tryin' to give you a little friendly advice, that's all. But if you're thinkin' about makin' it as a gambler strictly by sleight of hand, you've got a helluva lot more practicing to do."

"Why you old drunk, I'm thinkin' 'bout puttin' an extra air hole right between your eyes. A man don't accuse another man of cheatin' unless he's ready to back it up. You're wearin' a handgun, so I'm givin' you a chance to prove you can handle one." With his eyes locked on Scofield's, he stood up and pushed his chair back. The steady din of saloon conversation stopped immediately as it became apparent to everyone in the room that a challenge was about to be issued. A duel between two card players was not an uncommon occurrence in The Gateway Saloon, so the regular patrons remained silent in anticipation of the challenge to follow. They were not disappointed. "Old man," the young gambler pronounced clearly, "you're a no-account drunken liar and a damn yellow-bellied coward to boot. I'll have you take a knee and beg my forgiveness or stand up to me and go for that handgun you're wearin'."

"Now, there you go, tryin' to make a name for yourself by shootin' me," Scofield responded. "If you're as bad at gunfightin' as you are at cheatin' at cards, you ain't likely to last long enough to ever get to my age. And if you shot me, what good would that do your reputation? Hell, I ain't got no name as a gunfighter. You just called me a no-account old drunk. You ain't gonna get very famous for shootin' an old drunk." Scofield got up on his feet, holding onto the edge of the table to steady himself. "Damn," he swore, "that likker's hit me harder'n I thought. I might have to set down again to keep this saloon from rockin' back and forth." He looked the young gambler in the eye and said, "I'll not draw on you, young feller, so go on and find yourself another game."

The young man was not to be denied, however, and was not willing to be bluffed by the wobbly old man. No matter what Scofield had said, a kill was a kill, and that's all anybody would talk about. And this would be so easy he'd be a fool to pass up the opportunity. He stepped up in Scofield's face and poked his shoulder with his forefinger. "You ain't talkin' your way outta this, big mouth." The last word had barely dropped from his lips when Scofield's Colt Navy Model six-shooter landed solidly against the side of his face, knocking him unconscious and breaking his jaw in the process.

Clayton Scofield plopped back down in the chair and shook his head slowly, as if afraid it might roll off his neck. "Damn," was his only comment when Pete, the bartender, walked over to take a look at the unconscious man on the floor.

"I declare, Scofield, it's been over a year since you were in here," Pete said. "Don't look like you've changed a helluva lot." He paused to see if Scofield was even aware of his comment. When it appeared that he wasn't, or that he didn't give a damn, one way or the other, Pete shrugged and asked a couple of the spectators to give him a hand. He directed them to carry the injured man out the door and deposit him on the front porch of the saloon. Back to Scofield then, he said, "Best pick up your money and let somebody else take that chair." He glanced at the remaining two card players and they both nodded vigorously. Scofield looked to be a handful, drunk or sober, and the recent altercation with the young gambler verified it.

Scofield didn't protest. He was well aware of his incapacity after consuming such a large quantity of rye whiskey at a single sitting. He struggled to his feet once again, and with Pete to give him a helping hand, he made it over to a small table against the back wall. He settled heavily into the chair and smiled up at Pete. "'Preciate it. I'll just set here a little while. Do I owe you any money?"

"No, you're paid up. You need me to bring a spittoon over here for you?"

"Nope," Scofield answered with certainty, knowing that the sick part of his drunk would strike him in the morning, most likely. "I won't be here long." He felt confident in saying that, thinking that Clint was probably looking in all the saloons for him already.

"Might be a good idea to get outta here as soon as you feel like you can make it," Pete advised. "You clobbered that feller pretty good, but when his head stops ringin', I expect he's gonna be lookin' for you. And you ain't in no shape for a shoot-out."

"Ain't that the truth?" Scofield responded with another foolish smile. "I'll just set here and rest a spell."

On the street in front of the saloon, young Clint Buchanan pulled up to a stop at the hitching rail when he saw a black Morgan tied there. Seeing the prone body lying on one side of the porch, he at once thought his chances looked favorable for finding his uncle inside. He stepped down from the saddle and tied his horses up at the rail. Then, out of habit, he drew his Henry rifle from his saddle sling. He liked to keep it with him because the Henry rifle had just been manufactured and it was not easy to come by one. He stepped up on the porch, where he paused for a moment to observe the man lying there. After a few moments, he saw signs of life as the man struggled to come to. *I hope you ain't got nothing to do with Uncle Clayton*, Clint thought as he walked past him and went into the saloon.

Pete glanced up from the bar when the tall, strapping young man walked in. He was a stranger, but there was something familiar about him. So he looked more closely as he approached the bar. Then it struck him. He pointed to the little table in the back. "He's settin' right back there at the table, Clint."

"Much obliged," Clint said. "Has he caused any trouble?"

"Well, maybe a little bit," Pete replied, still marveling

at how a year had served to complete the rugged image of a competent young man.

"That fellow lyin' on the porch?" Clint asked and Pete nodded. Then he quickly told Clint about the incident during the card game. "And the other two players, they didn't say anything about that fellow cheatin'?" Pete shook his head. "You reckon he was?" Clint asked.

"I expect that he was," Pete admitted. "But the other two fellers in the game are in here playin' cards all the time and ain't neither one of 'em likely to call anybody on it." He shook his head and grinned. "But not ol' Scofield. I expect you've got a full-time job tryin' to keep him outta trouble, don'tcha?"

"No, for a fact, I don't," Clint answered, "just between runs. Uncle Clayton won't usually take a drink of whiskey when we're on the trail. All the way from here to Oregon, he's sober as a judge. Oh, there are some places when he feels the need to have a drink, but even then, he won't take more than two shots. That's just his way. The only time he wants to tie one on is when we get back here and then he makes up for all that time he's done without. He'll be sick as a dog tomorrow and we're supposed to meet with some people who wanna go to Oregon with us. I expect I'd best get him back to the hotel. Does he owe you any money?"

"No, sir," Pete said. "He's all paid up. You need any help gettin' him outta here? He drank an awful lot of whiskey."

Clint thanked him just the same, then walked back to get his uncle. Scofield opened his eyes when he heard his nephew approach the table. Seeing who it was, he fashioned a satisfied smile and announced, "Clint, I'm drunk as a skunk."

"I expect so," Clint replied. "Can you walk?"

"I'll give her a try," he answered and tried to stand up,

but found he needed help from his nephew to get up from the chair. "I ain't so sure," he confessed and tried to take a step forward, only to start to fall face forward. "When they built this dang saloon, they shoulda used a level on the floor. It's hard to walk when it's on a slant like this floor's on."

"No matter," Clint said as he quickly laid his rifle on the table, ducked down and caught Scofield on his right shoulder, then straightened up. He settled his load on his shoulder, then picked up his rifle and headed for the door.

"Goodnight, all," Scofield slurred cheerfully over Clint's shoulder, as he was carried past the bar.

"I want you to be real quiet now," Clint told him. "Don't say another word until I get you on your horse. Can you do that?"

"Anything you say, Clint," Scofield slurred.

When Clint walked out the door, he found he didn't have to worry about his uncle making a sound. Scofield was fast asleep. The injured gambler was now up on one knee, gingerly feeling his broken jaw with his fingers. When he saw Clint, he managed to spit out, "Is that him?"

"Yep," Clint answered. "That's the old coot who busted your jaw. He's dead, so you might as well go get that jaw fixed up. I'll take care of this'un."

"Whaddaya gonna do with him?" The gambler forced through clenched teeth.

"Bury him," Clint replied and slid his uncle off his shoulder to lie across his saddle. Wasting no more time then, he rode away from the saloon, leading Scofield's horse toward the hotel and the stable behind it.

Morning arrived a good bit earlier than Scofield had planned to greet it. He woke Clint up with his frantic efforts to pull his trousers and boots on in his haste to make it to the outhouse behind the hotel. He didn't waste a moment to consider the thunder-mug under the bed, knowing every evil he had trapped inside his body the night before would not be denied its escape. Clint had to get up to close the door his uncle had left wide open before he could go back to bed and try to go to sleep again. He finally dozed off, thinking how much he missed the freedom of sleeping on the open prairie.

Much to Clint's surprise, he was allowed to sleep until well past sunup when Scofield, fully dressed, roused him out. "Time to crawl outta them blankets, sleepyhead. Breakfast is cookin' and you're still layin' in the bed."

"Well, if you ain't somethin'," Clint replied, rubbing the sleep out of his eyes. "When did you come back in to get dressed?"

"About two hours ago. You was sleepin' like a baby. I went down to the washroom and cleaned up. And right now, I feel like I could eat half a buffalo. They got a nice outhouse, a two-seater, and that worked out real nice for me, because I was shipping outta both ends at the same time."

"I'm mighty glad you're feelin' so good this mornin'," Clint commented. "'Cause I was a little worried about you last night. I thought for a while there that I was gonna have to do the talkin' to these fellows from Springfield. And talkin' ain't my strong suit."

"Well, get your boots on and we'll go get us a big breakfast," Scofield said "I mean your moccasins." Clint didn't wear boots. "We're supposed to meet those fellers at ten o'clock at the Henry House Hotel."

For their breakfast, they went to the same place they had eaten supper the night before, a tiny little establishment called Mama's Kitchen. The hotel they spent the night in was small and offered no dining room, but Mama's Kitchen was only a short walk away. They considered having breakfast at the Henry House but decided their dining room might be too fancy for a couple of trail-hardened adventurers like themselves. The food at Mama's was to their liking, as Scofield put it, and it was bound to be a helluva lot more reasonable in cost. So, after a leisurely breakfast, they returned to their hotel. It was time to go to the meeting with the two men from Springfield.

"Mr. Scofield?" John Zachary asked when they walked into the Henry House lobby. He had been standing near the front door, watching for the wagon guide. When Scofield pleaded guilty, Zachary introduced himself and they shook hands. "It's a pleasure to meet you in person, sir," Zachary said. Then he signaled a man standing near a side entrance and he immediately hurried over to join them. "This is Emmett Braxton, Emmett's the other party I wrote you about."

"Glad to meetcha," Scofield said. "This young feller with me is Clint Buchanan. He'll be ridin' scout on this crossin'."

"Mr. Zachary, Mr. Braxton," Clint said politely and stepped forward to shake their hands.

"Why don't we go over there where we can sit down and talk about this trek across the country," Braxton suggested, knowing there were a great many questions he and Zachary wanted to ask. So, they went across the parlor to a sitting area and the meeting began. "To start with, John and I have definitely made the decision to make this journey. Right John?"

"Absolutely," Zachary replied. "We're goin', for sure,

and accordin' to your letter, you're gettin' ready to lead a wagon train out to Oregon Territory any day now."

"Well, sir," Scofield replied, "That's a fact. We've got some folks that are ready to go, waitin' on the prairie across the river. Some of 'em have been there for a week, but I'm just waitin' to give the grass a little time to grow. I set a date to leave on April the first and that's day after tomorrow. I'll be mighty happy to have you join our train, if you can get your wagons ready to roll by then." He paused to glance from Zachary to Braxton, trying to make a quick judgment of the seriousness of their intent. "Where are your wagons now? And your families, are they here in Independence?"

"Both families are packed up and ready to go," Braxton answered him. "They're parked down at the river, near the ferry slips. We were waitin' till we talked with you before we crossed over the river. So, I reckon we'll go ahead and cross over as soon as we leave here and join your wagons on the other side of the river."

Scofield had to chuckle. "I swear, I thought you were stayin' here in the hotel."

Zachary laughed with him. "No, I just suggested we meet here because it was the only hotel I knew the name of here in town."

Scofield laughed again and declared, "Me and Clint, here, will try to get you and your families out to Oregon as fast and as safely as we can. But you need to understand, this ain't no pleasure trip. There's gonna be hardships and maybe dangers we might have to face. But if a family's strong and willin' to make some sacrifices, there ain't no reason they can't make it. And what's waitin' for you on the other end of the journey is worth it. I sent you a list of everything you'll need to make it for four to six months. I hope you treated that list just like a bible, especially the part about the wagons. On the route we're takin', a light farm wagon does the best job over the flat prairie land we'll be travelin'. And like I told you in my letter, my trains are with horses or mules. Lotta folks say oxen are better, they got stronger pull and they can go longer without water, and oxen are cheaper to buy than horses or mules. But on the route I'll be leadin' you on, horses do just fine and there's plenty of water along the way. Oxen are too slow to suit me. Most trains that use oxen make about fifteen miles a day. That's the same as we'll make with our horses, maybe a little more. The difference is it'll take oxen all damn day and half the night to do it. We'll make our fifteen and stop at five o'clock in the afternoon for supper and rest. It'll make your journey a whole lot easier to take."

"You don't have to sell us on that. Emmett and I are both drivin' horses. How many wagons do you think you're gonna end up with?" Zachary asked.

"The same number I start out with," Scofield replied, then quickly chuckled to show he was joking. "Right now, I'll have twenty-seven wagons, counting you and Mr. Braxton. We might pick up a few more before we pull out day after tomorrow and we might not. But twenty-seven is a good manageable number. I've led trains of a hundred and fifty wagons, and I'd a heap druther go with a smaller number. I think you and your family will find it a lot more comfortable, too."

The meeting continued for quite some time until Zachary and Braxton ran out of questions. In the end, they shook hands with Scofield and Clint, and assured them they would be ready to join them on the day after tomorrow when the wagon train would roll out of Independence.

"Well, I expect John and I best get back to the wagons,"

Emmett declared. "Marcy and Sarah will be wantin' to get everything ready to travel."

Scofield and Clint walked them to the front door. "Seem like nice people," Clint commented to his uncle as they watched them depart.

"You'll find out for sure after they've been on that trail for a few weeks," Scofield replied.

Look for **GO WEST, YOUNG MAN**
on sale now everywhere books are sold.